Frost

Books by Donald Wandrei

Colossus
Don't Dream
Frost

Books by Howard Wandrei

Time Burial
Last Pin
The Eerie Mr. Murphy (in production)

Frost

by Donald Wandrei

Edited and Introduced by D. H. Olson

Illustrated by Les Edwards

Minneapolis, Minnesota
2000

Copyright © 2000 by Harold Hughesdon

Introduction copyright © 2000 by D. H. Olson
Artwork copyright © 2000 by Les Edwards

First Edition

Acknowledgements

"Frost" copyright 1934 by Street & Smith Publications, Inc. for *Clues*, September, 1934.

"Green Man - Creeping" copyright 1934 by Street & Smith Publications, Inc. for *Clues*, November, 1934.

"They Could Not Kill Him" copyright 1935 by Street & Smith Publications, Inc. for *Clues Detective Stories*, February, 1935.

"Bride of the Rats" copyright 1935 by Street & Smith Publications, Inc. for *Clues Detective Stories*, April, 1935.

"The Artist of Death" copyright 1935 by Street & Smith Publications, Inc. for *Clues Detective Stories*, June, 1935.

"Death Descending" copyright 1935 by Street & Smith Publications, Inc. for *Clues Detective Stories*, August, 1935.

"Impossible" copyright 1935 by Street & Smith Publications, Inc. for *Clues Detective Stories*, October, 1935.

"Merry-Go-Round" copyright 1935 by Street & Smith Publications, Inc. for *Clues Detective Stories*, December, 1935.

ISBN Trade Edition: 1-878252-42-9
ISBN Limited Edition: 1-878252-43-7

Layout and design by Felix Bremer

CONTENTS

vii	*Introduction*, by D. H. Olson
1	Frost
37	Green Man—Creeping
71	They Could Not Kill Him
109	Bride of the Rats
157	The Artist of Death
195	Death Descending
233	Impossible
269	Merry-Go-Round

INTRODUCTION

In August of 1934, Jean Moray, lithe, young and in trouble, slipped quickly through an iron-grille gate on State Street in New York City. After a thoughtful pause, she rang the bell at number thirteen and stepped inside. Moments later she passed through another doorway and into the presence of the mansion's owner, a curious, gaunt, hatchet-faced man with an engaging smile, a steel-trap mind and a taste for sharply pungent cigarettes of his own design. Thus was Professor I.V. "Ivy" Frost introduced, not just to Jean Moray, but to thousands of readers across the country.

To the Editors of *Clues* magazine, Frost was "a modern, American Sherlock Holmes;" to its readers he was its most popular and successful series character. To Jean Moray, he was an employer and a frustrating, never to be consummated or understood, love interest. But, to Street & Smith, publisher of *Clues*, I.V. Frost was pure gold. The series proved so popular that Frost was given star treatment, promoted to Hollywood producers and hardcover book publishers, and regularly featured on the magazine's cover to boost sales.

So, how did Ivy Frost come to be, and why? Firstly, one can blame editors F. Orlin Tremaine and Desmond Hall. Street & Smith was one of the largest and most important magazine publishers in 1930s America, yet its cornerstone mystery publication *Clues*, was a perpetual also-ran, routinely bested in the circulation wars by Pro-Distributor's *Black Mask*. To counteract this, the powers that be at Street & Smith decided they needed something new, something to draw readers in, issue after issue. To battle *Black Mask* and the various other mystery publications, like Popular Publications' *Dime Detective*, that often relied on series characters to bring readers in month after month, they needed a detective of their own. One unique enough to be notable. They were searching for a detective whose adventures would be violent enough to appeal to the sensibilities of *Black Mask's* hard-boiled readership, while also remaining cerebral enough for *Clues'* more traditional base. They also wanted something slightly off-the-beam, plots whose very strangeness would make the series memorable by way of its uniqueness.

Into this vortex of commercial creativity and early niche marketing walked Donald Wandrei, a young writer whose career in the pulps was still in its infancy. While he hadn't been working long as a true "professional," his reputation was already strong among readers of such science fiction and horror/fantasy publications as *Weird Tales*. Nor was he a stranger to Street & Smith's editorial department. Both Tremaine and Hall had first gotten to know Donald Wandrei (and his brother Howard) several years earlier while editing *Astounding Science Fiction*. For them, Wandrei had long since proven himself a valuable and important commodity, producing in 1934 "Colossus," a science-fiction story so formula-shattering and popular that it became an instant classic of the genre—a status it retains to this day, at least among lovers of pre-Golden Age Science Fiction. Since the hottest and best-paying markets in pulp-fiction were in the mystery field, and since SF and horror publications were mostly both unremunerative and notoriously slow in their payments, it's not surprising that Wandrei would eventually choose to expand into more rewarding markets. Nor is it surprising that Tremaine and Hall would do what they could to aid in the transition.

Donald Wandrei's first known excursions into the mystery marketplace were "Man Hunt" in Tower Magazine's *Alibi*, a magazine produced specifically for, and sold exclusively through the newsstands in Woolworth stores nationwide, and two short stories dutifully passed to the friendly editors at *Clues*. One, "Burned Without Fire," a tale whose plot involved the use of dinitrophenol, was never published, it's manuscript eventually lost. The other, "Dramatic Touch," appeared in the June 1934 issue of *Clues Detective*. Donald Wandrei was now a mystery writer and, in the eyes of F. Orlin Tremaine, a prime candidate to oversee the birth of Street & Smith's new series detective.

Having been given his task, Wandrei set to work. During the month of April 1934, he slaved over his new creation in a story entitled "Advertise for Death." Tremaine and Hall loved it, but thought it over-long. During a luncheon meeting on April 30, they went over the manuscript with its author and indicated those "few choice bits" they wanted removed and saved for later editions in the series. Wandrei, eager for both a paycheck and the security of a continuing series, was happy to oblige. He performed a minor rewrite and, on May 18, 1934, "Advertise for Death" was purchased by Street & Smith for $157. Retitled "Frost," it was quickly scheduled for publication in the September 1934 issue of *Clues* and announced with great fan-fare in their August issue.

There can be little doubt that I.V. Frost was exactly what Hall and Tremaine had wanted. Donald Wandrei was immediately sent to work on future installments in the series. To protect their own interests, Street & Smith also fiddled with their usual contractual terms for this (and presumably later) Frost tales. While Donald Wandrei would be recognized as full owner of rights should any book or movie deals be forthcoming, Street & Smith retained the right to make such sales on its own (with all monies going to Wandrei) while also preventing I.V. Frost stories from appearing in the pages of any competing magazines.

The support of *Clues'* editors for Professor Frost and his winsome assistant seems to have paid off. They were a huge hit with the magazine's readers, and the November 1934 issue of *Clues*, the one that included "Green Man-Creeping!," I.V. Frost and Jean Moray's second adventure, proved to be the biggest selling issue in the history of that magazine.

Soon Frost's success would birth a host of imitators as well. Wandrei, in later years, would often complain about those whom he felt had "plagiarized" from his creation. While too circumspect to actually refer to such miscreants by name, one was undoubtedly John Franklin Bardin, whose critically acclaimed *The Deadly Percheron* (1946) boasts a plot uncomfortably similar to those of the first two Ivy Frost adventures. While perhaps unintentional, the strong similarities in the stories, as well as the over-lap of some very unusual plot elements, makes it appear likely that Bardin was familiar with Professor Frost's adventures even before beginning work on his own.

Other unnamed offenders, at least from Street & Smith's point of view, were some of the contributors to Popular's *Dime Detective*. In January of 1936, for instance, Tremaine presented Donald Wandrei with a copy of that month's *Dime Detective* and indicated that no fewer than two of its stories were direct imitations of I.V. Frost. Such imitation may not have been actionable, but it did reassure *Clues* editors that they had been well repaid by the trust they'd placed in Donald Wandrei.

Between September 1934 and September 1937, a total of eighteen I.V. Frost adventures appeared in the pages of *Clues Detective* magazine. The first eight of these are reprinted here, with the remaining ten slated for publication in a future collection. While the series proved remunerative for both Wandrei and his publishers, it never quite achieved the level of success that F. Orlin Tremaine had envisioned. No I.V. Frost motion picture was every produced, though, in early 1935, Street & Smith was approached about a possible serial deal. The idea was for *Clues* to sponsor a "half-a-dozen two-reel mysteries to be nationally distributed." The production was being pursued by an outside agent who would handle the "scenario and picture," while *Clues* magazine would receive an on-screen credit tie-in. The apparent purpose was to produce a series of short films in direct competition with "the *Black Mask*-Warner Bros. series of mysteries" then being produced. In the end, the deal fell through. If it had not, I.V. Frost and Jean Moray would have soon appeared on screens all across the country, for Tremaine had decided early on that a series character would be the best way to proceed—and his clear first choice was Wandrei's Professor Frost.

Likewise, no collection of I.V. Frost stories was ever forthcoming, in spite of Tremaine's efforts to interest several of his friends within the publishing business. One problem, as Wandrei himself knew well from his days with E.P. Dutton, was that the New York publishing houses had little interest in story collections. In 1936, Donald Wandrei, at Tremaine's urging, considered remedying this situation by writing a full-length I.V. Frost novel. He developed a plot line, at least mentally, but, overcome by the need to write for his regular markets, and the income they provided, no such novel was every really begun.

So how do I.V. Frost and his adventures stand up after all these years? Amazingly well, as readers of this collection will soon discover. While certain elements in these stories may strike the modern reader as anachronistic, they are certainly no more so than those of Frost's contemporaries the Shadow and Doc Savage. In fact, a case may be made that they are, in some ways, more modern than either.

For what you now hold in you hands, the editor would like to thank Cindy Rako and her father, Tom Soben, for transcribing the stories collected here. I would also like to thank Harold Hughesdon and his family for their support in what I now refer to as the "ongoing Wandrei project," as well as to Messrs. Fedogan & Bremer for deigning to bring Wandrei back into print. A belated thank you also to Steven Stilwell, whose name I can never seem to spell properly. I would also like to thank

Donald Wandrei and the Minnesota Historical Society for, without Donald's correspondence with his father, much of the information related above would have been lost forever. One might also add that the quotes appearing in the preceding article are taken from those letters. Finally, and perhaps most importantly, I would like to thank the readers and fans of both Donald and Howard Wandrei, whose ongoing support and enthusiasm make projects like this well worthwhile.

D.H. Olson
La Fonda de los Lobos
Eagan, Minnesota
May 23, 2000

FROST

A GIRL TURNED the corner into State Street. Keeping to the inside, she walked swiftly. Only a trained observer would have seen anxiety in her hurrying stride. To the average passer-by she would merely have given the appearance of a young woman walking briskly.

At this fairly late hour, State Street was almost deserted. Doormen lounged inside the entrances of huge apartment buildings that lined the first half of the block. A couple of cars were parked along the curbing. The last half of the block was occupied by private houses, half a dozen mansions of the sort that require moderate wealth to keep them up, each isolated from the others by iron grille fences or stone walls, each set in its own small grounds.

The girl hurried past a street light. It shone briefly on a velvet wrap clasped at her throat. The slinky lines of a glowing red evening gown flowed below the wrap. Her pumps were flame, dusted with gold. They were costly things that she wore, but lifeless, negligible compared with her lithe beauty of figure and the strikingly individual loveliness of her face.

Her gray-green eyes were a trifle wide. They gave her an expression of cool and determined intelligence. Her cheek bones were a bit high; her cheeks held only a faint curve. The corners of her slightly full mouth turned in. Her complexion was a shade from that warm color of ripe wheat which only the sun can give. Not even the expert hands of the hairdresser could have concealed the willful poise of her head. No cosmetician's art could have created in her face its distinctive but indefinable natural quality; the bloom was still on the grape.

Hurrying past street lights, keeping to shadow whenever possible, the girl continued walking toward the Hudson. The drone of riverside traffic grew louder. When she reached the second mansion, she slipped quickly through an iron grille gate.

A weak, overhead bulb shone on the engraved nameplate: I. V. Frost, Sc. D. The girl hesitated, hovering for a moment in the shadows at the side of the porch. All windows were shuttered. From one on the ground-floor left, emerged bars of light. They permitted no glimpse of the interior when she came up the walk.

She stared back at the street, listened a full minute. Then she stepped forward and rang decisively, insistently. The stone retreat was well built. She could not hear the ring of a bell. Having no means of telling whether the bell was working, she rang again, waited a few seconds, and knocked on the door.

It opened silently. The girl stared at an odd hall, neither long nor wide, but occupied by an amazing number of objects—table, oriental vases, small settee, pictures, umbrella stand, book-and-magazine rack, a couple of singularly carved chairs, and a few miscellaneous items. Most singular of all was the fat and benign Buddha that squatted in a niche at the end of the hall, some twenty feet from her.

But there was not a person in sight. Tense, the girl stood in the doorway. Her face showed alertness, but neither fear nor perplexity.

"Please step inside, Miss Moray," an oddly muffled voice suggested. "There is nothing to fear, and you will be perfectly safe while you are here."

The girl entered. It must have required extraordinary self-possession to conceal her surprise that her name was known. She returned to her purse an envelope that she had half removed.

The voice continued: "If Miss Moray will be so kind as to leave her automatic on the table—"

The visitor's poise was admirable. She betrayed no emotion as she took the weapon from her purse and obeyed instructions. It was an authoritative but not unpleasant voice.

"Thank you," the hollow voice spoke again. "Now, if you would be obliging enough to remove the pearl-handled toy from your right thigh."

The girl lifted her gown, took the tiny automatic from its sheath just above her knee, and laid it beside its companion. Not even a start, or a glint of eyes, indicated any reaction. She looked with apparently naïve interest at the Buddha. To all appearances, she accepted it as a matter of fact that some one she had not yet seen knew in some magical fashion what weapons she had and where she concealed them, as well as who she was.

"Thank you," the muffled voice said. "Will you kindly walk to the end of the hall and enter the first door on your left, where Professor Frost will receive you?"

The girl followed directions. When she was three feet from the door, it sprang open with a *clup* of compressed air and without visible agency. The door, like the front door through which she had first passed, slowly closed behind her.

The girl entered a library complete in sumptuous furnishings, from Astrakhan rug to built-in bookcases lining every wall to the ceiling, from mahogany table to Minoan amphora. The only unoccupied wall space lay between the two front windows, and there an antique print of Sir Francis Bacon overlooked a pedestal on which stood a bust of Socrates. Yet the room was so spacious that it did not seem crowded, in spite of its furnishings, objects, and thousands of books.

A man had been leaning back in a huge overstuffed chair with an air of abstraction, chin resting on interlaced fingers. He unfolded like a gaunt specter when she entered, until he stood fully six feet four. The girl was convinced that he could not possibly have been sitting in that chair for more than thirty seconds, yet he rose with the reluctance of one who had been comfortably meditating for a long while.

He was about as unlovely a specimen as the girl had ever seen. He had a gaunt, hatchet-thin face, excessively high cheek bones, an ascetic mouth, and a nose like the beak of an eagle. His eyes were inscrutable under immense black eyebrows. He towered like a loose-jointed scarecrow, of large bone and little flesh, and his beautiful, almost feminine, hands were a startling contrast to the rest of him and to his nondescript clothes. Corduroy trousers that looked as though they had not been pressed since he bought them—and that might have been a decade ago—blue shirt past its prime, and a leather jacket bearing the scars and stains of many a mishap, clad the specter.

In spite of his appearance, he smiled one of the most engaging smiles the girl had ever seen as he bowed her to a seat; and in spite of his impersonal manner, his air of scientific and emotionless detachment, there lay, deep underneath, the impression of some great human dream. Even the mission that drove her and dominated her thoughts could not prevent her from feeling slightly piqued; there simply was no response to her personal beauty. She might have been an old hag or a lump of inanimate stuff.

"Allow me to introduce myself. I am Professor Frost."

"It doesn't seem necessary to tell you that I am Jean Moray. And I presume you know that I came in answer to your advertisement?"

She took out of her purse an oblong strip torn from the "Help Wanted—Female" columns of a newspaper. The advertisement asked for the services of an:

> Assistant for criminal investigation; young woman of exceptional appearance, personality, courage, health, intelligence, without close ties, for dangerous but exciting work with private criminologist. Reply in detail. High salary to right person. Box Z, 149.

The girl also removed a sealed envelope, addressed to the professor, which she handed him. He laid it aside without opening it, saying:

"Your reply made a very favorable impression which my attorneys inform me was amply confirmed by the appointment they arranged. In fact, you are only the fifth applicant recommended to me out of some five thousand replies."

"Thank you. May I enquire just what the nature of the position is?"

The professor laced his fingers. The lids half drooped over his eyes. The girl's glance strayed toward the windows, and she edged forward in her chair, listening in vain for sounds from outside that could not penetrate within. The window slid part way up as if to answer her wish. Her gaze darted back to the professor. If his hands had moved to some hidden button, they had done so instantly when her attention wandered, for they were again laced under his chin.

Professor Frost spoke slowly and precisely, each word the result of cautious selection: "I am seeking an assistant to further my researches and to help carry on various criminal investigations. In addition to the qualifications listed in my advertisement, the successful applicant should have a scientific background and an unusually analytical mind. Since I hold no official positions, I am acting entirely upon my own initiative. For that reason, the position entails more than ordinary danger and personal risk.

"However, some of my work has started at the request of friends in office who desired aid in solving obscure cases. I have begun other investigations for private individuals, though I prefer as a rule not to handle such matters. Much of my analysis is voluntary, involving problems abandoned by others as hopeless of solution, or peculiarly puzzling affairs cited by the newspapers, in which events I offer my services if desired.

"Laboratory study of material clues, microscopic analysis of data, the trailing and even apprehension of criminals, are only a few phases of the work. I have as many bitter enemies as friends. The danger cannot be minimized."

"I see. Can you mention a specific instance? A case or two that you've worked on? That would give me a more definite idea of what to expect."

The professor drew a special cigarette from a case, offered the girl one from a different pack of common brand, which she declined in favor of her own. He exhaled a cloud of sharply pungent smoke. A peculiarly hard glitter entered his eyes.

"Not long ago, State Senator Kyle was killed, apparently by a hit-and-run driver, on the eve of pressing for passage of important labor legislation. The laws died in committee, with his influence removed. Several large industrial plants in that State are now having violent labor disturbances as a direct result. Unless there is a special session of the legislature, riots of the most serious character are likely to occur. There were circumstances suggesting criminal planning behind the occurrence. This is typical of the lines that my research follows."

The professor's face was grim. The girl sensed in his carefully chosen phrases an ulterior motive, a deeper mystery.

"It sounds as if all these, at least, might be linked to a single source," she suggested, with a rising inflection.

"Possibly. My purpose is not to theorize, but to prove."

"I should think that you would find masculine aid more valuable."

"No. A man could only offer qualities that I already possess. I want a woman who must be alert, intelligent, a keen analyst, one who can circulate in places where a man could not, and who through her beauty and magnetism of personality can quickly obtain information that it might require even the most brilliant of men longer to acquire. No; my assistant must be a woman because she will have the only additional qualifications of value in my work, those springing primarily from the difference between the sexes.

"For instance, she should be of such striking beauty that if we were seated at a table, and some one entered intending to kill me, her appearance would attract admiration for just a brief moment. That fractional second would be all I need. The position, I repeat, is full of constant peril. My assistant would never be free of danger. The salary, one hundred dollars a week and all living expenses, is small compared to the menace. Incidentally," he asked with seeming irrelevance, "how much do you weigh?"

"123 pounds, stripped."

"That's correct."

"Of course it's correct," she exclaimed. "Why, how did you know"

"When you entered the front door, you stepped on an electrical weighing device which registered your weight as one hundred and twenty-five and one half pounds. Allowing a pound for clothing and a pound and a half for your hardware, the result could be only a few ounces off."

"And what's the good of that?"

The criminal investigator shrugged. "It enables me to find out, for instance, whether truth or vanity predominates when I ask a simple question."

"I see. And the same device is sensitive to the presence of metals, which told you I was armed?"

"Your reasoning faculties bear out the report of my attorneys. Yes; the presence of metals being established, I press a button which sets the Buddha X-ray at work. In thirty seconds, I know the exact postion of every weapon my visitor has."

"I gather that your visitors are well prepared to defend themselves?"

"If you wish to put it that way. But I have outlined the nature of the position. Perhaps you would now like to tell me a little more about yourself and why you think you are qualified."

"Since my parents died, I've been on my own for several years. I have no close relatives. A little money was left me, and I finished my college education, receiving my B. A. and M. A. I majored in science—chemistry, physiology, and psychology. Then I decided I didn't want to teach. I wasn't interested in business, but tried various jobs for a while. Up to a month ago, I modeled until the art school term ended. Then when I saw your ad—"

While the girl rattled on, the professor's eyes, as they had ever since she arrived, continued searching her from head to foot, as if she were a human book, or a fly under the microscope. She felt that keen scrutiny rove over each feature, register it indelibly, read its meaning, extract each secret.

He produced another of his pungent cigarettes and exhaled a cloud of smoke. He drawled with a crooked smile: "That is a very interesting little speech, Miss Moray. It seems to say much about you, but actually it is couched in the broadest and most general terms which convey a minimum of information. You did not come here to tell me that pretty fable?"

The girl's face tensed. "Is that a hint for me to go? I presume you would not be interested in employing some one whose word you did not trust."

"True; but truth is a relative matter. A trained observer can extract truth from mere appearances and actions. Then, too, any one's private life is a matter of his own concern, about which he is at liberty to keep silent or tell any evasion he prefers. It does not concern me what your private life had been or your reasons for concealing it.

"I already know that you possess the requirements I wish, are completely trustworthy, and cool in emergency. You are quick-witted and intelligent. The part of your story concerning your educational background and scientific bent is true. You have the major qualifications for the position. Are you able to accept it?"

He studied her intently as she thought over his unusual proposition. "I wouldn't worry about it, if I were you," he remarked. "No one will ever see the scar, and one vaccination mark is all that is necessary to provide the one flaw which will emphasize your otherwise perfect figure."

The girl stared at him, started to ask a question, then looked down. While listening, she had unconsciously been rubbing the spot above her right knee.

She looked up at Professor Frost with a glint of admiration. "That is good observation."

"It is nothing of the sort, though I compliment you on your quick understanding. It is good observation, analysis, and synthesis. Observation tells me that you are in splendid health, possess a most enviable figure, and a very beautiful face. I observe your hair which is the color of a rare rye whisky. I analyze it and discover that it is a natural color. Observation presents only the surface of things. Analysis goes to their heart. Synthesis takes their real significance and relates it to other objects, events, or patterns of existence.

"I observe your formal attire. You will admit that it is distinctly unusual for a young woman to apply for a job in such clothing and at this rather late hour. Furthermore, while costly, even attention-arresting, the color harmony is not quite suitable to your personal characteristics. Analysis, synthesis, induction, and deduction, all convince me that you wear this particular raiment by somebody else's specifications, and that you came not so much to apply for the position as to ask for aid, if you could convince yourself of the advertiser's good faith.

"I can assure you without fear of contradiction that your story was largely fabrication, that you have been in this city less than a month, that you came from Minneapolis, that you have just been through a strange experience, and that you are right now in great fear. May I suggest—"

The girl sprang up. "It is true! I did not come here primarily for the position. I came because I had heard about your success in solving mysteries that baffled other experts, but I had to make sure I was not letting myself in for more trouble of the sort I got from answering the other advertisement. I'll make a bargain with you, Professor Frost. You want my help, and I need yours. Solve my mystery, and I'll go my limit in aiding your work."

"Suppose you tell me about it?"

II.

The girl moved closer to the window, began speaking rapidly. "Perhaps I have delayed too long already. I may not have time to finish. If I suddenly break off and go, don't try to stop me or follow me immediately. The rest will be up to you.

"I *am* in danger, but I don't yet know from whom or why. I arrived here two weeks ago with only enough money to last a week. The first thing I did was buy a paper. As you probably know, there were two identical advertisements. I wrote the same answer to both. I received an answer from both. The first came two days before the answer from your lawyers.

"I had an interview at what purported to be another law firm. It was in a small office on Broadway near Forty-second, and there was only one ferret-looking man there when I called. I got the job. I was paid a week in advance. I was to do nothing but follow a few simple orders. He explained that the first week would be a test of my courage, ability to follow orders, and general merit. He gave me some further instructions and told me not to come back to that office.

"Nevertheless, I did go back the next morning. I had thought it all over and become suspicious. The office was empty. I found it had been rented only a week before. Right then and there, I decided to go through with it and see what it was all about. Besides, I had a queer feeling I was being followed, and I didn't know what might happen if I failed to do what I was told."

The professor lighted another of his peculiar cigarettes without shifting his gaze. From the intensity of the look that enveloped her, she sensed a more than casual interest.

"Following the ferret-faced man's instructions, I went to a jeweler's window near Fifth Avenue and Forty-second Street, at ten o'clock. A neatly dressed man, whom I never saw before or since, stopped to look at the trays and gave me further instructions together with five hundred dollars. I was to purchase some gowns and other things, turn myself into as seductive a siren as I could, go to Mardi's restaurant at three o'clock, take the table reserved for me, and at three thirty—but I'll tell you when I come to that.

"The man disappeared in the morning crowd. By this time I was more mystified than ever and determined to see the thing through. I've always loved excitement, and this promised plenty of thrills. I bought some lovely things and went to the best beauty experts. When I entered Mardi's at the cocktail hour, there wasn't a man in the place who didn't forget about his companion, though there were dozens of wealthy and attractive girls around."

"Yes; I can well imagine it. You would shine even among the stars," Frost agreed in a tone as if he had said: "Albany is the capital of New York."

The girl gave him an exasperated glance. "At three fifteen, a distinguished-looking man with a very florid face and a mole on his left cheek—"

Frost said: "Did he also have a triangle of white hair in his left eyebrow?"

"Yes! Do you know him?"

"Go on."

"He and his companion, a dizzy young thing with a sugar-face, took a table reserved for them next to mine. At three thirty, making sure that no one was looking in my direction, I carried out the fantastic part of my instructions. I lighted a cannon cracker in my lap and tossed it under the table so that it slid under the next table. It exploded like a gunshot. The young thing screamed, the man leaped to his feet with the whitest and most scared face I've ever seen, waiters came rushing up, and the place was in an uproar.

"I rose like several others and called for my check. The head waiter made profuse apologies to me as I left. A good many people looked at me, but I don't think any one connected me with the incident."

The professor leaned forward in his chair. "Very interesting," he murmured. "Go on."

"I'll have to hurry. Ever since, I've been given instructions from time to time, always at a different place and by different people. More than ever, I began to feel—I *knew*—that I was being followed, though not once have I been able to identify any pursuers. I even changed my address. But no matter where I am, I know that some one or some ring of persons is constantly near by. It's an intuitive feeling that I haven't much real basis for proving except the one possible clue of a sound."

"What sort of sound?"

"Just an automobile horn of a peculiar pitch. It's the first of the four notes that French horns have. Sometimes it comes merely as a honk at a pedestrian or a traffic snarl, but other times it sounds in short and long notes and pauses, like a definite pattern. I've heard it many times, but I've never been able to tell what automobile it comes from. Maybe it hasn't anything to do with the mystery, but it's distinct from other horns if I listen hard, and it seems strange that it should always be near, since I took the position.

"After the firecracker farce, I had nothing further to do that day or the next, except to round out my wardrobe. But the next evening I went to a theater, was met in the lobby by a man I never saw before or since, and escorted in. His tickets were in the sixth-row center. He made no effort to talk with me, except to whisper further instructions, and to say that my employer was satisfied with my work thus far. When the curtain rose he excused himself for a minute, but left a package on the seat which he asked me to watch. He did not return."

"Of course," Frost muttered. "Personal escort—to see that you not only went in but took the exact seat specified. Departure—to prevent suspicion from falling on him, and to make sure, in safety from the back of the orchestra, that you carried out everything to the dot."

Jean stared at him. "If I hadn't so much confidence in you, I would almost suspect you of having planned this. Anyway, some late arrivals took seats in front of me. In ten minutes, a wild clatter burst from the package. It was obviously an alarm clock. I leaned over and whispered: 'Everything is set, if you raise the ante.'

"The man in front of me whirled around with wide, scared eyes. He was the same man of the firecracker incident. Then I seized the package and made my way out. The play fumbled along. The whole audience was restless. Two ushers hurried down the aisle toward me. All in all, I don't suppose there's been a madder audience or a more harassed woman on Broadway this season.

"It then seemed clear to me that my strange assignments were concerned with the man I had twice seen, but who he was I hadn't any idea, or what was behind this fantastic rigmarole. And I didn't have any friends here close enough to take into my confidence.

"For the next three days, I had only insignificant things to do. I did try giving my unseen shadowers the slip by dodging into a motion-picture house and leaving by a side exit. For half an hour I felt free, and then—I heard the horn.

"Yesterday, after the three days of trifling around, I had another curious assignment, the most disconcerting of all. Early in the morning, a singular bird was delivered to me. It had beautiful colors of green, gold, purple, and scarlet, looked somewhat like a macaw or parakeet, and possessed a flowing tail of pastel feathers at least a yard long.

"I strolled down Fifth Avenue with this extraordinary creature perched on my shoulder, and you can imagine the sensation we created. Still obeying orders, I walked along until a taxicab drew up at the curb beside me. It honked twice and then once. I climbed in. The taxi moved on slowly. It circled a block and slid into a parking space just off upper Fifth Avenue. After a while, some one came out of the nearest big apartment house and entered a waiting limousine.

"We followed it down Fifth Avenue. Below Thirty-eighth Street, my driver swung out in front of the limousine. It was skillfully done. The two cars locked and banged against the curb. My driver nonchalantly got out and vanished among the passers-by. I waited until the limousine door opened and the owner came forth. He was the same man of the firecracker and alarm-clock scenes. I stepped from the cab and said: 'Make it a million, or else—'

"His face turned positively green. A second man came threateningly toward me, but the first man shook his head. The bird on my shoulder cackled harshly. I pushed my way through the gathering crowd. A cab, waiting around the corner for me as promised, took me across town before the nearest policeman arrived. I saw by the evening paper that the wrecked cab had been stolen. I was surprised that only the chauffeur of the limousine was mentioned by name.

"That is the whole story so far, except that I think I succeeded in giving my pursuers the slip twice more—once when I went to your attorneys, and a while ago before I came here. But I feel that the mystery is coming to a head any hour now, and I'm worried. This is the last day of my trial week. I'm in too deep to draw back, but I'd stay, anyway, just to satisfy my curiosity.

"My last instructions were whispered to me this afternoon by another stranger."

"What were you told to do?" Frost asked.

"To-night at midnight," she said slowly, "I am to—"

The girl's voice broke. Through the window had come the sound of an oddly pitched automobile horn.

The girl dashed for the door.

The criminologist rose.

"No! Don't try to follow until I'm clear!" the girl cried. "They're catching up with me again. I've got to get out of here before you're drawn into it directly. I'll try to telephone you soon. But it's a bargain—clear this mystery, and I'll join forces with you. Yes?"

She spoke with breathless haste. From the doorway she gave him a quick look, provocative, challenging, questioning—an expression of diverse moods, her face glowing with a more hectic beauty from the fever of the chase.

"Yes." The professor smiled, and she was gone, snatching her weapons as she fled.

Frost watched her through the window, after adjusting the shutter so that he had a clear view. She melted like a shadow into the other shadows of trees, then into the sidewalk shadows of buildings. She darted to a parked taxi. It immediately sped off, whirled around the nearest corner. A sedan raced in the same direction, sloughed around the same corner.

Ivy Frost strode across the room, passed through a door opposite the windows.

His laboratory gleamed with the instruments of science. One entire wall was shelved with thousands of bottles of chemicals, pure and in compound, of drugs, acids, and alkalis. The tables were strewn with microscopes, slides, retorts, furnaces, Bunsen burners, electrical equipment of every kind, a great variety of sensitive measuring instruments from micrometer calipers to interferometer, complete sets of draftsman's, surgeon's, and carpenter's tools, radio materials, photographic supplies. Long rows of filing cabinets stood against the walls. There was an immense quantity of miscellaneous items that appeared to cover every conceivable category of science.

Frost moved without hesitation to a short-wave television set and turned on the power current. He watched a metal screen into which a room gradually swam and focused.

"F calling JV, F calling JV," he intoned into a microphone.

Within a half minute, a man wearing a lounging robe hurried into the other room and moved to a duplicate set.

"Hello, F!"

"I want the address of the girl who—"

John Vogel, senior partner of Vogel, Vogel, and Brant, attorneys, interrupted with a chuckle. "I thought she would make an impression.

Just a second, I have it in my coat." He left, reappeared in a moment. "She gave it as 609 West 75th."

"Thank you. She's moved, but I'll have to start from there. Good night!"

He lifted the receiver from a telephone and dialed the central telegraph office. "I'd like the following message delivered in exactly twenty minutes. Can it be arranged? Good! To Jean Moray, 609 West 75th Street, City."

Frost picked up a telephone directory as soon as he had given his telegram message, hunted another number, and called it. He heard central buzz repeatedly before an answer came.

"May I speak to Mr. Hastings?"

"Mr. Hastings is not in. Whose name shall I give him?"

"Professor Frost. Can you tell me where I can reach him? It is urgent that I communicate with him at once."

"I am sorry, sir, but Mr. Hastings did not say where he would be this evening. However, if you wish to leave a message—"

"Which is a plain lie," the criminologist muttered as he hung up.

He dialed another number. "Jerry? Ivy talking. Glad I found you in and sober—what, you're not sober? Sorry I cast aspersions. I want some information as fast as possible. Can you find out where Sam Hastings is to-night? Yes—the power behind Coin Machines, Inc. It's very important. Leave his home out—I just tried there."

"Absolutely!" the answering voice said. "If nobody on the *Press* staff knows, some of my columnist friends will. It'll take a while. Want me to call you back?"

"No; I'll be on the move. Can you find out by telephoning around? Fine! I'll call you again at fifteen-minute intervals. Also, find out who's in charge at the central station to-night. Calper? You're positive? Thanks! Call you later."

He passed from section to section of his laboratory. Into a small valise he carefully placed his selections. From the gleaming apparatus and stoppered vials of science, he made his choices instantly, without hesitation.

Within five minutes he took the wheel of his car. It purred out of the basement garage. He sped downtown and at Eightieth Street halted to phone Jerry Travis again from a drug-store booth. Travis reported Hastings' movements up to nine o'clock and was still on the trail.

At the West Seventy-fifth Street address, Frost climbed the steps of a grimy brownstone house near the river road. Prolonged ringing brought a hag, reeking of beer, and wrapped in a greasy, torn kimono.

"Is Miss Moray at home?" Frost asked suavely. "I'm sorry to intrude at this late hour, but I've only now arrived from out-of-town."

The harridan stared at him sullenly, suspiciously. "No one here by that name."

"She has moved? Where can I find her?"

"I don't know, mister. Write her a letter." The door banged.

Frost returned to his car and waited. In five minutes, a messenger wheeled up with his telegram and roused the crone. He argued with her for a moment, then jotted a notation on the envelope he carried. He remounted his bicycle and pedaled downtown, with Frost following. In West Sixty-third, the messenger stopped at another brownstone. He talked to some one, left a delivery notice, and then wheeled back toward his office with the telegram.

The professor made a quick selection from the contents of his valise. Carrying a bundle under one arm, he mounted dilapidated steps that were grooved from the tread of generations. A red-eyed hunchback answered his ring and studied him overtly with glittering pupils when he inquired for Miss Moray.

With a shrug as if it was none of his funeral, the dwarf mumbled: "Third-floor front, No. 31." Then he scuttled back to a dimly lighted rear recess.

Frost climbed the worn stairs. Stillness enveloped the rooming house. Not another person except the hunchback seemed awake. There were no lights shining through transoms or under the bottom of any door that he passed. The silence was uncanny.

At the head of the stairs on the third floor, he paused and listened, but still heard no sound. No. 31 was in the front. The scientist made his preparations with precision and speed that required only seconds. He unrolled the bundle, pocketed a few items, and donned an all-protective garment. He carried no firearms.

Frost strode soundlessly to the door of Room 31 and gently tried the knob. The door was unlocked. He opened it and faded inside.

III.

By the weak light filtering in through the single grimy window could be seen a typical cheap, furnished room. Frost twisted his head sharply aside. The blackjack raked the left side of his head, and a dark blob closed in on him. He raised his two forefingers and jabbed the blob. An explosive cry jerked from its throat. It doubled over, straightened again, stiffened rigidly as though in the convulsions of epilepsy, and jackknifed against the wall. From a chair tipped backward against the far corner of the room, a second dark shape raised a silenced automatic and fired with cold-blooded aim. They were all direct hits. The first *whammed* against the scientist's chest, one *panged* his forehead; the whole clip was fired and wasted on the bulletproof metallized cloth of his protective suit. The only damage was bruises from the force of impact.

When the shots ended, Frost acted. The second blob grunted in surprise as the strange specter plowed in, unharmed by six direct hits at close range. The second man yanked at another gun, but never used it. The scientist knocked him clear out of the chair. The world-be killer could take it, if only because he had to.

As he came up, the first hoodlum groaned on the floor. The professor's long arms were as deadly as pile drivers. As calmly, carefully, and methodically as if he was perfecting an experiment, the criminologist broke the second man's nose, laid open his right cheek, stuffed a few teeth down his throat, and sent him to oblivion with a smash that sounded as if it cracked his jawbone.

The first victim was still groggy when Frost returned and plunged a hypodermic needle into his arm. He treated the more badly damaged killer with a similar dose. As the stiff injections of morphine took effect, the breathing of the two men became regular and they passed into a state of deep coma from which they would not emerge for many hours.

They were gangsters, two of Joe Blake's gorillas. It was a rule of Blake's that his men keep away from dope. The rule was rigidly enforced. Death was the penalty.

Frost dragged one of the bodies in front of the door. He pulled down the window curtain and then turned a light on. He hauled a good-sized suitcase from under the bed. Next he went through the room with swift but minute care, packing all the girl's belongings in the suitcase. If he had needed any corroboration of her strange story, it was partly borne out by the amazingly gaudy bird that perched in a tall cage and cocked a sleepy eye at him.

There were no interruptions. Frost removed the protective cloak and hood which he rolled into a bundle. He scrutinized the insulated caps for each forefinger, from which the needles had been broken off when he jabbed the first man. He removed the caps, loosely bunched the wires that led from them, and stuffed them into his pockets beside the powerful, compact batteries to which they were connected.

Frost's face wore the expression of a man satisfied with a job well done. After dragging the body out of the way, he turned out the light and raised the window shade. He carried the suitcase with him when he left.

On the ground floor, he summoned the dwarf. "You have an extra room to rent now. Miss Moray will not be back."

The hunchback squinted evilly.

"Also, there are a couple of uninvited callers in Room 31 who need attention." Frost's features hardened. He bluntly ordered the crooked man: "I think you had better move—fast."

The dwarf glared, turned without a reply, and padded up the stairs.

The bundle and the suitcase went into the rear of Frost's car. Three blocks away, he stopped long enough to use a coffeepot phone booth to call Travis.

"Hello!" came the reporter's slightly worried voice. "Everything O.K.? That's good. You're ten minutes late in calling, and I was beginning to wonder if something happened. I got the dope all right, from Win Morro. You know, the human keyhole. He says he got it by calling some of his girl friends at the hot spots. Hastings blew in at the Golden Goblin twenty minutes ago with John T. Dellener, the political boss, and a couple of Eves in tow. I can't guarantee that he's still there, but when Win says something is so, I'd hate to put up money against him. Anything else I can do?"

"That's all, thanks. I'll see that you get some of your favorite Scotch to-morrow."

Back in his car, Frost drove to the Golden Goblin, a gyp-joint nude-review rendezvous in the blistering Fifties, before twelve thirty. He parked at the nearest space and hurried inside.

The hat-check siren stared at him in disgust as he sauntered along the lushly carpeted and ornate lobby without even having noticed her. Several people glanced his way in surprise. It was a tribute to his impressive carriage that, however startled strangers might be by his disreputable clothes, they never smiled.

A hostess hurried toward him with polite but firm intentions. "I am sorry, sir, but it is one of the rules of the club—your clothing is—"

Frost looked through her. She suddenly stuttered, lost the power of speech, lapsed into silence.

In the main room, an orchestra was evoking low music, wearily feverish. The floor show had gone on. As he entered, a chorus of platinum blondes, flood lights spotting only the upper half of their bodies, undulated through involved patterns.

The head waiter approached, eyeing the gaunt intruder doubtfully.

Frost dismissed him with a gesture. "No table, I'll be here only a few minutes."

He lounged by an enormous rubber plant. After a few seconds he shifted his position and scrutinized the booths beyond the floor show.

Frost smiled a crooked smile as he spotted Jean Moray. She was outstanding even in this haven of beauty. Her mobile, intelligent face expressed something original. She struck a new note. Her rye-whisky hair was a welcome exception to the run of artificial blondes and smoky brunettes. For an instant his gaze lingered on her, as she sat alone, in a small wall booth. She was flirting outrageously with every man in the place.

His scrutiny advanced. Hastings and his three companions occupied the next booth to Jean.

The professor's searching analysis reached across tables to the wall booths diagonally apart from Miss Moray and Hasting's party. A man and a moon-faced doll sat in one of the booths. They seemed no different from other patrons. Only Frost in all that crowd saw the barrel of the gun that crept in the direction of Hastings' booth from apparently folded hands. Even waiters glanced at the review while the orchestra wailed to a saxophonic triumph.

The woman rose, passed in front of the booth, walked away. There was a quiver of recoil from the stranger's gun at almost the same instant that Frost fired from the hip. Neither *sput* of the silenced automatics was loud enough to attract attention, but the killer yelped. A few waiters stared. Holding his shattered hand, he rose, hurried after the girl friend, vanished through a door near his booth.

Dellener wabbled and slumped over his table. The lights went out, stayed out for what seemed ages while Frost plunged across the room. Some one screamed. A weird chatter swept up from blackness, a babbling staccato of inquiries and forced banter.

Frost jerked out a flashlight as he ran, bumped into a table, collided with some one before the beam stabbed forth. Three other beams sprang into existence from other parts of the floor.

The lights flickered on. Jean Moray lay sprawled upon her table, a red streak searing eye to ear across her left temple. Her purse was open. An automatic rested at her finger tips. Frost dived for her, saw instantly that she was only stunned from a minor scalp wound. He whisked around to Hasting's booth. The Eves, wise in their way, had vanished. Hastings, white-faced, was trying to claw his way past Dellener from the inside of the booth. Blood trickled from the unconscious man's head. A deep gash laid open the top of his skull. Frost grabbed a clean napkin, wrapped it over the wound. He had shot barely in time to spoil the killer's aim.

"Out of the way, you!" grated a harsh voice. "I'm taking charge here."

It was a plain-clothes detective. Another was reviving Jean Moray. A third ran up. The Golden Goblin burst into an uproar of babbling guests and scurrying people.

"Certainly, take charge," Frost said, "but this man is injured if not dying. He must be taken to a hospital immediately."

"I'll take care—"

"I'm taking him now. Come along if you wish."

He lifted the unconscious man and carried him out. The detective hesitated, issued crisp orders to the two others, and trotted after Frost.

"How the hell do you get in this?" the detective demanded.

"The name is Frost—I. V. Frost."

"I've heard of you." The detective's attitude stiffened in the wary fashion of the man who bagged a black panther and didn't know what to do about it.

Frost honked a couple cars out of his path and stepped on the accelerator. His car swung from the curb. He sped to the corner and turned left.

The detective opened his mouth.

"Clinic Center Hospital," Frost drawled. "Keep an eye open for traffic police. If we're flagged, flash your badge."

"What the hell!" the detective exploded, but followed instructions.

"Did you trace the telephone call to headquarters?" asked Frost. "By the way, I didn't catch the name."

The detective squinted. "Seeley. Say, what do you know about that call?"

"Nothing. But there's no reason why three extra plain-clothes men should be detailed to the Golden Goblin. Some one must have phoned in that something was going to happen."

"You know too much for a guy who just wandered along in time for the fireworks."

"The fact that some one phoned headquarters doesn't mean it was the only place he called. I'm doing some investigating, too."

The car shot up to the receiving ward of the hospital, a fifteen-story masterpiece of architecture set in its own block of ground, one of the most celebrated and progressive medical units in America, with lawns and landscaped shrubbery on all sides. It occupied a short cliff bordering the river road.

The intern made a rapid examination of Dellener, summoned a night surgeon who treated the wound. He shook his head.

"The patient has an even chance of recovery. Hemorrhage may occur. Concussion of the brain is undoubtedly present. A trepan may be necessary later, but there is nothing more to be done now but keep the patient absolutely quiet."

Frost turned to Seeley. "Want to stay here in case he regains consciousness? Or come with me?"

"I'm sticking."

The scientist asked the surgeon: "Are there any escape-proof rooms here, aside from the psychopathic wards?"

"The best and safest of the private rooms are on the eighth-floor rear. The windows are not barred, but, even so, there is not enough bedding by which any one could conceivably make a sheet rope long enough to reach the ground, and it is impossible to scale the wall. But there is no chance of the patient's recovering consciousness for hours."

"Take Dellener to one of those rooms. If you stay with him, Seeley, keep a guard outside the door. If you leave the room, see that some one else stays inside with Dellener. A double guard must be kept."

Seeley glowered. "You kind of like to give orders, don't you?"

"One attempt has already been made at murder. There may be another because it failed. Whoever is behind this has brains and uses them. If Dellener vanishes from the hospital, I would regret being in your shoes when headquarters heard about it. I can't waste any more time here now. I'll be back later."

As the injured man was wheeled down a spotless corridor, Frost went out to his car. Five minutes later he was well on the way to the central station.

The city's night life had begun to subside fast. Theaters long dark were joined by the dimming lights of restaurants and taverns that closed. Traffic was so diminished that the harried pedestrian could cross streets in safety at almost any point. Even the inevitable cruising taxis became of reasonable infrequency, after one o'clock. The roar of noises, traffic and miscellaneous, passed from a loud confusion to a separate intermittency, as subdued as they ever were in midtown.

Frost parked by police headquarters. It was now nearly an hour after the Golden Goblin mess. A clock chimed one-fifteen as he climbed the steps.

The captain at the night desk was an elderly, slightly florid, rather thick-featured man. Calper had gone up and down in the ranks during long service. He played politics. When his party was in, his fortunes and promotions went up. When a rival administration held power, he generally found himself reduced or transferred to the sticks. He had been on the carpet several times, for investigation or censure. Like many men on the force, he had a general dislike of private investigators and a particular grudge against Frost.

Calper stared over the desk top with bland interest as Frost entered.

"Good evening, Captain Calper."

"What can I do for you?"

"A friend of mine, Miss Jean Moray, has been detained, I believe, in connection with some incidents at the Golden Goblin an hour ago. I would appreciate her release."

"Would you? That's interesting. Any more friends of yours around that I can turn loose for you?"

"It is only by mistake that my friends spend even an hour here."

"I'm afraid that you'll need a better excuse, perfessor. The lady knows plenty about what happened in that joint."

"I presume she's held both as a material witness and under direct suspicion?"

"So you're in the guessing game now?"

Frost leaned over the desk. "Calper, that young lady happens to be my assistant. She was there for the sole purpose of helping me not only prevent what happened, but of catching the criminals on the spot. That the police arrested my assistant while the guilty escaped wouldn't look so well in the papers, would it? And I don't suppose it would help certain reputations."

"If that's so, she should 'a' told us to begin with. And if she does know something, she better put it in the hands of the proper authorities."

To Captain Calper, it seemed as if the figure of the scientist suddenly expanded, achieved a more towering stature and a more implacable power.

Frost's dark eyes burned with the fire of an irresistible will. "Calper, I want that woman. *I want her now.*"

He got her. In that uncompromising ultimatum, backed only by the strength of Frost's personality, Calper read the finish of his career unless he yielded. Without another word, he issued the order for Jean's release.

IV.

Three minutes later, the abrasion on her temple taped, but otherwise looking cool and self-possessed, Jean sat beside Frost in the car.

As it swung north, she asked: "Where to, now?"

"Clinic Center Hospital, where I left Dellener."

"Who is he?"

"Political boss of his party—didn't you know?"

"I'm afraid I'm still pretty much in the dark. After I left you, I followed the instructions that had been given me by my employers and went to the Golden Goblin where I took a booth that they had reserved for me. As I expected, the man I had already been thrown against three times was in the next booth with a party. The time hadn't arrived for the stunt I was to do when the lights suddenly went out. Something hit me on the head.

"The next thing I knew, detectives were rushing me off. They claimed I had shot somebody and the gun was at my finger tips. But they wouldn't tell me anything more. They tried to make me confess that I knew who was shot, and why I did it, whereas it's still as much a mystery as when I came to you. But you know what it's all about, don't you?"

"It was a fairly simple problem," Frost admitted. "If you had lived here for a longer period, I am sure you would have seen the answers yourself."

Jean looked at him curiously. "How did you know I came so recently?"

"If your story had been true, and you had been in town a month ago looking for a position, you would have answered the first advertisement which appeared in the Sunday papers three weeks ago. That was no advertisement of mine, however. For reasons of my own, I inserted a duplicate notice in the following Sunday's papers, when a repetition of the first also was printed. You answered those two, thus indicating that you had begun looking for a job between three and two weeks ago.

"Your accent, even your use of words, was sectional. New England, the South, the Mid-West, the Far West, all have regional peculiarities of language, and within these districts speech may be further localized by its varying degree of colloquiality. Your usage was definitely Mid-Western.

"Furthermore, young women here do not carry new purses with the label of a Minneapolis store. It might have been a gift, but considered with the two facts I mentioned and a half dozen others that I won't bother detailing, it was evident that you had bought a new purse in that city just before you came East less than three weeks ago."

The professor stopped for traffic lights, kept the motor idling.

Jean remarked: "It seems like a miracle that you picked up my trail so quickly, especially since I left without telling you where I would be."

"As a matter of fact, you need not have left so suddenly, when you heard the horn. That was a deft bit of psychology on the part of your employer. Impress on the mind of any given individual a certain factor, such as this sound, which is associated with another factor, such as fear of pursuit, and if that individual eludes watch, one merely meeds to repeat the factor at random. The victim, by association, believes that he has been caught up with and is startled from cover."

The car leaped on again as the lights changed.

"You could have stopped me"—Jean began, then interrupted herself—"but of course not. If you had, you would have prevented the plot from coming to a climax, but by letting me go, you stood the best chance of catching the people behind it."

"Exactly! And I was confident I knew who they were. It was mainly a matter of identification. Your remarkable story suggested criminal activity in the first place. Legitimate affairs are not conducted by such fantastic means. Your description of the man identified him as Sam Hastings, owner of Coin Machines, Inc., and not generally known as a leading public enemy and one of the most influential racketeers in the country. His company controls ninety per cent of all slot machines, with an estimated 'take' of some ten million dollars monthly.

"The second major clue was your statement of the number of strangers who issued instructions to you. That indicated a large but well-organized group, which could only be Joe Blake's gang, whose twenty-three members, now twenty-one, dominate the city's underworld. The third important point was your phrase, 'Make it a million.' That of course referred to dollars.

"The slot-machine racket cannot thrive without political protection. A law is now in committee before the legislature to outlaw slot machines. That law will fail or pass according to the wish of the State boss, John Dellener, the man who was shot. Add to these the fact that the man who shot Dellener was Sam Orny, a paid killer, and you have the main essentials. Now do you understand?"

Jean wrinkled her brow. "Partly. Hastings was evidently dickering with Dellener, bribing him to use his influence to defeat the slot-machine bill. In return, Dellener would get a million for himself or to build up his party's power."

"A million a month," Frost corrected grimly.

"But I don't see where I fit into the picture. There is no reason why Blake's gang should use me to annoy Hastings. It's plain, though, that my mysterious assignments were meant to draw attention. Dozens of people would remember me in connection with Hastings. It looks as if somebody intended to railroad me and Hastings for the killing of Dellener.

"But why? And if a rival gangster did the shooting, there must have been a double cross somewhere. Why shoot Dellener with Hastings around? Whether he lives or dies, the newspapers are bound to raise so much trouble that the slot-machine law will be passed. And that will be killing the goose that laid the golden egg. It begins to seem as if there is a deeper mystery behind this."

"Come in and we'll have a look at Dellener," Frost said as the car halted at the hospital.

They had scarcely entered when the scientist exclaimed: "Seeley! What are you doing down here?"

"I have to report to headquarters now and then, see? I'm keeping track of developments at the other end."

"Is any one guarding Dellener?"

"Of course somebody's watching him. I know my business. The door's locked, and there's a guard outside."

"How long have you been gone?"

"Say, can the Sherlock Holmes stuff! I haven't been gone more'n a half hour. Dellener won't come to for a long while yet, the doc said. Nobody can get past the guard without permission, and I hope you don't think some bird is going to hop through an eighth-floor window."

"A half hour!" Frost groaned. He tossed the keys of his car to the girl. "Keep the motor idling for a quick start." He raced to the self-service elevator.

Seeley snarled: "Listen, Frost, I don't like your airs, see? The guy can't get out because he's unconscious, and nobody can get in through the door because the guard's there, and nobody can get in through the window because it's eight floors up. Is that clear? Or want me to draw a diagram?"

Frost gave Seeley one short glance. Seeley squirmed and subsided. It was strange how that raking gaze made him feel like an inferior bug on a pin. Frost wore an air of abstraction until the elevator stopped.

While Seeley puffed after him, the lank scientist raced down the hall to the one door in front of which a guard was lounging. "Quick—open the door!"

The guard hauled out a key and inserted it. He swung the door open. His eyes took on a queer, baffled look. Seeley opened his mouth and remained on the verge of speaking. Frost alone swept the room with a glance.

It was empty.

"I knew Dellener would be gone. You should have carried out my directions." It was less a rebuke than a simple statement of fact. Frost turned and sprinted for the elevator.

Seeley found his voice: "Hey, you! Come back here! How'd the guy get out? Where you going?"

"There are at least four means by which he might have left. I'm going where he is now. I gave you all the instructions you needed an hour ago, and you didn't follow them. Now find out for yourself what happened." He slammed the elevator door, punched the starting bell, and dropped while Seeley fumed behind.

He tore through the ground-floor corridor. Jean, with beautiful teamwork, had the car under way and shifted to high before he climbed in. She deftly slid out of the driver's seat, and he took the wheel.

"What's the trouble?" she asked.

"Everything! Because an obstinate detective wouldn't remember the alphabet, Dellener is gone, and we've got to start all over." He sketched the situation rapidly.

"It sounds impossible, but I suppose the guard might have been bribed or doped," she speculated.

"That's one possibility."

"A helicopter plane could have landed on the roof, and some one slid down a rope to the eighth floor."

"Number two."

"And a human fly with suction cups like the man who walks upside down at the circus might have scaled the side of the building."

"Good alternative number three," Frost approved. "You have at least three hundred per cent more brains than that unimaginative ass behind, which I'll admit isn't much of a compliment."

"What's the fourth? I can't think of any other reasonable explanation."

"The kidnaping was maneuvered in a highly ingenious manner. One man with a coil of strong, light rope carried a balloon, or more likely a duralumin shell filled with gas under high pressure, the lifting power of which equaled his weight. Dellener's room was in the rear of the hospital facing the Hudson. The kidnaper, unnoticed in the dark night and at this late hour, stood under Dellener's window and leaped straight up.

"Guiding himself by pressing his hands down on the wall, using suction tips on his fingers, he simply drifted up to the eighth floor, lowered Dellener to his confederates, then stepped out of the window and floated to the ground. It could be done easily in five minutes."

The girl objected. "It sounds plausible enough—except for the fact that the balloon had to be made, prepared, and filled, even before it was taken to the hospital. The feat could not possibly have been accomplished in the short time since you left Dellener here."

"The balloon was ready. The mind that engineered this coup was not trusting anything to chance. He had foreseen and prepared for everything."

"No mere gangsters could be as clever as that and so well equipped with scientific supplies—"

Frost interrupted: "Can't discuss it any more now. I'll be gone three or four minutes. That gown you're wearing would be a fatal hindrance. You'll have time to change before I return."

"Change? To what? Where?"

"In the car. I forgot to tell you I took everything out of your room. Your things are in the suitcase on the floor behind us. Your life would be worthless if you ever returned to the Sixty-third Street address. I own both the houses adjoining my State Street address. They are rather crowded with material of all sorts, but you are welcome to the use of either one."

The car shrilled to a stop in front of Frost's laboratory. He hurried inside without waiting for a reply.

The girl moved as if she was trying to rival the speed of light. She was on pins and needles for fear that Frost might be back before she had changed. She sensed that feminine appeal was wasted on him. Though men succumbed to her, she knew that the professor considered her only as an added impersonal quantity to be fitted into his plans.

She flung open the suitcase, wriggled from the gown slipped into a tweed suit, and changed to sport shoes. The transformation was completed just as Frost came running out with a load of apparatus which he set carefully on the rear seat.

Gathering speed, the car streaked north toward the outskirts of the city.

"Where are we going now?" Jean asked.

"Why don't you try telling me?"

"Because I still don't see where I fit—" she began, but her voice trailed off. Sudden enlightenment brought a startled expression to her face.

Frost, watching the girl from the corner of his eye, nodded agreement. "Now you understand it. For the time being, call X the agency behind all this. X has larger plans in view, but works through Blake's gang to have them kidnap Hastings, fasten suspicion on you, and leave you to face the music. Then X hires a killer to accomplish one of the real aims—the murder of Dellener, leaving both Hastings and you to answer in court.

"You can imagine what would happen if you told your story in court. Your beauty attracts attention, even without such bizarre elements as that tropical bird. Dozens of people would remember your behavior at Mardi's, the theater, and in the cab collision. It would be as sensational front-page stuff for days as the press has ever had.

"Murder, the mysterious woman, fantastic explanations, crime and politics involved, suspicion of mental derangement—at least I can admire the imaginative audacity of that plot. And while the papers issued reams of this spectacular stuff, X could put across crooked schemes that would slide unnoticed by the public while it devoured the murder mystery of the century. Unfortunately, I spoiled the schedule."

"Then X must have been in the Golden Goblin at the time of the shooting!" Jean took up the thread excitedly. "By now he must know that you are in the picture. When he saw his plans miscarry, he had you trailed to the hospital. But there doesn't seem to be any reason for kidnaping Dellener, except for the sole purpose of drawing you on so that X and Blake's gang have a chance to remove us once and for all, using Dellener as bait. If they caught us, they could again fasten suspicion on me, and they would be free of a dangerous enemy by killing you."

"It is disconcerting to have one's sudden departure from this existence discussed in so casual a fashion, but for a young woman you have a very good head. The most dangerous part of our work lies immediately ahead.

"In the course of a lifetime devoted to criminal investigation, I have accumulated a vast mass of information and data, much of which even the police do not possess. I doubt whether they know that the house on Tucker Lane where we are headed is the clearing point for all Blake's activities. Dellener has unquestionably been taken there.

"It is strategically situated off the main highway, and a mile from the nearest habitation. It stands in a clearing so that a surprise raid is impossible. It can be surrounded, but it has three long underground tunnels leading into the adjacent woods, so that, if ever raided, the gang could still escape in safety."

The everlasting lights that streamed toward them as they sped through the outskirts of the city became more infrequent. A wall of wind seemed to be pressing against the car with a roar. They shot beyond the city limits, racing northward along a deserted highway. Only their headlights pierced the darkness.

"Ah! The first attack—and just about where I thought it would be!" Frost breathed.

He shot past a crossroad. The lights of another car suddenly blazed out. A long, powerful limousine swung after them. Frost stepped on the accelerator. His car leaped faster, but the pursuers roared faster still. Two radiating series of cracks spread across the rear window of Frost's car. The *pang* of metal came repeatedly. Fifty—fifty-five—sixty—sixty-five—seventy—

"The tires!" Jean cried.

"Built-in and protected. This car is armored, and the glass is bulletproof. Let them shoot all they wish—it's the last time they ever will shoot."

"They're still catching up! Can't you go faster?"

"Certainly! I could leave them out of sight in five minutes, but I want them to catch up. The best way to meet a threat is not to run away from it but to eliminate it altogether. Less than a mile ahead, the road is elevated over a cross-highway. If you're not used to sudden, violent death, you'd better not watch."

The girl watched.

Frost's car zipped down the middle of the road. The pursuing car raced nearer, nearer, swung clear over to the left side of the road, edged on foot by foot as the scientist let them catch up. The wind droned past as in a gale. The girl looked into the death car, saw three murderous faces in the rear seat, another in front beside the driver, and all four men armed with submachine guns.

A blast raked the whole side of Frost's car. The flaming gun was followed by a spitting clatter that raised a dozen round spots with radiating cracks on the windows. The bridge loomed ahead. The limousine edged closer to Frost's car, forcing him farther to the right.

Then his hand flicked to the dashboard, punched a button. At the same time he swerved his car sharply to the right, and for a moment it rocked wildly along the edge of the road. To Jean, his face in profile seemed as stern as destiny itself.

The two right tires of the limousine exploded. Its front plowed toward Frost's car, fell a foot short. Its rear sloughed away. It careened, rolled sidewise over and over, slanting left across the road. It mounted the slope at a tangent and piled into the concrete retaining wall. It stood on its nose for a sickening second, and a dark, limp figure hurtled through its smashed top and sailed down like a grotesque bird. Then the limousine toppled to the lower roadbed, while Frost's car sped across the bridge.

Jean, white-face and wordless, wrenched her eyes away, stared at the road ahead as they raced on.

Frost snapped: "Don't waste any sympathy on them. That was a service to society. Did you notice the swarthy-faced man sitting beside the driver? He was Spike Leone, one of three members of Blake's gang who specialized in kidnaping. The others in the car were more of Blake's gang—strong-arm men, killers."

"What did you do?"

"Perhaps you noticed that the front bumper is tubular? I merely released one of two springs. It ejected a couple of quarts of tacks, nails, broken glass, and scrap iron from the left side of the bumper. Momentum did the rest."

V.

Ten miles north of the city, Frost cut his speed. He halted just before a curve, and told the girl to await his return. He vanished noiselessly into the darkness, came back ten minutes later. A pleased expression hovered on his face.

"The second waiting committee sleeps," he remarked, as he drove around the bend and approached a semiprivate side road that wound through the woods. He left the arterial highway and followed it. "A lookout was posted at the juncture. He made the mistake of smoking a cigarette." Frost commented, as if that explained everything.

The headlights dimmed and, progressing at scarcely more than a walking pace, he drove at last off the rough road into a thicket.

He lifted a pile of apparatus from the rear seat. "I'll need your help. Move as quietly as you can," he cautioned and led the way into the forest.

She followed silently in his path.

"Where did you learn the woodsman's art?" he whispered.

The girl's answer, almost voiceless, came with a hint of laughter: "One doesn't spend summers on canoe and camping trips through the Ten Thousand Lakes district without learning a few things."

Frost halted. Ahead of them, in the midst of a clearing two hundred yards across, loomed a house, dark save for one window on the ground floor which was open to a brightly lighted room.

Frost climbed a tree and perched on a limb. "Hand me the things," he whispered and leaned down.

The girl passed up to him the camera, plates, and telescopic lens.

While he busied himself for several minutes, Jean studied the house. She could make out the head and shoulders of a seated man. He looked powerful, ruthless. He had a crooked nose and a frog's face and his hair was whitish. A shadow might have been thrown by a second man, or an article of furniture. She could hear no voices, and the quiet of night remained unbroken except for the faint, mechanical sounds made by Frost. They were inaudible more than a dozen feet away.

The professor at last lowered his materials to her and cautiously descended.

While again transferring the things to him, she whispered: "Did you see Dellener?"

"He is lying on a couch, still unconscious. Beside him is Stocky Mason, chief lieutenant and killer of Blake's gang."

"Who is the third man? Or is the shadow only—"

"Quiet!" the professor insisted impatiently. "Stay here until I return. But if you see any one leave the house, come back to the car and let me know. Have you a gun? Then take this. I shall be gone for twenty-five minutes."

Carrying his equipment, Frost melted into the blackness of the woods. The minutes dragged on, doubly long now that she kept vigil. The girl centered her gaze on the lighted window. Mason hardly moved. He sat half facing the window. She wondered why he did not shift his position or raise his hands into view even once. He seemed to be waiting, so far as she could tell.

Keyed-up and alert though she was from the tension of the night, and from her feeling that the strange events in which she had become enmeshed through answering advertisements were coming to a head, she wondered if there might not be more at stake than the criminologist had yet explained to her. She felt privileged to have become his assistant in games where death was always a part—until a flash of insight destroyed her pleasure.

The first advertisement had been inserted by some one who deliberately sought to make her a victim of circumstantial evidence in a crime of far-reaching results. But Frost had inserted a duplicate advertisement a week later. Why? Because inevitably one or more applicants who at least had an interview with the agent of the first advertiser would also come to Frost.

Yet she could not be sure. Had Frost duplicated the first advertisement primarily because he recognized the germ of a deep plot? Had he actually wanted an assistant and simply used the opportunity to serve both purposes?

And who was the X, the unknown quantity, that Frost had postulated? Was he hunting bigger game than gangsters, or had he merely used the symbol to designate some grafting politician who protected Blake's gang, or even to designate Joe Blake?

Frost was gone a long time, fifteen minutes, a half hour—Jean could not tell. Her eyes began to ache from the strain of watching. She wondered what Frost was up to. She consoled herself by thinking that, whatever the motivation, Frost had definitely offered and she had just as definitely accepted the position. But then, positions may only last a week, she thought wryly.

No one emerged from the house, and no unusual sound broke the silence.

She tensed and almost ran when the professor suddenly stood beside her like a bleak specter from the darkness. Then she felt a sense of absolute security, so strong was the force of his personality.

The scientist handed her some things and whispered his last instructions: "The trap is set for us, all right, and we are going to spring it. Slip into this bulletproof cloak and hood. They will protect you against ordinary pistol fire when we rush the house. Keep this shield in one hand. The suit is not proof to submachine gun or rifle bullets, but the armor-plate is.

"Drop this automatic in the outside pocket of the cloak and keep the other gun in hand. You'll need both. Above all, shoot at any lights that appear outside of the house. Now put the gas mask on and keep it on. Are the instructions clear? We won't be able to talk after the masks are in place."

The girl nodded. They made the transformation in silence. The atmosphere became electric. She felt the thrill of imminent and all-powerful danger. Yet her nerves remained steady, and she liked the way in which she had been accepted as a working partner.

Frost made no idle chivalrous gesture, did not try to persuade her to stay behind or to back out. She liked, too, his positive methods; his bold counterstrikes, the scope of his analytical imagination that enabled him to make definite and sure preparations for any eventuality.

One on each side of the lighted window, they broke from the woods and stole toward the house. There came an almost inaudible click, a sudden faint hissing, when they were still eighty yards from their goal. At fifty, the grounds sprang into blinding radiance from flood lights on the roof. A rifle cracked above. Frost staggered.

The girl calmly aimed at the spot of the flash on the roof and fired. A scream pierced the night. The figure of a man spun from the roof and toppled, twisting, to earth. The girl flung herself face-down, held the protective shield in front of her. The light in the window vanished as Mason's hands came up with a submachine gun. Flame spurted to the accompaniment of a staccato bark. Bullets clipped the ground, whined overhead, *panged* and flattened against the shield. Her hand stung from the vibration.

Frost picked himself up, warily advanced, running low behind his shield. The more infrequent but deadlier bark of a rifle again sounded from the roof. Through a slit in the shield, the girl emptied one gun and two of the four flood lights shattered into darkness. A startled rabbit bounded across the grass. Suddenly it wabbled and fell inert. Jean thought it had been hit, but there was no trace of injury. Then she remembered the hissing noise, and Frost's insistence on the gas mask.

The girl raked the remaining flood lights with her second weapon. Crash of glass and *zing* of metal. The grounds plunged into blackness. The roof sniper fired again, and Jean jerked as a slug tore off a heel.

From the darkened window, the submachine gun poured its livid spurts; the air whistled and the shield quivered. Jean sensed rather than saw the professor run toward the house. His arm swept back, curved forward, three times, almost as fast as the eye could follow. The gas bombs hurtled through the window and broke with dull plops. Some one cried out, whether in warning or fear or pain was impossible to tell. The firing abruptly ceased. Jean reloaded both automatics and raced after the professor.

His long, loose-jointed form swung easily through the window as she ran up. He produced a flashlight from his pocket and played it around the room. Mason lay sprawled on the floor. A faint, thudding noise, as of a dead weight being dragged, came from far away. Dellener had been abandoned. Frost stooped, lifted the unconscious man, and returned to the window. He lowered Dellener to Jean who sturdily supported him while the professor dropped down to her side. He cast one quick glance at the huddled figure of the man who had toppled from the roof.

Dellener's breathing was so faint as to be almost indetectable. Frost carried the body again and stumbled off in an obvious but unexplained hurry. Jean took the cue and ran beside him. They were scarcely forty yards from the house when a terrific explosion blasted the night. Frost immediately dropped to the ground, but the girl was blown from her feet.

A wall of wind roared from where the house had stood. Plaster, bricks, debris began to rain everywhere. Frost staggered to his feet and carried Dellener to the protection of the woods. Jean, stunned, slowly regained her senses and followed.

The sight of a stain spreading down the professor's shoulder brought her sharply back to reality. She tore off her mask. She swayed dizzily, then recovered. The scientist removed his own mask.

The girl cried: "You're hurt!"

"Just a flesh wound, painful but not serious. The bullet passed through, and I have already staunched the flow. Miss Moray, hereafter, in the presence of anaesthetic gases—"

"Please, Professor Frost, credit me with enough intelligence to know that an explosion as strong as that one must have blown the gases away. Are we safe now?"

"Not entirely. Keep your automatic ready while I carry Dellener to the car."

"Then you don't think the blast killed them all?"

"Rather, it was intended to destroy us. Mason, who was probably gassed by the bombs I tossed in, must have died, as well as the second sniper on the roof. It's just as well. The law has been saved from the necessity of prosecuting Mason and the first sniper—the two other kidnapers. But the mind that planned to-night's work may have got away. When we entered, did you hear the sound of some one's dragging a body? He had time to reach the underground passageways, and thought we would search the house or delay long enough to be blown up with Dellener."

"How were they warned so quickly? I thought we were very quiet when we started across."

"Do you remember hearing a faint click?" Frost asked, as they approached the road. "We crossed the beam of a photo-electric eye and thus announced ourselves by breaking the circuit."

"That's strange. I didn't see any beam of light."

"There are several kinds of photo-electric cells, including one that works only by infra-red rays which are invisible to the eye. If we have time, I'll make a survey of the grounds, but I really see no need for it. That is the only automatic way by which our advance in the darkness could have been recorded. The cell-operated relay was undoubtedly connected with the buried gas containers.

"The mistake lay in thinking that we might escape the death car, the lookout, and even the gas, but not the shooting. They overlooked the possibility that I might go them one better by not only coming prepared for defense but also by bringing my own gas bombs."

"I should think they would have worn masks, if only because their own gas might drift back into the house."

"The wind drift, what little there is, is away from the house. Even so, they counted on shooting us in mere seconds and then closing the one open window until the gases had dissipated. The plan was thorough—but not thorough enough."

Frost strode from the woods and went toward his car. The gray dusk of dawn was just beginning to lighten the air. Frost stopped abruptly and laid Dellener on the ground.

"Is something wrong?" Jean asked anxiously.

"Just one of the precautions I took when I left you at the clearing."

He searched along the roadside until he found the wire he had left connected with the ignition of his car and pulled it. It was still fastened. He unscrewed the bulb of his flashlight and scraped the wire across the exposed battery. It sparked.

Forty feet away, his automobile leaped into the air in a cascade of flame and exploding debris.

Frost's eyes were grim. "Some one has been active while we were gone. Now—"

The motor of a car purred to life farther down the road. Frost raced to one of the two hiding places where he had concealed the plates of the photographs he took and returned with three in hand.

A car gathering speed swung around a curve fifty yards off. The glare of headlights fell on them. Low, powerful, and armored, the car swept ahead and glided to rest a dozen feet away, its motor idling with a deep-throated purr.

"Professor Frost and Miss Moray, I believe? Be so good as to drop your weapons." The soft, triumphant voice slurred from the impenetrable blackness in the car.

"The pleasure is mutual; one encounters you so seldom."

Frost's sardonic answer had the hardness of metal. He and Jean dropped their guns. The girl felt as if she were in a nightmare that went on and on, but, even now, her nerves did not crack, though she faced death. She had confidence that the dominant figure in the nightmare was still the scientist, weird in his protective garments.

The bodiless voice continued: "Your automobile appears to have been wrecked. That is a pity. It was such an ingenious little laboratory in itself."

"And a greater pity that we were not in it when the unfortunate accident occurred?"

"Not necessarily, for there might be an unexpected but altogether satisfactory pleasure in silencing your efficient, but annoying, partnership, now and for ever."

To the girl, the personal antagonism underneath this polite interchange was like a lighted fuse, crackling swiftly to the final explosion that would end the nightmare.

"Wish-fulfillments do not often occur in life," Frost replied suavely.

"But frequently by death."

"Before that sad event takes place, perhaps you would be interested in viewing some most unusual photographic plates I have here."

Silence from the car for only a moment. Then a single shot came from the interior of it. The three plates burst into fragments, and the bullet flattened against Frost's cloak.

The voice murmured with mock regret: "What a pity! I am sure that the plates would have been most entertaining."

Jean, staring at the sinister car, felt that a sardonic smile must have crossed the professor's face when he drawled:

"Fortunately, those were the spoiled plates, though the figure of Dellener was clear enough. The three others, the perfect three, the most compromising three, clearly showing Dellener, Mason, and a third person, will doubtless be of remarkable interest to the police and the press."

"They would be, indeed—if they reached such hands. But, of course, it is difficult to extract information from a corpse. And those who do not know what or where to hunt, do not hunt."

Frost's voice took on a slur of satisfaction, as if he and he only controlled the situation: "Surely, if you were thoughtful enough to plant a bomb in the ignition system of my car, you were observant enough to notice the built-in developing outfit, and the wireless transmission set under the rear seat? Nor should it be necessary to remind you of the high-tension wires a hundred feet from here which furnish ample power for sending.

"It was close to an hour ago that I wirelessed the location of this place and of those valuable plates. I should say that fifteen minutes at most would suffice for the arrival of certain persons who would think nothing of spreading those pictures on the front page of the nation's press. The least of results, of course, would be the utter ruin of one hitherto brilliant career."

"Your imagination is far-sighted," the voice from the car answered, "but in fifteen minutes, one may investigate a considerable area."

"True! The problem is quite simple. You may kill Miss Moray and me, then hunt for the plates. If you do not find them, and I can assure you that you will not, you may be trapped on the scene, which would be most unfortunate, or if you departed, your own legal execution would be only a matter of limited time as a consequence of the incriminating plates.

"Much as I regret doing so, I am afraid that I must give you an opportunity to escape," Frost remarked with cool and ironic effrontery. "Since it is undeniable that you could destroy us now, I shall, before my friends arrive, be so careless as to smash the plates. You will be considerate enough to continue on your way. The mutual profit of the action should be immediately evident to an intelligent mind. I might add that instant action is desirable. Fifteen minutes was my maximum estimate, not the minimum."

The voice from the car spoke for the last time: "I have always held a high opinion of your extreme resourcefulness, Professor Frost, and of your gifted mind. I trust, indeed, I anticipate meeting you again. It is both a liability and an asset that you have the one weakness of always fulfilling your promises."

The motor roared. For an instant, Jean had an impression that she had reached the permanent end of the nightmare, that the drone of the engine would drown the spitting racket of a submachine gun. The car swept past and disappeared around a bend. Its deep purr suddenly died down. There was silence for a minute, then a burst of shots. The motor faded away.

"What did that mean?" Jean demanded.

Frost shrugged. "The lookout will never awaken, now. Those who sleep on guard duty, no matter what the cause, have no place in Blake's gang."

"It was not Blake who spoke from the car?"

"It was the voice of the mind behind to-night's work, a mind that conceived a perfect plot," Frost replied. "Whatever happened at any point, he could still turn the developments to his purposes. Even now, though this case is closed."

"How can he profit now? We have Dellener. The kidnapers are dead. You have made it impossible for them to make me the victim of circumstantial evidence as they planned."

"Yes; but to-day's papers will carry headlines on the attempted murder, the kidnaping, the rescue, and the persons involved. Under the glare of publicity, public opinion will force the passage of the anti-slot-machine law."

"But that means that an immensely profitable source of revenue will be cut off from crooks and racketeers. Grafting politicians will lose some of their easiest money."

"Precisely! They won't surrender fat profits as readily as that. With bootlegging gone, and the enormous slot-machine income erased, only one result can occur: a great increase in burglaries, bank robberies, kidnapings, business racketeering, hijacking, blackmail, and other criminal activities. But this is no time for a post-mortem. Let's be off."

"Aren't you going to wait till your friends arrive?"

A mirthless smile twisted the professor's lean features. "I am afraid it would be a waste of time. I neglected to inform our recent visitors that when I used the wireless some time ago, I was unable to obtain any answer. But let us account for the other plates."

Jean's hair, tousled and wind-blown, framed a face all the lovelier for its glint of admiration at the successful bluff, as she accompanied Frost to the second cache, where he had left the remaining plates under leaves near a great boulder.

A piece of twisted metal from the wrecked car lay over the hiding place. The plates had been shattered into bits.

Chuckling silently, the scientist lifted Dellener. The girl walked beside him as he strode slowly toward the lightening east and the main highway to hail a car.

GREEN MAN—CREEPING

AS HIS ALTOGETHER too good-looking assistant entered, Professor I. V. Frost continued to stare indifferently at a point somewhere beyond the ceiling.

"Here is the mail—if I'm not disturbing you." Jean Moray hoped she was, but knew perfectly well that hopes were futile so far as the rangy, beak-nosed criminologist was concerned.

He did not bother to turn around. "Is there anything of consequence in it?"

"A Mr. Blane, of various corporations, offers a retaining fee of five thousand dollars. His idea seems to be that substantial proof, to be acquired by you, will be needed of his wife's indiscretions for divorce proceedings."

"Not interested. I do not handle such cases."

"The Women's City Club wants you to address them on the fifth. The topic suggested is 'The Solution of Crime.'"

Frost massaged the tip of his nose. "Tell those good ladies that unfortunately I shall be in Peoria on the fifth. And, if necessary, I *will* be in Peoria."

Jean glanced at another letter. "A kid at the General Hospital says he heard about your work in the Golden Goblin affair, and when he gets out he wants to see you so that he can tell you he thinks you're a swell sleuth."

Frost shifted his position. "Disillusion him."

"Here's a terse message. Somebody who signs himself 'Ishmael' writes that you have interfered with the destined order of things and are therefore marked for death. Upon him has fallen the honor of being the agent."

"Let me see it."

The girl handed him the note. He tossed it back after studying it for a few seconds.

"Well?" she suggested.

"Fairly interesting, but not important. It bears out a belief of mine that deductive logic is almost worthless by itself."

"Why?"

"The threat is written on cheap, soiled, ruled paper, with a scratchy pen. The last part is in pencil. Various words are misspelled. Deduction would indicate that the letter was written by a poor, illiterate man who was munching a sandwich held in his left hand, and who had biblical delusions. But the matter is not so simple as that. A highly intelligent man could have written the letter. He might have gone to great pains to obtain just such a piece of cheap, dirty paper. The misspellings could have been the result of deliberation rather than ignorance. However, there is no need to waste further time on a trifling note."

He unfolded from the chair, slouched to a window. Even when half stooping, Frost seemed taller than the average man. He hooked a heel on the radiator cover, rested an elbow on his knee, and bent over, cupping his hand under his chin while he stared moodily outside. Lines of boredom creased his lean features. His black eyes looked lusterless.

"Little things, odds and ends that any competent police force or detective agency could manage," he fretted. "Why do people bother me with these run-of-the-mill affairs? There surely must be strange, terrible, and almost incredible crimes taking place in the world every day. A city of this size must be rotten with them.

"But where are they? Nothing unusual has come to my attention in a fortnight. Either the perplexing riddles are not occurring, which is contrary to human nature and to all probabilities for a city as large as this, or they are taking place but not coming to light, which also stretches the laws of probability.

"If I am exposed to these dull episodes much longer, I may be compelled to invent or arrange bizarre events. There might be some stimulus in watching others attack a knotty problem."

"I hope you don't," Jean returned. "If you did start something, nobody would ever find the answer. So what fun would there be in that?"

Frost continued to stare moodily out of the window. A sport roadster turned the nearest corner, rolled slowly along State Street, and came to rest in front of No. 13. A hectic young woman in her middle twenties stepped out. Frost's glance raced over her. His boredom dropped away like magic. A glitter entered his eyes. His sagging frame tautened, and animation returned to his face. He whirled around.

"Stuff those letters out of sight. Empty the ash trays and powder your nose in ten seconds flat," he ordered crisply.

As Jean flitted to obey, she complained: "It might help if you'd tell me what part of the house is on fire. Maybe the world was made in a day, but you can't expect me to polish it off in a second even if the enemy is coming."

"Miss Mae Ellen Hollister is almost here. She has just come through a remarkable experience. It was so terrifying that she decided not to ask police aid for fear of disbelief. Her nerves have gone completely to pieces. She is not only distressed. She is in such a state of hysteria that she may collapse with a nervous breakdown. I want you to admit her. And, by all means, stay at her side and use every last gram of feminine understanding you have while she is here, or at least until she has had time to tell her story."

Mingled expressions held a field day on Jean's face. When she did manage to straighten her thoughts, the bell rang sharply before she could speak.

As she left, with a last glance at her compact and a pat for her already perfectly arranged hair, Frost plucked a cigarette from an ivory case. It was one of unusual length and emitted smoke of a peculiar and stimulating aroma. While he inhaled, his frame took on a deceptive repose, but his eyes glittered more brightly under the bushy black brows, and his features lost their pallor.

Jean introduced Mae Ellen Hollister. The visitor, fighting for control, dropped limply into the nearest chair. Her face was bloodless. Her eyes hardly seemed to see the criminologist. She was obviously near the end of her resources. She acted like a person in a dream or suffering from shock, with mechanical motions, blazed pupils, countenance alternately quivering and then set in a mask of stone. She was attractive in the way of her kind—expensive clothes, slim figure, a wise, thin curve to her mouth, sophisticated hazel eyes, the discontent of having so much that there is nothing left to want.

Frost took one look at her and disappeared into his laboratory.

The visitor sat trembling, unable to speak, exerting the full strength of her will to keep from going over the edge. Frost emerged with a glass of pinkish fluid that he handed her. She gulped it down. In five minutes, an indefinable change took place. The shock and the terror remained, but her manner became calmer, more detached. She seemed just a trifle drowsy.

"It was a terrifying experience, wasn't it?" Frost meditated coolly. "But the explanation is so simple that you will wonder how you were ever frightened so badly."

"Do you think so, really?" The girl looked up with anxious hope.

"Of course! The strangest things in life are often easiest to explain. I remember a time years ago when my car broke down on a lonely road late at night. I started walking, and when I came to a cemetery I knew that a town would be not much farther on, but I was tired and leaned on the fence for a rest.

"While I was looking at the tombstones, a white figure suddenly rose, a misshapen, ghostly thing that seemed to issue straight from the ground. If I had been frightened and ran away, I would have sworn to this day that I saw a ghost at least eight feet tall rise out of the ground. But I went over to investigate and discovered that some tramp had wrapped himself in an old sheet and gone to sleep. He became cramped and stood up to stretch about the time I happened along. Your experience will prove to have just as natural an explanation, once all the facts are known."

"I hardly know what to say or where to begin," Mae Ellen Hollister replied slowly.

She fumbled with a small package and stared at it with the fascination of horror before nervously sliding it onto a table. Her eyes continually strayed to it while she talked.

"I've lived a pretty fast life," she went on at last. "I've never thought much about anything except what my crowd went in for—parties, sports, clothes, and the rest of it. A pretty pleasant and carefree sort of life with plenty of everything. Now, I don't know what to believe. Half the time I think I'm going mad; the rest of the time I feel that some awful force actually exists in a form ever so much more worse than just ghosts. If it was only something supernatural, I could pretend it was a dream. But it's the hideous reality of this that sent me to pieces."

"Suppose you start at the beginning and tell me what happened." Frost urged.

"It began shortly after my father died, four years ago. He was very wealthy, and when the stroke carried him away, he left most of his property to my mother. We were away cruising in the Caribbean at the time, and the interment had taken place before we returned or even had word of it. Separate trust funds were established for my sister, my brother, and myself. In addition, there was a big annual income in royalties from some mining and manufacturing patents that my father owned.

"After his death, we continued living in the town house, except Paul, my brother, who married an adventuress and set up a place of his own more than a year later. Paul of course dropped in to see us from time to time."

The visitor took a deep breath. Her voice trembled.

"My father died on April 9, 1930. Nearly a year later, on April 6th, before Paul left, I was awakened long after midnight by a shriek from my sister's bedroom. I won't call it a shriek. It was a continuous sound, appalling. Of course I jumped out of bed. I could hear the servants already pattering down from upstairs. I heard the door to my mother's room open. How I heard is a mystery to me because that cry never stopped.

"I was the first to reach Ann's room. The door was locked. She never locked it for any reason at any time that I know of. When the servants came up, they broke the door in. The lights were on. The window was wide open. Ann was out of her head, staring at the open window and still screaming, but in a raw sort of voice now.

"She kept on screaming. We called our physician, had her taken to a sanitarium. She never recovered, never talked. She died two weeks later. Her voice was only a dull whisper by then."

Mae Ellen Hollister closed her eyes, as if to forget an unforgettable memory. Jean leaned forward, all sympathetic attention. "Ivy" Frost puffed his cigarettes with the peculiar aroma. The lids drooped over his eyes, but they glittered keenly under the black brows.

The visitor resumed, speaking in a low monotone:

"If it will help, I can give you a general idea of our town house. It is three stories high, built in the early years of the century, of stone exterior, and surrounded by lawns, trees, and shrubbery. The ground floor contains the reception room, tea room, ballroom, conservatory, library, dining room, and kitchen. On the second floor are our bedrooms and the guest rooms, eight in all, and some closets and storerooms. On the third floor are the servants' quarters. None of the second-floor rooms have adjoining doors. You must go out into the hall to reach another room."

"At the time, none of you had the least inkling about what frightened your sister, but you discovered later," Frost remarked.

"Yes; I am coming to that. Naturally we were alarmed and mystified. We couldn't imagine why her door was locked. The best guess seemed to be that some intruder had entered, locked the door, and done something that terrified Ann. But we looked at the ground under her window, and there was no trace of anything there, not even the marks of a ladder."

"He who comes by the roof leaves no trace on the ground," Frost murmured, exhaling a cloud of smoke.

"We even thought my sister might have been the victim of a hallucination, but though we were all a pretty high-stung, nervous family, she had never shown any such tendency before. We thoroughly examined the house, but nothing was missing.

"After the interment, we gradually returned to our usual mode of living.

"A year passed. The depression grew worse, but it did not affect us nearly as much as it did many of our friends, partly because of sound investments, and partly because the companies leasing father's mining and manufacturing patent rights found them so valuable that they could not stop payment of royalties without losing the leases to rival companies and perhaps being forced out of business. We had that fixed income so we kept our town house open and went on pretty much as usual.

"One night, on April 15, 1932, mother asked me to go shopping with her the next morning. Of course I said I would. She said she was tired, though, and would I mind waiting until she wakened.

"For some reason, I didn't sleep well. I heard mother moving around at one time in the night and decided she hadn't been as tired as she thought. I rose early for me, about eight o'clock, had breakfast, and was surprised when mother still had not come down by ten o'clock. I don't know why I didn't ask a maid to look in her room, but I suddenly decided to run up. I tapped on her door. There was no answer, but instead of turning away, I tried the door. It was locked. My heart felt so heavy I thought I would faint. I called the servants and had them break the door open.

"Mother was dead. There was an awful look on her face. The doctor said that it was a case of heart failure, and her expression was simply the result of muscular contraction and *rigor mortis*. Perhaps he was right, but why did she have heart failure? She was not subject to heart trouble. Why was her door locked when I had never before known her to lock it? And that awful look on her face—it reminded me only too closely of the fate that had taken my sister. But there were no signs of an intruder, except the wide-open window, and nothing was missing. I had no tangible evidence to support my suspicions.

"I thought many times of moving from the house. I began to feel as if a curse hung over it. But I stayed on for sentimental reasons, and, after all, one must stay somewhere. It was a good place to entertain in, too, and I often had friends for week-end parties. After this, my brother Paul began to drop in more frequently, and his scoffing at what he called my wild ideas made it easier for me to stay. He was having his own troubles.

"His marriage soured. His wife turned out to be a greedy little gold digger, played fast and loose with other men, and constantly nagged him for ever larger sums and more expensive things, to a point that brought a definite financial strain. A divorce became inevitable. I believe there was a pretty bad scene the night of the break. The upshot was that Paul abandoned his apartment and moved back into the family mansion.

"I felt a greater sense of security then. Time slipped by, and I began to be my old self. I convinced myself that mother's death had been from natural causes."

The girl paused, fumbled in her purse. Frost offered a case of cigarettes, but she preferred her own. Inhaling nervously, she resumed her story.

"In April of 1933, I was invited down to Washington to spend a week with friends. I left Paul in charge of the house.

"When I returned on the morning of April 11th, I knew something was wrong the minute I drew up at the house. I hurried from the cab. There were police around. Winton, the oldest of our servants in term of service, had even telephoned to Washington to make sure I didn't extend my stay.

"Paul had disappeared. According to the servants' stories, they heard a scuffle and cries in his room about two in the morning. Then there was a bumping sound. They came down to investigate, found the door locked, and pounded on it. After a short interval, they heard what they described as a stirring within, then Paul answered in a faint voice and said everything was all right; that he had been walking in his sleep and tripped over a chair.

"But as they were leaving, the door opened and Paul raced out of the house, jumped into his roadster, and sped away. He did not speak or give any clue to his actions. The servants say his face was dead-white and that he had a nasty bruise on his forehead.

"When he had not returned by morning, they called the police and gave the license number of his car. An hour later, the car was found abandoned at Elmwood Cemetery. That is the site of our family crypt. The police of course made a careful examination of the grounds. They found Paul lying in the partly opened crypt. He had been killed by a blow that crushed the top of his head. It might have been struck from the front or behind or either side.

"Who, if any one, had been in his room? What was the scuffle? Why did he run wildly out of the house in the dead of night without a word of explanation? Why did he go straight to Elmwood Cemetery as he apparently did? For what possible reason was he trying to open the vault? Who killed him and why? Did he accidentally discover some one else trying to enter the vault? Or did some one know that he was coming and lie in wait for him? Did he have an appointment there, for some unguessable reason? What inexplicable purpose lay behind his actions, if they were rational at all?

"Why? Why? Why? I nearly went mad asking questions. I found no answers. There were no clues, no weapons found at the vault, no positive evidence of who the murderer could have been, no signs in his room to indicate the cause of the scuffling sound or the presence of a second person.

"There was trouble with the servants. Two of them left, though they had been generously remembered in the family's wills.

"This last death, the fourth in the family in three years, almost finished me. I was now absolutely alone. I felt I could not remain any longer in the house; that a fatal destiny had settled on it. Yet neither could I quite bring myself to sell it; it had been my home for so long, and I had so many memories connected with it. At last I left it in charge of the servants and took a month's cruise.

"That did me a lot of good. I came back determined to stay put. As I said, I was the only remaining member of the family. If there was some malign purpose behind the deaths, it would be next directed against me. But also I felt reasonably sure that I had nothing to fear for a while at least. It seemed to me to be significant that the fatalities had all occurred around the anniversary of my father's death. On that assumption, I would not need to worry until this month.

"I busied myself in a hectic round of activities, morning, noon, and night. Parties, dances, teas, luncheons, bridge, theaters, travel, sports—anything to keep me busy. Maybe I shouldn't have gone the pace so hard. It left me little enough time to think and that prevented me from worrying, but I don't suppose it helped my health any.

"This year, as April approached, I began to grow nervous. Time and again, I thought of leaving on a long cruise, but I've never been one to run away from things. Better to face the issue and either prove my fears were groundless, or find out what the trouble was, I decided. So I stayed. I bought an automatic pistol, though, and kept it under my pillow. Father's old six-shooter I put in my vanity table for extra protection.

"There was even a heavy old sword in the den, which I took to my room. I bought a couple of flashlights. There is a high, iron fence around our grounds, but I was taking every precaution I could think of, so I bought a pair of police dogs and turned them loose each night. I felt pretty secure then. I was still nervous, but confident I could handle any situation that might rise."

II.

The last of the Hollisters paused and drew a deep breath, as if about to plunge into icy waters. Her face was bloodless. Her voice sank to a lower monotone. Her eyes roved restlessly from her lap to the package on the table, from Frost to Jean Moray. The pupils of the professor's eyes seemed brighter in a blacker fashion. He had smoked at least a dozen of his pungent cigarettes.

Jean listened in rapt attention. She hung on every word of their client as if she was living the narrative and intuitively placing herself in Mae Hollister's place. It was a keen, sympathetic response that obviously served as a sustaining chord for the visitor.

Mae Ellen Hollister resumed speaking: "Through the early days of this month, I felt an increasing tension. I would lie awake for hours, but nothing happened, and I would drift off into a troubled sleep. Because nothing happened, I would feel more strongly that something would take place the next night. When I kept the lights on, I couldn't sleep. When I turned them off, I pictured all sorts of terrible things coming toward me in the darkness. I thought of asking one of my girl friends to stay with me. But if she did, and something happened, I would have deliberately drawn an innocent person into danger. I did nothing more about it.

"Yesterday, April 9th, the strain reached a point where I saw my physician. He gave me a prescription which he said was a sedative. When I took it, I would quickly fall into a deep sleep. I didn't take it last night. I couldn't. I kept thinking about all the things that might happen if I was in a drugged sleep. I could die without ever knowing how or why, but no matter how much it hurt, I wanted to fight the battle out.

"So I went to a dinner party, theater, and dance, with some friends. I got home after one. The dogs barked when I came in. I was pretty tired and took to bed almost at once. Every one else seemed to have retired. The house was absolutely still.

"I didn't sleep well, I thought of the prescription and decided against it. I opened a dull book on sociology. I counted sheep. Nothing seemed to help. I tossed around for what dragged like ages. I must have dozed off.

"I don't know when I woke up. I had a drowsy feeling that the window was wide open. Then I became fully awake. I distinctly heard a weight fall on the floor. I strained my eyes, but I couldn't see a thing. I stared and stared, but there was no moon, and it was very dark. I reached over to the light-switch and clicked it, but nothing happened. I grew alarmed, and a panicky feeling swept over me. Some one was crawling across the floor. I sat up and fumbled around until I found the flashlight under my pillow and turned it on."

Again the girl took a deep, nervous breath. Her eyes remained fastened now on the little parcel.

"I don't know if I shrieked when the beam leaped forth. I don't think so. I was too paralyzed by the shock of horror such as I never dreamed of.

"A green thing, like a man, was creeping toward me. It resembled the corpse of my father, Franklin Hollister, only bigger, more—more—enormous. The thing was dead, as dead as anything can ever be that has been buried four years. It crept toward me, slowly, the stiff limbs hooking crab-fashion on the floor, a few inches at a time. I felt my scalp prickle, and I shivered I was so cold. I had the strangest roaring in my head, yet I could hear every little sound that the thing made.

"It was halfway to me when I moved, but I couldn't seem to control myself. I sprang clear out of bed in a single leap. I pulled the door, but it was locked, and I couldn't find the key. I jumped for the automatic, but I was trembling so badly that I knocked it off the bed.

"And still the green man crept toward me, its dead eyes shining dully, its face set in the dreadful rigidity of death. The noise in my head swelled to a great roar. I have a vague memory of clutching the sword on the wall and trying to wield it. Then I sank into infinities of blackness."

The girl was shuddering again now. Not even the powerful bromide that Frost had mixed could counteract the terrific shock she had received.

Her voice came faint and trembling: "I don't know how long I was out, but I don't think it could have been very long. The first thing I realized was that I was clutching a sword. I couldn't remember why. I got up and turned on the lights in a heavy sort of way as if I was numb all over.

"There was a hand lying on the floor—a green hand. For a long time, I couldn't bring myself to go near it. I noticed in a mechanical kind of fashion that the window was wide open. Then I wondered why the lights worked when they didn't earlier. I tried the door. It was still locked. That scared me. I went around the hand to shut and bolt the windows. I found the door key lying on the floor. I don't know how it got there.

"I stared at the gruesome thing in the middle of the room until I thought my eyes would pop out. I was going to call the servants, but, for the first time in my life, I was up against something so abnormal and appalling that no ordinary help would do. I thought of calling the police, but I could predict in advance what stock they would take in my story. I racked my brains, and the one person I had heard of who might help in getting to the bottom of this was you.

"So I mustered up courage and took some stockings which I dropped on the hand. I simply couldn't bring myself to touch it directly. Even so, I could feel its awful reality when I dropped it into a box.

"Then I began wondering why the dogs hadn't barked. It was getting light now. How I ever found strength enough is beyond me, but I threw on a robe and went downstairs. It was dreadfully quiet. I slipped outside. Bingy and Carl had been poisoned.

"I went back and sat in my room for hours. I can never express all that this terrible experience did to me. I would sit in a sort of mad ecstasy of horror, drifting midway between unconsciousness and insanity. Again and again, the memory of that frightful scene when I turned the flashlight on congealed me in a waking stupor. Then my thoughts would veer crazily back and forth across the years.

"I knew now what frightened Ann to death, what caused mother's heart to stop beating, why Paul rushed from the house a year ago. I could not believe, I would not believe, yet I had to believe against all the reason I could summon. Reality and unreality spun around me. I would pretend I was dreaming, wait to wake up, only there was no waking.

"Time and again, I started to call the servants, to call the police. I tried to get up enough courage to drive out to Elmwood Cemetery to see if—to see—" Her voice broke. She stared straight into the eyes of Frost. The utter demoralization and appeal in her face outweighed everything she had said.

Frost straightened a little in his chair. "During the latter years of you father's life, do you recall that he ever made a point of disappearing for a period in April?"

The visitor thought hard. "No; not that I remember. But, then, I wouldn't know. We always took a Caribbean cruise in April. Father insisted it was good for our health."

"He accompanied you?"

"His business affairs kept him here."

"Excuse me for a few minutes."

Frost rose and took the parcel, with which he vanished into his laboratory. Miss Hollister, her face bloodless, sat with staring eyes. She looked numb, crushed.

The criminologist came back in less than five minutes, wearing a faint and enigmatic smile of grim significance.

Mae Ellen Hollister clutched the arms of her chair as if to keep from screaming. Her voice rasped in a shrill and rising plea: "Isn't there anything you can do to help me? Isn't there anything—"

Frost bent over and laid an extraordinarily slender, almost feminine, hand on the young woman's clenched knuckles. "Do? There is a great deal to be done, Miss Hollister. You did a splendid job in putting me in possession of all the information I need. I know how the atrocity was committed. I know why it was committed. Within twenty-four hours, I shall identify the persons behind this and bring them to justice. I shall say nothing more now because only in this way can I prevent any mischance and avoid even the least inadvertent motion that knowledge might cause you. I can assure you that the explanation is simple, through not pleasant. Cease worrying."

The girl relaxed a little. The lines on her face sagged from released tension.

Frost continued, speaking in a matter-of-fact manner: "Does your household know you came here?"

"No; I told them nothing."

"Good! Then go back and act as naturally as possible. You have hired a new servant. Her name is Jean Moray, but you will hire her as Jane Armstrong. She will arrive about an hour after you return to your home. You will carry on an extended conversation with her about her previous employment, her references, what she can do, and so on. Try to have at least one of the servants within earshot. You will then take her on for a trial, assign her to her quarters and duties, and introduce her to the staff. You will also take her over the entire house from cellar to roof. Have you bought any dogs to replace Bingy and Carl?"

"No; but I thought—"

"Do not do so. To-morrow you may if you wish."

Mae Ellen Hollister gave him a queer look. "You seem to know what I am thinking even before I have a chance to tell you. You said your assistant would be coming to the house shortly. May I expect you, too?"

Frost mused, with an air of abstraction. "No; not until considerably later. Let me see, the library will require several hours, then it will take an hour or two for the drive out and back, and I may need to spend as much as two hours at the circus. All in all—"

"The circus!" Mae Ellen Hollister rose, her face white and furious. "I come to you for help when I need it most, and you talk about going to a circus! Why, you would think—I think—" But her voice trailed off.

The air of abstraction had vanished from Frost the moment she exclaimed. She stared into eyes blackly glittering and deep, with pupils so expanded that the iris virtually disappeared. The effect was hypnotic. Yet Frost spoke with a calm authority that instantly restored the woman's confidence.

"You have been through a frightful experience, Miss Hollister, and it is a miracle that you have controlled yourself as well as you have. In the circumstances, I can understand how irrelevant my actions may seem to you.

"I am attacking the problem with my own methods. My visit to the circus is absolutely necessary. It has a direct and vital bearing on your welfare. You are in very great danger of death, or were, as you must have realized. The terror that has been menacing your family ought to be eliminated now. I shall accept the responsibility only on the condition that I have an absolutely free hand to do exactly what I deem best, however incongruous or fantastic it may sound. As I remarked before, I do not care to tell you more now, simply because there will be no slip-up in my plans so long as they are known to myself alone.

"Now, return to your home. Do not worry. Jane Armstrong will arrive soon. I shall announce my presence when I come."

Jean accompanied the last of the Hollisters to the door.

Bursting with curiosity when she reentered, Jean demanded: "Why in the world are you going to the circus?"

Frost flung over his shoulder: "Come into the laboratory."

In spite of air conditioning and the ozonator, the place smelled of acids, reagents, chemicals, and solutions. Microscopes and slides, X-ray machine and spectrographs and fluoroscope occupied the first table. Mae Hollister's parcel also lay upon it.

The professor, donning a pair of rubber gloves, and inhaling continually his private cigarettes, tossed aside some hose that Jean looked at enviously. They must have cost ten dollars a pair—beautiful things. She would have loved to wear them. Then the criminologist, his graceful fingers holding it as if it was a work of art, lifted from the bottom of the box a severed, green hand.

"Here," he remarked, "is the answer to your question."

Jean did not take the loathsome object while she studied it. That it had been detached from a corpse long dead was too gruesomely clear. The yellowing finger nails, the greenish color of the skin, the film of mold that had begun to develop, the faint odor of formaldehyde and embalming fluid, the purple-black hue of arteries and veins, the stagnant aspect of flesh and muscle—all were unmistakable evidence of the grave. The hand may have been attractive during the life of its owner. In death and decay it was only repulsive, a detestable relic, a thing of ugly and sinister nature.

"What does it suggest to you?" Frost inquired.

"Why ask? I think you know already."

"I should like to hear you tell me."

Jean shuddered. "It is so obviously what Miss Hollister said it was that I'll have to believe the rest of her story, incredible as it sounded. There is nothing imaginary about that hand. I wish there was. It is so real that it makes the affair more horrible than I ever thought anything could be. Like Miss Hollister, I believe it, and yet it is unbelievable. It cannot be, but it is. It's so strange and abnormal and so much beyond anything I've come across before that I simply can't think of a reasonable explanation."

Frost replaced the relic in its container. "You have as much information as I have. All the clues necessary to provide the motive and explanation of the crimes, and to indicate the course to follow in trapping the fiends behind this, lay in the woman's story and in a scrutiny of the hand. Eliminate the impossible answers and what remains must be true, however unlikely or improbable or exceptional it may seem.

"When you are installed in the Hollister place, make a note of every room and every individual in the house. Take any action you think best, until you hear from me. I do not know when I shall arrive, but not until I have completed the outside work."

Frost's shaggy brows were knit as in contemplation of some perplexing and abstract problem. Jean, feeling both mentally and physically dismissed, started on her way. Her last glimpse of the professor showed him still rapt in his thought, but walking about and selecting with unhesitating choice various items from the immense and exhaustive stocks of his laboratory.

III.

Jean, installed in the Hollister house as second maid, had surveyed the entire place from cellar to attic by late afternoon. Mae Ellen Hollister showed her through. Still suffering from the effects of shock, she moved with tired but nervous steps, keyed-up, jumping at the least sound. She made an effort to repair the ravages of strain and loss of sleep; cosmetics helped little. Jean had taken pains before she came to remove her make-up; but, even so, her natural beauty of face and figure obviously impressed the mistress of the house.

That was a help. Envy and a slight irritation of jealousy tended to bring the Hollister woman back to the petty, familiar things of life.

"Make-up is *such* a help," she remarked in the basement.

"I'll take care of mine when I reach my purse," said Jean.

"Oh, that wouldn't do at all! My maids do not use cosmetics," Mae Ellen hastily replied.

In the living room, the last of the Hollisters inquired: "Just who is Professor I. V. Frost? I've heard a good deal about him and his work, and he seems like a rather strong and confident person, but then I don't know whether I can count on anything after last night. Is he all he's said to be? What sort of man is he?"

"That," Jean sagely commented, "is a question to which no one will ever really know the answer. He doesn't talk much about himself, doesn't say much, but you can consider the mystery just about solved right now. He has his own methods of working. He always seems to be a couple of jumps ahead of everybody else."

In her second-floor bedroom, Mae Ellen fidgeted, ill at ease. Merely being in the room caused added strain, so overwhelming had been the shock of the previous night's horror. Jean's vitality and positive manner afforded the only support that kept Mae Ellen from breaking. Jean led the way out after a quick survey.

The servants' quarters on the third floor, and the roomy attic with its ladder to a roof skylight, completed Jean's once-over. It fixed the exact location of rooms and windows on her memory, but offered little to enlighten her. From Miss Hollister's own narrative, it had been evident that entrance and exit could have been accomplished in a number of ways. The house as a whole was a great capacious thing of large rooms and long corridors, the sort of structure that was built around the turn of the century. It had front and rear staircases.

More interesting than the house were its occupants, a curious ménage. Mrs. O'Linn, the cook and general housekeeper, was a quiet old soul who seemed lost in dreams of Irish hills. Miss Hollister's personal maid, Adrienne Gallis, looked frustrated. Winton, the butler, resembled a certain type of clergyman. He had a round face, placid blue eyes, an air of pompous dignity and self-righteous virtue. He looked twice when Jean passed.

The housemaid, Winton's wife, was a morose, pudgy person who would have disliked Jean because of her youth even had she been completely lacking in beauty. The caretaker and gardener, Olaf, appeared incomprehensible and stolid. He had colorless hair, vacant eyes, and knotty fingers.

Of this singular group, not the least noticeable was William Gallis, the chauffeur, who devoted most of his time to taking cars apart, putting them together again without the loss of a piston ring, building shortwave radio sets, and reading all the science and aviation magazines.

So far as Jean could determine, these individuals, including the Wintons and the Gallises, lived separate lives and might have been so many persons brought together by mere chance in a rooming house. Yet Winton had dwelt here for twenty years, his wife twelve, and the others from nine down to the chauffeur, who had come only a year previously.

The more Jean thought about it, the more baffled she became. The terrifying picture of a dead, green man creeping absolutely paralyzed rational action. It was so utterly at variance with reality as she knew it; so gruesome a thought that even yet she could scarcely believe. Yet there rose in her mind the image of Ann Hollister, screaming her life away in an asylum; Mrs. Hollister, dead from shock; Paul Hollister, found murdered in a cemetery after inexplicable incidents behind the locked door of his room.

Had this same dreadful nightmare afflicted them all? Was there a legend, a curse, a taint, or a psychopathic strain in the family? Or—and Jean faced the thought with dismay—was some new and infinitely evil force, of another realm entirely, bringing the dead back from the grave?

She wished Frost would come or call. There was no word from him. What could he possibly have meant by his cryptical allusions to his plans for the day?

The hours dragged. The house was like a tomb, an inhabited tomb. The frequent jangle of the telephone seemed an alien, discordant note. The servants attended to their tasks with noiseless and secretive efficiency. Mae Ellen Hollister went out in the afternoon to a cocktail tea, returned as sober as when she left. Neither stimulants nor narcotics would affect her much until the profound first effects of her grisly experience had begun to wear off. From shock such as she had received, she would never fully recover, whatever the answer might be.

Mae Ellen Hollister summoned Jean at six thirty to her boudoir. She seemed nervously distraught, unable to reach a decision. Her face was haggard. Yet a slow lassitude accompanied her hectic and over-wrought condition. "I had decided to spend the night with friends," she began abruptly. "I can't make up my mind. I don't want to stay here another night. It will be hard on me to stay, just as bad to leave. What can I do?"

Jean answered quietly: "I've already thought of that. Professor Frost would never have insisted on my coming here as a member of the staff if he hadn't been sure that our investigation should be as indirect as possible. If you leave and I remain, it will be obvious to any interested person that there is a connection between the two events. Aside from that, it might prove more difficult or impossible to take action if you went elsewhere and were again menaced.

"It will be better if you act as though nothing had happened. If there is no word from Frost by ten o'clock, retire to your room. As soon as the servants are asleep, I'll slip down and tap four times on your door."

The Hollister woman seemed relieved, content to let some one else assume her burden of worry.

Dining with the staff was an experience that Jean had no desire to repeat. Mrs. O'Linn looked at her with a wistful air that she could not quite analyze. The Irish came out only to the extent of a few impersonal questions, a kindly interest in seeing that the new member had enough to eat. Adrienne Gallis, staring with depressed fascination at her husband and at Jean alternately, volunteered no remarks. William Gallis rattled on about connecting rods and piston rings, compared different makes of cars, gave a resumé of the last science-fiction story he had read, studied Jean with direct and observant eyes, and appeared pleased with his contributions to life.

Winton ogled Jean, tried to be agreeable and managed to be unctuous while Mrs. Winton maintained a stony silence. Olaf peered blandly at every one, his big, pale eyes serene and vacant as an idiot baby's.

In the midst of this ill-assorted, curious, and secretive group, whose talk was purposeless and awkward, Jean felt as much a stranger as if she had intruded upon the private habits of so many newly arrived visitors from alien lands who spoke no language but their own. She doubted whether Freud had ever encountered a finer set of neuroses, or whether Bellevue ever had a better assortment of psychopathic cases. That these people had lived in the same house, however spacious, for years without being more intimate was as inexplicable a vagary of human aberration as that, preserving this isolation, they had not plotted each other's death long before.

Jean welcomed the end of this trying meal. She went directly to her room where she wasted an hour in a vain attempt to get a start somewhere in unraveling the weird mystery of the green man and the queer reticence of the servants. She merely succeeded in working herself into a state of exasperation. About nine, she took a shower and felt refreshed. Studying her face in a mirror, she decided to improve it, but could not find her compact. She recalled that she had had it during dinner.

Descending the rear staircase, she met Adrienne Gallis.

The maid frowned. "If you hear of another opening, take it." Her voice rattled like dry peas in a pod.

"Why?" Jean's voice expressed curiosity rather than the surprise that the maid's unexpected remark caused.

"You won't like it here."

The maid went her way without another word.

Jean, still wondering what the maid had in mind, reached the second floor just as Winton strutted along the hallway.

"Ah, Miss Armstrong!"

"Yes?" Jean practiced a meaningless inflection.

Winton purred: "Couldn't we have a talk? It is just possible that I might be able to tell you some very interesting things."

"Yes?"

"Not here, of course. Oh, in strict privacy. How would—"

"To-morrow. I'm very tired to-night."

"Very good!" Winton seemed not at all taken aback as she continued on her way.

Mrs. O'Linn was drying dishes when Jean entered. She looked up. "If you came for your compact, it's there on the table. I was going to bring it to you when I finished here."

Jean took the compact. "It was good of you to think about it. Can I help you with the dishes?"

Mrs. O'Linn polished a plate. "No; I'll get along all right." She appeared to be thinking about other and far-away matters. Jean moved toward the door.

Mrs. O'Linn spoke softly: "Miss Armstrong, you are new here. You aren't used to our ways. If I were you, I wouldn't walk around after ten. I wouldn't leave my room."

Jean stopped. "I don't understand. Why?"

Mrs. O'Linn carefully dried a saucer. Her face was hidden by the back twist of her gray hair. Her voice, reflected from the sink, had a muffled sound. "When you leave your room, lock your door, Miss Armstrong. But don't lock it when you are inside. Good night!"

Jean almost stayed, but Mrs. O'Linn, busy with her work and her thoughts, gave no further explanation of her enigmatic words. Frost's assistant, after a few seconds' hesitation, departed, a bewildered and puzzled young woman.

Closing the door behind her as she left the kitchen, Jean thought she heard the sound of receding footsteps. She listened, ran lightly and rapidly through the dining room and living room to the front staircase. In the dark area of the turn, she was sure she caught a glimpse of a figure, or the shadow of a figure.

She hurried noiselessly up the thick-carpeted steps. She heard something like the faint sound of far footfalls, but they died away. She cautiously explored the second floor and the third floor, but saw no one.

Had there been an eavesdropper? What did Mrs. O'Linn mean by her cryptic warning? What sort of household was this, where each individual appeared to lead a private life, separate and isolated from the others? Where was Frost?

In her room, Jean undressed, donned black pajamas. Black would be least conspicuous if she had to do much wandering through the halls.

A thousand suspicions and speculations ran through her head as she sat in darkness, waiting till the household was asleep. Dominating every thought, the image of the creeping green man clung like an evil incubus. What had Adrienne Gallis meant? What was Winton's purpose in furtively accosting her? How much did Mrs. O'Linn know?

At eleven, she palmed a tiny automatic, a deadly and efficient weapon that she could handle better than a .32. She carried a flashlight in a pocket of her blouse. She opened the door and slipped through. From long experience on summer trips in forest and lake wildernesses, she moved with the soundless ease of a phantom.

As she passed the door of Mrs. O'Linn's room, she paused. The woman, apparently the only kindly member of the staff, seemed to possess suspicions or knowledge that must have been well-grounded, or she would never have mentioned them. Perhaps if Jean could speak to her in the privacy of her room, she would give more specific information.

On impulse, Jean twisted the knob, wafted silently inside, whispered: "Mrs. O'Linn!"

She heard no answer. She moved to the bed, played the small beam of her flashlight around. The room was empty.

Puzzled, she returned to the hall, melted wraithlike along the black corridor.

Why was Mrs. O'Linn not in her room? Where was she? Why had there been no word from the professor?

On the second floor, about to go toward Mae Ellen Hollister's boudoir, Jean hesitated. Again she changed her immediate goal. She descended the rear staircase to the kitchen. The darkness made her progress slow. She did not wish to use the flashlight except when absolutely necessary.

She heard no sound. The eerie silence and the darkness got on her nerves. She felt like a ghost in a catacomb, as she trod with noiseless steps, listening for creaks that did not come, for sounds of people stirring, for any sign of human presence.

She waited till she had felt her way into the kitchen before she flicked the button of her flashlight.

"Mrs. O'Linn!" she gasped.

Mrs. O'Linn did not reply. The Irish cook made no answer because she was leering at the open window. Her dress ran red with blood from the gash that sliced her throat. Her spirit had returned to the Irish hills.

For a long interval, Jean stared at the lolling head and leering face of the dead woman. An appalling silence pervaded the house. With a great effort, she mastered an impulse to cry out, to run away. Silently she advanced and studied the corpse. It was cold. Mrs. O'Linn must have died an hour ago, without a struggle or scream.

Had she surprised some one or something in the act of entering the house? That seemed unlikely, for she would have had time to give the alarm. Had some one she knew entered and taken her utterly off guard with a sudden attack? A possible answer.

But the more Jean thought, the more she became convinced that Mrs. O'Linn had been murdered to silence her. If this was so, it implied that some one had overheard her talking to Jean, and Jean's thoughts flashed back to the retreating footsteps she had tried to follow at the time. The set-up became clearer. Mrs. O'Linn had been caught off guard and slain brutally, without warning. The placing of the body and the open window were plants to throw investigators on a wrong trail.

But who? And why? All the servants profited handsomely through Hollister wills. And any one of them might be a homicidal maniac—Mrs. Gallis, jealous, frustrated, neurotic; Olaf, the incomprehensible ox; Winton, the self-righteous and pompous, with a flair for young women; Mrs. Winton, sour, taciturn; William Gallis, skilled mechanic, ingenious at making things. As fine a crew of potential cutthroats and nervous wrecks as ever manned a house.

Jean did not dare rouse the household or summon the police. If she did, Frost's plans, whatever they were, would be ruined. She feared to disturb the body, could not take it upon herself to do more than spread a napkin over the hideous face for the sake of Mrs. O'Linn's kindly efforts to warn her.

Knowing now that some one had been watching her, wondering how much of her other brief talks had been overheard, she strained her ears to make sure that no one was at hand before she carried out her next move. Here she felt stymied. She originally started out for Miss Hollister's room, must still go there, but the murder of Mrs. O'Linn threw a new and major interference in her schemes. The cold-blooded ferocity of the murder was proof enough that she faced a criminal dangerous and swift to strike. The knife-wielder plunges for the heart. The man or woman in this case struck with deliberate reason for the throat—so that any cry would be choked.

Afraid to use her flashlight in the hallways lest she give herself away, so anxious to breathe silently that her heart pounded, redoubling her caution, she paced slowly, apprehensively, up the stairs. Her senses became preternaturally keen. She heard the faint swish of silk against her own ankles. And suddenly she felt sure that she was followed.

The one thing she must not do was to make any move toward Miss Hollister. Whatever peril she met, she must not drag it straight to the woman she was trying to protect. Thinking fast and coolly now that she sensed a definite encounter, she determined that the wisest course was to return to her room. She could leave the door ajar. There she could listen, find out if she was being shadowed, and slip quietly to Mae Ellen Hollister's room in half an hour or an hour.

Jean reasoned while she climbed. Softly and as quickly as she could, she mounted the stairs and glided down the third-floor hall in almost total blackness. The feeling of being observed grew on her—an unpleasant enough sensation in daylight or in a crowd, a morale-shattering impression in darkness and alone.

Solely because of the accuracy with which she had studied the house, she sensed when she was opposite her room. She listened, imagined a dozen sounds, but heard nothing definite. She groped along the wall and found her door. She opened it slowly, without creak or protest, and melted within.

A hand closed her mouth. She fought like a demon. She bit, kicked, clawed. She flicked her right arm up to fire over her shoulder. Fingers like steel springs tore the automatic from her palm. A sweetish odor filled her nostrils. She held her breath. She twisted and wrenched. Her pajama-top tore with the sleazy sound peculiar to silk. Her feet kicked vainly. If only she had worn pumps, she could have brought a yelp of pain with a dig of their sharp heels. The hand pressed harder, relaxed. She bounded away. A dull, tremendous weight fell on her head. Cushioned into flame-split blackness, she went out like a burst shell.

From nightmares and dreams, from visions of vast armies of dead, crawling green men swarming toward her out of crimson and infinite hells, Jean struggled to consciousness. Her head throbbed. She tried to raise a hand. It would not move. She tried to lift her other arm. Then it dawned on her that her wrists were knotted beneath her back; as thoroughly knotted as if bound with steel and set in glue. She attempted to open her mouth. It was plastered with adhesive tape. She tried to roll over, but her legs were tied to the foot of the bed. A rope encircled her neck and held her to the head upright.

She ceased her attempts in momentary panic when the knot tightened around her throat. Struggle only made her precarious position worse. She was as effectively out of the running as if she had been set in plaster. But she refused to give up. She could not call for help. She could not make use of teeth or feet. She could not double over. She could not bring her hands around. Yet she determined to free herself.

More angry than frightened now, her mind working swiftly and methodically as her head cleared, she concentrated on the problem of escaping from apparently unescapable bonds. She moved her hands tentatively. She arched her back, swung her bound hands a few inches sidewise. This was the only action she could take without garroting herself. It was enough.

With numb fingers, she plucked at the sheet, thread by thread. She split a finger nail, tore through the sheet in a few minutes.

The mattress was harder going. She gritted her teeth. Her arms wearied. Her fingers felt raw. She broke two more nails before she opened the mattress. Bit by bit, she plucked the wadding out. Her back became a solid ache from the strain of taut muscles. The rope around her neck tightened a little more. It was difficult to breathe. Bit by bit, a piece of wadding between thumb and forefinger, out, drop it to one side, down into the hole again, bit by bit, minute after minute.

Then the bottom of the mattress, and another finger nail gone as she shredded through the tough fabric. With a hole in the mattress just large enough for her hands, she had little play in this awkward position, but she moved them an inch from side to side until her sharp middle finger nails cut through.

Her heart beat exultantly. The spring consisted of rough, parallel wires composed of several smaller strands tightly twisted. The parallel wires, an inch or so apart, were fastened in pairs by metal clips at intervals of a foot. She dropped her wrists on a wire, forced her hands through the inch-wide space on either side, slid them toward the foot of the bed, drew them back. The wires scraped her skin, cut into her flesh; but the wire between her wrists frayed the rope slowly.

The effort proved agony. Pain dwelt in every part of her body. Her hands felt like raw fire. Patiently sawing her wrists down and back, tortured by every motion, hurrying lest her assailant return, Jean persisted though will alone now kept exhausted muscles working.

She had no idea how long she had been out, or of the real lapse of time since she began her efforts. It seemed hours. Actually, it might have been little more than a half hour before the bond snapped, and with cramped, throbbing arms she drew her bleeding hands out.

Another minute or two, and the neck and ankle ropes came free. The tape proved more resistant. She wasted several minutes peeling it from sensitive skin.

She did not turn the lights on. Accustomed to gloom now, she hunted in darkness for her flashlight and automatic, found them lying on a bureau. With difficulty she made out the hands of a clock. It was nearly twelve thirty. She wondered if the sheets would tear into enough strips to reach the ground, since she expected to find the door locked from the outside, but it opened without trouble. Surprised, she slipped into the deserted hallway.

Her bare feet made no sound on the carpet as she sped along the hall and hurried down to the second floor. Miss Hollister alone lived on the second floor, but Jean took no chances. Fading along the corridor, she did not even attempt to knock as she had promised, but silently entered Mae Ellen's bedroom.

Jean had fears of what she might find—anything from a strange corpse or a green man to a dead Hollister; but the reality proved so mystifying that she stood just inside the door for at least a minute trying to think straight.

Mae Ellen Hollister had vanished. Her clothing lay tossed over a chair. The bed, mussed, had obviously been occupied recently. But Mae Ellen Hollister was gone.

Jean searched the room, examined closets, peered in corners and under the bed, in all likely and unlikely places for some clue to what had happened. She ended as perplexed as she began.

Had the Hollister woman lost her courage and suddenly departed from the house for the night or for good? Had she lost her mind and wandered away at random, on irrational impulses? For that matter, was the last of the Hollisters already deranged, a psychopathic case who might herself be responsible for her fantastic story and these puzzling occurrences? Had she worried over Jean's delay in coming and left to find her? Had she been murdered here, or lured elsewhere to death, and her body hidden? Above all, where was Frost?

Tormented by doubts and haunted by fears and utterly unable to find a starting point for untangling the weird, sinister, and complicated web of mystery that enveloped her, Jean began a half dozen different schemes, but abandoned each in turn. She thought of exploring the house again; the risks seemed great, the potential profit small. She considered going to her own room and awaiting the almost certain return of her assailant. She would have got in touch with Frost if she had the slightest inkling where the professor could be reached.

She remained where she was because she saw no better course. If the Hollister woman had left for some temporary reason, her return might come momentarily. If Mae Ellen had been slain, Jean could do nothing for her, except try to trap the criminal. All factors considered, it seemed better to stay put. Some one or something, unaware of her absence, might make another attempt on her life here.

Jean flopped on the bed. Her nerves ragged, her body weary, she hung between the sleeplessness of mental excitement, the oblivion of exhaustion. She could not get out of mind the memory of the dead woman still keeping a leering vigil in the kitchen; the attack in her own room, as unexpected as it was savage; Mae Ellen Hollister's astounding narrative; the green hand; and now this inexplicable disappearance of the last of the Hollisters.

Jean dozed, waked into apprehension, walked around. She sat in a chair, nodded. She returned to the bed and slept fitfully while deciding to remain awake. At one thirty, she poised in a detached, sleepy mood. Her aching muscles demanded rest. She was too healthy a young animal to resist. She stirred vaguely with the idea of walking around again, but she drowsed. She did not dream.

She wakened suddenly, fully. She wakened because she heard a sound and knew she was no longer alone. She wakened because all her faculties shrilled a warning of immediate and deadly peril. She wakened and stared, and for one freezing, timeless moment felt the impact of such panic as had swept Mae Ellen Hollister to the verge of collapse.

A great, dark blob sprawled on the floor by the window. The blob moved toward her. She turned her flashlight on it, and it sprang into hideous reality. Edging forward, creeping, slithering along the floor, bloated and dead, a greenish corpse inched toward her. Its left hand was missing. The light wavered as the flash trembled in her nerveless fingers. It flickered on dead eyes and glistened on corrupt flesh that belonged to the grave.

Sick and appalled, weak with horror, Jean crept out of bed, aimed, fired. The bullet plowed true into the thing's forehead. No blood oozed. No sound came after the bullet's plop. The thing, remorseless, evil, horrible, crept on.

The door opened behind her. Jean whirled. A flying form bowled her to the floor, hurtled across the room. The flashlight was shattered. She lay stunned, unable to move, pain flashes streaking her vision. A powerful figure leaped on the green thing, struggled, heaved. Something misshapen, repellent, like a gigantic rat, scuttled away. The dim figure lunged after it. It poised on the window sill, leaped. A wail pierced the air, and then followed the sickening sound of a body smashing.

The figure turned, raced across the room, dashed out of the door as Jean struggled to regain vision and consciousness. She had managed to sit up when she heard what sounded like two quick, distant shots. She was on her feet when racing steps approached. She had her gun ready when the figure plowed in.

"Frost!" she cried. She had never been so glad to see any one.

"Quick!" he whispered. "It's all over, but I want this out of sight before the servants arrive."

He hurried to the gruesome object on the floor, bent over, opened something he carried. There was the shuffle of feet on the floor above. Frost straightened, heaved. A bag slung over his back, he strode toward the door.

"This won't be a pleasant job, but you had better come along," he told Jean. "The police will be here before I return. You might not have an easy time of it if you stay. I'll straighten things out when we return."

He spoke without emotion, without ego. They were statements of fact and made solely as such. He did not slacken his pace, did not wait for any debate on Jean's part.

IV.

Jean trotted along beside him. There was more scuffling of feet, growing activity, cries, far away. Jean opened the front door and walked with Frost to the street. The professor turned, walked a block, turned again, stopped at a parked car.

A disheveled drunk, staggering down the street, stared owlishly at a curious illusion. He thought he saw a towering, hatchet-faced person, with eyes like black coals and an immense sack swung over his shoulder, walking beside a ravishing vision in the shredded remnants of pajamas. The lank person dumped the sack in the rear seat of a car. He climbed in, and the dream followed. The car sailed away. The disheveled drunk reeled after it, muttering incoherently until a fire hydrant reached up and bit him.

The car gathered speed. Jean relaxed, took a cigarette, inhaled, and let out a thankful sigh.

"The grand-stand finish was simply swell," she said. "I don't know who won or what the score was or what it was all about, but it was a swell finish."

Frost smiled faintly. "As Alice might have said, your speech grows curiouser and curiouser," he observed. "How did you make out at the Hollister house?"

His thoughts seemed to be elsewhere, yet he listened intently. He nodded approvingly at one or two points in her narrative.

"Exactly what you should have done," he agreed when she spoke of not disturbing the corpse of Mrs. O'Linn.

"In the circumstances, that was a careless way to enter your room," he remarked with disapproval when she was telling of her flight from the unknown pursuer. Jean's voice became meeker, less enthusiastic. But when she described her escape from apparently fool-proof fetters, he drawled:

"Ingenious! Not all people would have had sense enough to see what could be done, or perseverance enough to do it."

Jean's voice became excited again as she continued her story.

"So there you are," she finished. "Maybe I'm dumb and don't know it, but the Hollister affair is a big, nasty mess as far as I'm concerned, and I'll admit it. I don't know what it's all about, and I can't believe half of it yet."

The car hummed on. Frost, his eyes glued to the road, did not turn his head.

"That admission does you credit," he said. "Estimating reality at its face value is a gift that few persons have. The frank statement of one's ignorance is often a sign of intelligence."

Jean pouted. "I don't want a lecture on philosophy. I want to know who and why. Maybe the case is ended in your opinion. It isn't in mine. How in the world did you get started and what magic did you use?"

Frost settled lower in the seat. Driving with one hand, he pulled a cigarette out of his pocket, lighted it, and exhaled a patch of pungent, aromatic smoke. His eyes took on a deeper gleam.

"When Miss Hollister arrived yesterday, she gave all the information needed to deduce the broad outlines, the explanations, the course of action to take, and the probable solution of the case—"

Jean interrupted: "How did you know who she was? You mentioned her name before she arrived."

"I make a point of remembering the names and faces of prominent, wealthy, or important people, and members of their families. Certain types of crime, including blackmail, extortion, bribery, and kidnaping, are most prevalent in this group.

"Even before she reached the house, it was obvious that terror brought her. Her extreme agitation, strained features, nervous actions, and other indications were so plain that it required no very alert mind to read them. If she had already asked police aid, there would be no necessity for coming to me. Since she could have employed the services of a detective agency at a fraction of my fee, it was evident that money meant nothing, and that her experience had been of so extraordinary a nature that ordinary assistance would not help.

"Accepting her complete story as an accurate presentation of the case, analytic reasoning then broke it down into probable cause and result. Let us begin with the most striking part of her narration—the creeping green corpse.

"In general, only three theories were tenable. Her story might have been pure invention or delusion or dementia. That category I discarded because of her serious condition. Her collapse was not responsible for hallucinations; but something was responsible for her collapse.

"The second category was that of a supernatural occurrence, not subject to known laws and explanations. This I also dismissed. There may be supernatural manifestations, but I have never witnessed any connected with crime. I would have recourse to such an alternative only if all other methods, approaches, and investigations utterly failed.

"The third possibility was that she *had* actually seen what she claimed, that a corpse *had* crept toward her, that it *was* the body of her father, though dead four years, and that a logical purpose and human motives lay behind the outrage.

"Several suggestions about how the phenomenon was achieved occurred to me. I was convinced I knew the truth, but I desired further investigation and objective proof to substantiate the theory I had formed."

Jean grabbed the door handle, steadied herself as the car turned a corner and sped on over an almost-deserted highway.

Frost continued speaking in a calm, lucid, incisive fashion: "Discarding for the moment the various ways in which the seemingly impossible could have been brought to reality, and accepting a rational explanation as certain, let us consider Miss Hollister's recital in the light of motives.

"First, why was the green man creeping? The answer is apparent. Miss Hollister stated that she came of a high-strung, neurotic family, some of whose members were subject to heart trouble. Such individuals are usually short-lived. They die of apoplexy, overexertion, hemorrhage, or shock. Only a ruthless and cunning mind, plotting murder, knowing the victims well, would create so novel a device for achieving his purpose.

"If the device failed, more direct means could be employed. It failed on Paul Hollister. Seeking the truth, he was beaten to death. If the device succeeded, as it did in two instances, a murder without clues and without physical violence was committed.

"Now we have a result to be achieved; the death of Hollisters and a method for achieving it—the animated corpse, with more direct and violent means in reserve. But we have also a weakness in the plan. A corpse *walking* would be infinitely more paralyzing, outrageous, and terrible than a corpse slowly *crawling*. An astute observer, after the first shock would conclude that the corpse did not walk, because it could not; that it had nothing to do with the realm of the supernatural; that dead it was and dead it would be; and that its semblance of life appalling had no inexplicable basis. Consideration of this detail added further support to the theory I had formed.

"The means and the result having assumed a logical sequence, I next turned to the cause or motive. It should hardly be necessary to point out the purposes that were deducible and obvious in Miss Hollister's narration. By her own statement, the servants were generously remembered in Hollister wills. Every death meant a direct, worth-while, financial gain to them. Furthermore, Paul Hollister had married a shrew and a spendthrift.

"There were now nine or ten suspects in the case. By elimination, I reduced the number to six. Paul Hollister's wife could immediately be dismissed as having no connection with the affair, since he did not marry her until *after* the death of Ann Hollister. The servants who had left could also be dismissed, since the crimes continued *after* their departure. Since they were under no suspicion, there was no need to leave; and, by leaving, they sacrificed bequests from subsequent wills and would not profit by subsequent deaths. The criminal, therefore, should be sought among the remaining staff of six."

His body relaxed, but his gaze fastened on the highway and, zest in his drawling, educated voice, Frost pursued his résumé with relentless logic: "The more I thought about it, however, and taking into account other elements of the situation, the more evident it became that the solution was by no means as simple as this. Money, even in a large amount, did not seem sufficient to justify the remarkable circumstances, the extreme and fantastic lengths, to which the criminal had gone. I was convinced, then, that there must be not one, but two motives; not one, but two criminal units working together; that this was both an inside and an outside job.

"It was significant that Franklin Hollister sent his family away in April during the latter years of his life. Why? It was significant that the corpse of Franklin Hollister made its appearance in April around the anniversary of his death. Why? It would have been more effective if the manifestations had come on the exact anniversary.

"Here another statement of Mae Hollister's offered a clue, and the case rapidly became clearer as the details filled in. Miss Hollister asserted that her father's wealth came chiefly from some valuable patents that he controlled. Not that he *invented* but that he *owned*.

"A tentative theory at once offered itself. Franklin Hollister obtained the rights to, or patented, the inventions of some one else. He got them illegally, or did not pay for them in proportion to their worth, or did not pay for them at all. The unknown person tried repeatedly to gain some part of the fortune to which he was, or felt he was, entitled. He came in April because he was in town only in April. Franklin Hollister knowing that the person would be in the city every April and would see him or try to see him and wrangle over the patents, sent his family away.

"When Franklin Hollister died, the inventor lost all chance of obtaining redress for the wrong done him. It must have preyed on his mind, demented him, until for revenge he determined that the Hollisters should never enjoy the ill-gotten fruits of his labors. And Franklin Hollister himself, dead and buried, was to bring ironic justice, be the terrible instrument of vengeance, the curse and destroyer of his own heirs.

"This demoniacal scheme would be difficult to carry out by one not intimately familiar with the Hollisters and their habits, or by one limited to short visits to the city in April. It would require coöperation, inside help, from some one who stood to profit by the action. Presumably, the unknown person and one of the servants came to know each other during the former's successive visits at the Hollister house."

The look of admiration growing on Jean's face vied with expressions of absorbed attention and marveling as the tale unfolded.

"With this theoretical outline from which to start," Frost continued, "the next step was a matter of taking action in the most effective way. If the previous sequence of events continued, it would be a year before the next apparition of the corpse. But I had excellent reason to believe that the sequence was broken and that another visitation would occur to-night.

"Consider the green hand. It lent not only physical confirmation to various phases of my working hypothesis, but also gave circumstantial support to other parts. Close scrutiny showed it to be in a state of deterioration assignable to a body long dead. At one time, but not recently, it had been treated with theatrical grease paint, the green type which is generally used for shadows. In addition, the hand was covered with a fine layer of greenish mold.

"I must digress for a moment. There are a great number and variety of molds, fungi, films, and sporous growths which may accompany decay. Even in thoroughly refrigerated storage rooms of medical colleges, the cadavers will develop such growths unless they are treated with alcohol, formaldehyde, or other chemical substances. The green mold on the hand might have been such a spontaneous growth, but it was most unlikely. The mold was more likely to have been artificially developed. A chemist could easily have done so, and not merely on a hand, but over an entire body.

"These interpretations were of major importance. The grease paint indicated some one familiar with stage make-up. The mold suggested some one familiar with chemistry. The Hollister patents were of a chemical nature. Of the different performers who use grease paint, the class that fitted must be one which came here every April. Legitimate actors, motion-picture actors, concert artists, and so on, are here the year around. But every April, the circus pays us a visit before swinging around the country. You may have noticed the current advertisements and publicity about it.

"I now had a good picture of the outside criminal. He was a former inventor who knew something about chemistry. He had so limited means that he had to accept employment and had been connected with the World Circus in recent years.

"Now, to return to the severed hand. Why had it been left behind when the corpse disappeared? It could have been by accident or design. It seemed incredible that the loss of the hand was not noticed when the sword amputated it. Therefore the abandoning of it must have been intentional. Why?

"To the criminal, Mae Hollister had fainted. When she recovered consciousness, she might go to pieces, she might have hysteria, she might persuade herself that she was the victim of a nightmare. But if she saw the hand, the sight might finish her. If it did not, it would prey on her mind. If she went to the police, she would very likely be turned over to a psychopathic ward for observation.

"If the police did investigate, there was no one upon whom to fasten suspicion. If Mae Hollister departed, another indirect or direct attempt on her life could be made later. If she remained, the best time to strike, from a psychological or any other viewpoint, was to-night. The inside criminal could check up on her actions. The partnership had much to gain and nothing to lose by abandoning the hand.

"Concluding that another atrocity would be committed to-night, if conditions were favorable, I saw to it that they were. If I had gone to the Hollister house, the warning would instantly have been given. Nothing would have happened. But it was necessary that Miss Hollister return to her home, and that she have protection and some feeling of security. Going as a servant, you would be suspected, but even the criminal is prone to look with favor upon beauty. As a woman, you would not be regarded as dangerous as a man. There was a good chance of your being accepted for what you were supposed to be."

Jean made a noise in her throat. The car streaked toward less congested parts of the city.

Frost, engrossed in his analysis, and absorbing a curious excitation from his peculiar cigarettes, approached the climax. "After Miss Hollister and you had gone, I took a few things from the laboratory.

"I first stopped at the library and checked a number of records and files. I examined the reports of the patent office. I found the application of Franklin Hollister for three patents. Exception was taken, some months later, by one Kurt V. Raim. Exception was denied, and final patent was granted to Hollister.

"I studied the April files of all the newspapers here. I found that in each of the last ten years, the World Circus arrived in the second week in April and left at the end of the month for its tour of the country. Among the publicity and advertising, I discovered a reference to Kurt V. Raim seven years ago, another two years ago.

"Having substantiated parts of my theory, I then drove out to Elmwood Cemetery and talked to the caretaker. I got a key to the Hollister vault and entered it. The casket of Franklin Hollister was empty, further proof that I had made a correct analysis.

"I returned to the city and made some arrangements with a mortician. I then spent a couple of hours at the World Circus. I discovered that Raim was still associated with the circus.

"It was then dark and time to set the trap."

Jean broke in: "Haven't you eaten since breakfast?"

Frost replied indifferently: "It didn't occur to me. The case was so unusual that it held my attention exclusively.

"I left my car a little distance from the Hollister house and entered the grounds," Frost went on. "Light shone from a second-floor window, thereby identifying Mae Hollister's bedroom. Directly under the window, I placed the battery I carried. The light-bulb was screened so that only infra-red rays formed the beam which, of course, was invisible.

"In the rear of the house I found an open window. I discovered the body of Mrs. O'Linn when I entered. A brief inspection produced ample proof of what had happened. The murder also testified that one of the criminals was becoming desperate, and that another attempt on Mae Hollister's life was scheduled for to-night.

"I ascended the rear staircase to the attic, thence to the roof. The light had gone out in Miss Hollister's bedroom, but I had accurately fixed its location. Under the eave, and directly over the bulb on the ground, I placed a small photo-electric cell, sensitive to infra-red rays. I pressed a couple of thumb tacks in to hold it. I ran a wire around under the eaves to the opposite side of the house and let the loose end hang down to the room opposite Miss Hollister's.

"Working in silence and encountering no one, I reëntered the house. In the unoccupied room opposite Miss Hollister's, I fixed the wire to a simple relay. The contact was closed. It would open the moment anything tried to enter her room and interrupted the beam.

"It had been apparent from her own story how entrance for the manifestation was effected. The slain dogs, the lights that failed at crucial moments, the very avoiding of detection, were indicative of an operator inside the house. There were no tracks on the ground. Entrance must have come from inside the house or from the roof. The Hollisters did not lock their doors. In two instances, the corpse came down by way of a rope from the third floor, in the other instances it came down from the roof.

"The crimes could have been prevented. But Ann Hollister, crazed, could not tell what she saw. Mrs. Hollister died of heart failure. Paul Hollister was not so easy a victim. He advanced to the corpse, struggled with it, and was knocked out. Finding nothing when he regained consciousness, he rushed out to Elmwood Cemetery. The inside member of the crime partnership was no fool. He could easily guess where Paul was headed, and warn the outside member, who thereupon took cruder means of preventing Paul from finding the truth, and of satisfying his bloodthirsty vengeance. Mae Hollister fainted long enough for the corpse to disappear.

"All I needed to do was wait until the contact broke, allow enough time for entrance to be accomplished, then go in and trap the guilty. There was, however, very real danger that another shock might finish the woman. I decided that she should not be exposed to the risk.

"She was sleeping very lightly when I entered. I administered enough anesthetic to put her in a deep coma, before carrying her across the hall. She continued to sleep soundly while I waited by the relay.

"After a while, I heard the door to her room open and close so faintly that it would have escaped detection if I had not been keenly concentrating. You did an expert piece of work. It was obvious that it must have been you, since the visitor did not come out. Your presence there admirably suited my plans. If the criminals checked up before acting, you would, in darkness, be taken for granted as Mae Hollister. The criminals made one fatal error—they thought you were securely tied. They did not make sure by a second visit. The rest you know."

V.

The car slowed down, halted. Frost took a small parcel from the rear seat, got out, and slung the large sack over his shoulder as Jean joined him beside the entrance to Elmwood Cemetery. A figure rose out of darkness.

"Hello, Johnson! Everything's all right."

An anxious voice answered: "Did you succeed, Professor Frost?"

"Yes. Is Connolly here?"

"Waiting inside."

"Good! Have him come to the vault. Give me the key. If you don't mind, I think it would be better for you to keep watch here and see that we are not molested."

The caretaker handed a key over, glanced dubiously at Jean. "But the young lady——"

"She is my assistant."

"Well, I mean——" The man hesitated.

Frost looked at Jean, his glance encompassing her for the first time. "Do you generally go around wearing as little as that?" he inquired, curious.

Jean defended herself. "Well, you told me to come along and you didn't give me time to change or grab anything," she began, but Frost was already striding through the cemetery.

Slightly peeved, she nevertheless trotted meekly after him. She didn't feel that he was at all properly appreciative of beauty.

Frost flashed the beam of his light on the Hollister vault. They entered and descended. An eerie sensation crept through Jean as she looked at the caskets in the gloomy interior.

"I still don't know the rest," she whispered. "You practically knocked me out when you barged in."

"Kurt V. Raim fell to his death. I reached the third floor in time to see Winton shoot his wife in a last effort to save himself. He was a trifle slow in aiming at me. He died."

Frost opened the sack, grasped it by the bottom, eased its contents out. "There is the answer," he remarked.

Jean shuddered. The entire front torso of the corpse had been removed. One look was more than enough for her. She felt ill.

"Now do you understand? Franklin Hollister was a large man, but Kurt V. Raim was a midget, a strong midget, but one of the smallest dwarfs of our time. It was his crazed brain that conceived this fiendish means of revenge. It was Winton's greed that made him help. It was Winton who killed Mrs. O'Linn and assaulted you, and whose wife was a tacit partner to his evil. It was Winton who lowered the corpse and Raim, once from his bedroom, once from his wife's bedroom, which were directly above the rooms of two of the dead Hollisters, and twice from the roof.

"It was Raim the dwarf who, protected by a rubber sheet from direct contact with the body, was willing to endure what must have been a ghastly experience for the sake of satisfying his insane desire for vengeance. It was Raim the inventor who conceived so weird a revenge. It was Raim the chemist who doctored the corpse to make it more gruesome, and who built the air-tight, chemically refrigerated box underneath the surface clothing in that big chest in Winton's room."

Steps sounded. A man of untroubled composure entered, followed by another bearing a load of clothing and materials.

"Hello, Connolly! This won't be a pleasant task, and it must be done fast. Can you use some assistance?"

"Thank you, but it won't be necessary, Professor Frost. I brought another member of our firm. We shall be through in an hour. You understand that it is a delicate matter for a house as respectable as ours to handle."

"I understand perfectly. Here is the key. Be sure to send the bill to me, and go to any expense necessary. The hand is in the small parcel."

As they left, the two morticians were already at work with the undertaker's magic that transforms a mutilated corpse into a dignified and unblemished body, seemingly asleep.

"To-day," Frost prophesied, while the car gathered speed, "we shall bring Miss Hollister here, if she wishes, and show her the casket containing Franklin Hollister. We will tell her a fable about wax dummies and mechanical contraptions that make them move. If necessary, we shall make a wax hand looking real but decayed, and return it to her as the one she brought. The guilty are dead. The police will be mystified, and after much speculation they will call it a case of attempted burglary and murder, which just happened to occur in the same house during the same night as a suicide pact."

The bright glitter of his eyes was beginning to wane. Jean, drowsily curled up and about to fall asleep, knew that days of boredom lay ahead for him, now that the case was closed.

THEY COULD NOT KILL HIM

WHEN JEAN MORAY tripped up the steps of 13 State Street, entered, and threw off her wraps, she powdered her nose and gave a fluff to her hair. She surveyed herself critically in the hall mirror. She approved what she saw, from immaculate complexion on a wise, youthful face to the nonchalant tilt of her head, from hair the color of an old rye whisky to hands that would have graced a nail-polish ad.

She was young and beautiful and sophisticated and full of the devil, with just enough of naïveté to perplex an observer. She was exceptional even in a city noted for its attractive women. Her face glowed.

She held the evening paper in one hand and floated into the library. She felt like humming. Had not her escort paid every compliment to her beauty over the dinner table at a night club? His admiration lingered in her heart. But she had deftly turned aside every advance, checked him on the verge of proposing, taken the fruits of victory while granting nothing. She liked the sensation of being loved, but conquests came easy, too easily. With perverse reaction, she would never respond save to some one completely indifferent to her appeal.

She danced through the library and into the laboratory.

Professor I. V. Frost did not look up as she entered.

The criminologist, carelessly dressed in old corduroy, blue shirt open at the throat, and the stained leather jacket that he always wore around his laboratory, was studying an object on a table. His back, half turned to Jean, concealed the object.

His sharp, hawklike features were etched against a table light. The immense and shaggy black eyebrows stood out in ridges. Bent over though he was, slouched toward the object, he yet conveyed an impression of latent power in every part of his long, spare figure.

It was obvious that the professor's immediate interest lay elsewhere. Nettled, Jean decided to get some attention.

"Can I help? Am I intruding?" she asked with sweet innocence.

Professor Frost straightened and glanced at her. She felt herself raked by eyes that pierced and probed. He smiled faintly.

"Perhaps you will not always have the good fortune to obtain as dinner companions men who are gentlemanly enough to let you parry their advances, even to the extent of thwarting an intention to propose," he observed calmly.

"Well, I size 'em up pretty well first," Jean began defending herself. Then she flushed. Rattled by this man who studied her and told her where she had been and what she had been doing, she burst out: "You talked to him?"

Frost shook his head. "No. Nearly every person carries on his features and in his actions the impress of his recent doings, and even of his thoughts. I doubt whether there are half a dozen individuals alive who can successfully disguise or conceal their character and habits from the trained analyst.

"But tell me what you make of this. I found it lying on the sidewalk."

He handed her the object. It was a woman's purse. She scrutinized it carefully. The contents were a mess—powder case open, coins and compact and handkerchief and lipstick and miscellaneous girl-things jumbled together. Jean tried to get a mental picture of the owner.

"To begin with, the woman was slovenly and untidy," she guessed.

"Wrong. Go on," Frost placidly contradicted her.

"These things are about the most expensive you can buy. The gloves would be fifteen dollars a pair, the perfume forty-five an ounce, and the platinum compact at least fifteen hundred. She was a wealthy woman."

"Wrong, but continue."

Jean pouted. "She was a blonde. A natural blonde. Hair about the color of clover honey."

"Right."

"And she didn't have enough money for a cab, so she was walking to a bank to cash a check when she dropped the purse."

"Wrong."

Jean gazed at him steadily.

Frost's cool voice had no reproof or pride. He stated facts and corrected errors, so far as Jean could tell, with the same merciless, impersonal, and accurate logic by which he tracked criminals and solved the most baffling of mysteries.

She returned the purse. "I don't seem to be doing so well," she commented with a trace of irritation.

Frost continued in his detached manner: "Do not let it worry you. Your method is correct, and if you carried it far enough you would arrive at the truth. Logic, whether inductive or deductive, can be one of the most powerful aids to the scientific investigator. It can also be a source of profound error and confusion when improperly used, or when employed without possession of all the facts. Logic is not only an aid to science. It is a science in itself.

"I told you I found the purse on the sidewalk. You began with the assumption that it had fallen from the arm of its owner. You then made other deductions which would have been true had the initial premise been true. But the starting point of your analysis should have been—how did the purse come to be lying on the sidewalk?"

"How else could it get there if it didn't fall? It certainly wasn't deliberately placed there."

"I did not say it did not fall. I merely challenged your assumption that it fell from its owner's arm: If you examine the end of the clasp closely, you will find it scraped and twisted. The gleam of the metal combined with the presence of a few embedded grains of concrete indicate that the dent is fresh and was caused by the purse falling with considerable force to the ground. The logical explanation is that it was accidentally knocked from a window ledge several stories above the sidewalk.

"In falling and striking, its contents became jumbled. Far from being a slovenly person, the owner was actually fastidious and possessed of great pride in her personal appearance and in the neatness of her belongings."

Explanations were easy, Jean thought, when Frost made them.

"Again," he went on, "your deduction that she was a woman of means and that she was on her way to a bank was incorrect. Obviously she could not have been on her way anywhere if the purse was dislodged from the window ledge of her apartment.

"You next determined that she must be wealthy because her belongings were costly. You thought she was on her way to a bank because she had no bills and only a few coins in her purse, but did have an uncashed check for one hundred dollars.

"Now, if you had examined the check carefully, you would have noticed that it was made out to 'Cash.' If you had thoroughly investigated the signature, you would have discovered that no such person as 'T. J. Williams' exists. The woman's initials, 'M. M.,' you of course noticed on her handkerchief.

"Husbands are not in the habit of signing fictitious names on checks for their wives; neither, as a rule, do they make out such checks to

'Cash.' The conclusions are inescapable that 'M. M.' was kept, that the valuable belongings were gifts, and that she had only such means as her friend allowed, through an account set up for safety's sake under a fictitious name. I will have the purse delivered to her to-morrow.

"Is there anything unusual in the paper?"

Jean tossed it on the table. "Just the usual run. Gangster killings, suicide pacts, a love murder. They haven't found a trace of the gang that got away with the four hundred and thirty-five thousand dollars haul at the Midtown Bank yesterday. Nothing that sounds as exciting as the case of the Green Man, or even the Golden Goblin affair. Do you suppose we shall ever hear anything more about that?"

"Possibly. Joe Blake and the remnants of his gang are still loose," Frost replied in a perfunctory voice. "That was a clever raid on the Midtown. While crowds gathered at the fire a block away, the gang entered the Midtown, scooped up the cash, and got away without a shot being fired. They took the teller at the R-Z window with them. The fire, of course, was incendiary."

"That's what the fire and insurance investigators announced to-night. But to return to the raid, the police have given up hope of finding the kidnaped cashier alive. They think he was slain to prevent his identifying the criminals."

"Or to avoid giving him his share of the loot," Frost suggested.

Jean looked at him intently. "You think he was in league with the gangsters?"

"At the angle of his cage, he could not have been shot from the point where the leader trained a submachine gun on the place. The teller in that particular cage could have ducked and set off the burglar alarm."

Jean wondered about the professor's expression of returning boredom as he slouched from the laboratory. Only in the grip of some knotty or abstruse problem did his features light up.

From the amazing knowledge that he sometimes displayed in the most offhand manner, Jean guessed that pursuits of the pure intellect afforded him the stimulus that lesser men found in simpler ways. Yet she had not elicited a single item about his life, or obtained anything from him that he did not choose to give, or learned anything except what he allowed. His was as enigmatic a nature as that of the great stone Sphinx.

In the months that she had served as his assistant, she had discovered little even about his habits. He sometimes disappeared, leaving no clue to his destination when he left and volunteering no information when he returned days later. He had no detectable schedule. In the solving of strange and perplexing crimes, he went without food and sleep until he had answered the riddle, whether it took one day or three.

During these periods he appeared to subsist on nervous energy. The only stimulus he received at such times seemed to be the peculiar cigarettes that he smoked incessantly then, but never on other occasions. He made them himself. Jean did not know what they were or what he put into them.

Of what he thought, or how his mind worked, she knew absolutely nothing. When he chose to explain the steps and processes by which he arrived at his deductions, they seemed surprisingly obvious. But when he did not explain, she floundered in darkness. She felt, with unreasonable irritation, that she would never penetrate beyond his external appearance.

For all his indifference to what he wore, his striking but unlovely aspect, the long, lank figure of the professor possessed an extraordinary fascination.

She could not specify or isolate even this quality—whether it came from his personality, or from his latent power and his inexhaustible reserves of nervous energy, or the hyperneurotic complexity of his nature, or from the compelling strength of his features.

The hatchet-thin face, with its high cheek bones and sharp features, its shaggy eyebrows, and the black eyes that on different occasions varied from a listless lackluster to a hypnotic intensity, had stamped itself indelibly on her memory the day she came. A strange man. A remarkable man. A personality more baffling and incomprehensible than any problem she had yet seen him solve.

A curious sound broke her chain of thought as she followed him from the laboratory.

An alarm clock was ringing stridently. She halted in surprise. The sound rasped from somewhere outside, buzzed through the partly open latticed windows, made a harsh undercurrent to the noise of late evening traffic. Why would an alarm clock be going off, apparently on the grounds of 13 State Street, at this hour of approximately eleven P.M.? Was it something for which Frost had been responsible? She watched him.

He had paused and listened intently for just the briefest of moments. The next instant, he plunged for the door faster than she had ever before seen him move. She raced after him.

The drone of traffic swelled louder as Jean darted into the cool night air. The glow of the sky, the reflected glare of the city, the illumination from street lights, would have been more than enough even without the beam of the flashlight that Frost turned on the thing at his feet in the middle of the lawn.

Jean felt sick. She experienced a nausea in which revulsion and horror and pity left her weak. For once in her life, she could have done without all the light on earth. The buzz of the alarm clock came with sinister harshness while it was running down. And neither the alarm clock nor the noise of traffic could drown out the indescribable bubbling bleat that issued from the man on the lawn.

Dark blood spouted from his severed hands and feet. It crept from the raw stubs of his ears. It dribbled from his tongueless mouth. His inarticulate, writhing agony became more dreadful because no pain could be expressed by his eyes. There were only gaping sockets where his eyes had been. An alarm clock, tied to the victim's waist, lay face up on the ground.

Jean's hand flew to her mouth. She bit a white, clenched knuckle to stifle a scream.

The hands of the clock pointed to five minutes to twelve. The significance was hideous. The tortured man had only five minutes to live—five minutes to die. A challenge to Frost had been flung at his doorstep for reasons unknown, by persons unknown. Was it a gesture of brutal contempt? How could any one, even Frost, extract information from a deaf, dumb, blind, limbless, dying man with less than five minutes to live?

II.

Frost snapped, in a voice harsh and cold: "Search the grounds for any possible clue."

He knelt and in one continuous motion scooped the alarm clock on the dying man's chest, lifted the body, and hurried toward his laboratory. Gouts of blood dribbled to the ground. The dying man's head lolled, rolled feverishly. The blood bubbled and frothed on his lips, clotted in his ears, bathed his sockets with ebbing life. His wordless gurgle held a more awful and sickening plea than any shriek Jean had ever heard.

In the faint light—or was it an illusion or distortion of her overwrought nerves?—Frost's features took on an expression of stern, implacable, and relentless purpose. Yet even now, in the presence of a gruesome crime, Frost's reaction seemed less emotional than rational; as if the laws of reason had been violated, so that the ultimate resources of mind, the acid bite of logic, must be summoned to restore the true pattern of things. And while wondering what demons they were who had flung this wreckage at Frost's door, Jean experienced a shudder at the thought of the fate awaiting them if Frost caught up with them.

His long, spectral form, bent from the weight of his burden, erased the distance to his laboratory in great strides.

With the flashlight that he had left, Jean began a systematic and minute search of the lawn, foot by foot, in an ever-widening circle around the spot where the body had been found. She hunted for footprints, for crushed blades of grass, for cigarette butts, scraps of paper, anything that might prove helpful.

She found only Frost's and her own footprints, and one curious fact. There were glistening drops of blood in a line extending away from the spot and toward the sidewalk. The last of the splashes was approximately eight feet from the stained area where the body had rested. The sidewalk was twenty feet distant. But the grass was not trampled at any point between the body and the sidewalk.

How had the drops of blood come there, in that line extending from the body? It was incredible that the man had threshed around in such a fashion that a trail of blood had been flung out in a singularly straight line. Why did the trail end or begin at that particular point? If it marked the direction from which the stranger had come, why were there no signs of his struggle? And if others had brought him, why were there no footprints?

By what agency had he arrived, and why? What sinister purpose lay behind his mutilation? How could even Frost, in spite of his immense resources, solve this riddle, unravel the mystery of the tortured stranger, and bring the guilty to justice?

Jean's exhaustive survey of the grounds revealed no clues. With a last swing of the flashlight, she abandoned further search and returned to the house.

Frost had just emerged from the laboratory. He carried a valise. His expression was inscrutable. By the long, pungently aromatic cigarette that he smoked, Jean knew he had found a crime worthy of his attention. The hunt was on. Wherever it might lead, into whatever danger it might hurl them, there would never be a moment's let-up in Frost's remorseless pursuit.

"Remain here until I return or until you hear from me," he commanded as he strode toward the cellar garage. "Did you find any clues?"

"No. No footprints, nothing. The only suspicious fact was a trail of blood extending from the spot toward the upper sidewalk for about eight feet. The man——"

"Died a few minutes after I brought him in."

Jean's face fell. "Then there is nothing to go on," she said in a disappointed tone.

Frost flatly contradicted her: "On the contrary, there is a great deal to go on. I know his identity, why he was mutilated, where he lived, how he came here, why he was brought, and who is responsible."

Jean looked incredulous. "Did he carry all that information with him?"

"His pockets had been emptied and every mark of identification removed."

"But you said—how in the world could—"

Frost cut her short, and stated calmly: "I obtained the information I needed from the man himself before he died."

Jean burst out: "But he could not talk! He could not hear or see or write! He—"

The door closed on Frost's departing figure. Behind him he left a bewildered assistant who floundered around in mental dead-ends in a hopeless attempt to visualize the magic by which Frost elicited all the information he wanted from a tongueless, earless, eyeless, limbless, dying man.

Frost climbed into his car. Driving out of his garage, he turned north on Broadway. He watched in the mirror the headlights of a sedan that swung along behind. Sometimes he speeded up for short bursts, sometimes he drifted along at twenty or thirty miles an hour. The sedan kept pace a block behind him.

The professor settled into a more comfortable position. He drove toward upper Manhattan, his eyes occasionally flicking to the mirror to watch the trailing sedan. He made no effort to elude it, and it made no attempt to overtake him. A bleak, mirthless smile hovered on his features. He smoked one cigarette after another.

He turned into West 180th Street. He stopped in front of a cheap apartment building. The sedan sidled to the curb, still a block behind.

Frost entered the vestibule and punched a button marked "E. L. Troff." The latch clicked almost immediately.

The professor climbed one flight and rapped on the door of apartment 2C. A lock turned and the door opened cautiously.

"Who are you? What do you want?"

A worried-looking woman in her passing thirties faced him. She was plain-faced and a bit plump. She looked like the average, middle-class housewife. Though midnight had passed, she was fully dressed.

"I came to talk to you about your husband."

"I've already told the police all I know."

"I am Professor I. V. Frost, a private investigator. I have been drawn into the case. I can and will help you."

Frost was halfway in when the woman said: "Come in."

The professor did not sit down.

"Do you know where Everett is? Have they found him?" the woman asked anxiously.

Frost did not reply directly. "We are on the trail. Can you tell me offhand who some of his best friends were?"

The woman rattled off several names. Frost listened idly until she named "Ganther."

"The former district attorney?" he interrupted.

"Yes. It was mostly his recommendation that got Everett the job."

"Let me use your telephone."

Frost reached the instrument without waiting for a reply and dialed a number. A full minute passed before the intermittent buzz in the receiver was broken.

"Who is it? What do you want? What do you mean by disturbing a man's sleep at this hour of the night?" an irate voice exploded.

"Frost calling."

"Oh! Why didn't you say so? Where have you been hiding all these months? Get a fellow out of bed at this hour. You ought to be ashamed of yourself. What are you up to? Where are you? Why don't you say something?"

Frost wore an amused expression. "What's your opinion of Everett Lucius Troff?"

"Did you phone just to ask me that? Are you on the case? What the devil difference does it make? Where are you? Have you——"

"What do you think of Troff?"

"Don't believe a word of it. Can't trust the papers nowadays. Everett's a fine fellow. One of the best. I got him that job. I'll stake my reputation on him. It's a lot of stuff and nonsense. It's——"

Frost broke in: "I merely asked. The papers say he was kidnaped. Why spring to his defense when he is under no suspicion?"

"You should ask me that. You wouldn't be calling if his name was clear. Where is he? What have you found? Anything I can do? Why——"

"You'll get the details later. Right now you need the rest of that sleep you were sputtering about."

When he hung up, Mrs. Troff, who had been anxiously listening to his side of the conversation, stammered: "Everett—do you know—is he——"

Frost replied, gently: "I cannot say. If he has not been heard from before this, I would be prepared for bad news."

The woman, dull-eyed, despondent, sank into a chair as Frost left.

The hall was clear. He went down the rear stairway to the back entrance of the building. He studied the dark areaway. After a moment, he slowly and silently opened the door and put a wedge under it.

Flattened against the wall, he waited while minutes dragged. A cat meowed. A rat scampered in the black shadows. The sound of faint breathing came from beyond the door.

Frost struck first and eased the inert body to the ground. One look at the thug's face sufficed. The professor handcuffed the killer's hands to his ankles behind his back.

Swiftly crossing the areaway, Frost entered the building opposite and emerged in 179th Street. He headed for Broadway where he hailed the first cab he saw.

A few blocks downtown, he halted at an all-night restaurant. His first telephone call went through to the night desk of police headquarters.

"Let me speak to Inspector Frick. . . . Hello, Frick? . . . Frost calling. Will you take a couple of men and meet me at the Midtown Bank? . . . No. I'm merely doing some investigating. The bank will be opened by its president, in our presence. Time is important. It might be too late if we waited till morning. . . . Fine! In three quarters of an hour."

He dialed another number. "Tell Mr. Stafford that Professor I. V. Frost is on the phone." Frost listened. His voice hardened. "Tell Mr. Stafford that Frost wants to speak to him. Now."

A long pause. Then, "Yes?" came a noncommittal answer.

"Professor I. V. Frost speaking. I—"

A suave voice interrupted: "Sorry, but you must have made a mistake. I have not the pleasure of—"

Frost drawled: "You will have, within an hour."

The suave voice sounded hostile: "I am not accustomed to being disturbed by strangers at this hour. You may speak to my secretary in the—"

"The police are waiting for us at your bank. I am working with them on the Midtown Bank robbery. As president of the bank, you will be there in three quarters of an hour to open it in our presence."

"But I'm—"

"Then get dressed."

"But I haven't—"

"Get the keys. Be there in three quarters of an hour. We appreciate your coöperation," Frost sardonically finished.

He glanced at his watch. Returning to the cab, he ordered: "Drive slowly uptown."

He peered out of the window as the cab rolled along. At 180th Street, he suddenly commanded: "Turn left here."

The sedan was gone. Frost's car stood where he had left it. Making sure that the street was clear, he dismissed the cab. He entered the vestibule of the apartment building again. The glass of the front door had been shattered over the knob. Frost shrugged his shoulders and departed.

After a quick inspection of his car for bombs, Frost drove downtown. On his way, he stopped at the same restaurant to call headquarters again.

"Has Inspector Frick left yet? . . . Let me speak to him. . . . Frost calling. There is the body of a murdered man in West 130th Street. . . ."

The professor talked for a minute. He then drove leisurely toward central Manhattan, his shaggy brows frowning while he hunched low in his seat. The air in the car became thick from the fumes of his odd cigarettes. Whatever stimulus they gave showed in the brightness of his eyes and in his deceptively dreamy expression.

A squad car already waited at the curb in front of the Midtown Bank when he arrived. A wiry, crisp little man with a military carriage bounced out of the car.

"Hello, Frost, glad to see you again. What's the news on the stiff? When did you find him?"

"I didn't find him."

"What the heck! You called in, didn't you?"

"On my way to that address an hour ago, I was trailed by a sedan. It parked a block behind me. It was supposed to be curtains for me when I came out. They planted the man in the rear entrance, just in case. I left by the rear entrance and knocked him out. I left him handcuffed. After calling you the first time, I went back to get my car. The sedan was gone. The glass in the front door of the building was knocked in. You know the rules in Blake's gang—the penalty of failure is death. I didn't need to go back to the areaway."

A car drew up behind them. A huffy gentleman emerged. He wore impeccable clothes. His face was of the bland, confident kind that makes small depositors believe that God's in His heaven and all's well with the world of banking.

He greeted Inspector Frick politely and bowed coldly to Frost. The professor eyed him searchingly and lighted another cigarette. Frick sniffed dubiously. He started to speak, but held his words.

Frost looked up at the burglar alarm. He drove his car onto the sidewalk underneath it. Vaulting to the top of his car, he stood up and removed the alarm casing. With the aid of a flashlight, he inspected the mechanism.

Leaving the casing off, he dropped to the sidewalk.

"What's the idea of that?" Frick asked.

"I'm going to test the alarm, without making any more racket than necessary." To Stafford, he suggested: "Now open the doors."

The squad-car men kept guard outside while Frost, Stafford, and Frick entered the bank. Stafford threw a light switch, and the floor sprang into desolate clarity—long marble aisles, deserted cages, untenanted desks. The bank, by night, seemed only less dismal than a tomb.

"Which was Troff's cage?" Frost demanded.

Stafford pointed out the teller's window.

"And where did the first gunman issue orders?"

Frick took a position. "Right about here, from what the witnesses said."

Frost studied the two spots. He walked over to the teller's cage and stood inside, facing an imaginary line of depositors. He faced the door. Then he turned his attention to the burglar alarm, worked by foot pressure, that jutted from the floor of the cage. He pressed it. The mechanism outside whirred. If the casing had been on, there would have been a terrific clangor.

"If I hadn't fixed it up at headquarters, the place would be swarming with radio cars right now," Frick remarked, with an element of pride at the efficiency of the service.

Frost halted the alarm, tried it out a couple of times. With a thoughtful look, he knelt by the foot button. He took a couple of instruments from his valise and dismantled the object. Lifting the top part off, he stared down. With a few swift motions, he made some adjustments and then replaced the top part.

He rose, holding an innocent-looking metal-and-composition gadget, with a couple of springs on it. "Here is the answer."

Frick and Stafford inspected it curiously.

"What in blazes is it?" Frick asked, frowning.

"A simple type of interference spring, with an automatic catch so that it locks after one shift."

Stafford wrinkled his forehead. "I do not quite follow you."

Frost explained: "When the floor button was pressed, with this thing under it, the button pushed against the composition. The composition is a nonconductor. The burglar alarm would not ring. But when pressure was released, this spring automatically pulled the metal part into position and locked at the same time. The metal being a conductor of electricity, the alarm would go off every occasion thereafter."

Light dawned on Frick. "How long would it take to install the thing?"

"Anywhere from two to ten minutes, depending on the skill of the workman."

Frick asked Stafford: "Would it be possible, during banking hours, for the teller in the cage to install this thing without attracting attention?"

Stafford nodded slowly, with grave features. "I am sorry to agree, it would be entirely possible."

Frick pocketed the gadget. To Frost, he stated: "It looks bad for Troff. He installs this, makes a phony play at pushing the alarm and goes through a phony kidnaping. He splits with them and lights out, or he turns up in a day or two, goes back on the job, and takes the gadget out when he has time. But the chances are he's flown, with his share of the split."

"It sounds possible," Frost admitted.

"I wouldn't have believed it." Stafford shook his head ruefully. "And now, if you gentlemen have finished your business——"

Outside, after Stafford had left, Frick said, with a note of genuine regret: "The force could use you, Frost. Any time you wish, you can just about name your own position and pick your own cases."

"The police are efficient. I prefer freedom of action and the use of my own methods."

"You find out things that even we don't know, Frost. Any time you need us, call me at headquarters. Good luck!"

The squad car moved off.

The hum of the city was at its low ebb. Skyscrapers and gigantic buildings raised their dark towers to the always faintly luminous sky. At infrequent intervals, a lone passerby hurried on his way. From time to time a car roared down the wide avenue. The pulse of life never wholly ceased in the great metropolis, but it had become as quiet as it ever was.

Seated in his car, the professor opened the valise and made some quick changes. They took but a minute. When he had finished, he drove uptown.

He had not gone two blocks, and was still gathering speed, when a tire blew out. Frost did not seem in the least surprised, as he eased the car to the curb. He climbed out and surveyed the damage.

"Stick 'em up!" snarled a harsh voice.

Frost's hands rose slowly as he turned. Out of the black shadows of doorways emerged two men with submachine guns. A sedan streaked to a halt in front of Frost's car.

"Get in!" barked the leader.

Another submachine gun poked its ugly muzzle through a window to emphasize the command.

"You aren't afraid of me, by any chance, are you?" Frost ironically asked. "By the way, did you know that army officials figure one machine gun as equal to the attacking power of two hundred troops? I believe I see three submachine guns."

The leader viciously jabbed a gun in his back. "In, or you'll get it here!"

Frost entered, a strange, tight smile on his features. The car picked up speed, roared north.

III.

They were rats. They looked like rats. Behind a spitting submachine gun, they could be brave. They could even be brave if they merely had a sawed-off shotgun to train on an unarmed man. They were brave now. Did not a man sit on each side of Frost with muzzles aimed at him. Did not a third killer keep him covered point-blank from the front seat? They were taking him for a ride, and the driver's foot stepped with relish on the accelerator.

"Pull those side curtains down!" barked the leader. "We don't want any dumb cops lookin' in."

The curtains were drawn. The car shot on toward the outskirts of the city.

"The great Ivy Frost goin' for a ride!" jeered the swarthy killer on his right. "Just another fall guy."

The professor made no reply. He sat still, hands folded, the strange, enigmatic smile still on his face.

"Wipe that grin off your mug!" the swarthy gangster growled with an angry prod.

"Cut it out!" the leader curtly ordered. "It's the last chance he'll ever have to smile at anything."

"Let's give it to him here."

"Orders are orders. He'll keep."

The car roared on, and still Frost sat with that puzzling, mirthless expression, as if he enjoyed some huge joke. His lips were tightly compressed. He seemed to have a little difficulty breathing through his nose. The car streaked out of the city limits and off to a little-traveled road.

"Bulletproof clothes, huh? They don't help much when your mug gets riddled. Won't talk, huh? You don't need to. You're never gonna talk again. Ivy Frost takin' a ride like any punk," the swarthy rat mocked.

The car wabbled.

"Keep your eyes on the road, Sam!" clipped the leader.

The driver shook his head, muttered: "Aw, what's eatin' ya? Can't miss all the bumps."

The swarthy man jabbed Frost again. "So you were gonna find out what happened to Troff, huh? Save your time. We'll tell you. We did the job. Anything else you'd like to know?"

The car lurched wildly.

"Say, I got a headache," moaned the man on the left.

"What the hell!" muttered the leader. His voice was thick. His eyes had a peculiar look.

The expression on Frost's face did not change. His features were rigid. There was something almost unearthly in his bearing and implacably menacing in his silence.

The swarthy killer opened his mouth to speak and talked incoherent syllables. The gangster at Frost's left moved a hand to his collar, but the gesture was listless. The driver suddenly slumped in his seat and his hands slipped off the wheel. The car lost momentum, skidded crazily out of control. The leader made no protest, no effort to seize control. The gun fell from his hands. His head lolled. His dying eyes stared with a look of reproach into Frost's glittering black pupils.

And now the professor bent forward with a swift motion and grasped the steering wheel. The driver did not stir. The leader had slumped beside him. The man to the left of Frost sat hunched over, head and knees on the floor. The dark-faced rat tried to keep the submachine gun trained on Frost, but he had trouble holding it. It wobbled around. His finger hung on the trigger, but the finger was nerveless. His jaw sagged. He gaped at Frost with dull bewilderment and strove to rise. He lurched and slid dizzily to the floor, gasping.

Tight-lipped, the mirthless smile gone like a prophecy the meaning of which the killers would never know, now, Frost straightened the car and guided it till it came to rest. The motor choked and died. As coolly as if he was completing a common experiment, the scientist stooped, shifted the gears from high to neutral, and pressed the starter. The motor idled.

With swift, expert fingers, so nimble that they seemed possessed of a life of their own, Frost searched the four gangsters. His nostrils quivered and his breathing was slow.

The pockets of the four yielded large sums in bills which he inspected briefly and stuffed in his coat. He glanced at papers and memoranda, but did not keep them, and did not take time to copy even the important numbers he observed.

He left the car, motor still idling, and shut the door. The moment he emerged, he gulped a deep, satisfying breath of air, and for some minutes, as he strode along the rutty road to the main highway, he enjoyed the night air with keen zest. His gaunt, spectral figure, striding down the lonely road, would in itself, and by its forbidding nature, have been defense enough against most mortal assaults.

Fifteen minutes brought him to the highway. A pair of headlights streaked toward him. He planted himself in the middle of the road and hailed it. The car sped on. When hardly a dozen yards distant, its brakes squealed, it veered sharply, and accelerated. Frost made a flying leap to the running board as it attempted to pass him.

A white-faced driver cringed, slammed on the brakes. "D-d-d-don't shoot. I-I-I was only foolin'."

"Drive on!" Frost briefly ordered as he climbed in. "I merely want a lift. I'm on police business."

The fat-faced driver did not seem much reassured. He glanced doubtfully at his newly acquired passenger. "Going far, mister? I'm kind of in a hurry, and you see, the way you jumped on, I thought—"

"I'll tell you when to let me off," Frost silenced the man. Volunteering no further explanations, he maintained an air of abstraction until they entered the city limits.

"I live in the Bronx," the driver began.

Frost looked out. "All right. Let me off here."

The stranger, relieved, did not wait to accept the bill Frost was fishing for, but drove off in a remarkable hurry.

The professor entered a restaurant and telephoned his own private number. There was no answer. He hung up, tried again. Still no answer. He frowned and dialed the listed number of his assistant. Still no answer. He tried a different number, and this time got a reply.

"J. V.? Frost calling."

The sleepy voice of John Vogel, an old friend and his personal attorney, answered plaintively: "Don't you ever sleep?"

"This is urgent, J. V."

"Everything you do is urgent. I wish my life was as exciting."

"Try the television set and see if you can get any response from my house."

Protracted silence. Frost deftly flipped a cigarette from deep down in a pocket, produced a match, and lighted it, in a continuous movement born of long habit, with one hand.

Vogel's voice at last came through, "There's no answer and I can't get anything on the screen."

"I expected as much. As soon as possible in the morning find out and send these over—the serial numbers of any or all bills known to have been taken in the Midtown Bank robbery; the market quotations on Midtown stock for the past two weeks; the credit rating of Stafford, and whatever else you can dig up about his financial affairs."

Hurrying out, Frost took the first cab available. "State Street and Riverside Drive. As fast as you can make it!" he flung at the driver.

The car shot downtown, clipping through light changes, screeching around curves and corners. Frost brooded, but the driver, occasionally glancing into his mirror, was unable to tell what went on behind the inscrutable expression of his fare.

The driver wasn't sure he wanted to know what those thin, sharp features concealed. He felt, on the whole, that he would not even care to make an issue of a tip. There was something about the passenger that made him leery. He had handled tough birds and hard customers in his time, but never one with quite the peculiar character of Frost, or one who proved so difficult to size up. He would be a bad one to tangle with.

"Quite right," Frost spoke aloud, and lapsed back into silence.

Badly shaken, the driver pushed his cab for all it was worth. As a rule, he didn't care much one way or another about fares, but he was damned glad to beat it after dropping Frost.

The professor melted into the shadows along the inner sidewalk, and faded into the grounds of the house at 15 State Street. Moving warily, his keen eyes probing every place of concealment, he crossed to the grille fence inclosing No. 13. He went through a section that suddenly opened at his touch.

No. 13 was dark. Satisfied that no one watched him, he crossed the lawn, stepped lightly across the driveway, and stopped at an ornamental pillar on the side of the porch.

Again he listened intently before touching the pillar. It opened noiselessly and revealed a compact mechanism. From a tray at the bottom, he lifted several wet films which he studied by holding them against a tiny red bulb set in the mechanism.

The first negative showed two masked men crouching on each side of the door. A third man, erect, unmasked, had one foot forward toward the opening door.

The second negative showed both masked men still crouching. The door was closed. The next film showed both entering. The fourth was merely a picture of the doorway. The fifth outlined the two masked men emerging. They carried the body of Jean Moray, who might have been unconscious or dead. The sixth was another blank.

The seventh negative showed four husky thugs carrying a huge crate. Number eight blank, on number nine the four were coming out empty-handed. Ten blank, eleven saw the same four entering with smaller parcels. Twelve was blank, but thirteen indicated four of the gang leaving. The last film was blank.

Eyes narrowed, face drawn into tight, hard lines, Frost dropped the wet films back in the tray. He tore off a strip of paper from a spool. It was stamped with figures that ranged from 12:58 to 1:33 in fourteen separate notations.

Jean Moray had been kidnaped between 12:58 and 1:33 A.M. by a gang numbering at least five persons.

IV.

Frost straightened. From the upper compartment of the pillar, he lifted a small earpiece with one hand and pulled out a tiny disk with the other. He pressed two buttons almost simultaneously.

"Drop the gun and throw up your hands!" he ordered in a low voice.

He listened, heard nothing. He replaced the items and closed a power switch, before sliding the movable section so that the pillar looked as innocent as before.

Speed now marking every action, he vaulted over the porch railing and reached the door in a few strides. He whipped an automatic from his coat. He inserted a key and turned it with his left hand. He shoved the door open and kept his automatic trained into the brightly lighted hall.

The heavy brute stared up. He gave a last tug at his gun that lay curiously immovable on the floor. The gun slid only a fraction of an inch. The killer scrambled to his feet, face working, hand streaking to his pocket. It all happened in fractions of time, but Frost, slouching outside, a sardonic twist on his face, did not fire.

"Hands up and come out," he threatened, "or I shoot!"

The ugly one made a final, desperate tug at his second weapon. He could not seem to budge it from his pocket. His eyes bulged. Sweat popped out on his forehead.

He gave up and marched forward as commanded, his features twitching. Frost turned him around and handcuffed him.

"Get inside."

The killer entered. As Frost followed and closed the door, he clicked a button. He removed the captive's second gun. He walked over and picked up the fallen weapon.

The gangster's eyes stared. He ran his tongue over dry lips. His face had the sickly color of old cabbage. His mouth twitched, and the muscles of his throat corded. Frost strode toward him.

The prisoner's voice broke out: "Whatcha gonna do? Whatcha gonna do? I ain't done nothin'! Honest, I ain't done nothin'! I'll talk! Lemme go an' I'll tell ya all ya wanna know. I'll tell ya where the girl is! I'll—"

Frost's words cut like lashes: "Shut up! You can tell me nothing that I do not already know."

The captive shrank unnerved against the wall. He could face any human opponent. With gun in hand, he could meet any ordinary emergency. But he had waited in darkness, waited for hours, with those other things all around, until his nerves got fidgety, and nothing happened.

Then the hallway had been mysteriously flooded with light. From the walls, the ceiling, nowhere, came a muffled voice commanding him to drop his gun. As he peered around in amazement, the gun was suddenly torn from his hands with a terrific jerk. He dived for it, but could no more lift it than he could have budged the Statue of Liberty. And even while his wits, trained in the gutter school of crime, tried to fathom events wholly beyond his comprehension, the door opened, and it seemed to his panicky gaze that a nightmare had become real.

The prisoner cowered against the wall. His handcuffed hands clawed. He cringed, knew the terror of silence. Frost came on, wordless. The criminologist taped his captive's lips, shackled his feet and left him lying on the floor.

Then he spoke: "You'll have plenty of time to think things over, Squinty. When I want you to talk—talk!"

Ignoring the gangster, Frost faced the door of his library and studied it speculatively, as if debating a problem. He walked toward it. "Squinty's" eyes took on a momentary crafty gleam, then went white with terror.

Frost laid his automatic on a table. He broke the chamber and extracted the first bullet. He roughened its nose and smeared it with some paste that he took from a vial in his pocket. He replaced the cartridge.

Gun in hand, he stooped by the soundproof door to his library. Squinty twisted and squirmed on the floor. A weird, nasal moan shrilled from his nostrils, and blood trickled from his torn lips as he tried to open his mouth to scream.

But Frost flung the door wide, pressed the light switch on the wall within, and threw himself flat on the floor. The entire motion was completed in a second.

The panther sprang, eyes blazing. It sailed overhead with a mad snarl. Frost fired from the floor. The bullet tore into the great cat's neck. It landed in the hallway and for a split second glared at Squinty. The helpless thug quivered in the paralysis of horror.

The beast whirled and leaped savagely at Frost. But the professor had whipped into his library and flattened himself against the wall inside the door.

The jungle cat, its leap oddly short for its power and the fury to kill in its hunger-maddened eyes, sprawled on the rug, pawed crazily, and spun around. A scream poured from its throat. It shook and tried to leap. It went limp after a last contortion in a death agony.

The professor inspected the carcass. Even in death, the giant cat was a thing of beauty, in its own sleek, savage fashion.

In Frost's harsh features was no sign of relief or surprise as he walked to the door of his laboratory.

Hurling it open, he switched on the light and dashed to a wall panel. He closed a control. The hum of a powerful air-conditioner arose. The stagnant, chemical-sodden air stirred and cool drafts circulated. Still holding his breath, Frost paused just long enough to grasp an empty bottle and stopper it before racing from the laboratory. Ten minutes would allow an ample margin of safety.

The rear entrance to his house led to the kitchen, from which also led the stairs to his basement garage. The kitchen could be reached both through the laboratory and from the hall. Conserving time, Frost returned to the hallway. Squinty Maginess' eyes rolled, still wide with the unnerving terror that had swept him when the panther seemed ready to pounce.

Frost, every movement exhibiting the calculation characteristic of the scientist who tackles a problem to which only one solution is ultimately possible, walked to one of the doors beside a stone Buddha. Its fat face had a placid smile.

The door, unlocked as he had left it hours ago, yielded readily to his shove. He pushed the light switch. His eyes probed into corners and nooks, studied every inch of floor, walls, and ceiling. He took a step forward.

From under a cabinet, something small and coral streaked like a flame. Before its venomous head struck, it was buried under the folds of the garment that Frost dropped. Methodically he trampled on the cloth, crushed the writhing snake into pulp.

Out of the radiator coils ran something tiny, black, and hairy. Sprayed by the liquid pump that Frost turned upon it, it was dead before it reached him. Its mate never left the coils into which he wafted death.

One task remained in the process of repossessing his house—the most dangerous task of all. They were innocent-looking parcels that rested, precariously balanced, on horizontal wooden laths that had been nailed to the jamb of the cellar door and the outside kitchen door. The strips of wood jutted halfway across the door. Had the door been pushed even slightly open—

Frost gingerly lifted the parcels, one at a time. He carried them outdoors. Nothing was ever handled more gently. Darkness still remained, though dawn was not far distant. Picking his way carefully, avoiding every possible tripping point with unerring accuracy, the professor set his parcels in the middle of the lawn behind his house.

Using a shaded flashlight, he unwrapped the parcels with sensitive fingers. After a painstaking study of its construction, he dismantled one box. The second parcel proved less difficult. It contained a bottle. This he opened, tilted, and let the yellowish fluid seep gradually into the ground. He had completed a task as deadly as it was simple.

Returning inside the house, he tore off the wooden strips. Then he lighted a cigarette and inhaled deeply. His eyes glittered.

For some minutes, he was busy collecting things. A trail of pungent smoke swirled after him. He made a detailed examination of all rooms. A half hour later, in the gray of coming dawn, he lowered himself to an easy-chair in his library and surveyed a remarkable assemblage.

These specimens comprised: one Squinty Maginess, alive; one panther, dead; a large, iron-barred cage, and its crate; a coral snake, dead; a small wire-mesh cage, and its crate; two black-widow spiders, defunct; a tiny wooden box with perforations in the lid; a heavy metal container that had once held gas under pressure; one stoppered bottle with a sample of cyanide gas; parts of a dismantled dynamite bomb; a bottle to which only a bare trace of nitroglycerin adhered; fourteen wet films; a piece of tape on which fourteen time indications were stamped; eighty-seven thousand dollars in bills; the shrouded corpse of a mutilated man; and a couple of automatic revolvers with silencers.

To these might be added the cards on each of the crates, which merely bore the stenciled address: "To Professor I. V. Frost, 13 State St." On a sheet of paper, Frost jotted the significant numbers he had seen among pocket memoranda of four gangsters who had raised no objection to his search.

"They are an interesting lot, aren't they?" he remarked to Squinty. "Remember what you have just seen. Think hard about what might happen to you. And when I tell you to talk—talk!"

V.

For hours, Frost sat in a reverie. The captive's eyes were closed. Frost seemed unaware of his presence. He smoked incessantly. The air grew hazy. The ash trays overflowed with butts. Ashes sprinkled his jacket, his old corduroy trousers, littered the floor. He looked dreamy, almost benign, and quite without worry. If anything, so far as observable, his features expressed the same detached air, the same attitude of serene contemplation, that was chiseled on the marble bust of Socrates upon a pedestal at one end of the library.

Occasionally the professor shifted into an easier position, but always with his legs doubled up on an ottoman.

If the mysterious appearance by mysterious means of a dying man outside his house caused him any perplexity, it did not show. If the pursuit of the black sedan and the episode of the waylayer waylaid in a building on 180th Street were cause for speculation, no one could have guessed.

If the ride that ended in death, but not for the intended victim, motivated whatever plans he had, he gave no indication of it. If the kidnaping of Jean Moray, or her subsequent fate, commanded his attention, only he knew it. And he must already have dismissed from his calculations, so Squinty thought, these recent occurrences in his house, since the professor plainly took no notice of the considerable array of objects around him.

The telephone rang. It was not yet seven o'clock. Frost reached out a slim hand and lifted the instrument.

"Frost? Thank Heaven!" came the relieved voice of Inspector Frick. "Your car was picked up on Fifth Avenue and I thought—"

Frost cut in sharply: "Let no one know that you have talked to me. Hold the car until I call for it. Do not give out any information. This is highly important. I'll call you later in the day."

The professor sank back in his chair and studied the long ash of his cigarette. He stretched for an ash tray. The ash fell to the floor. It was ever thus.

Fifteen minutes later, the phone ran again.

"What the hell!" exploded the voice of Inspector Frick. "We got a report from a guy in the sticks of a stranded car. And what do we find when we get there? Four stiffs and a note in one mug's lap, 'Call Frost immediately.'"

"Thanks for calling," the professor replied. "Can you keep it out of the papers for a couple of hours?"

Frick protested: "I'm going off duty at eight. How did four of Joe Blake's gang come to die way out there? And from what looks like carbon monoxide? Understand, we aren't shedding any tears, but just the same, there'll have to be some routine stuff."

"That can wait. Can you withhold the information from the court reporters and from the papers until ten o'clock? . . . Good! No; it isn't necessary, but if you're going to stay on the job I'll drop in around noon."

An hour passed. Squinty made a poor pretense of sleeping, but at last abandoned the effort.

A bell tinkled. Frost sprang from the chair. In his laboratory, he closed a power switch. Minutes later, the round face of John Vogel blurred into the television screen and focused.

"Hello, Frost! I have the information you wanted."

The professor glanced at a clock. "You needn't have stayed up all night. Mid-morning would have been time enough."

"Yes," replied the senior partner of Vogel, Vogel & Brant, attorneys, "so you said. But your cases have a habit of ending rapidly the minute you possess all the facts. Here are the serial numbers of the bills." He read them off.

"Now, as for the price range of Midtown stock, it held steady all last week at thirty-one. On Monday it opened at thirty-one but spurted up to thirty-six. Tuesday it opened off, dropped to thirty, and on Wednesday slid to twenty-six where it has stayed since."

"Did you find any reason for the fluctuation?"

"Yes. The Midtown had applied for a government loan. There were rumors Monday that the loan had been approved, but after the market closed, it was announced that the loan would not be granted."

"Exactly!" Frost agreed.

"Eh? You knew this?"

"No; but it was the only theory that the facts could have fitted," Frost drawled.

Vogel floundered. "Don't you mean it the other way round? Theories fit facts, don't they?"

"Sometimes they do," Frost conceded. "But any fact, merely as such, is worthless. It has no value unless it bears a relation to some other fact. It has no meaning except in so far as it concerns other truths. The interpretation of facts, truths, and series of events is a matter of mind and logic, which analyze them and understand them in terms of ideas, concepts, or theories.

"Thus far, the process is inductive. But from there on, the light of pure, analytic, deductive logic comes into play. It must, or the facts never would have significance. Therefore I say, and agree with a celebrated English scientist and philosopher, that facts must be tested and proved by theory."

"Many an innocent man has died from a good theory." Vogel's eyes twinkled.

"Circumstantial evidence never yet convicted an innocent man; wrong interpretation of such evidence has, or failure to discover all the evidence has, but those miscarriages of justice are the fault of facts, not of theories, and the fault of incorrect or inferior reasoning. But let us save the discussion for an evening next week. I shall be finished with this case before then.

"You might drop into a pawnshop Tuesday afternoon and purchase a number of old trinkets. We shall use those things, those facts, to discover solely by logical analysis and deduction the one true theory that presents us with an understanding of their previous owner or owners, the habits and characteristics of those owners, and the reasons whereby the trinkets found their way to the pawnshop.

"But there is a matter that I must attend to this morning. What else did you find out?"

John Vogel complained: "Just when the discussion becomes exciting, you abandon it. Stafford, in a dummy account carried in the name of a friend, speculated heavily in Midtown stock, expecting a rise after the government loan. It was a complicated business involving some skullduggery. He lost heavily on the decline. His affairs were further complicated by the fact that his bank has made some questionable loans that might not stand investigation, and that he himself has a large indebtedness to meet to-day."

"Which he is ready to meet," Frost observed.

And John Vogel added wryly: "The facts appear to confirm your theory in every detail."

"You did an excellent job of obtaining valuable and not readily available information in a short time at unfavorable hours."

Vogel stated simply: "The legal and the medical professions have traditions pertaining to the confidences of clients. Those traditions can work for injustice as easily as for justice. There is only one living person to whom I would freely divulge everything I could, for I know that such information will be devoted only to the attainment of justice."

The face of John Vogel, bland and approving, faded from the screen when Frost and he cut off power from the duplicate transmitters.

VI.

The attitude of repose sloughed from Frost like a discarded coat. The inactivity of hours vanished. The air of abstract meditation disappeared. In no single, definable, specific way did the change come. It was more than a matter of motion. It represented the difference between potential and kinetic energy.

The professor came out of the laboratory with a number of tools and appliances. He wore rubber gloves. The telephone received his concentrated attention for a few minutes. Testing the results, he found them wholly satisfactory.

Returning to the laboratory, he strode to a maze of switches, controls, screens, dials, and electrical equipment. He pressed a button and a small section of wall opened. Another, and the fat Buddha lost part of its anatomy. Another, and the front door swung open. Frost threw a switch. Satisfied with what he saw, he closed all portals.

Taking further instruments, he descended to the basement and worked for several minutes on the wiring of an electrical switchboard.

His task completed, he plowed through an accumulation of odds and ends from which he took a battered trunk. He carried it upstairs.

Walking to the front door, he pushed the bell button. The action accomplished, he returned to the library and put through another phone call.

"Let me speak to Mr. Ransome. . . . All right. I'll hold the wire." A minute passed. "Hello, Pete! Frost calling."

"Say, why'n hell didn't ya tell the dumb cluck it was you? I'd 'a' been here in two jiffs."

"Night school, as I have observed before, would, on the whole, improve your vocabulary, but, on the other hand, it would eliminate a certain picturesque quality indigenous to one phase of the American scene."

"That's swell, chief, but whaddaya mean? I don't get them six-bit words."

"Never mind, Pete. Can you get away for an hour or so with the truck? Just starting out? Good! I want you to stop at my house, 13 State Street, and pick up a trunk. When you arrive, do not ring the bell. You will find the door open. I shall be gone before you arrive. Remember, *do not ring the bell*. Walk in. A trunk is standing just inside the door. The address where it is to go will be on it. Close the door tightly as you leave and take the trunk straight to the address. Just leave it there. Is that clear? Repeat it."

The professor listened. "That's the idea." He looked at a clock. "It's nine twenty-five now. Can you manage to be here exactly at ten? Good! The envelope on top of the trunk is for you."

The gaunt figure of the criminologist vanished into the mysteries of his laboratory. When he emerged, with an assortment of objects, the hands of an ancient grandfather's clock stood at nine-forty.

Frost stood over the prisoner. "Squinty, I told you to talk when the time came. That time is now. Do precisely what I tell you, but say it in your own words."

He stripped the tape from Squinty's mouth with a deft motion. He unlocked the handcuffs. His eyes, inscrutable black slits, burned into the thug's. He toyed with an automatic.

"Now, listen carefully. The bullets in this gun are explosive. One false move, one change made from what I tell you, and you die in pieces."

Frost issued orders. Squinty moistened his lips. Frost finished: "And remember the password, 'Frost and thirteen.'"

Squinty's eyes, imbued with a brief crafty gleam, turned dull again. "O. K.," he mumbled. His right hand went shakily to the phone. He dialed a number.

Frost lifted the receiver of the duplicate phone he had just installed, and listened. He kept the gun point-blank on Squinty.

"It's Maginess. Lemme speak to the boss," the thug mouthed.

"It's about time you called. Hold the wire," a disagreeable voice snarled.

The line went dead. Frost aimed at the crook's face.

A soft voice slurred over the wire: "Yes?"

"Listen, boss, it's Squinty. I want—"

"Aren't you forgetting something?"

Frost's finger quivered.

Squinty hastily mumbled: "Frost and thirteen. I got 'im as he was comin' in just now. Nope; I dunno what took him so long. He was alone. He's out cold and sewed up."

Frost groaned through his nose.

"What was that?" the voice asked sharply.

"He's comin' to. I got 'im handcuffed and taped his mug just in case. Want me to finish the job?"

"If you do, you'll die the way Troff did, and it won't be pretty. Finishing Frost is a pleasure that's going to be all mine, understand? Stay there. I'll send four or five of the boys over. Don't pay any attention from now on to the phone or doorbell until they get there. Four short rings will be their signal."

The line went dead.

The criminologist snapped: "Now address this card as I tell you."

Frost glanced at the clock. Ten minutes to ten. It was nine minutes to ten when the gangster lay on the floor, more securely tied than before. The professor took the card and the items he had selected from the exhaustive stocks of his laboratory. He did not look back at Squinty, or the panther, or at any of the queer assortment of objects in the confusion of his library as he strode to the hallway door.

The gangster watched the door close. He was left alone with dead things, a musty animal odor, and air full of stale cigarette smoke that made him giddy.

VII.

Pete Ransome stopped his truck in front of 13 State Street and lumbered up the sidewalk. He was a tremendous person. He had a bull neck, a flat nose, and crazy ears. He had been a prize fighter once, until he got in a jam. He had been framed on a murder charge, but a guy named Frost had proved that Pete simply did not have brains enough to commit murder by the use of spoiled antitoxin serum. Pete always admired him for that.

Pete thumped up the steps and across the porch, and was about to jab the bell when he remembered Frost's instructions: "Do not ring the bell." He pushed the door open.

A battered old trunk stood in the hallway. A heathen idol squatted in a niche at the end of the hall. A nutty piece of junk. There was an envelope on the trunk. It contained ten ten-dollar bills. The card tacked on the trunk read: "From I. V. Frost, To Oversea Export Co., 227 Front St." The trunk was so worn that part of the lock had gone.

Pete shouldered it and plowed out. What was it the brainy guy had said? "Be sure to close the door." Pete pulled it shut with a bang, and without bothering to set the trunk down.

His delivery route lay in another direction, but Pete drove the truck south. A big car with some tough-looking customers swung into State Street as Pete turned the corner.

"I'd hate to have those guys sore at me," he thought.

He cut across town and headed down the East Side. He passed Fourteenth Street and ran through slum districts where the streets swarmed with dirty brats. The air was full of exhaust fumes, the stench of refuse and litter, food smells.

Driving through the tenement section, Pete swung over to Front Street, almost at the East River, and followed it toward the tip of the island.

No. 227 proved to be a dingy place with windows so covered with grime that Pete could see nothing inside. The building had not been painted since the year one. It was only three stories high. If it had been four, it would have collapsed. The gilt letters on the window had long ago faded, and some had peeled off entirely, but the legend was still plain—"Oversea Export Co." in a half moon over the numerals "227."

Hardly anybody was around. Most of the buildings in this section had gone to ruin and were deserted. All were run-down. They had a depressing effect, though the roar of traffic surged loud only a couple of blocks away. Pete climbed out. He took the trunk and shouldered his way in through a filthy door that creaked.

It was a dim, musty room that he entered, a small room that had once been an office. Paper peeled off the walls in scabby splotches. The floor was bare. Dust lay around. Some rickety chairs and the wreckage of a desk might have been discarded by the last tenants.

A pasty-faced tough got up with cold, venomous eyes. "What the hell you doing here?"

"I got orders to deliver this. Here it is." Pete dropped the trunk and turned to leave.

"Who's it from? Wait a sec, guy." The pale tough looked at the address card, scowled. "From Frost? That guy is poison. Squinty's writing. Come on, punk; march upstairs and tell it to the boss."

Pete hesitated.

The evil-looking one yelped, clapped a hand to his neck. "You damned rat!" he snarled. "Try to get funny, will you? Maybe this'll teach your ugly mug a lesson."

His hand snaked to his hip. Midway in the action, he crumpled to the floor. A tiny sliver was sticking from his neck. A drop of blood oozed out.

Pete did what he had wanted to do—took Frost's advice and lammed.

The lid of the trunk came up. Frost stepped silently out and went to the rear of the room. A door on the left opened on a flight of stairs leading up. A door on the right was locked. After listening, Frost went to work on it. In less than a minute, he had it open.

The dark interior contained old boxes, papers, junk. Frost played a flashlight on the ceiling. When it reached one spot, he turned it down to the floor opposite. The floor was bare there and filmed with dust. Frost scrutinized the area intently, prowled around a section about four feet square. He found a couple of loose knots in the floor strips, and dusty holes where other knots had sunk. He probed these with a fore-finger.

When he poked into the third knot, a section of the floor swung down, noiselessly. He caught the section as it was swinging back and shoved against it with a heel.

The beam of his light played into a cellar. A pile of rags lay below him. He gauged the distance and dropped. Holding the trapdoor with one hand, he kicked away the pile of rags. Only smooth concrete lay underneath them. He swung the flashlight around. Débris, cobwebs, furnace, pipes, rubbish, dank walls, sprang into fleeting view. A staircase. A rear door.

He hoisted himself through the trapdoor and continued to force it down against the steady pressure of the electrical device. He squeezed thumb and forefinger in the knot hole beside it, and twisted the wires free. Skin and flesh tore but the trapdoor suddenly hung perpendicular, stayed down.

There was a rear door to the room. He tried it. Locked. When he finished working on it, he looked into a rubble-strewn areaway. Soundlessly, he devoted a minute to his task before locking the door.

He avoided the yawning hole and locked the front door of the first room when he went out. The front and rear doors were the only entrances to the room.

The pasty-faced savage lay where he had fallen. Frost crossed toward the staircase and opened the door.

He mounted, a step at a time, examining the walls carefully before each step. The light was only short of darkness, but he did not use his flash. Less than a third of the way up, he halted and assumed a curious posture. He lay flat on the steps and inched himself up for approximately a yard. Then he carefully stood erect once more.

There was a door at the landing. The staircase continued up. Frost mounted as painstakingly as before. Again he flattened and edged his way up for a short distance. He trod with the precautionary ease that eliminates squeaks.

The stairs ended at the third floor landing. A vertical iron ladder reached to the roof. A single door faced him. Frost remained on the landing for a brief interval. When he descended, as phantomlike as before, he again lay flat on his back, rigid, and slid down with slow care at the same spot as previously.

On the second-floor landing, he listened. The sound of voices came from behind the door. He kept an automatic in his right hand. With his left, he gently turned the knob and tried the door. It was unlocked. He flung it open and stepped inside.

The room was large and almost empty. There was no rug on the floor. The varnish had long ago worn away. A dozen cheap chairs stood around a couple of tables. Toward the rear of the room, a desk put up a tawdry front all by itself. A dozen feet beyond it, the only window, frosted glass over a wire mesh, was so covered with the grime of years that light could not pierce through. An overhead bulb emitted a blinding flood.

A curious man wearing spectacles sat behind the desk. He looked like a scholar or student, with deep eyes, an intellectual forehead, a wedge chin, thin lips, and a frown on his face. He might have been thirty. His hands were not visible. He looked up and stared at Frost with something of the interest that might be expected of a fossil expert who had discovered the bones of an unknown species.

The only other person in the room had been leaning back in a chair. Dapper in appearance, cruel of face, he had the strange look that dwells in the eyes of the irresponsible killer. Joe Blake, for years a crime lord, racketeer, mobster, public enemy, and menace to society, the leader of a gang notorious for its ruthlessness, butchery, and cold-blooded efficiency, let his chair tilt forward and stood up.

The action had no rational basis. It resulted from hatred—hatred of the man who had ruined his immensely profitable slot-machine racket during the Golden Goblin affair. It rose from a desire to be free of his hampering position, a lust to kill. It rose from surprise and anger and fury. Above all, it rose from fear, the fear of the trapped and doomed rat caught in its hole, faced by its most dangerous enemy at the moment it felt most secure.

In that interval of electrical tension, no word was spoken. Ivy Frost towered in the doorway like a hawk about to strike. The man behind the desk looked up like a college instructor interrupted in the midst of a lecture. Blake stared at Frost with slitted eyes. His lips twitched as if to speak.

No use speaking. No use arguing with Frost. Nothing was any use while that hound remained alive. He got you in your own hide-out when you thought you had him out of the picture somewhere else. And in that menacing attitude, Blake sensed something tougher and more inflexible than anything he had ever before faced or any one he had ever put on the spot.

Nothing soft in that guy. Frost didn't need to speak. Blake's gorillas never gave a break, never took a chance. They killed for efficiency and ruled by terror. Four of them had been told to erase Frost. They hadn't yet come back. Frost's house had been turned into chambers of death.

The rest of the gang was over at Frost's place now. No telling what was happening there. But they wouldn't come back. Blake knew they wouldn't come back. And what about Tony Valency downstairs? But Frost didn't need to speak. Joe Blake knew. It was take it or give it. Something fell into the palm of Joe's right hand. The hand lifted at the wrist, imperceptibly.

"Your arrival was most opportune, Professor Frost," the man at the desk spoke in educated tones.

Frost was not staring directly at Blake. Blake shot. The bullet smacked into the floor. That was strange. That wasn't where he wanted to send it. And Joe Blake, dying, like the rats he had taken for rides, realized only that the sound of his gun had blended into the sound of Frost's and that the room was spinning into eternal blackness.

From the floor above came a cry and a sound, the sound of a thud, like that of a body falling.

"Nice work, Frost," said Gordon, guessing the downfall of the guard. "You always were a jump ahead of the game."

The implacable aspect of the professor's face remained as unyielding as Gibraltar.

"It is perhaps unfortunate, Gordon, that society does not give to its sores precisely what it gets from those sores."

Gordon seemed indifferent. "I suppose you are referring to our work on Troff. He was an easy out for Stafford and me. It doesn't look so good now."

Frost prophesied: "Stafford will commit suicide to-day."

A trace of petulance entered Gordon's face. "It seemed like a novel idea at the time. I've hated you, Frost, ever since you half wrecked the organization and spoiled our profits. I should have killed you that night at our country place. I've planned ever since to kill you. Troff was innocent and a stranger to you and it struck me as a bright idea. He made a lot of noise when we—er—prepared him in the balloon. Useless things, balloons."

The satanic perversity of the man showed in his casual tones. "I wanted to give you a riddle you couldn't solve, Frost. Just to satisfy myself that I could think up something you couldn't answer. I would be ready for you and kill you if you did get the answer. By the way, how did you work it so fast? Or did Troff live longer than the few minutes I allowed?"

Frost answered harshly: "I shall tell you nothing, Gordon, except that you are going to die by your own hand."

"Really! I think not. It doesn't matter. When you left your house, we trailed you to see if you were on the right track. You were. But you got out of the trap on 180th Street. Too bad that Sam slipped up on his end of the job. It was his last slip. So we lost your trail, but I sent the boys over to your house, Frost, and fixed it up for you in case you returned. And we got that kid assistant of yours. I wish we had gone to work on her, Frost. I had pretty things planned for her and for you. But I was frankly afraid of you, afraid of what you might do when you found out, and if you escaped us. She's upstairs, you know."

"I know all this. I am merely waiting for you to destroy yourself."

Gordon mused: "We picked up your trail again when Stafford got in touch with us and told us you had just ordered him to the bank. I suppose you found what we did to the burglar alarm. Stafford thought he was safe. He thought his tracks were covered. To-day he was to get his part of the loot, but in other money of course, not the 'hot' bills. I didn't bother to disillusion him. He won't commit suicide, Frost. He was the kind who'd squeal. We took care of him."

The complacency of the criminal had something inhuman, something fiendish. Blood and death and torture and crime all appeared to be simply parts of some mathematical problem in his twisted mind.

"You are wasting time," Frost drawled.

"Perhaps. It looked like a good set-up. Four of the boys were told to shoot your tires and take you for a ride. If you got out of that trap, you would either be caught by Squinty or killed in your own home. Good work, Frost. I don't know what happened to the four. I presume you eliminated them. When Squinty called, I sent the rest of the boys on. Except the four of us, here. I figured on playing safe. I don't know how you got past Squinty or what you did. I don't know how you got by Tony downstairs, or why the infra-red photo-electric cells on the stairs didn't warn us you were here. But it doesn't matter, now."

"It doesn't matter, for now you are going to kill yourself."

Gordon murmured: "Am I? You're clever, Frost, damned clever, but even the best of us can't guess right all the time. I don't think I will be so obliging as to do what you ask."

The killer vanished. Frost walked forward. A fearful scream tore up through the closing trapdoor, a sickening smash followed. Frost held the trapdoor open a moment and looked down along the beam of a flashlight, down through the trapdoor that he had sprung and left open on the first floor, down onto the concrete basement where pulp lay.

"I told you," he echoed grimly, "that you would have the pleasure of killing yourself."

He gave only a passing glance to the desk, and the button that operated the trapdoor, and the signal light connected with the invisible eyes that he had avoided on the staircases. He paused upstairs only long enough to free the girl. Not much the worse for rough handling, she eased the tape off her mouth.

"Say, I didn't think you'd ever come." She bounced up. "Let's go."

VIII.

On the way out, Frost tied Valency. In the cab, he sat silent, almost morose.

Jean rubbed her wrists, chafed her ankles to restore circulation. She felt her lips gingerly. Pulling adhesive tape off did not help a skin or complexion any.

"Here a girl gets herself knocked out and kidnaped and tied up and things," she complained, "and she practically doesn't get any attention and nobody even wants to know if she's all right. I bet if I got shot and was practically dying and blood just pouring out and things, you'd just stand there and go into a lecture on how many kinds of blood there are and—"

"As a matter of fact," Frost remarked, "the analysis of blood is a special study. Biochemists have not done nearly enough in exhausting its possibilities. When the science is sufficiently advanced, it will be possible, by microscopic and chemical analysis, to determine from a single drop of blood the sex, health, and racial admixture of the person from whom it came. Furthermore when—"

"There you go!" Jean sighed, exasperated. "I don't want to hear about blood. I want to know how you get information out of people who can't give any information, and what this is all about, and why I get knocked out and carried off by a lot of men I never saw before and don't ever want to see again."

Frost straightened, a little less morose. "For a while, it was rather interesting," he returned. "But it seems strange that Gordon with his intellect and you with your good mind could not guess the answer to so simple a question."

"Who's Gordon?"

"De Lancey Gordon was a brilliant protégé of Henderson, the noted physicist and chemist. But Gordon, like occasional other brilliant men, had a mental quirk, a distortion, a warp that turned his abilities toward evil ends. There is something about crime that fascinates the most intelligent minds.

"There is a challenge, a lure, that can overpower the restraints of sane thought. Gordon was such a person, gifted with a keen mind, of scientific bent, an excellent student, but with a taint. Most scientists are poorly paid. Few of them receive the thanks or the appreciation of the world that they do so much to improve.

"Gordon used the help and the aid and the knowledge he had got from Henderson to turn on him. Henderson would have nothing more to do with him and withdrew all support. Gordon, then, devoted all his talents to the pursuit of crime. He had a delusion that he was the arch-genius of crime, that he could combine the tools of science with the ambitions of the gangster. He enlisted Joe Blake's gang, because it was the strongest in the city. He became the brains behind its operations. He was the one who plotted the Golden Goblin affair. He was the mysterious voice you inquired about."

"But about the dying man?" Jean persisted.

"From the first, I suspected that it was the work of Blake's gang. Blake and Gordon and part of the gang escaped from the Golden Goblin episode. It was inevitable that they would strike back. The singular circumstances surrounding the finding of the dying man, Troff, were indicative that he had been placed there as a challenge and gesture. Blake and Gordon were the two who had most reason to wish me out of the way.

"Because of the man's condition, it was hopeless to try to save his life. Considering the limitations of time, I did the best possible thing. I took him into my laboratory and spoke into an amplifier that literally blasted sound through his blood-filled eardrums. Then I simply asked him questions which he could answer with a nod or shake of his head."

Jean looked admiring and disgusted simultaneously. "It's so darned plain I could kick myself for not guessing."

Frost went on: "I first asked him if his last name began with a letter in the first half of the alphabet. A shake. Then I raced from M down the line until he nodded at T. When I had T-R-O-F-F, which sounded as if it might be a name, I asked him if there were more letters. A shake. I asked him if he was listed in the telephone directory. A nod. I asked him if his residence was Manhattan. A nod.

"I then found out the numerals of his address. I inquired if he was connected in any way with a recent crime. A nod. I discovered, by this process, that he was not a criminal, but was concerned with the Midtown Bank robbery. He died then, but I had all the information I needed to bring his murderers and the robbers to justice. The rest, of course, is evident." He gave a resumé of subsequent events.

"No; it isn't plain," Jean contradicted. "I never listened to such a disconnected story. I'll admit you succeeded, but I don't see the explanations. Why did you go to Troff's place first of all?"

Frost began to look bored. "I went primarily to draw the criminals into the open, to test the validity of my deductions, and to find out whether Troff's replies were all truthful. Since the sedan made no attempt to attack on the way uptown, it was logical to assume that they were ready to act when I came out. They would have the rear entrance guarded for safety's sake."

Jean pouted. Frost's logic was an exact science, merciless. He gave the only answers possible. And yet the answers were always obscure until he explained them.

"I had the bank opened because, on the basis of the knowledge I had accumulated, Troff appeared to be innocent. He would have, must have, touched off the burglar alarm. It failed. I wanted to know why. The only answer possible, of course, was that the mechanism had been tampered with in such a way that Troff could try to give warning and fail, but all subsequent attempts would succeed. The device I discovered was precisely what I expected.

"It was now clear that the bank robbery had been more than a raid by Blake's gang. There had been inside assistance. It had not come from Troff. For subtle reasons so detailed that I won't go into a long explanation, but involving actions, reactions, attitudes, and so forth, my suspicions fastened on Stafford. If Stafford was the man, then he undoubtedly had got in touch with the gangsters immediately after I called him. Naturally I prepared for another attempt on my life. The attempt came a short distance from the bank when one of my tires was shot. As I expected, the hoodlums were not anxious to get rid of me there, with a radio car in easy hearing distance. I was taken for a ride."

Jean exclaimed: "And you came back! It sounds incredible."

Frost remarked: "It was quite simple. To escape detection from even chance observers, gangland cars keep the windows up and sometimes the curtains down as well, in such circumstances. Carbon monoxide gas is odorless and deadly in as little as seventeen parts in one thousand of air. The interior of an automobile may contain anywhere from sixty to two hundred or more cubic feet of air. Assuming a high average of one hundred and fifty, only 2.6 cubic feet of carbon monoxide gas would be dangerous in a closed car. I carried four cubic feet under pressure in a special vest the valve of which I loosened when I stepped out of my car."

"But how could you foretell so exactly what method or procedure they would use?" Jean burst out.

"I am surprised that you ask. I was not prepared for one particular emergency. I was prepared for all emergencies. So long as I had the saturated cotton wads in my nostrils, the gas could not harm me; and if I had not been taken along, I was ready for other methods. A trained analyst, knowing that he is to be murdered, can forestall any attempt."

"So——" breathed Jean. "But tell, tell me—how ever did you get out of the traps set in the house."

"That was a problem involving many possibilities and probabilities," Frost admitted. "There again I was prepared for several emergencies. And yet the pattern became clear, under the scrutiny of analytic logic. It was evident from the films—one exposure each time the door was opened or closed, a purely automatic process of infra-red photography—it was evident that one member of the gang remained behind. It was also evident that other traps had been set if that failed.

"The presumption was that I would enter through the front door, as most people do. Therefore the gangster would be waiting for me there, in the hope of possibly capturing me alive. I turned the hallway floor into an electromagnet. The gangster's weapons became useless.

"That danger past, the others became simpler of solution. The large crate suggested an animal. I threw myself on the floor when I opened the library door, because an animal springing would pass overhead; because any other concealed crook would shoot overhead; because the force of an explosion would be upward and outward; and so on.

"But explosives, if used at all, must logically be at the outside doors of the kitchen, so that if I entered, the force of the explosion would not extend to the front hall where Squinty waited. And if I escaped Squinty and entered the kitchen through the hall, the presumption was that I would notice the explosives, walk toward them, and be struck by the snake or spiders while my attention was diverted. But if I avoided Squinty and killed the panther, the presumption was that I would expect some other living thing in the laboratory. I would be killed by the gas while I was searching for something else."

Jean mused: "And of course you used Squinty as the means of splitting the rest of the gang into two parts. And I suppose the ones who started out for your house killed Squinty."

"No," Frost told her; "they didn't kill Squinty. They joined him. The only one who escaped was the driver of the car. The others hurled themselves into an escape-proof, stone-walled room the moment the doorbell was pushed. If they haven't killed each other by now, Frick may have the personal pleasure of carting them away.

"And with the enemy divided, the last step was carrying the battle into the heart of their camp. At most, there could be not more than four or five gangsters remaining. I employed the most efficient method of entering their headquarters without observation. It was then an easy and instantaneous matter to render Valency, the lookout man, unconscious by blowing through a tube and through a broken lock of the trunk a dart tipped with an aconite paste.

"The logical steps from there on must be self-evident. When I found a trapdoor in the ceiling directly over another in the floor, the obvious answer was that it was an ingenious mode of escape, which in turn informed me that Blake or Gordon or both must be directly overhead. The building had but three stories. Therefore, you and a guard would be on the third floor. Thus, in case of a raid or of being surprised, the leaders would drop out of sight through the trapdoors, and the man on the third floor would have time to kill you and leave by way of the roof."

Jean grimaced. "The way you talk about the most depraved spectacles, you'd think I was a cat or something that the humane society ought to put out of misery."

Frost ignored the interruption. "When I reached the third-floor landing, only one problem, of course, remained. I could not risk the chance of creating any disturbance in eliminating the guard, or the leaders on the floor below would be warned. The solution, naturally, was to make such arrangements that when I entered the den of the leaders, a disturbance would be created there, and the man upstairs, drawn out to investigate or to try a flank attack, would be automatically felled."

The cab slid into the curb. Frost got out.

"And what earthly means did you use so that he would obligingly take himself out of the picture?" Jean demanded.

Frost replied: "I have some matters to talk over with Inspector Frick. It seems to me that I am doing all the explaining. I will leave you to cope with that little problem. I may remark that it is capable of more than one solution."

Jean had a bright idea. "You know what?" she called after the professor's retreating back. "I bet I don't even guess one!"

BRIDE OF THE RATS

Jean Moray wore a frown of irritation on her lovely face as she skipped up the steps of No. 13 State Street. Adversity could not change nor displeasure mar the breath-taking eloquence of her features, even though everything had gone wrong this morning.

She was quite capable of suppressing her feelings, with that exasperating flair for deception that is a native talent in most women. But being young and beautiful, possessed of a lithe and luscious figure, with a face the more strikingly attractive for its combination of naïveté and sophistication, and independent in a willful fashion because she usually got what she wanted without the necessity of doing anything about it, she took no pains to hide her annoyance.

Anyway, what was the use of trying to conceal her feelings? Men were easy to handle—but not Frost. She had originally become his assistant in the investigation of crime as the readiest way out of a mystery in which she had become hopelessly entangled. She expected, then, to cut loose and drift on her way.

But she stayed. The cases he handled were of so fascinating and frequently bizarre a nature that they made life as exciting as the Arabian Nights. And the character, the remarkable personality, of Professor I. V. Frost, both challenged and baffled analysis.

He didn't give a damn about the way he looked. Every time she saw the old corduroy trousers and the chemical-stained leather jacket that clad his lean, unlovely figure, she suffered qualms. He was long and thin. He had a hatchet-shaped head with a hawk nose, shaggy eyebrows, and piercing black eyes. Any one could notice these externals. No one ever got beyond them or found any more about his thoughts and methods than he himself chose to tell.

But Jean at the moment was irritated past caring much what even he thought. Little things had upset her, the little things that do not count but that upset empires. She twirled her hat in her fingers, idly.

Frost, lolling in an easy-chair and with his hands interlocked under his chin, shifted his gaze from the bust of Socrates and surveyed her with what appeared to be a casual glance as she entered the library.

"You ought to be grateful to the dentist for saving that dying tooth," he drawled.

"Well, I'm not. It hurt like sin and it'll keep aching for a while. I almost wish I'd told him to extract it."

"We are sometimes ungrateful to those who help us," the professor mused. "And it is really too bad that you don't like the hat you bought, but of course you can return it to-morrow."

"To-day," Jean decided.

"If I were you, I would forget about the man who seized your arm when you were leaving the subway train. Such incidents will happen, but it is seldom worth while making an issue of them."

Jean complained: "Sure; but that doesn't change it any from being a disagreeable experience."

"It is also unfortunate that you didn't enjoy the chocolate malted milk at Mardi's, but, then, it would naturally start the tooth aching again."

"It was worth it, and I had some aspirin along," she returned. "Except at Mardi's, the malteds are as thin as milk in this neck of the woods. I wouldn't think of getting one anywhere else."

Frost dangled a leg over the arm of his chair, swung it indifferently. "Ill luck sometimes runs in streaks. I can sympathize with you over the loss of your purse. Annoyed and upset as you were, it was an easy thing to forget when you left Mardi's, but no doubt they are holding it for you at the counter. Naturally, worked up as you were, and having decided to walk back here, you didn't miss it until you had arrived almost at the door."

Jean pouted. "At that, I darn near went back. Everything's gone wrong."

A look of surprise and exasperation suddenly drew her face into a grimace. She opened her mouth, only to click her teeth as if biting something with relish. She blurted out at last: "Have you been having me trailed? How did you know what I've been doing?"

Frost smiled. "The facts and evidence indicated that certain events had occurred. I deduced them and found them supported by your answers and testimony." He made it sound as if she was the all-important key in a chain that would have been useless except for her proofs.

She looked somewhat mollified but argued: "There doesn't seem to be much point in carrying on a conversation with you. You know all the right answers. I might just as well sit here a couple of hours and then listen to you tell me what I've been thinking. It's uncanny. How did you know I had a dying tooth? I didn't say anything about it. How did you know the dentist filled it instead of pulling it out?"

Frost relaxed. "Nothing could be simpler. There was a slight swelling in your upper right cheek when you went out. You took an aspirin tablet. Aspirin is one of the fastest known agencies for the relief of toothache. An extraction would be followed by a small flow of blood until the clot had formed. Some gesture, if only the use of a handkerchief, would be natural. You have taken no such action. Furthermore, definite traces would remain if any local or complete anesthetic had been given. In the absence of these, I conclude that the dentist filled the tooth."

"It does sound easy," Jean admitted. "I should have guessed."

Frost calmly contradicted her: "It isn't a matter of guessing."

"Well, it's good observation." Jean attempted to minimize the ingenuity of the rational masculine mind by reducing it to a merely sensory basis.

The professor shrugged. "Observation? Yes; but only as a starting point. Any one can observe day and night; then, like Ptolemy, offer the simplest explanation. It takes a man like Copernicus to evolve a true theory of celestial motions. Daily life is crowded with facts and incidents that need not only to be observed, but also to be interpreted, related, and compared with other truths until their absolute value is apparent. Observation, synthesis, analysis, induction, and deduction are equally necessary in the process.

"The hat you hold will serve as a good illustration. And one who observed it casually would assume that it was part of your wardrobe. Only if he noticed its unspotted and uncrinkled newness, its fresh label, its failure quite to harmonize with your ensemble, the fact that you carry it instead of wear it, and that it is not the hat you had when you left, would he conclude it had been newly bought. It would also be evident that while you walked along the street, looked at your reflection in shop windows, and noticed the critical expression of passers-by, you decided it was not quite suitable after all."

Jean nodded slowly. "What made you think a man grabbed my arm on purpose? How do you know I didn't stumble and somebody was only trying to help me?"

Frost interlaced his fingers at the back of his head. "If you had tripped, the tips of your shoes would be scuffed, and there would be other corroboratory evidence. But your shoes are in impeccable condition. The sleeve of your upper left arm is both mussed and soiled. The palm of your right hand is slightly reddened. It must have been a hard slap to leave an impression that still lasts.

"The facts suggest that some one accosted you when you were on the way to the dentist. Such an encounter would be unlikely on the street at that hour, or when you were entering a subway car. The best opportunity would be at the point of leaving the train. Then, if the advance was successful, the stranger could accompany you, but if repulsed or if you made any outcry, he could easily vanish in the crowd."

The telephone rang. Frost lazily lifted the receiver. "Yes? . . . Speaking. . . . Yes. . . . Excellent. . . . Thank you, and good-bye." He frowned slightly as he hung up.

Jean tossed her head, "'Yes and thank you,'" she echoed. "If I said that over the phone while you were listening, you'd promptly tell me who I was talking to and what was said. It sounds easy when you do it, but neither I nor anybody else could get to first base given the same lead."

Frost objected mildly: "Your diction is as confused as your figures of speech. In baseball, it is impossible for the batter to have a lead. After he is safe upon first base, and when he has become the runner—"

Jean's eyes gleamed, but all she said when she interrupted was: "What about the malted milk and the purse I lost?"

"The evidence behind those deductions was, I admit, of less tangible nature and more nebulous except for the spot on your cuff. The spot is of a creamy color, fresh, and obviously has passed unnoticed. It alone, considering the usually fastidious care you take of your attire, would imply that you were upset to the point of overlooking details, and consequently that it must have followed the incidents that annoyed you.

"Dental pastes have a whiter color, milk has a thinner consistency, and while various fluids or chemical compounds might have left such a spot, they are rare in daily life. A chocolate malted milk would leave just such a spot; and if this deduction was true, it followed that you must have gone to Mardi's which you once said was the only place you would go for the beverage."

"Do you ever forget anything you see or hear?" she asked perfunctorily.

The professor glanced at a clock. "When you entered the library, you unconsciously held your left arm as if you were holding a purse, in the manner you have always used. If you had deliberately set the purse on the hall table, or left it near by, your mind would be at rest. Furthermore, you felt a twinge of pain from the tooth a few minutes ago. You grimaced. Your right hand moved toward the spot where your purse would normally be, and which would contain aspirin tablets. Also, the pocketless ensemble you wear would absolutely require the presence of a purse at all times for common necessities like a handkerchief and cosmetics and change.

"Your failure to have a purse is subject to three different explanations. You could have purposely left it somewhere, you could have lost it, or it could have been stolen. If you had left it near by, you would have gone for it before now. If it had been stolen—"

The doorbell rang.

"Bring Mrs. Hossner in," Frost murmured.

II.

For a moment, Jean looked as if she would refuse unless he divulged the magic that enabled him to predict who stood outside, but she turned around without speaking. Seconds passed. Voices sounded in the doorway, indistinguishable words. The door closed. Click of heels, then a woman entered ahead of Jean.

She was passing from her twenties and inclined to be a bit plump, but still on the voluptuous side. She had a roundish face, but her eyes were set close and possessed a peculiar, stony blankness in their pupils of mottled gray. She had neither coat, hat, nor purse, and her clothing was soiled. Her plain brown hair needed a few hairpins and some attention. She breathed unevenly and walked jerkily, with uncoördinated movements.

"Be seated, Mrs. Hossner," Frost gently urged.

The visitor betrayed no surprise that he knew her name. She did not ask how he knew it. She did not seem to care whether he knew it or not. She sat down stiffly and said, abruptly:

"The alienist Clehr sent me to you. I started to tell him what was wrong. First he thought I was crazy. Maybe he still does. He said it might be a case for investigation. He told me to see you. You are Professor I. V. Frost? He told me to come back after I talked to you."

The woman spoke in clipped sentences, jerkily, like her motions. There was no continuity of thought. Frost studied her with a deceptively careless glance that passed for merely interested attention. She kept her hands tightly clasped. Her whole attitude had something wooden and unnatural, even psychopathic. The far-away look in her eyes bordered on the abnormal and partook of invisible worlds.

Frost helped her along: "Clehr is exceptional. He would not have sent you to me unless he believed your story and thought it worthy of investigation. By all means, continue."

The woman did not move, showed no emotion, and persisted in her trancelike state. Her lips barely moved as she stated tonelessly: "I began breakfast with an antelope."

Frost sat up, tense and alert. He reached into a satinwood container and extracted a cigarette of unusual length. By that gesture, and the sharply spiced fumes that he exhaled, Jean knew he had found a case to his liking, a mystery with fantastic overtones.

"Did you say canteloupe?" Jean demanded, thinking she might not have heard correctly.

Mrs. Hossner repeated "Antelope," and stopped.

She began and ended with that preposterous statement. She sat with impassive disregard of what effect her words had. Jean stared at her, incredulous, skeptical, wondering what sort of lunatic they now had on their hands. Frost waited, a bright glint in his eyes, until it became obvious that further information would have to be pried out of her.

The professor inquired: "Have you ever before had breakfast with this or any other antelope or any other animal?"

"No. I never want to see the creature again."

"Just where did the incident occur?"

"I reached across the table for some grapes. The door opened and the antelope came in. It was a beautiful creature."

The visitor again ceased speaking. Jean tried in vain to extract some grain of meaning from these absurd and irrational assertions.

Frost persisted: "Where did this happen?"

"In the castle. The antelope and I were in the castle."

"What castle?"

"I don't know."

"Where is it?"

"I don't know."

"How did you come to be there?"

"I don't know."

"How did you leave it?"

"I ran away."

"Why?"

"It was bad enough when the rats kept me awake. I couldn't stand it any longer when the organ played as the antelope came up to me."

"Why did the organ annoy you?"

"Because there was no organ in the castle."

And in this baffling manner, this group of apparently unrelated dream-images like a nightmare and a fairy tale combined, this queer jumble of contradictions and meaningless ravings, began one of the strangest riddles that Professor I. V. Frost was ever called upon to solve.

Jean, listening with growing exasperation to the toneless statements of Mrs. Hossner, nevertheless felt pity for the woman who was either suffering from dementia or had been made the victim of some savage hoax.

But Frost, sitting forward, firing questions like bullets as if to jolt the woman out of her daze, and inhaling whenever possible the fumes of his odd cigarettes, showed no skepticism whatever. He exhibited only deep interest and curiosity in the information he was eliciting.

"Would you recognize the route by which you ran away from the castle?"

"No."

"Why not?"

"I couldn't see because of the tears."

"You were crying?"

"I don't know why."

"But you ran away and left the antelope in the dining room?"

Mrs. Hossner replied: "I was frightened. I ran into the hall. The organ music frightened me. It sounded like demons muttering. I ran to the door. The first door I saw. I had my hand on it when something hit me with a plop. I couldn't scream. There was no one to scream to. I cried so hard that the tears blinded me. I ran outside and ran and ran. I thought I heard steps. I bumped into bushes and trees. I tripped and got up. I ran and ran.

"Then I heard a squeal of brakes. Somebody said 'What's the trouble, lady?' I said 'Take me to New York.' Somebody said 'Sure, but stop crying.' I think it was a truck. We rode a long time. After a while I stopped crying. I looked out. We were on Fifty-seventh Street. 'Let me out here,' I said. They stopped the truck and I jumped out and walked to Dr. Clehr's office.

"I thought I was going crazy. I had heard his name somewhere; I didn't know him. I looked him up. I had to talk to somebody. He gave me money to come here."

The woman stopped. Jean, hopelessly mystified, but inclined to ascribe the whole story to the ravings of an unbalanced mind, squirmed uneasily. Did Frost believe these incredible assertions?

He asked: "You said there was no one to scream to. Were you alone in the castle?"

"I don't know. I saw no one. I heard no voices. But there was fruit on the table when I came down. I was hungry and wanted breakfast. Or I think I saw fruit. I wouldn't swear to it now. I must be mad. No; I didn't see any breakfast or antelope. It was all a dream like all the rest."

"Stop that!" Frost's voice cut with a harsh and stern command. His eyes glittered like black stars.

The woman stiffened.

"Mrs. Hossner, there is truth in your story. Tell me that truth without further doubts. You are unquestionably sane in spite of a terrifying experience. There must be and is a perfectly rational explanation. Give me the facts and I will find you the answers.

"When you left the castle, you ran along a path or road that you remembered?"

"I don't recall. Maybe I had a vague memory of it from the night before. I don't know."

Frost suddenly abandoned Mrs. Hossner's story: "Where were you yesterday?"

She showed some surprise. "Why, with my husband, of course. I suppose I was kidnaped and held for ransom. No. That doesn't account for the antelope."

Frost snapped: "Forget the antelope. Have you seen or talked to your husband to-day?"

"No. We had no phone. I had to tell somebody my story first. Somebody who wouldn't think I was crazy. I wasn't sure of myself. I didn't know what I might find. Maybe he's gone, too. Maybe I dreamed it all."

"Have you tried to communicate with friends or relatives?"

The woman sighed. "I have none here."

The criminologist inhaled more deeply than ever of acrid smoke while a gleam of what looked like keen relish dwelt in his black eyes. He ceased his questions for the moment and wore an air of meditation, as though putting together the parts of a verbal jig-saw puzzle. He flipped a glance at Socrates, and Socrates placidly gazed across the room with calm and dispassionate inquiry in the eternity of marble.

Frost resumed the Socratic method: "You mentioned rats. Did you see any rats?"

"No. I only heard them. They kept me awake. Running, running, running. I heard them in the walls and halls. Maybe they were part of the dream."

"How do you know there was no organ?"

"Because the chords were just as loud when the dining-room door was open or shut. They must have come from the room I was in. I looked. There were no pipes or keyboard or organ."

Frost nodded approval, though of what Jean had not the slightest idea. If the matter was in her hands, she would have summoned an alienist. Yet Clehr had sent this patient to Frost. And Frost did not waste time chasing rainbows. In spite of herself, the eerie feeling grew on her that she was wrong, that the woman told truths, impossible truths, baffling truths, truths that bore some unknown relation to each other and to some unknown crime of gnarled and devious nature.

Frost took up another tack: "You are positive you were with your husband yesterday?"

"As usual, we spent the whole day together. We had breakfast in, but went out toward noon. We had lunch, tea, and dinner at different places, all new ones to me, of course. We went to the zoo in the afternoon and a movie in the evening."

"What happened last night?"

Mrs. Hossner looked weary. "Nothing."

"The most trivial detail may be more important than you think. Exactly what happened after you got home?"

"We talked about the day. He said that when the weather got cold and I got tired of the city, we could fly down to Florida or Cuba."

"Your husband, I take it, has no regular occupation?"

"No. He's retired. He has plenty of money. We turned in about eleven. I had a headache. I took an aspirin and a glass of water. I fell asleep after a while. There were strange, blurry dreams, but I can't remember them clearly. I half awoke and thought I was somewhere else. I did not recognize it. It was dark. I thought I was alone, but I was terribly tired and dozed off.

"It was lighter when I became conscious again. I listened and heard rats running, rushing, scampering in the walls and floors. I was afraid to cry out. It was all too strange. I dozed and half awakened from time to time. It is hard to tell what was dream and what was real. I wanted to move but didn't. It was so easy to stay in bed. And always I heard the rats scampering.

"When I next opened my eyes, it was much lighter. I saw I was in a big, dark room like a prison. With an effort I went to the window and looked out. The window had bars. What I could see of the building made it look like a prison or castle. Yes; I wondered then if maybe I hadn't been there a long time; if maybe there had been something wrong with me. I saw the sea. The sea was blood-red."

"From the rising sun?" asked Frost.

"No. The sun wasn't up high enough. But the sea was blood-red just the same, by itself," Mrs. Hossner insisted. "I went back and slept again. It was daylight when I got up. I went to the door and opened it. I didn't see or hear any one. I crept downstairs and opened the first door I saw. There was fruit in a big bowl. I suddenly realized how hungry I was. I went in and took an orange from the bowl. Then I heard a sound by the door and I whirled around. The antelope was coming in. The door was closing. I heard the organ thunder. I guess I lost my mind and began running."

Antelope and rats—blood-red sea and organ music without organ—disappearing home and mysteriously appearing castle—these were the material of fantasy.

But Frost stared at the woman with ever-deepening interest. His first eager attention had given way to an air of abstraction, and now something grim, ominous, entered his attitude. The lids drooped half over his eyes. However crazy the narrative sounded to Jean, it must already have assumed some definite pattern for him.

He suddenly demanded: "Where was your apartment?"

"At 16 Logan Street."

"Tell me more about your husband. Who is he?"

"Fritz Hossner."

Frost shifted impatiently. "Have you been married long?"

"No, for only about——"

The doorbell rang sharply. The woman broke off in mid-sentence, made a wild dash for the laboratory, but Frost was there first.

"Delusions of persecution on top of all the rest!" Jean thought as she went to answer the ring.

Looking in the hall mirror as she passed, she approved of her lovely self. Nevertheless, she reached for her compact, remembered that it lay in the lost purse, and continued toward the door with a feeling of irritation. She firmly believed that nature was never so good that it could not be improved.

A curious little man stood on the porch. He couldn't have weighed more than a hundred pounds. He looked like an idiot gnome. He had vacant eyes of pale, watery blue and skin the color of a grub. A tuft of fuzzy hair, lemon-yellow in hue, sprouted from his chin like the whiskers of a goat. His cranium was barren of shrubbery, foliage, or the least sign of life—a naked plain stretched tightly over bone. His hands made fluttering motions in the air. Though his lips moved, he spoke not a word, but peered vacuously at Jean.

"What do you want?" she demanded.

His fingers did odd bends and dances, as if possessed of separate lives. And Jean realized that he was a deaf mute.

The stranger magically produced paper and pencil. He scrawled a note, in handwriting as devious as the worm tunnels in rotten logs.

"Let me have that," Frost ordered.

She had not heard him approach, but there he suddenly was, beside her.

The note read: "Is Professor I. V. Frost in?"

Frost looked at the little gnome whose lips moved and whose fingers danced. Frost shook his head with a frown. He wrote: "Who are you? Who sent you here? What do you want?"

The dwarf scrawled a reply. As Frost took it, the stranger's hands made a few last flutterings, and, as if of their own volition, his lips writhed.

Jean ventured to the professor: "Well, it's some comfort to know that you're at least partly human and can't do everything, such as reading lips and sign language."

The dwarf peered at Jean, peered at Frost.

The Professor lifted his eyebrows in a calm manner that made his assistant feel like a fly on a pin. He turned his attention to the note. It said: "I am D. S. Higgs. Dr. Clehr sent me. A dead man has been threatening my life. Will you accept the case?"

Frost wrote in answer to this extraordinary communication: "Previous engagements make it impossible to discuss the matter now. At four this afternoon?"

Mr. Higgs nodded, bowed, and departed. A hat came out from under his arm and concealed the painfully bare, bobbing cranium of that retreating personage.

Jean mused: "Clehr must have taken to sending all the screwy ones here. Or else he seems to be becoming a regular gold mine of freak cases."

"Doesn't he?"

Something in Frost's tone made her look up sharply. "Why did you send him away? Threatened by a dead man. It isn't any goofier than Mrs. Hossner's yarn. It sounds like a honey, just up your alley."

"Doesn't it?"

Jean bit her lip. "Higgs is crazy, she's crazy, I'm crazy, everybody's crazy," she chanted.

Frost wore a sardonic smile as he turned away from the door. Jean did not see what amused him. He reëntered the library, strode across to the laboratory door, and pushed. The door stuck. He heaved it open far enough to slip through. The smile vanished from his face, to be replaced by a grim tightening of cheek bones. Jean raced after him, her heart pounding.

It had been a mad morning, mad events, anything could happen, but she knew what had happened, what must have happened, to set those implacable lines on Frost's features.

She squeezed through the aperture. "What's wrong?" she asked anxiously.

She did not need an answer. Trained in the hard school of life and reality, having seen death in violent forms, she neither screamed nor fainted. She stood stoically regarding the corpse while Frost clipped the words out savagely:

"Mrs. Hossner has been murdered."

III.

The woman lay face up, with contorted limbs, her body still warm. An expression of agonized surprise was fixed in her wide-open eyes. She had been telling her incoherent narrative only a few minutes before. She had dashed for concealment in the laboratory when the doorbell rang. No one could have entered through the fortified windows of the laboratory. Mr. Higgs, the visitor, had not for a moment been out of sight. He had never got beyond the outer doorway where she and Frost met him.

Mrs. Hossner could not have been murdered. Of that Jean felt sure. But dead the woman was, and it seemed no more unnatural than the preceding events, which had no relation or reason and possessed no connection with each other or with this.

Frost snapped: "Get Clehr on the phone for me. Initials L. S. In the Crayman Building."

Jean stepped back into the library. She returned after a minute and reported: "Clehr has not come back from lunch yet. I left word with his secretary to call you as soon as he came in."

Frost nodded, continued his careful, detailed study of the body. He missed nothing. Whatever caught his special interest immediately underwent inspection and enlargement to a hundred diameters through a lens he had taken from his equipment. He studied the woman's hair, eyes, mouth, make-up, every spot on her clothing. He examined her hands as if they were a masterpiece of art. He gave her shoes the care that a connoisseur would bestow on a newly discovered painting by Ryder. Even the slight grime under her finger nails received attention.

"Could it have been heart failure? Or did she commit suicide?" Jean suggested.

Frost straightened. "Neither. She killed herself without knowing it. She was murdered as definitely as if a bullet had been put in her heart. It was simply an accident, an unfortunate accident, that the place happened to be here, and the time had to be now. It might as easily have occurred before, in which event I would have lost a most unusual case, or it might have occurred later, in which event I would have obtained more information, perhaps prevented this death, and certainly shortened the time requirements. No matter. It is done. And I have all that I need to bring her murderers to justice."

"And just how was she so obliging as to murder herself without knowing it?"

Frost pointed to an open aspirin tin. It was empty and lay near the body. "Don't touch it!" he warned.

Jean frowned. "It doesn't mean much to me."

"Look at the thumb and forefinger of her right hand. Look at her face and position."

Jean looked. "Yes; the white powder certainly indicates that she took the tablet, but I don't see how she died from aspirin."

Frost almost groaned. "Because she took a tablet from an aspirin box, does it follow that it was an aspirin tablet? Isn't it significant that the box contained only one tablet? She took what she thought was an aspirin; she had a terrible convulsion and met death instantly. So would any one who took five grains of strychnine.

"In her blouse, I found this key. Does its presence strike you as having any significance?"

Jean glanced at it before handing it back. "Not particularly," she decided.

It was a serrated key of common type, evidently for an apartment door.

Frost said: "The woman came here with an extraordinary tale. She came without a purse. By her own words, she had no money. She borrowed from Clehr in order to reach us. Yet her pocket contained a key, unquestionably to her apartment, and a box the one tablet in which was sufficiently deadly to kill several persons."

Jean protested: "It would only be natural for her to keep the key on her person—" Then she caught herself.

"Exactly! Your mind is beginning to function," Frost agreed. "She retired in one place and awakened in another. From her story, it was not clear whether she found herself dressed or still in her night-robes when she awakened. The point is unimportant.

"Most women keep keys in their purses. But even if Mrs. Hossner had some exceptional habit of carrying a key and a box of aspirin on her person, you will notice that hers is a sport blouse of the slip-over kind. Her jacket has no pockets. She could not conceivably pull the blouse off without spilling the contents of the pocket.

"It is just as inconceivable that she would put them back, or that she would keep on spilling them out at night and replacing them in the morning. But if, when she put the blouse on in the morning, something fell out, she would automatically put it in the pocket; and if nothing fell out, she might not know for a considerable period that anything was in her pocket. Her mind would be preoccupied by her nerve-racking mystery."

"It's too much for me. Shall I call the police?"

"No; not yet. In the interests of a larger justice, we'll have to accept responsibility for any difficulties that may arise. Bring me Throckmorton's 'Historic Sites of Long Island.' Tenth book from the left, third shelf from the top, second section in the library."

When Jean brought the desired volume, she found Frost absorbed over a microscope.

"Drop the book on the table. Get the missing-persons bureau and find out if a Mrs. Hossner has been reported as missing within the last day or two, and if so, by whom," he ordered, without looking up.

The sunlight, sliding through western windows, chiseled his features into bleak profile. In some intangible way, some invisible manifestation of personality, he suggested relentless power; not a merely physical energy; not the strength of those who live by brawn alone; not the smugness of those who by wealth or influence control other destinies; but the power of that most merciless weapon ever at the disposal of the mind of man—the use of pure logic based upon an exact knowledge of facts in the quest for absolute truth.

He was a strange one, Jean sighed, a rare one. He took no one, not ever her, his assistant, into his confidence, admitted no one to his thoughts, and divulged only as much as he cared to, if the spirit moved him. The smoke of his nameless cigarettes eddied about him, cast a pungent disguise over the smell of chemicals and acids in the laboratory.

Jean reported: "The missing-persons bureau by its Sergeant Hays says Mrs. Hossner was listed as missing early this morning. Her husband, Fritz Hossner, gave the alarm."

"What!" Frost exclaimed, whirling toward her.

"That's what they told me," Jean repeated. "Mr. Hossner expressed the fear that his wife had either been kidnaped for ransom or taken away to a fate unknown for reasons unknown. He awoke in the middle of the night, saw a stranger in the room, started to get up, and was slugged unconscious. When he came to, he was alone.

"The police sent a detail over, taped a bump on his head and promised to keep hands off until he got some word from the kidnapers. The thing has been kept out of the papers so far. I got the information only by using your name. Hays wants to talk to you. He's still on the line."

Frost strode out, returned after a few seconds, his face expressionless. He picked up the Throckmorton guide and skimmed it swiftly till he found what he wanted. He opened a closet and took out a couple of garments, looking somewhat like leather jackets, one of which he tossed to Jean.

"We've a great deal of ground to cover in a rather short time," he explained. "Take this. It's a bulletproof vest. Perhaps you won't need it, but wear it.

"Here's fifty dollars. Take a taxi to Clehr's office first. If he isn't there, talk to his secretary and find out anything she knows about Mrs. Hossner's appointment and his conversation with her. Find out who his patients and all other visitors were to-day.

"Then run out to the zoo and get some antelope hair. On your way back, stop at the Chemical Products Co.'s main office and buy a flask of liquid air. It will be heavy, but I think not too heavy for you to manage. Handle it with the greatest care and bring it here."

Jean mulled over this diversity of errands. "Anything more?"

"That's all." Frost was already striding toward the door.

"Will you be here? Or where can I get in touch with you if necessary?"

Frost paused briefly, mused. "First the library, then the marriage-license bureau—"

Jean interrupted. "Don't tell me you are going to take out a license?" she inquired maliciously.

As if sprung from a catapult, Frost bolted out of the room with an expression of pure horror on his face.

IV.

At the main library, Frost called for Landon's "Architecture of Old English Manors." The library's sole copy resided in the reference room from which the President and an Act of Congress together could not have removed it. Impatient at the delay, he carried the volume, a large folio, to a table for perusal. In the back was a series of folding plates through which he rapidly flipped until he came to the one he sought. He studied this minutely and read every bit of descriptive detail which lay in the text proper.

From the library, he continued his way downtown to the City Hall. In the marriage-license bureau, it took him less than ten minutes to rifle through the records, retrogressing day by day, until he obtained the information he was after.

Leaving the City Hall, he drove to police headquarters and entered the offices of the missing-persons bureau.

Sergeant Hays had nothing to add to the information he had given over the phone, but gave the gist of the report again.

At the conclusion, Frost nodded ambiguously. "Is any watch being kept over Hossner?"

The sergeant, a rugged, ruddy-faced individual with square jaws and a ponderous manner, shook his head. "No. As the thing stands, we don't know what we've got on our hands. Kidnaping, maybe. Maybe another man in the case. Or maybe she herself just slugged him and walked out in the middle of the night. Sounds goofy, but you never can tell, and of course he isn't much help. Anyway, he asks us to lay off just in case a ransom note does turn up.

"Hell," he fumed, "you know how it is, Frost, and what we're up against. If we tail the guy and it is a kidnaping, sure as fate we queer the negotiations, the victim gets hurt or killed, and then we've got the whole damn press as well as the family hollerin' about the way we messed things up.

"Besides, there's no phone in the place. For all we know, they may both have been slugged by a burglar. She comes to, sees her husband out cold, and goes tearing for a doctor. Meanwhile, he comes to, and hot-foots out to report that his wife has vanished.

"Come to think of it, you haven't yet told us how you're in on the case."

"She was a client of mine," Frost truthfully replied.

"Client of yours, eh? What's the set-up?"

"That," Frost drawled succinctly, "is precisely what I am interested in discovering."

He abandoned the missing-persons bureau in favor of the homicide-squad offices.

"Is Inspector Frick around?" he asked the man at the desk.

"No; he went out on a call. Due back any minute, though, if you want to wait."

"I'll wait." He took a seat and consumed two of his cigarettes, by which he deduced that approximately twelve minutes elapsed before Frick bustled in, to find Frost surrounded with an aura of pleasantly pungent fumes.

The inspector, a wiry, crisp little man with a decidedly military carriage, immediately trotted over to Frost.

"For cripes' sake," he whispered anxiously under his breath, "why do you want to take chances smoking those infernal things in here of all places?"

Frost crushed the butt absently. "I hadn't thought about it. I've got something I want to talk over. Busy?"

Frick nodded his head. "I'll say I am. Can't you let it wait?"

"It's important. How long will you be occupied?"

"That's hard to say. This Clehr mess is as bad as the Lingle case."

The abstraction disappeared like magic. Frost snapped "What Clehr mess?"

"Where have you been hiding? Clehr was murdered this noon."

"What?" the professor barked.

"I said murdered. The papers have been yelling it all over town. Thought everybody knew by this time. Interested in the details?"

"Go on!"

"Clehr left his office in the Crayman Building at twelve fifteen according to his secretary. He must have mingled in the noon crowd and turned south on Fifth Avenue. Somebody let him have it as he started to cross the corner of Forty-eighth Street on a traffic change, at twelve twenty-three. No witnesses so far found, and no clues except the slug which we turned over to a ballistics expert.

"He just crumpled over. For a couple of seconds, they thought he had stumbled. Somebody stooped to give him a hand and let out a squawk. Then the panic was on. He stopped just one slug, but he stopped that with his heart, and it came from behind. Coat powder-burned. Whoever did it simply stood right behind him and walked off in the crowd. It's going to be messy."

"Why?"

"Clehr was a big man in his field, psychiatry and that sort of thing. Nervous old ladies and society dames could run in and tell him all about the big bad dreams they had after eating too many chocolates or soaking up too many Martinis," Frick said dryly.

"He had some big clients, some of the biggest names in town. They told him stuff about their private lives, and what they did, and what they thought they were going to do, that they'd never think of telling us.

Confidential stuff, love affairs, family skeletons, and the rest of it. And Clehr kept it all card-indexed, case history for each.

"We took a look at those files when we went over his office. There were plenty of cranks of all sorts who came to Clehr. It's entirely possible that some one turned sour on him, or decided he'd given away too much dangerous information. We're working on that angle, hoping we can pick some leads up, because so far we haven't a thing to go on. Chances are he had made enemies, too.

"That makes it messy enough. But, on top of that, there've been a dozen people, powerful people, who've already pulled strings and brought pressure to bear not only on the higher-ups but on the papers and anywhere else it might do some good. We're sitting on a powder keg."

Frost nodded serenely. "That makes it much easier."

"Easier!" Frick snorted. His already perspiring face took on a somewhat redder hue. The clouds of wrath gathered.

"Easier all around," Frost added genially. "The murder of Clehr is solved. Those who are quaking lest their sins be discovered and broadcast," he continued in a lightly mocking tone, "can rest in peace until they feel the need of telling all about their latest fixations and complexes to another psychiatrist.

"However, while solving the mystery of why the highly important Dr. Clehr was murdered, I'm afraid that at the same time I must present you with the mystery of why a hitherto obscure, unknown, and unimportant Mrs. Hossner was killed."

"Any connection between the two? Where?" Frick asked impatiently.

"There you have the answer," Frost agreed. "In my laboratory."

"What! In you l-lab——" Frick stammered in his haste. It was his turn to be astonished.

"I would suggest," Frost urged, "that we lose no time. We'll need the photographer, coroner, and the rest of the crew. And have them do the job as fast as they can."

V.

The bustle of police headquarters was gone. The noise of mid-afternoon traffic was gone. The corpse was gone, and with it the photographer, the fingerprint expert, and the rest of the homicide squad.

Only Frick remained with Frost in the restful quiet of his library, while Frost told precisely as much as he chose, and no more, of the circumstances in which the dead woman had come to him and the circumstances in which she had died.

"Hence it is plain," Frost concluded, "that Clehr was murdered because the woman had told him some or all of her experience, and because some one as yet at large did not want that experience to be investigated. It was a needless murder, in many respects, and indicates that the killer is becoming panicky."

"You should have phoned us the moment you found she was dead," Frick said. "There'll have to be a lot of explaining now. It might have saved Clehr's life."

"Nonsense!" Frost exclaimed. "Your own examiner places the time of death for the woman at approximately one o'clock. As a matter of fact, it was exactly fourteen minutes and twenty-one seconds before one o'clock according to my watch. And, by your own testimony, Clehr had already left his office at twelve fifteen."

Frick yielded the point. "I still don't see why the woman picked your laboratory of all places, intentionally or otherwise."

"Why not? She was so wrought up and nervous that it is probable she never knew she had the aspirin box in her pocket. Remember, she had been wandering around, until she went to Clehr, who sent her to me. When some one rang the doorbell, she made a dive for the laboratory, as if she was afraid of being seen, or of being pursued. I told her she would be absolutely safe there, that she had nothing to fear, and that the laboratory was soundproof. Then I went to see who was at the door.

"In the meantime, she experienced a relief of tension and found the box in her pocket with the poison tablet. It appears that she did not even think about a glass of water. She could have got one from the laboratory faucet, but the indications are that she swallowed the tablet as soon as she found it."

The inspector frowned. "You think some one put the box in her pocket without her knowing it? Some one who thought that she would take the tablet sooner or later and that the death would be checked off as suicide?"

"Exactly!"

"But why? Why? If it's a case of kidnaping, nothing is gained by killing the goose that might have laid a golden egg. And if Clehr was killed because of knowledge he might possess about the woman, why aren't you and Miss Moray in danger of the same fate?"

"We are."

"Have you been attacked? Do you know them? What's behind this, Frost?"

The professor replied: "I don't know them. I know the cause and result, the motivation, even the identities of one or two persons involved. The identity of the real criminal remains to be found. I have my suspicions, but I want proof. Rather to my surprise, no attempt has been made on my life. In the absence of any other explanation, I am inclined to believe that my assistant was the object of an attempt that failed, and the criminal or criminals then decided on a change of tactics."

"Don't you think it would be wise to pay a call on Mr. Hossner at his apartment?"

Frost glanced at his watch. "I have merely been waiting for my assistant. If she is not here within two minutes, we shall leave without her."

"Why two minutes?"

"Greater delay would enable some one from the missing-persons bureau to be ahead of us. I should like to arrive there first, for reasons of my own."

"You haven't told me anything very definite about why the woman came to you or what she told you," Frick recalled.

"For the good reason that you would declare her crazy. I will repeat it when I have definite, physical evidence to substantiate it."

"Come now, Frost, you can at least give me an idea of what she told you."

Frost answered, with a gleam in his eye: "Of course, since you insist, inspector. She had breakfast with an antelope this morning in a castle by a bloody sea to the accompaniment of organ music from an organ that did not exist."

Frick glowered suspiciously. "Are you kidding me?"

"Certainly not!" Frost denied with a bland air. "That was her story and, in the vernacular, we are stuck with it."

"She was crazy as a loon!" Frick grunted in disgust.

"That is precisely what I told you your reaction would be," Frost remarked. "Time to go."

As they left the house, a cab drew up in front. Jean popped out, breathless and excited, but anger only made her the lovelier. Frost ran down, took the container of liquid air, and deposited it in his laboratory. He rejoined Frick and Jean in the official car.

"I see I was right," Frost observed.

Jean glanced at him. "You probably are, whatever you're talking about. Listen to this. I took a cab to the Crayman Building. I got out at the corner and was walking toward the entrance when I felt a stiff jolt in the middle of my back. I jumped into the doorway and looked around, but I couldn't find any one whose actions were suspicious. There was the usual crowd on the sidewalk. I felt around, and if it hadn't been for that bulletproof vest—" She shivered slightly. "I pulled the slug out—here it is."

Frost pocketed the flattened pellet.

Jean continued: "I suppose you know about Clehr. The cops had already been there and gone before I arrived. The secretary was all excited and not much help. Maybe she'll remember better when she calms down. I did find out that Mrs. Hossner was the only patient who came without appointment to-day."

"What floor is the office on?"

"Tenth."

Frost mused: "He could have got off the elevator at the same time and sauntered along as if looking for some particular office until he discovered which one she entered. Perfectly easy, since she would not know him."

"What are you talking about?" Frick cut in.

Frost said to his assistant: "What else did you find out?"

"Nothing of any help. His secretary had never before seen Mrs. Hossner, did not know the purpose of her visit, did not hear a word of the conversation, and could not find any record of it. Clehr apparently decided the case was outside his province and did not keep his usual index card. That's all. You already have the liquid air. Here are the antelope hairs."

Frick looked as if he was about to have convulsions. "Do you mean to tell me that all this stuff ties up?"

"I do not recall making any such statement," Frost replied. "This, I believe, is 16 Logan Street."

Frick parked the car directly in front of the address.

It was a noisy street. Trucks continually pounded its pavement with heavy loads from the wholesale market not far away. This block, however, aside from the noise, appeared to be a fairly respectable residential district of three-and-four-story stone buildings. According to the owners' whims, each building, though contiguous, had been painted a different color to distinguish it from the others; but the browns, reds, blues, and greens merely lent the street a pied effect, since all the buildings but one were more or less newly painted, and that one was 16 Logan Street, which thus distinguished itself by default.

Frost scanned the directory. Hossner was listed in Apartment 1A. The superintendent dwelt in subterranean crypts, the basement rear to be exact. Frost poked the Hossner button, received no answer.

He tried the entrance door, the lock of which proved to be out of commission. They entered a rather decrepit hallway, none too clean, and found the apartment to their right in the front of the building.

Frick looked down the hall, but out of the corner of his eye watched Frost insert a key in the lock and open the door. It did not open fully. That was because dead men do not care whether doors are pushing against them or not. And the dwarf was as dead as any one could be who had a hole in his forehead.

But even the dead are sometimes not lonely. Another man sat across the room facing the doorway from a swivel chair, his back to a desk. He did not, however, rise to greet the visitors. That was because dead men do not care whether they have visitors or not. And the second man was as dead as any one could be with a bullet in his heart.

VI.

The dim light of the autumn afternoon, straggling through the edges of the lowered curtains, cast a gloom not greatly less than that eternal darkness which the two had entered. The rumble of trucks had a muted sound, here in the chamber of death. The stage was set and the curtain ready, but the leading characters had already taken their last bow.

Jean was first to break the momentary silence of shocked surprise. "Higgs!" she cried out, staring at the nearer corpse. "It's the man who called on us this noon!"

Frick turned to the professor accusingly. "You didn't tell me about Higgs."

"No; I didn't," Frost agreed. "Miss Moray, if the superintendent and his wife are in, bring them up."

Frick hesitated, seemed to debate many matters, then announced to Frost; "There's no phone here. I'll have to go out and put in a call for the homicide squad. Keep a close watch over everything."

Jean walked out with him. She gave him an appraising glance. "Isn't the procedure a bit irregular for a murder case?"

Inspector Frick did not give a direct answer, but there was a note of finality in his voice: "Once in a great while, somebody comes along who stands head and shoulders above the rest of us. Whatever his line is, he's got what it takes, whether he's an inventor, a poet, or anything else. When you spot a genius, my dear young woman, give him all the room to play in that he wants. Rules and regulations aren't for men of that caliber. They make their own rules. They don't play the game according to Hoyle, but they always come out winners. Frost knows what he's doing. And he'll do it better if he has the chance before half a dozen other people go tramping around the room."

The inspector strode briskly toward the nearest telephone in a corner drug store.

Jean found the superintendent's wife in, while the superintendent achieved a doubtful distinction by being both in and out. He was sprawled in bed, and out completely from a successful attempt to decorate his interior with a new coat of whisky. The wife, whose slovenly appearance was rivaled by her sour disposition, glared suspiciously when Jean told her she was wanted upstairs, but finally plodded in the girl's wake.

Frick and another man were entering the front door as Jean headed down the hall from the rear-basement stairway.

"Lieutenant Flaherty of the missing-persons bureau. He was here this morning when Hossner reported his wife as missing," Frick explained.

Frost lounged just inside the door to Apartment 1A, as if he had remained there during the whole of the two or three minutes that the others were gone.

Flaherty let a low whistle escape him. The superintendent's wife, Mrs. Wod, launched the first gasp of what had the earmarks of a three-octave screech, which Frick stopped with a curt:

"Cut out the noise. They're dead and neither you nor anybody else can raise 'em."

He gave the room a rapid inspection. He bent over the man at the desk for several seconds, eyes glued to something he saw there. He strolled back to the group in the doorway with a more positive bearing than he had hitherto worn.

"You," he pointed an accusing finger at Mrs. Wod, "ever see this man before?" He indicated the body of Higgs.

Mrs. Wod shook her head.

"Ever see the fellow sitting in the chair?"

She peered across the now brightly lighted room. "Yes. That's, let me see, the chap who moved into 1A. What was his name? Hossner, that's who it is."

"You're sure?'

"Positive."

Frick asked Flaherty: "Did you ever see that man before?"

Flaherty inspected the corpse briefly, answered: "Yes. It's Fritz Hossner. There's the patch we put on that bruise on his head."

Frick turned to the professor. He demanded and received what information Frost possessed about the late Mr. Higgs. He asked Mrs. Wod if she had heard the shots fired, which she flatly denied.

Frost offered a suggestion: "It's a noisy street, with heavy truck traffic. Any one who heard the shots would undoubtedly ascribe them to back-firing and pay no attention to them or to the time."

"The police surgeon can probably fix the time of death pretty accurately," Frick decided.

"Approximately an hour and a half ago, for both of them," Frost stated.

"You saw the note Hossner was writing just before he was killed?"

"I saw a note on the desk," Frost admitted. "If I remember correctly, it read: 'To whom it may concern—I have carefully thought it over. I have decided not to pay the ransom. The kidnaping racket must be stopped. I will try to capture him when he returns and force him to tell me where my wife has been taken. It may be foolish but—' The note abruptly terminates. There is a spatter of ink where the pen was dropped."

Frick announced, looking at the professor: "Well, it looks as if the case is clear now, motive and all."

Frost said: "An unfinished note lying on a desk need not necessarily have been penned by a dead man found at the desk."

Frick's face fell. He asked grumpily: "Mrs. Wod, would you know Hossner's handwriting if you saw it?"

"Spare yourself the trouble," Frost cut in. "I can identify the handwriting. It is identical with that on an application for a license to wed, made out by Fritz Hossner."

"That clinches it."

"Indeed?"

Frost's inflection conveyed nothing but interest. He had been smoking cigarettes incessantly, and with such speed that the lighted tip seemed to race toward the butt, which he then used to ignite another cigarette. A cloud of spicy fumes eddied around him. All his faculties seemed to be keyed up, and while the fumes appeared to make the others a trifle giddy or drowsy, the only visible effect upon him was a brightening of his eyes, a sharper alertness to every detail—word and action.

In spite of his announced conviction, Frick spoke rather as if he was on the defensive. "Hossner is sitting at the desk writing the note. He has his automatic ready. He hears a sound at the door, whirls around, sees Higgs, and fires. Higgs sees what's coming and fires at the same time. It's a double killing. They've happened before."

"I believe the door was locked when we arrived," said Frost.

"What of it? Hossner may have left it ajar. If you notice the lock, you'll see it's the kind that automatically works when the door is shut, so that anybody inside could get out just by turning the knob, but anybody outside could get in only with a key."

"Precisely what I observed," Frost agreed. "Did you happen to observe that the weapon beside the man at the desk has been discharged once, whereas the automatic in Mr. Higgs' hand has been fired thrice?"

"I expect the ballistics expert to certify that Hossner's bullet is in Higgs' head, and one of Higgs' bullets in Hossner's heart."

Frost persisted: "And the other bullets? I failed to find a trace of them in the room."

Frick hesitated a moment. "That puzzled me at first, but I wouldn't be surprised if one of them turned out to be the bullet that got Clehr."

"I would be not only surprised but positively astonished if one missing bullet was not found in Clehr's body and the other stopped by my assistant," Frost said. "And I am confident that Higgs' fingerprints will be found on the gun in his hand, and Hossner's on the gun beside him."

"What the devil else would you expect?" Frick snapped with some exasperation.

"When Mrs. Hossner left Clehr's office, only she and Clehr knew that she was coming to me. If Higgs trailed her all the way, it is most improbable, aside from time limitations, that he then immediately rushed back to ambush Clehr, and promptly returned, after the murder, to my address."

Frick argued: "Higgs could have followed her and loitered by the taxi. He could have overheard the address she gave. Or he may have had an accomplice. Snatches are seldom the work of one man, usually two or more. He could have told the accomplice, if he had one, to follow the woman while he took care of the doctor. Better still, if he was deaf and dumb as you say, he wouldn't even need to be close to the woman. He could read her lips from a little distance and see the address she gave."

Frost exhaled a cloud of smoke. "Ingenious!" he commented, in a noncommittal manner. He dropped the idle remark: "Did you note that only five of the sixteen apartments in this building are rented?"

"What of it?"

"The building doesn't seem to be well-kept-up. I presume you are aware that this is on the ground-floor front, and that the superintendent's quarters are in the basement rear?"

"What are you driving at?"

Frost suddenly turned to Mrs. Wod. "You don't find much to do around the building, do you?"

The woman yapped: "None of your business."

There was an acid, withering effect in Frost's drawl: "The voice and the attitude are exquisitely true to the nature of their proud owner. By the way, you frequently saw Mr. Hossner?"

"No; I didn't." The woman's attitude had become a good deal more helpful. She developed a profound respect for and fear of that lean, towering, dominant person. "I saw him when he came to look at the apartments. And one morning I saw him and his wife go out."

"How long have they lived here?"

"He rented the apartment five or six weeks ago."

Frost said irrelevantly: "I believe the apartment has been recently cleaned. Vacuum-cleaned, in fact."

Frick put in: "it's a quaint modern custom."

Frost mused, with an imperturbable air: "How bright the woodwork and furniture! What a truly excellent job of polishing even the brass fixtures!"

The inspector wore a harassed face with acute discomfort.

Frost added: "I am sure that you will find the fingerprints of your Mr. Hossner upon the alarm clock that I observe on a table by the bedside. I am likewise confident that Mrs. Hossner's prints will be found on the empty water glass standing beside the alarm clock. Furthermore, I would be most astonished if the fingerprints of your Mr. Hossner were not found on the barrel of the fountain pen lying beside the unfinished note."

Frick looked fit to be tied, when a rush of feet announced the arrival of the homicide squad.

Frost declared: "Miss Moray and I must leave for some important research. We would appreciate your getting the routine questions over with. If you forget any, you will find me at home to-morrow."

Frick gave him a keen but wasted glance and obliged. The squad was hard at work when the professor and his assistant left.

"Will you be at home in case we want to call you this evening?" Frick inquired.

"In other words, what am I up to? I am going to descend into the dwelling place of rats," Frost cryptically replied.

VII.

The professor, in his laboratory, drove with smooth and unerring precision toward some objective that Jean had not yet fathomed.

He slipped something under a microscope, darkened the lights, connected the microscope with a projector. On the wall screen the image of what looked like a huge, fuzzy needle swam into view and focused. He inserted other tiny things under the microscope, and other images sprang into enormous magnification on the screen.

"What are they?" Jean asked.

"Hairs—antelope hairs. Three of them, you will note, are identical in appearance. The first I found on Mrs. Hossner's skirt. The second came from the sleeve of Fritz Hossner. The third was embedded with some dust and grime on the instep of Higgs' right shoe. The last is one of the specimens you brought from the zoo. You will notice that it is of identical type with the three others, thus establishing proof that the others *are* antelope hairs, but that its coloring is darker and that it differs in minor characteristics."

"And what does this prove?"

Frost snapped: "Simply that Mrs. Hossner, Fritz Hossner, and Higgs have all been, and recently, at a particular place where a particular antelope was kept, probably as a pet."

He replaced the hairs in carefully marked envelopes, inserted new items under the microscope. Again fuzzy forms, like tree trunks, leaped out on the screen with giant enlargement. Frost studied them with a relish that was neither pride nor elation, but rather the eagerness with which a scholar, thirsty for knowledge for its own sake, pounces upon a new fact which is utterly useless by itself but of importance in relation to other facts.

"They're different in type from the others, and not all alike among themselves," Jean commented.

"They are human hairs. I took the first from Mrs. Hossner. It is identical with the second which came from the crossbar at the head of the bed in 16 Logan Street. The third was one of a few short remaining wisps that lived at the base of the almost totally bald skull of the late Mr. Higgs. The fourth I plucked from Fritz Hossner's head, while the last also came from the crossbar of the bed. The first and second are not only identical. Watch!"

Frost removed the twin hairs, inserted them in a spectroscope, focused a beam of light, adjusted a delicate mechanism of micrometrical graduation. "Look at the bands!"

Jean stared at a series of lines that sprang into view. "They're lines in the spectrum—meaning what?"

"Aspirin! If all other proofs were lacking, those bands alone would indicate that the person from whom the hairs came was a chronic user of aspirin. The body, among other means, attempts to eliminate absorbed aspirin through the follicles of the hair. Those bands help to explain why

Mrs. Hossner would unthinkingly swallow any tablet that came out of an aspirin box."

Frost returned the hairs to the slide under the microscope. "The third hair, from Higgs, has striking differences from the first two. Cross sections from all of them would show the differences even better, but I can't take time to prepare them now. They would tell the exact age of the individuals to which they belonged.

"The fourth hair, from Fritz Hossner, is likewise different from the others, you will notice. And the fifth, one of several similar ones that I found on the crossbar of the bed, also differs from the preceding four. In other words, there are five specimens from four individuals of whom only three, all dead, are known."

Jean's face lightened as understanding dawned. "I get it!" she cried out excitedly. "The hairs prove that Mrs. Hossner *did* live at 16 Logan Street and that some one else lived there who was not Higgs and who was not the man identified as Fritz Hossner."

Frost said: "There is evidence in quantity—dirt, grime, stains, hairs, scratches, and other marks and materials—to substantiate my interpretation in a dozen ways. Logic told what the truth must be, but logic is not enough for juries. The tools of science have supplied the incontrovertible evidence to solve these murders and have woven a web from which the criminal cannot escape. Now we shall use logic and the tools of science for another purpose.

"Bring me the metal flagon with the clamp top. It's over there, in the corner."

He disconnected the projector, switched the laboratory lights on again, replaced the evidence in individual envelopes. He took the container that Jean brought and into it carefully poured the liquid air from its original flask.

"Get the bottles of porcelain cement and binder from the second section of the chemical cabinets," Frost ordered.

Jean laid them on the worktable while Frost brought out a small machine and cylinder.

"Bring all the explosives in Drawer C," he said.

He took solutions and jars from shelves laden with powders, compounds, extracts, fluids, and chemicals of infinite variety.

Jean trotted off and returned gingerly carrying four sticks of dynamite.

"Not enough, but they'll have to serve," Frost remarked. "Don't be afraid of them—they won't explode unless you drop them."

Jean promptly got the jitters and almost spilled them all.

When she had safely deposited them, Frost said "Get the long cloaks from the closet," while he himself turned to other tasks.

Jean remembered them well—they were the garments, bulletproof, except to high-powered rifles, that had protected their lives the night of the Golden Goblin affray, when they raided the hide-out of Blake's gang in woods north of the city.

She paused for a moment, puzzled, before she laid them with the rest of the paraphernalia.

Frost was amusing himself in a singular fashion. He had a glass gun. Except for the fact that it was made of glass, it looked much like the water squirt guns that small boys play pranks with. It worked with a plunger action. The end of the barrel was sealed except for a tiny hole in the center. At Frost's elbow stood a pitcher of water. The professor dipped the glass toy in the water, held it there until the chamber was full, then aimed at a spot on the ceiling and squirted the stream at it. Three tries hit the spot every time.

"Good enough!" The professor seemed satisfied.

"Let me play, too," the girl chided.

"That toy may serve to get us out of a tight predicament." Frost did not elaborate his mystifying remark. "Have you anything like a blouse or sweater and shorts in your wardrobe?"

Sheer astonishment almost petrified the girl. "Why, yes. I also have the loveliest tweed outfit—"

"The devil take the tweed outfit! Sweater and shorts will do, just so you get out of the clothing you are wearing."

"Undress? Here?"

"I don't care where. I am interested only in your legs," Frost flung over his shoulder as he strode toward a section of trays and drawers.

"Goody, goody!" Jean called brightly. "I hope it's going to be assault even if it does sound merely aesthetic."

"Guess again," Frost retorted.

He opened a section, pulled out an immense tray, and lifted from it some sheets that gleamed with a silvery, metallic luster. He brought them back to the worktable.

The girl lay on the unoccupied side of the table, lazily stretching her arms and looking up with frank impudence. She had taken Frost's suggestion literally. Shoes, hose, and dress lay in a little heap. What little she wore was a theory rather than a fact and might just as well have been added to the pile.

"Nice legs, aren't they? You'll never see a better pair," she gayly prophesied.

"Fifty million women in this country alone have the same appendages," Frost dryly commented.

"But I'm not fifty million, thank goodness!"

"A sentiment in which I heartily concur."

Frost set to work. He took a sheet of the gleaming stuff, wrapped it around the girl's ankle and leg, molded it to form, clamped it in back and clipped it. Jean subsided momentarily in the fascination of watching his long, supple fingers, so graceful and symmetric that they seemed almost feminine, work nimbly at their task.

"What are you doing this for?" she asked at last when curiosity got the better of her.

"Time will tell."

The gleaming stuff flowed up ankle, calf, and thigh.

"'So the captain said, I'll sail alone. And he set his course for the torrid zone,'" Jean hummed.

Frost ignored the levity, finished the leg, set to work on the other.

The girl looked at the first critically, approved of herself, and cocked an eye at Frost, "You'll have to admit it's a swell figure, one of the best. It has everything," she modestly declaimed.

"Thin, flexible, and tough," Frost mused, and added as his assistant opened her mouth: "I was speaking of the metal."

He finished the job. "Try walking and tell me if it bothers you any."

She slid off the table, pranced experimentally, paused in front of a mirror. She looked at her reflection and laughed with glee. "I can see the headlines: 'Nude woman picked up on street. Claims silver-plated legs are latest style.' No; the stuff doesn't bother me to speak of. Next? What's left?"

"You'll be left unless you hurry," Frost threatened.

The girl gathered her things and skipped out, to return a few minutes later to find Frost ready to leave. The long cloak enwrapped his form.

"Take some of the smaller stuff. I'll handle the explosives and other materials," he ordered.

Jean was piqued as she donned the protective garment. He might at least have commented on how weirdly beautiful she looked with her blue blouse, white shorts, silvery gleaming legs, and her whole splendid figure emphasized by the impertinent young wisdom of her face. There must be a way. There ought to be a way. Or else there ought to be a law against men like Frost.

She trotted, not too meekly, after him toward the car.

VIII.

The lights of the city retreated behind them, and behind them lay the colossal glow that always hung over it by night, the reflected glare of all its millions of lights. The seemingly endless skyscrapers and the interminable blocks of apartments at last gave way to houses. Traffic lessened, they sped through outlying towns, and at length they emerged on a south-shore road.

Now came the distant surge of the sea and the ebb and beat of waters in the Sound. A stiff on-shore wind was blowing. It rushed through the trees and screamed into every crevice of the car that ambled along at a steady fifty.

They had left the city shortly after eight. It was now nearly ten. A haggard moon hung far down on the eastern horizon and crept higher with weary slowness.

Jean admitted: "It's a good thing I had some sandwiches this afternoon. As it is, I'm hungry enough to eat turkey and caviar. Where are we going? You get me all ready for the tropics and then go batting off toward the polar regions."

"We are not far from the castle now."

"Do you mean to tell me that you took the dame's whole story? That there is really a castle here?"

Frost did not take his eyes off the road. "There are a good many castles in America. Some have been built here, others have been purchased abroad, taken down stone by stone, and carried across the Atlantic to be reërected on this continent.

"Lind Castle is among the latter group. A wealthy eccentric bought it in England more than twenty years ago and shipped it to its present site on Long Island. It attracted some attention as a curiosity, but he died, the heirs sold it, and it was forgotten by a public more interested in the War.

"The woman's story of course brought it back to mind. I refreshed my memory about its location and other characteristics by reference to a couple of volumes, one of which was in my library."

Frost suddenly slowed the car on a curve. "Look off there, between the trees, into that bay."

Jean peered in the northerly direction he pointed. Farther out, the waters of the Sound were dark, and even in the margins of the bay seemed black, but pale and faint rays from the rising moon made a path across the wind-riffled bay, and the wave crests rose from depths the color of old blood and broke with eerily crimson tips.

"Why—Why the sea looks as if it was bloody!" Jean gasped.

"That is the woman's blood-red sea. In daylight, you would find the sight even more impressive. It is caused by a variety of marine vegetation, algae which sometimes multiply and concentrate in such quantity in local areas that the result you see is brought about."

"If all this was planned in advance, the killer must be something of a genius."

"Not particularly. He has a certain kind of low cunning. He is shrewd enough to take advantage of most factors. He uses opportunism. But first and last he is a rat, and when the chase grows warm he will be found, like rats, hiding in his lair."

Frost drove on, more slowly now, the lights dimmed. They had not passed a house or met a car in miles. Frost as usual kept his thoughts to himself, and when Jean glanced at his profile, she found it inscrutable.

But to-night there was a difference, an intangible quality that she sensed intuitively rather than saw. Frost was neither annoyed nor angry, neither moved by hatred nor revenge; not disgusted and not ruthless, yet a mood that suggested all these hovered in him.

Jean hoped that something she had done disturbed him, but in self-honesty she decided that the source lay elsewhere. Something, somewhere, past or yet to come in the tortuous windings of murder and mystery, had made him a close companion of the destroying angel.

Frost halted the car and extinguished its lights in a clump of bushes off the road. He divided the equipment into two unequal piles, the larger of which he carried. They trod noiselessly along a private road, obviously little used, that wound through woods. Only the faint moonlight illuminated their course. Frost led and hugged the shadows. The dim light passed into total darkness from time to time when clouds scudded across the moon.

They walked for several minutes before they came to a clearing. In its center stood a castle, Lind Castle, strangely anachronistic, a relic of medieval architecture, transplanted in alien soil. There were no lights shining in its iron-grilled windows, and it seemed to be deserted. It loomed like the dark towers of legend. It flung its casements and scarps against the sky, stood silhouetted against the bay beyond, where the waves endlessly beat.

Frost whispered: "Wait here."

He vanished in the darkness that a cloud cast. Jean thought she saw him move toward the rear of the structure. She heard nothing. The wind made confusion. Frost moved among shadows like a shadow itself.

He was gone for ten or fifteen minutes. He reappeared as silently and swiftly as he had melted away. "Wear the hood," he whispered.

She slipped it over her head.

They walked unchallenged to the front door, a massive thing of hewn oak. Frost tested it gently, and, to Jean's surprise, it opened. Frost pushed it only far enough for her to slip through. He attached something to its outside handle, then stepped inside and closed it with infinite pains. He locked it behind him.

He pressed the button of a flashlight, swung it. The circling beam picked out a great stone hall, with the solid furniture of a much-older generation. The hall had one doorway in each wall, and all the doors were closed.

Frost let Jean hold the flashlight while he pulled from the front door the iron key that rested in its lock. From the inner folds of his cloak, he took the porcelain powder, mixed it with the binder, poured the stuff into the keyhole. It hardened almost as fast as he rammed it in with the key.

The girl did not raise questions. It was not the time. All she knew was that Frost had made it impossible for them or any one else to leave by way of the front door without spending hours prying the rigid porcelain out, or bursting the door from its hinges. She could have understood his doing something to make escape easier, but she could think of no reasonable explanation for his present maneuver.

Catlike, Frost stalked to the door in the left wall, listened, and softly opened it. Soundlessly Jean followed.

The swinging flashlight picked out a smaller room, sturdily paneled, and containing stiff-backed chairs against the walls, with an oak dining table in a corner.

Frost strode toward the table, inspected it swiftly, then bent over and played the flashlight on its under side. Jean caught a glimpse of heavy braces and what looked like a cigar box, but which might have been merely another supporting block.

The professor whispered, in words difficult to distinguish through the thin slit in the hood: "Whatever happens, take your cue from me. We are approaching the lair of the rat."

He walked to a door in the rear of the room. Like the others, it opened to his touch. They entered without sound, halted again to listen. Frost played the beam around—

Light suddenly flooded the room, brought the kitchen into full view.

A thick, emotionless voice ordered: "Do as I say or I will kill you." The words sounded slow, labored, and held a trace of accent.

The barrel of a rifle was trained squarely on Frost. It projected from the partly opened door of a closet across the kitchen. The bullet from a high-powered rifle would penetrate their cloaks.

Jean thought of many things. She thought that if one of them made a break, the other might conceivably drop the hiding killer before he could bring the barrel around for a second shot. She thought ruefully of the loaded automatic in a pocket of her cloak. But much as she wished she had been holding it in her hand, she knew she could never have sighted the rifle barrel or possibly have hit the man behind it before he shot first.

Frost drawled: "Moderation is an excellent quality in using that instrument. You may find our aid indispensable in getting out of here before other persons arrive."

The voice commanded, in slow, distinct gutturals: "You will please walk straight ahead. Do not walk fast. Do as I say."

Frost obeyed, Jean at his side.

The professor replied, with a calmness and conviction of mastering the situation that made Jean wonder, and with something akin to a sardonic gibe: "It might possibly interest you to know that the front and rear doors are the only exits to the castle. If you so much as disturb either one, you will have the pleasure of blowing yourself into food for rats. However, do not take my word for it. I would enjoy your finding out for yourself."

The voice, more hesitant, said: "Walk. Do not talk."

Frost mused: "Iron bars are most effective. They serve to keep strangers out. On the other hand, they also keep those inside from getting out. It will take time to remove enough bars for escape. I have not allotted you as much time as you will need."

"Halt where you are!" the thick voice answered.

The floor dropped from under them. Jean gasped aloud. It was all she had time for in the second of that sickening plunge through Stygian blackness. She heard a throaty chuckle, far away, and a grinding of metal and stone. She had a horrible fear of falling through endless blackness to unfathomable depths. But all her terrifying near-thoughts were stopped by the abrupt end of her fall.

Jarred to her hands and knees, she inhaled a sickening stench as dreadful as anything she had ever known, an odor of decay and death and animal smells, overpowering in its nausea.

Then they were upon her with a rush of tiny feet and sharp teeth that tore at her, worried her hands and ankles. Furry bodies flung themselves at her. In the midst of darkness and terror, she thanked with all her heart the foresight of Frost that saved those ravenous teeth from ripping her limbs to shreds. She staggered upright.

"Miss Moray!" Frost's voice cut steel-like through the darkness. "There is nothing to fear! Are you all right?"

The flashlight swept around and she gasped without replying.

Walls. Stone walls. A chamber eight feet high, twelve in length and breadth. Rats. Hundreds of rats, lean rats, gaunt rats, hungry rats, giant rats, swarming and rushing and snapping with the ferocity of starvation. A mound of débris, terrible in its implications. Skeletons, long picked clean of flesh, inextricably piled together with litter and refuse that had accumulated for unknown years.

Jean's head swam. She wanted to faint but could not. She could only stare, in unnerved horror, at those gaping eye sockets and finger bones, those cavernous ribs, the wild horde of rats that surged at her with savage desperation, while her very breathing was poisoned by an indescribable, loathsome stench.

Nothing to fear? Only death by rats, or starvation, or slow suffocation in the stone walls of a prison as impregnable as Gibraltar. And outside—if by some miracle they did escape—a homicidal maniac.

IX.

Frost leaped in front of Jean. His hand flashed into a pocket, came out instantly, and swung in a swift circle, in one of those graceful, continuous motions so characteristic of him. He sprayed a fine stream, and in that deadly strychnine solution, the rats died as they leaped.

He flung a gray monster from his arm, kicked others clear to the opposite wall. He crushed the life from more than one, fought them with a weapon of science and with bodily skill alike, stemming their rush and beating them back with an efficiency more murderous than their attack.

As if by some strange, mysterious communion, they suddenly swarmed off, with squeaking and cries and the patter of myriad feet. There were holes in the walls, where the cement had been furrowed out between stones. They retreated, but they left dozens of carcasses among the débris that had nourished them. Some of them scampered around, or waited beyond range of the deadly spray. Their vigil held an ominous prophecy.

Frost turned the sprayer over to his assistant. "Use it if the rats return in numbers or attack."

He removed his hood, an example that she followed. The stench in the cell smote her like a blow.

The professor immediately trained the flashlight on the ceiling and played it over a small area. Even Jean, accustomed to his peculiarities, was surprised by the appearance of his face in faint profile against the light. Of fear, worry about their fate, alarm over the rats, or awe of the mysterious skeletons, there was none. He showed only curiosity, the curiosity of a chemist analyzing an unknown substance.

"That's interesting," he muttered.

"What is?"

"The trapdoor that dropped us here. I thought we might find something of the sort." He pointed to a block of stone in the ceiling, recessed, and with its visible face at a slant. A piece of rusty metal jutted over its lowest tip. "The block has been cut like a cube diagonally bisected. It is pivoted on a bar, part of which you can see on two sides in those crevices between it and adjacent stones.

"Normally it would hang with its wide, heavy side down and its narrow side up, but the catch prevents the heavy side from swinging down. It is controlled by electrical or spring action, probably both. Our hidden enemy simply pressed a button that withdrew the catch. The stone instantly pivoted of its own weight, and we fell. The catch then returned to position, forcing the block back to its original state."

Even while he was talking, Frost drew a stoppered bottle from his pocket, together with the glass gun. He uncapped the bottle and dipped the barrel into a brownish fluid within. As the chamber filled, an inkling of the toy's purpose entered the girl's head.

Frost raised the gun, aimed at the catch-piece, and squirted the fluid on it. He repeated the performance on the two crevices where the pivot bar was visible.

"Concentrated nitric acid, one of the most powerful corrosives known. It is attacking the metal already," he explained. "Don't let even a drop fall on you."

His voice echoed hollowly through the chamber. The damp, fetid air added a clammy weight to the semidarkness. There was never complete silence, because of the restless rats, but there were eerie quasi-silences at times. A slimy film covered the great stone blocks, and the cement that the rats had dug out lay in scattered damp patches. How far their runways extended was impossible to tell. If Mrs. Hossner was right, the house must be honey-combed with tiny tunnels. Perhaps those tunnels would at least save them from suffocation.

Frost drenched the metal parts with acid again. The gruesome mass of skeletons looked on with grins that would never vary, save as the slow encroachments of time and dissolution turned bone to powder and fleshless, mocking jaws back into original dust. There must have been seven or eight human skeletons in that pile. The bones of countless rodents were intermingled with them and littered all over the floor. On top of all lay the freshly picked bones of one large animal.

The professor asked: "Does anything about the human skeletons impress you as unusual?"

Jean shuddered. Her low answer had a tinge of exasperation: "No. Of course it's perfectly natural that they happen to be here and the only surprising thing is that there aren't more."

Among ghostly relics, Frost murmured with the mirthless ghost of a smile: "You may be more accurate than you think."

"If we ever get out of here, and aren't killed by that maniac above, and get out of the castle after that, all of which I have some doubts about, maybe you would give me an idea of why three and six add up to nothing," she retorted.

Frost bathed the iron with more of the concentrated acid. "Shall I start at the beginning? And yet, in the final analysis, there is really little to say. Everything has been said. All the clues were at hand. Words and events needed only comparison in order for the truth to appear."

"Yes? The truth is about as plain as the nose of a fish. For instance, just what did Mrs. Hossner's ravings mean to you?"

"It signified much by itself, and it implied more," the professor began. "At the outset there was a choice of alternatives—either the woman had gone through some mystifying experiences, or she had not. It was quite evident from her manner, and from various of her statements, that she was telling truths.

"The nature of those facts next came under consideration. What were they but a series of fantasies and improbabilities? How many persons would believe them or believe her if she told exactly what she had experienced? The answer could only be that those experiences were designed and planned for the very reason that the woman and her story would be discredited.

"This interpretation further implied that it was the police who would be expected to put her in a psychopathic ward rather than investigate the case if it came to their attention. On the other hand, it also seemed that the police were intended not to hear her at all, but that some one had planned with such cunning that if she did escape she would not find an audience."

Without pausing, Frost emptied another chamber of acid to attack the metal. "I say 'escape' because from her own story it was evident that she had been drugged, and that it had been planned to keep her in the castle for some ulterior purpose. But her own constitution and her habitual use of aspirin combined to counteract the sleeping potion to a limited degree. She was not carefully guarded. When she ran for the front door, a tear-gas bomb was thrown at her, blinding her. The door must have been unlocked, otherwise she could hardly have had time to fumble for the key and twist it before she would be caught.

"But surely it would be oversight of the most flagrant kind if some one made elaborate preparations for a crime and then left the door unlocked so that the victim escaped from an almost impregnable stronghold. That fact alone was ground for suspicion that, while a specific crime had been prepared, it was only one of a series, and that the criminal or criminals had grown somewhat careless from constant and easy success. It was taken for granted that she would remain in a helpless stupor.

"So far, of course, there was no certainty that any crime had been committed. But the very nature of the circumstances indicated that, regardless of this specific instance, it might lead to the discovery of hitherto unsuspected crimes. What could be the nature of such crime or crimes, and who was responsible for them?"

Frost stopped long enough to light one of the curious cigarettes of his own make and to exhale a stream of smoke that helped to disguise the intolerable odor of the cell.

"Kidnaping, abduction, extortion, and other types of criminal intention occurred to me, and also that, whatever the truth, there must be at least three persons involved. If the woman's husband was the schemer, it would be necessary for many reasons to have an accomplice in the castle, two accomplices for steady vigil. If the woman's husband was not involved, it would still require two persons for the actual kidnaping, and a third at the castle. The arrival of Higgs at the door, though indirectly responsible for the woman's immediate death, was directly responsible for giving me positive evidence of the identity of the criminals."

Frost wore a crooked smile. "In the first place, Clehr has always personally telephoned on the occasions when he has sent clients to me. Higgs stated that Clehr had sent him, but Clehr had not called me. It was presumptive evidence that he had followed the woman to Clehr's offices and trailed her from there.

"In the second place, Higgs made the mistake of assuming that, since I looked puzzled when his fingers and lips moved, I could not read either lips or sign language. I am thoroughly acquainted with both. I watched him while I was scanning his written message. As is not uncommon, his lips and hands were both eloquent, perhaps unconsciously.

"His lips said: 'So it's two here. Well, Fred ought to be done with his job by now, and the three of us can take care of you two in a hurry. And this time we'll see to it that the dame gets curtains for good'

"His hands talked: 'The game is getting too hot. Whether he likes it or not, I quit after this one. Fred and I should have turned thumbs down. No one would have believed her, and we're taking a big chance this way. Still, if it's all going to smash, a couple more bump-offs can't make it any worse.'"

Jean gave Frost a hard glance. So he read lips and sign language? Well, it would be a long time, practically forever, in fact, before she again assumed his ignorance of anything.

Frost continued: "I let Higgs go on his way because I knew I could find him when necessary. When I found the body of Mrs. Hossner, the hitherto missing crime became a reality, and at the same time the case entered, like a spreading disease, what might be called its malignant stage. Some one had arranged a plot. The plot had failed because the woman escaped. But it had been so carefully laid that no one would believe her anything but insane, and the chances were that she would unwittingly kill herself before she had an opportunity to talk.

"I now had a secondary crime, so to speak, but not the primary crime. I knew that three persons were implicated, of whom one was Higgs, one the man called Fred, and the third either Fritz Hossner or an unknown.

"Surveying in detail each statement made by the dead woman, I resorted to logic to explain some anomalies and to eliminate others. Deliberate staging had to be separated from accidentals and incidentals. The motive and the nature of the crime must be, and were, elicited."

Frost kept his gaze intently fixed on the pivot stone now, while he repeated the acid spraying at intervals. "The antelope was undoubtedly a pet. Whether it wandered along by accident at the time the woman entered the dining room, or whether it was directed there, was immaterial. It served its function. It could be dismissed as unimportant except in so far as it contributed to the fantasy of her narrative and to the unbalancing of her mind. This was efficient planning.

"The blood-red sea I also dismissed as a natural phenomenon known to science. The organ music was part of the staging and constituted one of the apparently inexplicable or hallucinatory stratagems employed to cast skepticism on the woman's story. You saw how it was done."

"I did not," Jean contradicted him.

"You saw the box under the table upstairs. That was the organ, actually a pipeless pipe organ. The box contained thyratron tubes about three inches long. The tubes are essentially radio tubes with a small percentage of added mercury. Each of the tubes was electrically connected to one of the keys on a toy console elsewhere in the house, probably in the kitchen closet. The console undoubtedly has a dial to regulate volume. Different tones are produced by adding electrical resistance, more resistance giving lower frequency and lower notes.

"When any one manipulated the console keys, chords with the full volume of an organ would thunder forth in whatever room the thyratron tubes were placed. The woman may have looked, may have seen the box, but ignored it as being only a part of the table's supporting blocks. As she said, she literally listened to organ music from an organ that was not there.

"The rats that she heard in such numbers in the walls impressed me as having a deep and sinister significance. It was possible but highly improbable that the occupants of the castle would ignore so great a nuisance. Was it not likely that the rats themselves were cultivated for a definite reason?

"From this point on," Frost continued, "the case rapidly became clear. Why had not the woman gone straight to the police, or to her husband, when she reached the city? The answer lay in her statement that she had not been married long. I verified that by the city records. Fritz Hossner took out the license on September 26th, only five weeks ago. He rented the apartment at 16 Logan Street on September 23rd, only three days earlier.

"Furthermore, the woman stated that she had no friends here; that she was a stranger. She spent the whole of her time with Fritz Hossner, exploring the city, moving from spot to spot. He introduced her to no one. His wife disappeared the night of October 30th. On November 1st, he intended giving up the apartment and moving to another address.

"All the indications were that the marriage was one arranged through a matrimonial agency. Most of the persons utilizing the services of such agencies have sincere intentions, but crooks are found everywhere."

Frost lighted a new cigarette from the butt of the old, as he continued: "The entire design was now evident. Fritz Hossner surveyed the lists of prospects until he found one who was lonely, friendless, and possessed of a worth-while sum in cash, negotiable securities, or jewels. This last assumption I made, not on the base of anything the woman had said, but as the sole motive that would explain the intended crime.

"If this motive and interpretation proved correct, then the sequence of events was plain. Fritz Hossner corresponded with the woman, had her come to the city to meet him. If the meeting was successful, he married her. If not, he tried correspondence with another potential victim. In this case, the meeting was successful. He married the woman.

"He lived with her for a month, became familiar with her habits, found out whether she had friends or was keeping in touch with them. He had rented the apartment only for a month, and when they both left, there would be no questions asked. He had picked the apartment carefully so that he could even control the matter of exits and entrances to a considerable degree and avoid attracting attention.

"Two nights before the month was up, he gave his wife a sleeping potion and took her by automobile to the castle. If he was noticed as he carried her out late at night, he could explain that his wife was ill and, there being no telephone at hand, he was rushing her to a doctor or a hospital. He was legally married. There would be nothing upon which he could be held.

"Having got her to the castle, he deposited her with his accomplices while he returned, collected all belongings in the apartment, and further made sure that his actions had not been reported or observed. If they had been, and he found himself under surveillance, you may be sure he had a prearranged plan with his two partners for release of the woman in some distant spot.

"But the woman escaped. Higgs and Fred trailed her to the city. One of them continued trailing her, the other went to Hossner's apartment. Hossner, realizing that the woman had confounded his plans by neither swallowing the tablet nor going to the police nor returning to him, but by visiting first Clehr and then us, knew the game might be up. He took a desperate chance in deciding to kill all persons concerned, except himself."

The story unfolded, and Jean almost forgot the grim setting, the killer still at large or perhaps free of the castle by this time, as Frost fitted the details into the larger pattern.

"Fred shot Clehr. Hossner had already made his own fake report to the police. Higg's arrival at our door was a blunder. His purpose was, presumably, either to gain entry and learn what had happened to the victim; or to hope for an opportunity to kill us if the circumstances were favorable. I am inclined to believe that he was acting on his own initiative, but the point is a minor one.

"Hossner, meanwhile, had prepared everything for his own purposes, by removing all identifying characteristics from the apartment, such as fingerprints and stray hairs, vacuum-cleaning it thoroughly, and then spraying it.

"All this, and the clues I called Frick's attention to, plus the identification of the dead man as Fritz Hossner, was proof to me that the dead man was not Fritz Hossner, but actually the person called Fred. The two were either close relatives, or Fritz had hired the other because of a striking personal resemblance.

"It must have been Fred who trailed you and tried to duplicate his earlier performance in the slaying of Clehr. He failed. He returned to my residence in the hope of breaking in, or finding out what had happened to Mrs. Hossner. I did not take time to look for his footprints outside the laboratory window, but knowledge of the woman's death must have been present in order to account for what followed. The position of the bodies, among other signposts, indicated that it was Fred who made the discovery of Mrs. Hossner's death."

Frost filled the gun and directed acid against metal for perhaps the last time. The fluid was almost exhausted. So far there was no indication that the quantity he had brought would suffice. The pivot stone held. The dank, miasmal odors assailed their nostrils even through the aromatic smoke of Frost's cigarettes.

Frost went on: "Fred returned to the Logan Street apartment to inform Hossner of the wife's death. Hossner kept him there until Higgs arrived and rang the buzzer or tapped on the door. Hossner then knocked Fred out with a blow on the head. He opened the door a mere slit, stepped back, and shot Higgs as the deaf mute entered. He took Fred's gun, shot the unconscious man with it, wiped it clean of fingerprints, and pressed it into Higgs' fingers. He wiped his own gun clean and put it in Fred's hand. He wrote the note found on the desk, and put Fred's fingerprints on the barrel of the pen. He took the patch off his own head and affixed it to the bump he had raised on Fred's skull, in almost the identical spot where he had slugged himself. He carried Higgs' gun away with him when he looked out of the window, peered through a crack in the door, and found that the way was clear.

"He had thus accomplished directly or indirectly the cowardly murder of Clehr, the double-crossing of both his partners and their deaths, and the killing of his wife. If there was no unexpected development, a totally different interpretation of the crimes would be made, the interpretation that Frick and the police were advancing when we were in the Hossner apartment. He not only would not be hunted. He would be listed as dead. He alone would enjoy and spend the profits of murder.

"But his cunning was limited. His best recourse was flight. Instead of departing elsewhere, he returned to the castle. There were incriminating clues that could be destroyed, others—"

Whatever Frost intended to say was never completed. He listened sharply, flattened himself against the wall. "Back!" he commanded his assistant. "Follow these instructions carefully!" He spoke a few swift, concise sentences.

From the ceiling came a sudden grinding tear and scream of tortured metal. From far away rose the quick, instinctive patter of countless feet, a rushing sibilance of rats. The great pivot stone settled, sheared through the acid-weakened bar, and smashed to the floor, crushing débris and bones alike as if they were so much mush.

Frost bent, lifted the girl by her thighs until her straining fingers caught the edge of the floor above. Half pulling herself, half boosted, she went through the opening. She sat on its edge, leaned down, and caught Frost's hand. She hauled until his own hands caught the edge and he chinned himself up.

The kitchen was still fully lighted. Frost raced to a wide window at one side and reached his hand through the iron bars. Immediately after this curious action, he raced back to the opening in the floor. He sat with his legs over the edge of the hole, his back to the door, his body bent down as if he was helping some one up.

Jean ran to the inside kitchen door and flattened herself against the wall the moment she was free. She held her loaded automatic.

The door opened wide suddenly, swiftly. The barrel of a rifle swung into view, and a hand was upon the trigger. Without warning, without compunction, now that she knew what cold-blooded murderer they had trapped in his lair, she followed Frost's instructions and fired. The rifle wabbled, discharged at a tangent, fell to the ground.

Frost was on his feet, around, and training his own gun at the doorway in one fluent motion. "Walk in. Make a false move and I will perform a service to humanity," the professor ordered with deadly sincerity.

Holding his shattered right wrist, blood dribbling down his fingers, a man stepped into view, a man who at first sight seemed like the corpse that had recently lain in a room at 16 Logan Street.

X.

There he stood at last, the rat cornered in his lair, the killer who preyed on the helpless and unsuspecting, who used emotions and dreams as the tools for enriching himself, who promised happiness and delivered death; the missing Fritz Hossner who had been identified as the dead Fritz Hossner; a perfect twin.

He was stocky in build like the dead man, with the same stolid face, the same small eyes, the same thin mouth, the same appearance of almost peasantlike simplicity combined with an impression of animal cunning. He had not made a cry or sound when the bullet plowed through his wrist. He made not a sound now, as he came, holding the wrist, his features emotionless.

"Stop where you are!" Frost snapped, and the captive halted ten feet away. "I told you I had not allowed you time enough to escape. You might have succeeded in wrenching the bars out or filing through them in another fifteen minutes. Before I deliver you to a justice that will send you to the electric chair, but will never begin to punish you for your crimes, you may utilize those fifteen minutes by divulging some information I wish to know. What day is this, Miss Moray?"

"Why, it's now the early morning of November 1st," she replied with a slight frown of puzzlement.

"For how many years have you been carrying on your marriage-murder racket?" Frost flung the question at Hossner.

No answer.

"Is your real name Fritz Hossner?"

Sullen silence.

"What were the names of these women whose skeletons lie in the cell? Those whom you made brides of the rats?"

No answer.

Frost's whole manner, as he stood on the edge of the pit, had been stiffening and tensing. Now, with a look of hawklike and ruthless determination, towering as if he longed for the captive to continue his stubborn silence or to make some break that would furnish excuse for giving the killer what the killer had given to his victims, Frost stated savagely:

"I want those names. I want them now. If necessary, I will get them by other means, the same means that enabled me to identify you by hairs that you overlooked on the crossbar of the bed at 16 Logan Street, hairs that will send you to the chair.

"I will photograph every set of teeth on those skeletons and circularize every dentist in the country until some are identified by bridges and fillings. I will gather up every scrap of metal, every button, every remaining piece of cloth, no matter how rusty or moldy, and place them under the microscope. I will study the bones and analyze them, until I have built up an accurate picture of the height, weight, appearance, and characteristics of the woman of whom they were part.

"I will set handwriting experts at work on the records of the license bureau, comparing your recent signature with every signature on every application for the last twenty years, until all the false names you have ever used are brought to light, and the names of all your victims.

"I will have all the files of all the matrimonial agencies in the country examined in detail for records of your handwriting, your photograph. I will have the police departments throughout the country compile, if necessary, a list of all women missing and never found. It will take time, but I will build up a web of evidence and mute testimony from which you will never escape the chair, if you escape mob vengeance. You can believe me.

"You may sit silent through trial, and I will send you to the chair. You may lie and deny everything, and I will send you to the chair. Plead insanity, and I will prove you sane beyond any doubt whatsoever. Now talk!"

The prisoner talked. He mentioned names and years, a woman from Okmulgee, another from Denver, one from Iron City. The first three he had buried in the grounds of the estate, but success came easy, the extra work seemed needless. Thereafter he simply turned the bodies over to the rats. No; he had not always used the same technique. He drove one of his brides to the castle, murdered her as she slept. In other cases, his technique was much like that employed on the latest victim. The obscurity of the victims, and his own reticence, were his best protection.

Yes; Fred was related to him, a half brother. Higgs had been hired more than twelve years before, included in the plan partly because of his physical defects. Higgs and Fred occupied the castle. Fritz went there eventually only to deliver the drugged brides.

Yes; he had always planned to get rid of Higgs and Fred when the need arose. No; his real name was not Fritz Hossner. Yes; the proceeds had been split—half for himself, half to be divided between Fred and Higgs.

"And you thought this would be a favorable opportunity to eliminate those two and to retire from activity?" Frost asked him. "The prize must have been unusually attractive. How much did the woman have? Five thousand? Fifty thousand? One hundred thousand?"

"Twenty-seven thousand dollars in bills. She did not trust banks," came the slow, stolid reply.

The man shifted slightly on his feet. Frost held the gun at his side, not troubling to keep it trained on the killer. The captive showed no emotion, no feeling, no regret. The crimes were only so much cash business so far as he was concerned. They served his perverted nature well and gave him an easy living.

Jean listened with a repugnance and loathing greater than anything she had felt, even over the rats, as he admitted the fiendish murders in a voice of brutal complacency.

The occurrences at 16 Logan Street had taken place just as Frost reconstructed them. From there, Fritz had gone direct to the castle. He killed the antelope and tossed it to the rats. He did not expect to be pursued, but he was taking no chances. He had long planned where to hide and what to do in case some one came to the castle in search of him.

It was incredible that Frost and the young woman had escaped from the cell. He had removed two bars from one of the smallest windows when he heard a crash and ran to the kitchen to find out what had happened.

"That is all," Frost abruptly terminated his questions. "Now we can be on our way."

The captive stepped forward.

"The other direction," Frost commanded.

The man moved—like a catapult, head down, hurtling straight on. Jean cried out, swung her automatic, knew in that fleeting moment that whether she fired or not, the hurtling body would still topple Frost into the pit. The professor neither side-stepped nor shot. There was no time for one and nothing to be gained by the other. Jean stared. One moment the professor had been standing—the next he was sitting on the floor, cross-legged; in some instantaneous fashion, his legs folded under him, he was down.

Hossner's head battered free space where Frost's shoulders had been, but Hossner's legs hit where Frost's shoulders now were. The killer went over head-first into the pit.

He uttered one bull-like cry before a sharp snap and a thud sounded from the cell underneath. Then there remained only the patter and scurry and squeaking and gnashing of hundreds of ravenous rats.

Sick, appalled, Jean looked away.

"Save your sympathy for a better cause. One is tempted to believe in cosmic justice," Frost remarked coldly. "The man was dead when he landed—that snap came from a broken neck."

Jean shuddered. "It's a pity he didn't live, if only to clear up the old murders."

Frost walked to the window, reached a hand out. "I can turn the dictaphone off now," he informed her.

He stopped the machine that he had suspended on suction disks outside and above the window, and returned carrying a small parcel.

Jean ventured: "And now how are we going to get out of here? Why can't we leave by the front or rear door?"

"Because if the front door is burst from its hinges, or bullets are fired through the clogged lock, the dynamite which I attached to the outside handle will explode. And if the rear door is opened, a weighted stopper will drop into the flagon of liquid air, and the clamps will then snap shut, holding it in place."

Jean frowned. "What of it?"

"Liquid air is a gas in an abnormal state. It constantly tries to return to its natural state by evaporating, expanding, and warming. In doing so, tremendous energy is released. Liquid air must be shipped and handled in uncapped flasks. A full flask will evaporate in a day's time. If the door is opened, the evaporation and expansion will almost instantly build up the pressure for a violent explosion."

He placed his parcel at the base of the door. "Wait in the dining room," he said.

He rejoined his assistant there a few seconds later.

"Now what? Some hard work prying or sawing bars out?" she asked.

Frost shook his head. "I left part of the dynamite with the dictaphone. I just lighted its fuse."

A dull boom came from the rear of the castle, followed seconds later by a second, sharper blast and splintering thuds.

Frost strolled to the kitchen, examined it with interested eyes. "I would like to have watched it," he said. "The dynamite of course blew the door out, and the explosion of the liquid air blew it back in."

Jean sighed. "It's uncanny the way you predict and prepare for what is going to happen."

"No," Frost answered, striding toward the spot where he had left the automobile. "I did not prepare for what was going to happen. A wise man does not prepare for a specific emergency. He prepares for all emergencies. A sequence of events occurred and was faced. If it had been any other sequence of events in the castle, it would have been met in other ways."

Jean kicked an unoffending pebble. There ought to be a way, she thought, or else there ought to be a law.

THE ARTIST OF DEATH

IT WAS A COLD, blustery morning, more like early winter than early spring. Gray clouds shrouded the sky. The wind whipped in from the Hudson. It whirled eddies of dust and bits of paper debris along the Drive. It blew around corners with great, irregular gusts that made walking hazardous. A man hiked after his gray fedora that skimmed away in long arcs like a jack rabbit. A woman started to turn the corner from State Street but the wind blew mightily. Her coat bellowed and she was forced back a few steps. She leaned against the wall of wind. It stopped blowing suddenly and she almost fell. She reached the turn and staggered weirdly as the wind yowled again.

The police car nosed along State Street and eased to the curb in front of Number 13. A blown sheet of newspaper slapped against the windshield, lay flat there for a moment under the pressure of wind, then peeled off and slanted away.

"Wait here, I'll be back in a few minutes," Inspector Frick ordered the driver. He climbed out and huddled his overcoat closer as the raw wind bore down. He hurried briskly toward the old mansion.

Inspector Frick was in no particular rush but he had a wiry appearance and a crisp, military stride that always made him seem to be in a hurry. He approached the door as though the wind drove him, or some urgent and important mission. But if it had been a mild day and if he didn't have a care in the world, he still would have hastened to the house in exactly the same manner.

Frick hesitated briefly before ringing the bell. After all, he had come, partly on impulse, with nothing of very great consequence to tell Frost. He might be disturbing the professor in some important work. Frost might be a little amused or a little annoyed at such an interruption, and the devil of it was that Frick never would know Frost's attitude. The professor, when he chose, which was almost constantly, could be as cold, impassive, and inscrutable as a sphinx, allowing no one a hint of what lay behind the enigmatic exterior.

The door swung open, silently. Frick shrugged as though relieved of a burden and entered. He hadn't pushed the bell, and there wasn't any one in the hallway. It had happened thus before, and it would doubtless happen again. Frick knew something of the precautions, and wonders of modern science with which the professor had protected his house, but each occasion impressed the inspector anew, and he took care to touch nothing, however harmless it seemed.

Another door, leading off the hallway, swung open without sound and Frick walked into the library room. "Good morning, Ivy—Hello, Jean," he added as the professor's assistant, Miss Moray, entered from the laboratory door.

Professor I. V. Frost was sitting sidewise in an armchair, his legs dangling over one arm, his back against the other. He didn't seem to be watching anything in particular and he looked vaguely bored. Most men would have found his assistant excitement enough, for Jean was young, beautiful in an exotic fashion, intelligent, and contradictory, but Frost ignored her as she gave a bright response to Frick's greeting.

His quick glance encompassed Frick, and he spoke with a certain detachment, in the purely observational manner of a statistician stating facts.

"I perceive that you still have monkeys on your mind. I would also hazard the opinion that the volume on the subject which you were unable to obtain at the library would not have proved helpful."

"Perhaps so," Frick conceded, "But I thought I might as well get a line on the different kinds. It's a queer business. It doesn't make sense. I don't suppose it's very important, but—the devil!" He looked perplexed. "What ever gave you the idea that I had monkeys on the brain or that I'd been checking up on them?"

"Nothing could be simpler," Frost remarked in an offhand manner. "Any one who reads the newspapers must have noticed the brief account in yesterday's papers stating that both police and the proprietor were puzzled by the actions of a thief who broke into the Acme Pet Shop and killed two baboons. There was a second item this morning to the effect that the body of an ape had been found in a vacant lot.

"When you entered this room, your glance was caught by an ivory monkey which you have seen dozens of times, but which, nevertheless, caused you to give a barely perceptible start. You frowned slightly and your left hand made a vague, unfinished motion toward your left coat pocket. There I observed the corner of a paper slip, with the letters 'i-c-k.' The slip is of the kind, color, and nature in use at the library call desk, and the letters suggest your name, 'Frick.' The inference follows that you called for a book which was either in use or already loaned, hence the slip was returned to you and you put it in your pocket."

The inspector said ruefully, "Right. The answers certainly do sound easy—after you've made them. I suppose I might as well just stand here without saying a word and let you tell me all the details of why I came and what's on my mind."

Frost shook his head. "Be seated and tell me about it. Deductive logic is a valuable tool at times, but like all methods, it has limits beyond which its usefulness does not extend. The time factor alone is its greatest weakness. Logic enables me to study you now and to infer certain truths concerning your current activities; but it would be worthless, except under extraordinary circumstances, for enabling me to determine what you had done a month ago, or what your views of the gold standard are."

"What is so puzzling about those anthropoids?"

Frick hesitated before replying. "I'm not sure that anything is. If you're busy, I won't bother you."

Frost waved him to a chair, but Frick remained standing. "I only intended to stop for a minute or two. You're right about the newspaper stories, but what the papers haven't printed yet is that four more apes were found dead in various places this morning. That makes a total of seven that we know of. There may be others."

The criminologist shifted position slightly. There was no apparent change of expression in his gaunt features, but he had developed a marked interest. Jean, scanning his impassive face from shaggy black eyebrows to hawk nose and stern chin, his thin face seeming fuller in three-quarter profile, decided that his eyes were a trifle less lackluster than they had been a few minutes ago. She kept a keen watch on his hands, but so far he had made no motion toward the box of special cigarettes which he invariably and continuously smoked, from the moment he became interested in a mystery to the minute when he had solved it, but at no other time.

"What are the details?" Frost asked.

Frick took some photographs from his pocket. "Here are a few pictures I had made of the last four when I got interested in the affair. The thing began night before last when somebody broke into the Acme Pet Shop and killed a couple of baboons. Owner claimed about two hundred dollars was missing from the cash register. We decided the apes started raising a rumpus and the burglar shot them so he could loot the place in peace.

"The third ape was found by some boys in a vacant lot last night. We don't know where that one came from.

"This morning, the keepers at the Whitney Zoölogical Gardens found that one of their three apes had been killed. The real massacre occurred in the spring quarters of the Haney Circus up at Ringdale. There they keep all the monkeys in a separate series of inclosed cages which look something like a rambling one-room house. The night watchman was slugged by somebody he never saw. When he came to and looked around, he found that three apes had been chloroformed and the biggest of the three knifed in a dozen places."

Frost mused, as he glanced up from the photographs that he had been studying, "Chimpanzee, baboon, and two mandrills. Did the first three apes resemble any of those in the pictures?"

Frick nodded and indicated one of the bodies.

"They were undoubtedly baboons," Frost stated.

The inspector asked, "What do you make of it? It's cockeyed, unless some nut on the subject is going around killing every ape he can find."

The professor straightened his long, thin form and looked at Frick with new intensity. "Was there any similarity in the nature of the killings, or the animals involved? Think of even the most obvious resemblances."

Frick said, "None that I know of except color. The dead animals were all dark brown or black. The first four were shot. The next two were chloroformed, and the last one was chloroformed and slashed."

"Do you happen to know if gorillas were kept at any of the different places involved?"

"I can't say for the others, but I did see one at the Haney quarters."

Frost remarked, "Good. What do you know about the two apes which were not molested at the Whitney Zoölogical Gardens?"

"Well, I only noticed them in passing, but I would say they were the same size, appearance, and color as the one that was killed."

Frost glanced at a photograph. "That's strange. If your memory is correct, the live ones are chimpanzees. What has happened to the carcasses?"

"Most of them have gone the way of the city garbage by now. There's a chance that the one in the Whitney Gardens won't be picked up until to-morrow morning. You think there may be more to this than appears on the surface?"

"It's too early to say. There are some interesting angles I would like to investigate. You may be right in your suspicion that this is the work of a crank, but suppose we visit the Whitney Gardens. Miss Moray, I will be back in an hour."

He slipped into a long ulster and pulled a battered old black fedora down over his forehead.

The wind whooped as they went out. Frick turned up his collar, but Frost seemed to be wrapped in meditations that made him oblivious to the weather.

They were halfway to the sidewalk gate when it opened and a stranger came through. He eyed the two men diffidently, looked hesitant as though of a mind to turn back, then asked, "Is one of you Professor I. V. Frost?"

Frost nodded his head. The stranger said, "I have an unusual request to make. It is really most unusual, but then, if you are busy—I could come back later—I would rather speak to you in private—"

The professor said to Frick, "Don't bother to wait. Meet me at the Whitney Gardens in a half hour if you like, otherwise I'll give you a ring at headquarters later."

"I'll be at the Gardens," Frick promised.

Frost studied the stranger with an oblique glance that seemed merely casual while they walked back to the house. Jean regarded them in surprise as they entered. The stranger was a nervous, emaciated individual of meek appearance. Pain burned in his eyes. He looked about forty-five, stood approximately five feet eight, and had a pale, tired face. Lines of worry creased his forehead. With his upper teeth, he continually chewed his lower lip.

The professor tossed his hat on a table.

The stranger eyed the girl with distinct disfavor. "I prefer to speak in private," he insisted in a worried voice that was not unpleasant.

Frost's disturbingly good-looking assistant smiled in ready acceptance and went out like an efficient secretary. The stranger seemed a bit relieved. What he did not know was that she had gone into the laboratory and pressed a button that accomplished two functions. It recorded every word of the conversation on a dictaphone, and also brought the speakers' voices to her through an earpiece. She had been with Frost for some months now, and was familiar with many of the electrical, photographic, photo-electric, and other devices that honey-combed the house at 13 State Street, but even she could not say that she knew them all.

When she left the library, the stranger fidgeted for a few seconds, stirred uneasily, and finally blurted, "I might as well get it out at once. I will pay you five hundred dollars to kill me."

Pure astonishment almost caused the girl to relax her hold on the earpiece.

II.

Frost countered with, "Yours is a peculiar request. Why do you make it?" He reached out a hand whose fingers, in striking contrast to the rest of his gaunt, unlovely figure, were slender and feminine in their beauty. He opened the container on a stand and picked up a cigarette that was longer and thicker than standard brands. He lighted it in the same continuous motion and exhaled a cone of fragrantly pungent smoke. His black eyes took on a brighter glitter. Like all great men, Frost was a neurotic, but one whose indulgences were designed to sharpen to their highest thin precision his already brilliant faculties.

The visitor said, "I can't tell you."

"You mean you won't tell me. Why?"

"Well, I won't tell you because I can't tell you."

Frost remarked, "You could go into any underworld hang-out and have yourself killed for fifty dollars, or even ten."

The stranger answered ambiguously, "That wouldn't do. It wouldn't be the same at all."

"Why do you come to me? Who sent you?"

"Nobody. I've read about some of your work. I only came as a last resort. I don't know of anybody else who could to the job just the way I want it."

"There is some particular manner in which you prefer to be killed?"

"Oh, no. Any way will do just so you make sure it can't possibly be considered suicide. Can you accept the offer?"

"No."

The stranger's face fell. "Isn't it possible? Couldn't you plan a perfect murder that could never be traced to you?"

"Of course. There are a dozen or more ways by which I could kill you without the slightest suspicion ever attaching to myself. I could arrange it to include a splendid motive and with clues pointing to some mythical person, or I could guarantee, if you wished, that the homicide would be absolutely and unquestionably classified as suicide."

The stranger looked more hopeful. "Is it a matter of money? I might be able to borrow a little, but five hundred is all I have to my name."

Frost drawled sardonically, "Many men have paid small or large sums for the death of other men during the course of centuries. Many others have paid heavily to avoid being killed. But your anxiety to purchase violent death is, I think, unparalleled in the history of crime. Who are you?"

The visitor hesitated, then gave an evasive reply, "Wouldn't it be better if you didn't know who I am? Then if you killed me and by some accident you were suspected, you could say you didn't know me."

"Perhaps. The difficulties of arranging the demise would, however, be immensely heightened by lack of knowledge about your life and habits."

The stranger thought this over. "That is so," he admitted. "I hadn't thought about the matter very carefully up to now. My name is Connaugh Wilder."

"That's a rather unusual name."

"It's partly Irish and partly German."

"What is your occupation?"

Wilder answered wearily, "I'm a clerk. With Gridley & Halsted for the past twenty years. No, I haven't embezzled any funds. Or at least nobody knows about it yet." The accountant became confused. "Do these details matter now? Can't you arrange it so that I could leave now or possibly you could come along with me and get the affair over with as soon as possible?"

If ever a man was in earnest, Mr. Connaugh Wilder was the prize example. He not only did not boggle at the prospect of his own deliberate, premeditated death by violence. He welcomed it and offered to pay in advance. He was eager to quench at once that precious flame of being which most people want desperately to keep to its last final flicker.

Frost lighted a new cigarette from the stub of the old. "Have you entertained the possibility of suicide?"

"Oh, yes, but I haven't the nerve. The sight of a gun makes me nervous. I simply can't kill myself. I want death to come without my expecting it or knowing it. I'm not at all well-known. I'm really a very unimportant person but if you manage the affair well I'll achieve a sort of posthumous fame as the victim of a perfect murder."

Frost asked, "Have you at any previous time tried to have yourself slain?"

"Only the past couple of days," Wilder admitted. He added as an afterthought, "I've been around killing apes."

If this statement was startling, or if it conveyed any hint of deeper significance, or aroused keener interest, not the flicker of an eyelash or the slightest change of expression was visible on Frost's face. Outwardly, he gave the same appearance of calm, impersonal attention, as though listening to a quite ordinary conversation.

The professor suggested, "I read something in the paper about two or three dead apes. Was that your handiwork?"

Wilder looked unhappy. "Yes. I killed seven altogether but it didn't work. I guess it was a crazy idea. At first I thought I would cause something of a mystery. Then I decided that if I was careless enough in doing the job, I might easily get shot and killed. But nothing happened. Nobody interrupted me. The watchman at the Haney place was asleep and when I made enough noise to wake him up I meant to hit him just hard enough so that he would think I was a desperate character and he would really shoot to kill but as it was I knocked him out. After that I decided they might catch me instead of kill me, and then they might think I was insane. Perhaps I am but I don't want people to think so."

Frost listened intently to the singular assertions of the man who wanted to be killed. The air was becoming misty with fumes.

Wilder asked anxiously, "You won't turn me over to the police, will you? And when can you arrange this thing?" There was an almost childlike trust in his manner.

"I have no intention of turning you over to the police," Frost assured him. "However, I wish to consider your offer carefully before I make a decision. Can you call at four this afternoon? No? Then leave your address and I will communicate with you later."

The criminologist continued his analytic study of the visitor as he scrawled on a piece of paper. No slightest detail of Wilder's dress or appearance escaped that probing glance. Yet the man was unaware of being scrutinized. When he rose, he ran fingers as thin as a bird's claw through his already disordered hair. He rubbed his sunken cheeks, and gnawed nervously on the little finger nail of his right hand. His actions were uncertain, disconnected.

"Stay here if you like," Frost urged. "I would suggest that you take a sleeping powder."

"No, No, I have a good many things to do. I must go," Wilder insisted and started for the door.

Frost walked into the hall with him. The professor stated cryptically, "Go straight to your house and wait there. When you hear from me, I believe you will change your mind about certain matters."

Wilder looked astonished for a moment. He opened his mouth, and chewed his lower lip but suppressed whatever he had begun to say. "Perhaps I will," he muttered, and walked across the stone porch. Frost was closing the door as he started down the steps.

Halfway down, he turned around. As he did so, his body jerked. Two bright fountains of red spurted from his neck. A *spat* sounded from near by. He opened his mouth, but this time he could not speak no matter how desperately he tried. Frost sprang to his side with a motion as swift as a panther's and caught his slumping body. He whirled him around and eased him back onto the porch. Wilder's eyes were already glazing, and there was neither pain nor terror in his face. Only sadness, and a kind of ghostly, dreamy gratitude dwelt on the dead features, as though the unknown murderer had done him a favor.

III.

Jean came running. Frost snapped, "The man is dead. Get the homicide squad. Call Frick at the Whitney Gardens."

His assistant vanished. When she returned a minute later, she found the professor deftly and swiftly finishing an inspection of the slain man's pockets. He straightened upright by the time two radio squads sped in quick succession toward the house. The wind whipped his hair, and whooped dustily across the porch, but he ignored its chill blasts. Jean shivered even in the coat which she had hastily wrapped around her when she came out.

Frost walked over to the left side of the porch and examined inch by inch the surface of an ornamental pillar. Jean shuddered in the momentary expectation that the sniper might shoot again, but Frost proceeded as calmly as though he knew exactly what events would befall.

The homicide detail sped into State Street while the prowl-car men piled out. Within five minutes, the street swarmed with police and the inevitable throng of the morbidly curious to whom violent death is a magnet.

Frost gave a staccato summary of the slaying. His coolness remained, but an intangible change had taken place. By the cold flame in his eyes, by the endless cigarettes whose glowing tips were whipped into showers of sparks by the wind, Jean knew that his faculties centered on a new and mysterious puzzle which he would abandon only when solved.

All the resources at his command, the tools of science and the weapons of logic, would shadow the criminal with implacable and relentless pursuit. The manifestation of those resources she would see in actions, she thought ruefully; but she would know nothing of the deductions that motivated them. Frost did not conceal clues or facts. He interpreted them in his own particular fashion, and kept silent until he could demonstrate their truth.

Obviously he was on the trail of a mystery with deep and fantastic windings, but what? She wondered whether he put any stock in the dead man's preposterous tale. Except for the murder itself, what was the significance of the case? Had Wilder told the truth about himself or were his statements irresponsible? If so, what could possibly be the real reason for the slaying of the apes?

Frost finished his brief résumé. "Miss Moray and I have a few things to do inside. Send Frick in when he comes. I'll give you any further details you want then." Without waiting for an answer to his crisp remarks, he hurried his assistant along with him.

"Time and speed are of major importance right now. This thing has already gone so far that we can't afford to sift out all the details." The words flowed automatically. His attention appeared to be elsewhere, but while his mind wrestled with some gnarled problem ahead, he told her what lay behind. "This is one case where investigation of some important phases must be left until after the mystery is solved. Call all the places in which apes were killed. Find out when and where they were obtained."

While Jean burned up the telephone wires, he took the *Who's Who* from its shelf and flipped it to the W's. Under *Wilder, Druo*, he found the notation: "Artist and painter . . . residence . . . single . . . brother, Connaugh, b. 1891. . . ."

He looked up a number in the directory and ordered his assistant to call the number immediately.

Jean tried, reported, "Operator says the line is out of order."

"Continue as before," came Frost's reply. He disappeared into his laboratory and was absent for several minutes. When he returned, Jean had completed her calls. She handed him a slip of paper. "The Animal Import Co. supplied all the apes except two at the Haney place. Those two were purchased more than a year ago from another concern. The Animal Import Co. delivered the others within the past week."

Frost ordered, "Get the company, find out how many apes they had a week ago and the sources of supply. Buy all that they now have in stock."

Jean stared at him in bewilderment, but obeyed instructions without protest. If Frost wanted to enter the wholesale market as a trader in the larger anthropoids, doubtless he could produce some excellent reason for an action that on the face of it seemed extravagant.

She put a call through and talked for some time. While the connection was still open, she informed him, "They had forty anthropoid apes a week ago, including a consignment of thirty-five brought back by the Ditzer Expedition. About thirty of these, for which orders had been placed, were shipped out immediately on arrival. The eight or ten remaining were bought yesterday by a Mr. Jones who paid cash and represented himself as the agent for several zoos. The only apes now in stock are a large number of monkeys. Do you want them?"

"No. Get a list of all the consignees."

Jean had just finished when the bell rang insistently. "That's probably Frick," she guessed, and the inspector strode in a few seconds later.

Frost said, "We haven't time to delay any longer. Miss Moray will give you the record of the dead man's conversation with me. Here is a list of all the places where apes have been shipped the past week. Some of them are out of town. Post a man at every one of these addresses in the city and get the cooperation of the police departments in the other cities. Wilder, the dead man, was the self-confessed killer."

Frick looked baffled. He asked dryly, "You want us to protect some apes from a dead man?"

The professor turned to his assistant. "If you aren't wearing your automatics, get them."

"I'm ready."

Frick protested. "But the dead man—Wilder—haven't you any clues about who killed him or why?"

"Just as many as you have. He was shot by a high-powered weapon, undoubtedly a rifle, from the ambush of a truck less than a block distant. The truck instantly drove off. Have your men question everybody in the district, but the day being what it is, I am afraid they will never find witnesses or any one who noticed the car. The bullet passed through his neck and severed the spinal cord. It ricocheted off a pillar. Judging from the angle of deflection, it now lies somewhere at the bottom of the Hudson."

"In other words, no clues?"

Jean handed the dictaphone record to the inspector and hurried after Frost who was already making for the door. Frick trotted out with them.

The professor said, "See what you can find in his pockets."

"They have already been searched. There was only the usual run of stuff—keys, wallet, letters, small change, receipts for bills, and personal papers. Plenty of identification, but nothing to help us much. We're starting a general check-up, of course, to find out if his books are in order and if he had enemies. But if we can't find the slug and don't locate witnesses who saw the actual shooting, we'll never be able to pin a thing on any suspect we might uncover."

Frost closed the issue. "Examine the evidence and have an autopsy performed. If I discover any new material, I will communicate with you at headquarters."

A minute later, he was driving his assistant downtown as fast as traffic and safety permitted.

IV.

For a while Jean kept silent in an effort to assemble a significant pattern from the haphazard, irrational, and seemingly irrelevant occurrence of the past hour. The harder she tried, the more confused she became, and the less relation she was able to discern between pieces which were mystifying by themselves. Finally she ventured, "It is rather a muddled affair, isn't it?"

"Not particularly. The structure is now plain, and all that remains to be accomplished is the capture of the murderer, after which the other details can be filled in." He kept his eyes on the road. In profile, his features looked harsh without specific expression. Whatever his deductions were, or wherever the trail led, he kept them secret.

Jean asked, "Did Wilder tell the truth?"

"He told part of the truth, concealed part of the truth, and added a few fictions. He spoke truthfully when he said he had been killing apes. He gave reasons that were false."

"He was not really sincere about wanting to pay to be killed?"

Frost snapped, "He could not possibly have been more sincere."

Jean, exasperated, added lipstick to an immaculate make-up, before insisting, "Why in the world would any one pay to be murdered?"

The professor had the answer. He always had the answer—several answers, she thought wryly.

"There are many possible reasons, among which I might enumerate six. First, he might be so tortured mentally or physically that death would be preferable. Second, he might sacrifice himself to save the life of another. Third, he might desire death, but own a life-insurance policy with a suicide clause. Fourth, he might be insane. Fifth, he might choose a novel method, by appealing in the right quarters, of ridding himself of an insoluble burden while at the same time calling attention to a greater problem which his death might unravel but which his life would complicate. Sixth, he might make the offer insincerely, for the sole purpose of drawing the person appealed to into an ambush, or into a framed murder charge. There are other alternatives, but these are the most obvious."

"Which is the real answer?"

Frost answered, with a faint, sardonic smile, "You ought to be able to deduce the true motive by taking into account the other crimes."

"The other crimes!" she exclaimed, startled.

"Certainly. It is obvious from the statements and evidence that at least one and possibly two other crimes must necessarily have been committed already. That is why speed is important. We must uncover those crimes, and forestall others by trapping the killer."

Jean prove skeptical. "What was there in anything Wilder said or anything that's happened so far to indicate another crime?"

The professor waited impatiently for a red light to change. "Connaugh Wilder was an obscure, unimportant man with almost no funds or resources. The name was unusual and suggested a somewhat better-known name, that of Druo Wilder. *Who's Who* proved that the two were brothers. Druo Wilder has made a reputation for his experiments in surrealism in painting. He is also an excellent painter of wild animal life and has been employed by a number of museums.

"Druo Wilder was single. That Connaugh Wilder was married was proved by a couple of letters in his pocket addressed to 'Mr. & Mrs. Connaugh Wilder.' If Connaugh Wilder or his wife became involved in trouble, their natural tendency would be to seek out Druo first of all. But it is less likely that they would be the object of criminal activities, than the older brother, the artist, who was better-known and better off.

"Furthermore, most of the dead apes were captured by the Ditzer Expedition. Such an expedition would be very likely to include in its personnel a photographer or a trained artist, or both, to depict wild animals in their natural setting. By proceeding with purely logical and rational methods, therefore, and on the basis solely of the information obtained from Frick and Wilder, we have arrived at the strong probability that Druo Wilder plays a more important part in this affair than Connaugh Wilder does.

"But the fact that it was Connaugh Wilder who appealed to us, and who has ostensibly been the key figure, offers strong evidence that Druo Wilder has already been attacked in some manner, and perhaps killed in the same cowardly way that Connaugh was shot. The inclusion of all possible alternatives permits the suspicion that Connaugh may have brought harm to his brother; but consideration of other factors, too long for detailed analysis now, eliminates that theory and returns us to an unknown killer who is still at large. It is more probable that Druo came to grief which enmeshed the obscure clerk."

Frost spun the wheel and drove into West Ninety-first Street.

Jean half wished that Frost would some day make a mistake, if only to prove that he was human. If only once the incisive, clear patterns that he deduced from the scantiest of information would turn out to be something else; if only once that brilliant mind, working with the cold and cutting accuracy of a micrometer precision instrument, would go astray, she would feel more at ease. It was irritating to be given the same material, the same information, the same clues, and to have the same opportunities that he had, but to make little or no headway with them. She admired the methods and faculty that set him apart. Still, being human and feminine and contradictory, she decided that she wanted him to make an erroneous deduction sooner or later. She glanced covertly at him.

"Perhaps I will," Frost abruptly spoke aloud, in enigmatic tones.

A little electrical tingle shivered through her. Had Frost's uncanny accuracy of observation, his hypersensitive powers of analysis and deduction, enabled him to answer her inmost thoughts? Had she betrayed her thoughts by gesture or expression? she studied his profile from the corner of an eye but found nothing to support or deny her speculations.

As though there had been no interruption in the general course of her thoughts, she asked, "What about the dead apes? You said that Wilder did not tell the truth in explaining his motives. What other reason could there be for killing apes? And why did you change your mind about buying apes?"

Frost retorted, "I did not change my mind. There were no apes available of the kind I wanted. Remember, Wilder was not killing lemurs, marmosets, or other small monkeys. Neither was he killing gorillas, nor all of the larger anthropoids, though he had the opportunity. True, he slaughtered two apes that had been with the Haney Circus for a year, but all the other carcasses had recently come from the Animal Supply Co. The inference is that he slew those two also because he could not distinguish them from the late arrivals.

"In the case of the Whitney Gardens, the deduction offers itself that he was able to detect the new addition, and killed only that ape. We are thus left with the further inference that he was slaying apes that came from a specific source, the Ditzer Expedition.

"Wilder killed apes that were larger than monkeys and smaller than gorillas—apes of the baboon, chimpanzee, and mandrill species, which all approximate four feet in length when full-grown. Why he did so remains to be proved.

"Aside from the reasons he gave, there are many motives for such an action. The apes may have carried the germs of a deadly, contagious disease. The killings may have served as a blind to detract attention from ulterior purposes. In the history of espionage, secret messages have been conveyed on stranger mediums than the skin of an ape."

"Which do you think is the explanation?" asked the young woman.

Frost said, "Here we are."

He halted the car in front of a narrow, three-story, brownstone house. A flight of six worn, stone steps led steeply up to a dilapidated double door that was unlocked. The wind rattled the mail box which contained a couple of letters. There was no card in the name slot under the single bell button.

Frost punched the button. A bell rang inside. They waited a few seconds and rang again, but obtained no response. Frost walked in. A small entrance lobby, scarcely more than four feet square, separated them from a massive single door. Frost tried it and found it locked. He took a group of blank keys from his pocket, selected one, and inserted it. He twisted it firmly and withdrew it. Jean peered at it and saw nothing, but Frost took a file and wore the notches down to the microscopic nicks his keen eyes must have seen.

Within three minutes he had the door open. A hallway led to a flight of stairs. Beside the stair case was a recess with a door at the end of it. A portiére opened off the hallway on their right at the front of the house. Utter stillness prevailed, a silence unbroken by even the ticking of a clock. The faraway, muted sound of passing automobiles, and occasionally a wail of wind, gave the curious impression of a background that emphasized the quiet.

Frost went through the closed curtains, Jean following in his wake. What had once been a comfortably furnished living room looked now as though vandals driven by vengeance or sheer lust to destroy had rioted through the place. Every chair was smashed to splinters, every pillow slashed and its stuffing strewn around. Vases, tables, and bric-a-brac lay in fragments. Even the walls had been mutilated.

Frost swept the room with a glance and plunged through another curtained partition in the right rear of the room. It led to a short passageway from the left side of which several doors opened. The first door exposed a dining alcove which had escaped unscathed. Frost rapped the table smartly as he passed. It gave off a metallic thump.

The next door opened to a small kitchen strewn with wreckage and debris. Flour, sugar, coffee, and a wide miscellany of foodstuffs littered the floor. Even the garbage pail had been dumped, and the old-fashioned ice box emptied of its contents. The vandals had missed nothing breakable in their destructive fury.

Again Frost took in the scene with a glance and hurried to the next room, a small lavatory which, like the dining alcove, seemed hardly to have been touched. The passageway ended in a door which he opened.

Jean gasped, while the professor towered in the doorway like a gaunt specter come for vengeance on the avengers.

The room looked immense, cathedralesque, because its only ceiling was the skylight roof three stories overhead. Two colossal, narrow windows rose a full thirty feet in the rear wall, windows curtained with drapes that swept to the floor. Paintings by the dozen hung on the walls and were tilted against the baseboards—paintings of living animals in their natural surroundings and of prehistoric monsters roaming through fantastic vegetation of the cycles before man. The majority were of recognizable objects, but other strange, morbid, wildly imaginative scenes suggested nothing so much as the irrational images of nightmare. A model's stand had been demolished. Odds and ends of débris lay scattered around. But the paradoxical note was supplied by the fact that none of the paintings had been harmed.

And the dreadful note was supplied by the corpse. Long dead, and with the ebb of life a dry, dark stain spread around the blackened hole in his head, the artist stared with wide-open, hellish eyes at the visitors he could not see.

V.

Jean stood motionless as Frost hurried into the studio and began a swift, penetrating examination of the corpse and its surroundings. Death always proved something of a shock, and death by violence held an added ugliness. The atmosphere, the silence, the eerie nature of the paintings, the body with its sightless eyes and rigid posture, momentarily shocked her to inaction. But she was not sure whether it was not Frost, most of all, who dominated and caused her reaction.

In the months that she had been associated with him, she had watched him solve difficult and gruesome crimes. She had seen him unravel murder with scientific and unerring methods whose all-inclusive scope left no chance for the criminal to escape. It was one thing, however, to start from a crime and proceed to its solution. What she now witnessed was an altogether different matter. Before Wilder had been murdered, Frost, solely from external evidence and statements, had deduced the existence of another crime, an undiscovered murder which he had promptly brought to light. The feat was an exhibition of rational genius which, more than any other single act of his, placed him in a category of his own in her estimation—a category separate from others, above others, and tinged with something of awe.

The spell snapped. She mentally damned herself for wasting thoughts. Frost was cold, almost inhuman, akin to the mathematician in his impersonal approach to problems. But she grudgingly admitted that she was only guessing. She didn't know. Nobody knew.

She forced herself to walk forward and look at the corpse. Death must have occurred a day or two before. A single shot had entered the brain above the right eye. The body lay in front of an easel which contained an unfinished canvas. The smock the artist wore, and the oil-color stains on his fingers, were testimony that he had been working on his last painting before the interruption that had ended in death. He looked superficially like the man who had visited them, but was older, partly bald, and far less emaciated.

Frost rose from a scrutiny of the corpse.

"What did you find?" his assistant ventured.

He replied, with an abstract air, "He has been dead about forty-eight hours. He was shot at the beginning of a struggle with his assailant. The murderer probed the death wound and extracted the bullet, before ransacking the house. At the time of death, Druo Wilder was convalescing from malaria. He had just returned from tropical Africa which he left about three weeks ago. The only other salient observations I care to make at this point are that the murderer stands approximately five feet ten, weights one eighty, has black hair, possesses tremendous physical strength, is a connoisseur of art but completely without scruples, is a deadly and accurate shot, familiar with all sorts of firearms, will commit murder again and again to obtain his ends, wears a nine shoe, and has blunt finger nails."

Questions sprang to her lips, but Frost had turned to stare intently at the unfinished canvas upon which the artist had been working at the time of his death. She moved to his side to get a better view. She saw now that what she had thought to be a canvas was in reality a painting on wood. The clamps of the easel gripped a large panel of natural mahogany, five feet by four feet in size, and a half inch thick. Upon this unusual base, Druo Wilder had painted a scene of bizarre and cryptic symbols.

A desolate, somber landscape swept to the far horizon. In the lower right foreground rose a clump of palmlike trees, from whose lofty fronds peered the simpering faces of naked men and women. At the base of the trees in a semicircle toward the lower left foreground sat eight white baboons, dressed in tuxedos, and peering sadly at a ninth baboon. The ninth baboon was buried from the waist down in the soil, and white like the others, but lacked a tuxedo. The right half of the visible body was human, the left half simian. In front of the rooted monstrosity lay a pile of coal, above whose top danced a pure flame. In the far background to the upper left rose the sun, enclosed in a glass cage, and giving the impression that it had been imbedded in a cake of ice. The whole fantastic landscape and figures were done in dull-grays, corpse-whites, dead-blacks, leprous-greens, and blood-reds.

Jean looked at other canvases laying around. Many of them exhibited the same crazy juxtaposition of unrelated objects, the same weird coloring and morbid imagination. Some of them looked as though the artist had simply put down whatever ideas emerged from the subconscious, without regard to their relevancy or unity. Others indicated a kind of deliberate opposition to reality, as in the case of two oarsmen who were rowing across a desert, while another painting depicted a nude girl swimming over a valley where a frying pan, two large fish-hooks, and a purple orchid rested on the ground.

She turned around, and was surprised to see Frost still standing in front of the unfinished wood panel, a frown of intense concentration on his features. For fully five minutes, he stood motionless as he stared with unblinking, unwavering, rapt attention at the scene.

Jean's own interest began to mount, not because the picture appealed to her artistic appreciations, though she granted it originality and talent of a macabre kind, but because Frost seemed to attach importance to it.

Of all the paintings in the room, it was the only one on wood. Did that fact have any significance? Did the scene itself have a deeper meaning than appeared on the surface? Had the artist attempted to convey a message in this last creative work he would ever do? Had fear for his life impelled him to leave a pictorial message, but in such veiled manner as to be hidden from the comprehension of the murderer, but apparent to some one who knew him well? Had Connaugh Wilder seen the painting? Like a flash it came to her—the nine apes; Connaugh had killed seven. But Frost said the Ditzer Expedition had brought back thirty-five apes. The sun inclosed in a glass cage—that might symbolize the bars of a menagerie, inclosing something that was never meant to be shut up. And why was the ninth baboon, the half-human, half-anthropoid monstrosity, rooted to the soil? She abandoned speculation at this stage. She decided that she would have bad dreams enough anyway, and if she thought about it much longer, she might become a good companion for the squirrels.

Frost suddenly snapped out of his reverie. "Wait here until Frick and the homicide squad arrive. I'll report the murder from the nearest phone. After they come, go to Gridley & Halsted, find out what you can about Connaugh Wilder's employment there, and find out especially what was the last day he worked. Then go to any newspaper morgue and see if you can obtain a picture or pictures of all members of the Ditzer Expedition. Ask Frick if any more apes have been killed, and if so, when and where. Stay away from 13 State Street. When you're through, wait for me at police headquarters."

Without a backward glance, the professor hastened from the room. Jean noticed, as he departed, that he still wore an air of abstraction and concentration. She heard his footsteps in the passageway, then the bang of the front door.

The muted silence, with the distant sounds of traffic and city noises seeming miles away, got on her nerves the moment Frost departed. She caught herself staring with morbid intensity at the corpse, half as though she expected it to move. The corpse stared back at her with dead, questioning eyes. She shifted her gaze to the wood painting, and studied it until she felt as if she were being drawn into the swirl of nightmare realms.

She listened, listened, staining her ears and unconsciously tautening for the pounding sounds that would announce the arrival of the police. Somewhere she fancied she heard a board squeak, and she jumped nervously, looking around. She backed away a trifle from the dead body. She hummed the Brahms "Lullaby" softly, but the song disturbed the silence curiously, and her voice broke after a few measures, dying away to stillness. She felt ill at ease and longed for the arrival of the homicide detail.

The indirect lighting of the room, whose illumination Frost had turned on when he entered, cast a soft glow which became secretive in the corners. She fancied shadows that did not exist, and imagined things where there was nothing. She wanted to succumb to an impulse to leave and wait for the police at the front door. She suppressed it because Frost had told her to wait here. He might not have meant this exact spot, but his orders were to be obeyed literally.

The stillness had a ghostly quality, as though the room had partaken of the mysterious borderlands, rooted deep in the subconscious, from which the artist had plucked fantasies for his enigmatic paintings. There was something both incongruous and yet oddly appropriate in the presence of the corpse here. Her imagination began to run riot. She had a creepy feeling that the artist was dead, but that his mind and thoughts lived in the paintings he had left. She stared anew at the last work as though it were indeed the enduring essence of the dead brain.

She was peering at that painting when the lights went out. A timeless and stifling terror welled up within her for the flash of an instant, but even if that immeasurably brief paralysis had not frozen her, she would not have had a chance.

A long, hairy, and powerful arm wedged her neck as in a vise. She clawed. Her finger nails gouged out skin and flesh, raked long scratches from which the blood came. That grip never relaxed. She tried to twist and squirm. She could see nothing, through dimming vision, of who or what held her. She kicked backward, furiously, again and again. The sharp heels of her shoes cut and dug and slashed at the attacker. She struggled for breath, but no air came. Fiery dots began to flicker against a swirling darkness. She swung both knees up in a desperate effort to clutch the automatic that nestled in a special holder on her right thigh. The action only brought all her weight on her neck, and her fumbling arm hung limp.

VI.

Frost raced out of the house toward his car but stopped and swept the street with a glance in both directions. A drug store occupied the nearest corner, slightly less than a half block away. He sprinted for the store, his coat flapping in the wind behind him, a shower of sparks flying from the tip of his cigarette.

"It's pity some folks don't break their necks," muttered a vinegary breeder, fat and forty, as Frost sped by.

A chap bucking the wind, head down and not bothering to give leeway to an approaching postman, swore irritably when a lean specter slid through the margin, dodged in front of him, and ran on while his flapping coat snicked the irritable one's hat off whence it sailed along the street.

Frost vanished into the store and into a phone booth. He dialed for the operator, "Police headquarters!".

He got the connection in seconds. "Is Inspector Frick in? . . . Get him off the other wire and onto this. . . . I don't care how important it is, tell him Frost is calling. . . ."

He opened a pocket case without drawing it out, removed one of the pungent cigarettes with nimble thumb and forefinger, plucked the stub from his mouth with middle and forth digit, inserted the fresh cylinder, and lighted it from the old. The motion was continuous. He crushed the butt underfoot. Acrid smoke poisoned the air in the booth. Frost inhaled with relish and sniffed the air with as much appreciation as if it were the purest breeze across a field of clover. But his knuckles beat an impatient rhythm on the edge of the telephone board.

Frick's voice suddenly came through, "Sorry to keep you waiting but we just got another line on the monkey business. Three more dead apes were found dumped behind some trees below the retaining wall on upper Riverside Drive."

"What!" Frost exclaimed.

"What's more," Frick went on, "one of them appears to have been pretty badly cut up. Damn it all, Frost, what the devil is the meaning of these crazy killings? Why pick on apes?"

"How long have they been dead?"

"How do I know? The report just came in from one of the park patrolmen who found them."

"Give me the approximate location and I'll take a look at them. Here's another murder for you to look into. My assistant and I just found the body of Druo Wilder at his——"

It was Frick's turn to be startled. "What! Why, the men have already checked up on Wilder's apartment and nobody was home. Then they——"

Frost cut him short, impatiently. "I know, but this is Connaugh Wilder's brother, and it's a different address. Take it down. . . . Send the homicide detail over and come yourself. My assistant is waiting there and will explain the circumstances. The man has been dead about forty-eight hours. I don't expect to be on hand when you arrive but I'll get in touch with you later."

He hung up for a few moments, then dialed another number. He got a connection with E. H. Wallace, city editor, brushed preliminaries aside, and asked, "What do you know about Richard Ditzer, the man who just returned from a hunting expedition?"

Wallace appeared surprised by the query. "Why, he's a quiet sort of chap in the fifties. One of the directors of the Anthropological Museum. Financed the last trip partly out of his own pocket. Why?"

"What does he look like?"

"Stands about five feet eleven; grizzled iron-gray hair; rather studious-looking; weighs around one hundred and fifty; walks with a slight stoop——"

Frost broke in. "That's sufficient. Do you know him well? Well enough to vouch for him?"

"Absolutely. He has independent means and makes a hobby of the museum thing. He's on the boards of several charities, and is as square as they come."

Frost closed with, "Thanks. I need some information and time is so valuable that I've got to take short cuts. I'm going to get him on the phone, in case he calls you back as a check-up."

Wallace's incipient question went unheard as Frost rang off and put through another call. Time dragged while he waited for Mr. Ditzer to be located in the halls of the museum. Less than a minute actually elapsed before he got his man.

The moment he introduced himself, Ditzer replied, "Professor Frost? You are the criminologist, are you not? I should indeed be happy to make your acquaintance at your convenience."

Frost hurriedly interrupted. "I will call for a few minutes to-morrow afternoon. In the meantime, I am anxious to obtain some information that I believe you are in the best position to supply. Who sponsored the expedition?"

"Well, it was a loose sort of thing. The museum paid for our passage. I financed all other expenses such as hiring native porters, miscellaneous costs of gathering and shipping specimens, and so on, which were directly relevant to our work. Mr. Gairth, who captures wild animals alive for different circuses and zoos, joined our party to assemble a supply of monkeys and anthropoid apes. A friend of his, a big-game hunter named Gensel, also joined the expedition. We three did all the financing."

"How many members comprised the party?"

Ditzer replied, "Eight," and named them, adding, "We jointly assumed the expenses of Druo Wilder, artist and photographer of the expedition."

Frost did not enlighten him as to the fate of the artist, but asked, "What route did you follow?"

"Why, we landed at Cape Town and made our way north through the Transvaal and Rhodesia, on to Tanganyika, then west into the Belgian Congo and northwest to the Gold Coast, Liberia, and Sierra Leone. The whole trip lasted four months."

"Did you happen to notice whether the tropic sun had any noticeably bleaching effect on members of the party?"

Ditzer's voice carried his puzzlement. "That is a curious question. Of course, we all got pretty tanned, but as for bleaching—no, I didn't notice particularly. We were all more or less blond types, except Gairth, Gensel, and young Walkner from the museum here. They are dark in hair and complexion, but I can't say I noticed any change. No, I'm afraid I can't answer the question."

Frost had a thin smile, as he inquired, "Did the party stay together?"

"Why, naturally it did. We joined forces to cut down expenses."

The professor asked patiently, in the same urbane tone, "I assume that the party functioned as a unit, but I wondered whether there were side trips en route, or whether it didn't occasionally break up for a day or so into two or three groups in order to cover more ground?"

Ditzer acquiesced. "I see what you mean. Why yes, we often worked that way. Sometimes Gairth would go off to bag apes while I went elsewhere for botanical specimens. Gensel disappeared for three days with Wilder at one point and they came back with films and some rare specimens of eland, fennec, and quagga.

"The longest separation occurred between the Transvaal and Tanganyika. Wilder decided that it would be easier to film and sketch wild-animal life with a minimum of followers. He took three of the black boys and trekked east. He was gone for a week and we were all getting pretty worried when he finally returned with some sketches and mandrills. The country there is unmapped, practically unexplored, and rather rough. After that, we decided against long absences."

Frost's eyes glittered brightly. "Did you have any trouble with your wild cargo?"

"No more that usual. It became something of a job to manage the monkeys and apes, but we had plenty of porters. The apes kept up a terrific chatter. One of them yowled for several days. It had injured itself and we talked about letting it free, but it recovered and stopped whimpering. I shouldn't ramble on like this. Do the details of the trip interest you? By all means, drop in and I'll be glad to reminisce.."

Frost persisted, "Just one more question. You all left Africa at the same time?"

"Well," Ditzer admitted, "most of us sailed on the same boat. But Wilder came down with malaria when we got to the Gold Coast. We were going to bring him back with us, but decided it would be better if he waited a few days till the crisis passed, when he had more strength. Gensel and Walkner agreed to stay behind and see that he had proper medical attention. There was another boat a week later. So the majority of the party and all the specimens came back on one boat. Gensel, Walkner, and Wilder returned after us."

"Sorry, sir, but your time is up. Five cents more, please," came the lilting voice of the operator.

"Thank you," Frost interrupted Ditzer's flow and soothed central. "Yours has been a most interesting account. I'll call on you to-morrow. In the meantime, do not mention our conversation to any one."

He hooked the receiver and dashed from the booth. His gaunt figure emerged like a specter from the fog of smoke.

He raced back to his car and was jerking at its handle when a radio patrol slid around the next corner. Frost glanced at the house. As though sprung from a catapult, he leaped across the sidewalk and took the stone steps in two bounds. The inner door halted him but an instant before his self-made key turned.

His eyes narrowed and his face was a mask as he plunged through. He sniffed with flaring nostrils while he dashed across the living room and into the connecting passageway. His long legs sped him on and into the studio.

Jean Moray lay in a huddled heap between him and the corpse of Druo Wilder. The last painting of the artist had vanished forever into the destroying flame of the turpentine that had been poured over it and lighted.

VII.

Catlike, Professor I. V. Frost dropped to his knees and accomplished three simultaneous actions. He listened for the beating of the woman's heart. His sensitive, agile fingers felt for a pulse in her wrist. His eyes probed the burning oil panel. Nothing remained of the weird painting. The wood itself, and the easel, gave off thick smoke and the red tongues of a hot fire.

He whisked a tiny hypodermic needle from his pocket, filled it with calculating glance to an exact level from a phial that he unstoppered, and plunged it into the girl's breast. He listened again. The stilled heart suddenly gave a great, convulsive beat, raced irregularly, then settled down to a deep, steady throb far stronger than normal as the adrenalin took effect.

The professor rose and caught up a scatter rug which he tossed over the easel. He beat various burning parts until the flames subsided to a glow that would slowly char out. His eyes searched the room and analyzed the floor and the unconscious girl.

Footsteps stomped from the front of the house, whose door he had left open.

Frost returned to Jean Moray. He watched the flutter of life in her eyelids, saw the red weal, rising like a band around her throat. He slipped a wax envelope from his pocket. With a nail file he deftly removed certain tiny bits of evidence from her finger nails. Those fractional specimens of skin, hair, and blood would be sufficient to convict her assailant.

Her eyes opened and she was struggling to arise when Frick and the homicide detail burst into the room.

Jean mumbled, in a dreamy whisper, "What happened? I was far away—floating off in darkness—I was so cold—and I saw——"

Frick barked, "What in Hades does this mean, Frost?"

Frost said, dryly, "Ask the man who staged it. It obviously signifies that the murderer returned for reasons of his own, that he was in the house when we arrived, and that when I went out to telephone he strangled Miss Moray and set the painting on fire. This is one instance where the time element and the need for swift action defeated their own purpose. I had no time to make a complete search of the house, and as a consequence, the murderer escaped, temporarily."

Whatever annoyance he had felt had passed. Things done were done. Jean knew that he never wasted time on regrets. A new problem had taken the place of the old, with one more score to settle.

The fingerprint expert, the cameraman, the medical examiner, efficiently went about their work. Frick looked puzzled. "Why would he go to all the bother of burning a picture?"

The professor answered, "Try infra-red photography. It may bring out some portions of the painting, though I fear it has been totally destroyed."

"What's the connection between this murder and Connaugh Wilder?"

"That is what must be established."

Frick shook his head. "The whole thing is crazy. Connaugh must have been out of his head. We played the transcript of your conversation. 'I will pay you five hundred dollars to kill me.' Baloney. And this business of killing monkeys—"

"Apes," Frost corrected him.

"—is sheer insanity. And where does this tie in? I don't get it. On top of all that—by the way, I didn't tell you when you called in. After we searched Connaugh's place, and couldn't locate his wife, we sent out a description of her from a couple of photographs we found. She was picked up about an hour ago sitting on a bench, of all places, in a lonely part of upper Central Park. She was out cold, doped, and they haven't succeeded in bringing her around yet. What have you got to say to that?"

"Excellent!" Frost exclaimed. "Splendid!"

The inspector bristled. "Look here, Frost—"

The criminologist stopped him with "Save it. I have no doubt that you will obtain nothing from Mrs. Wilder when she regains consciousness. Her story will be that she was lured from her home two nights ago by a telephone call telling her to hurry to a certain corner where her husband had been injured in an automobile accident. She will insist that she went there, and that is the last she remembers. Her story will be entirely true. I said excellent, because finding her eliminates a step and some necessary calculations from my own investigation." He did not offer to elaborate further.

The inspector eyed him critically. A mixture of reactions ranging from curiosity to utter mystification played across his features. "Suppose you—"

Frost asked the girl, "All right, now?"

She struggled to her feet and gingerly felt her throat. "I—I guess so." Her voice had a husky, raw edge to it. She herself looked surprised at the froglike croak which had replaced her once musical tones.

Frost propelled her toward the passageway.

"Wait a minute," Frick objected.

"Can't stop now. Too much to do and not enough time to do it all," the professor retorted. "Have your men cover the street. It's possible that some one saw the attacker come out and you might get a description of the man. I presume you already have some one constantly beside Mrs. Wilder to take down anything she may say when she regains consciousness. Search the house carefully. There may be clues. If it will prove of any help, this is an accurate description of the burned painting."

He gave a quick description of the scene and departed, leaving behind him some energetic members of the homicide squad, plus one baffled inspector who was becoming fidgety every time any one mentioned the word "ape."

The professor drove toward 13 State Street. Jean complained groggily, "I can't think clearly. He got me from behind. I didn't even get a glimpse of him. All I remember is waiting, with that dead th-thing staring at me and then suddenly the—the arm—"

Frost drawled, in acid tones, "Your voice will be all right in a day or so."

Jean stiffened and spoke hotly through clenched teeth. "I practically get my neck broken and—"

Frost interrupted harshly, "Your beautiful neck will also lose the bruise in a day or two. Really, Miss Moray, you should not let a trifling incident upset you so."

The flame of fury whitened her cheeks and brought a blaze to her eyes. The webs in her brain blew away. At that moment she hated Frost, hated him so violently that everything else was stripped from her thoughts. There remained only the clear, crystallized thought that she hated him.

In a voice quivering with rage, she whispered huskily, "If that is all you have to say, you can let me out here and now. My resignation is effective at once."

The professor smiled in an odd, satisfied sort of way. "Stern measures were necessary, but they sufficed," he placidly commented.

Jean Moray had her hand on the door. "This corner is as good as any."

Frost said, "Sit still. Your usefulness is restored. The fastest way to calm your nerves and bring you out of a daze was to stimulate a violent emotion in you. I regret the measures but I approve of the results."

She protested bitterly, "You'd think I was a brass monkey or something the way I get—"

Frost turned, stared at her with glittering eyes. He shouted in a voice of almost uncontrollable excitement, "A remarkable inspiration! A brass monkey! A stroke of genius! Just the words I wanted! Miss Moray, you are positively brilliant!"

Her cheeks had been white, but now a rush of color added a hectic quality to her beauty. She struggled for words, shook with anger. Her lovely lips parted, and her teeth gleamed as though she would bite. She snapped her head up, and the long lashes of her eyes flew wide open as she glared at him. "Professor Frost, nobody—"

But the violence of her resentment subsided in the presence of the energy that flowed from Frost. It lasted but an instant, that momentary flash of insight and knowledge, yet it overwhelmed her with its irresistible conviction of truth. She knew that she had made some contribution of priceless value to his speculations. She did not know how, what, or why, but she felt mollified in spite of herself.

He deftly swung the car into a space that seemed inadequate, and cut off the ignition.

"Do we get out here?"

His cool, inscrutable surface had returned. "We are going," he answered, "upon a tour of the art galleries."

"Of the art galleries?" she echoed.

"By proxy, so to speak. We will take adjoining booths in this drug store. You will commence with the A's and call every art shop, gallery, and museum in the borough, while I commence with the M's. You will ask each one what paintings or other work of Druo Wilder they have on exhibit, and keep a record of the answers."

VIII.

The Allerton Art Museum possessed a nude in oil by Wilder. The Carter Galleries offered two water colors and a landscape. A group of animal studies was owned by the Daw Foundation for the Preservation of North American Fauna. Jean had gotten to the Eblin Collections, which listed a number of Wilder prints and etchings. She was about to call the Edgeworth Gallery when Frost pushed the booth door open and told her to hang up.

His eyes gleamed with satisfaction and by the keen zest of his attitude she knew that the trail had taken a new twist that raised still further problems.

"We're on our way to the Paris Studio," he explained as he hurried her toward the door. She stopped to order a couple of sandwiches and got outside just in time to jump in beside Frost as he started the car. She offered him one of the sandwiches but he could not be bothered. A problem and cigarettes were sufficient for his needs.

"The end is near," he prophesied. "I ran into a bit of luck though it wouldn't have made the slightest difference. The woman I talked to wanted to know if I was the gentleman who had called a few minutes ago.

Naturally, I said I was. She explained then that she was wrong when she said the studio was closed for the night. She had since consulted the director, who would be pleased to keep the studio open late, or who would open it this evening if I wished to make an appointment. Tell me what you deduce from this information."

Jean hastily swallowed a mouthful of tomato and lettuce. "Well," she began slowly, "I don't see that there's anything to connect the two calls."

"Quite the opposite," said Frost. "It would be stretching coincidence altogether too far to believe that an innocent person just happened to telephone the same place at almost the same time for the same reasons that we did. No, I think we may safely infer that the murderer was off on the wrong track, that he returned to the scene of his crime for another survey of the painting, that he deciphered the riddle, and that he then destroyed the painting in order to check pursuit. We may further conclude that he is becoming desperate, that haste is as imperative for him as it is for us, and that he will not wait until to-morrow before paying a visit to the Paris Studio. The work of Wilder on display there is merely a loan exhibit, and not for sale. All the more reason why the killer is likely to show his hand to-night."

"Who is the murderer?"

"You mean the murderer and accomplice."

His unexpected reply shifted the trend of her thoughts. "And what gives you reason to believe there are two of them?" she demanded, a trifle truculently.

Frost remarked, "If I were shadowing a man, and that man might at any moment commit an action that would endanger my life, I would be prepared to act before he did. In a crowded city, I would not risk an open affray. I would have a small closed truck, driven by my partner in crime. From the interior of that truck, with a high-powered rifle equipped with a silencer or not, I would be ready to shoot the victim. But I would not shoot him while he was accompanied by a criminologist and an inspector of police. I would suspect him of betraying me, but I would wait until he came out alone. Then I would follow him to either a very crowded or a very lonely spot, unless I had urgent reasons for speed, in which case I would shoot him immediately."

It was well for society that Frost indulged in the solution of crime rather than the creation of it, Jean thought. With his talents, he could have been an international menace.

The professor continued, "Yes, I should venture to say that the most recent incident entitles us to several deductions and explains certain small points that were not without interest."

"Such as?" she prompted.

"I had been wondering how Druo Wilder, in spite of the fact that he was closely watched, managed to rid himself of something either dangerous or valuable."

Jean protested, "How do you know he had any such thing? How in the world can you possibly say that he was shadowed?"

Frost went on placidly, "The explanation is absurdly simple. I really should have deduced it some time before this. Druo Wilder simply telephoned the Paris Studio and arranged to have them pick up some items for exhibition. He then left his home and his enemy followed him. While both were gone, the Studio representative arrived and collected the package or packages which Druo had left in the vestibule. Simple, ingenious, and effective. I regret his demise exceedingly. He must have been a person with a clever, distinctive, and no doubt, eccentric mind."

Jean sighed inwardly. Frost was clearing up some points that she had not even known existed. "What else is solved?" she asked in a slightly piqued tone.

"We are now positive of what we only suspected—that Druo Wilder did indeed convey a message in his last painting. There again he was most ingenious. He possessed something which he did not intend to surrender. A demand had been made of him and he had refused. He knew that the demand would be made again, and that he might be killed. He decided to leave a pictorial message that would be more or less meaningless to the murderer and to other people, but whose significance would be apparent to one person. That person would naturally be his brother, Connaugh, who could be presumed to understand the way in which Druo's mind worked.

"Druo, therefore, adopted a novel method of conveying the message. Instead of writing it, he painted it. Instead of hiding it, he left it in open sight. Instead of making it small and obscure, he made it gigantic. Instead of leaving it in portable form, he left it on a huge and unwieldy panel of hard wood. If the murderer attempted to carry off so enormous a thing, he would draw the curiosity of every one he encountered and seal his own death warrant. He would need a good saw to reduce the painting to manageable proportions, and we may be sure that Druo left no such useful tool at hand. There would, furthermore, be not one chance in millions that the murderer would have such an instrument on his person. It was clever, damned clever. I feel a personal grievance against the murderer for depriving me of the potential company of a most unusual mind."

Darkness had begun to shroud the city. A fine sleet lashed by the wind stung the faces of pedestrians and made driving perilous. Frost brought the car through the rush of late afternoon traffic and berthed it near the Paris Studio.

The art gallery proved to be on the second floor of an old five-story building.

Frost took the walk-up flight of stairs three at a time. The only door on the landing opened into a comfortable, quiet room of considerable size, occupied by a variety of paintings and art objects, a bespectacled young woman at a desk who poked the keys of a typewriter with disinterest, and a fussy little man. The gentleman looked about forty-five, somewhat stout, and completely impractical. He wore a black toupee and clasped his hands tightly as though he feared one of them would wander off.

The professor conversed in low tones with Mr. Paris Studio, who fussed all over the place. He seemed to be objecting to something with a degree of asperity. Frost did some animated talking. Mr. Paris Studio suddenly began to beam, and finally nodded his head with such vigor that his toupee, unfortunately, slid down over his forehead to the great detriment of his dignity. He then trotted over to Miss Typist and whisked her into her coat.

He trotted back and shook hands with Frost with a singular jerkiness not unlike that of a dying piston in its last gasps. This quaint person then hastened over to Miss Moray, bowed weirdly, and announced, "I am delighted to have made your acquaintance, Miss Moray. Make yourself quite at home. Good day."

"You have done nothing of the sort," she thought, but Mr. Paris Studio was already bounding out with the haphazard typist in tow.

Frost seemed amused.

"What ever did you do to him?" Jean asked.

He chuckled. "I merely introduced myself and stated that I desired to have the run of the place to-night. I told him that an attempt at entrance might be made. He became disconsolate at the prospect of losing prospective purchasers, which he assumed we were. I placated him by commissioning him to purchase a Brueghel wood print which I have long wished to add to my collection. I then engaged him in a discussion of the comparative merits of Gaugin and Modigliani, who of course have nothing in common. When I remarked that Modigliani was the greatest artist of modern times, which he is not, but which Mr. Calyppi thinks he is, our host fairly overflowed. He departed, convinced that we are the only two real appreciators of art in America."

He studied the layout of the gallery. "Ah, the beauties!" he exclaimed, pausing in front of a tall display case that stood against one wall.

The "beauties," Jean thought, were about as repulsive as any work of art she had seen in a long while, but the moment she looked at them, she knew they were tied up somehow with the dark windings of the puzzle. How they tied up, or what their significance was, she could not say, but she appraised them with sharp interest. They were grotesque, stylized in a monstrous fashion, suggestive of savages and the jungle, utterly bizarre. In their deliberate exaggerations and frank symbolism, their cynical lines and artificial distortions, they achieved sophistication from elemental tribal beliefs of a kind alien to the Western world.

Upon the three shelves of the show case squatted nine black images, sculptured in wood. Eight of the strangely fascinating figures were definitely anthropoidal and Negroid. The ninth was a perverse and malignant thing, neither ape nor human; a flight of imagination into the dawn of history; a creature low in the scale of evolution, and vaguely akin to Neanderthal man. All nine statuettes were carved of polished ebony.

A card in the window announced: "Loan Exhibit of African Primitives by Druo Wilder."

IX.

Frost made a quick tour of the gallery rooms which occupied the whole of the comparatively small floor. He returned in a minute and decided, "We will concentrate our defense here, since this room will be the object of attack. I would prefer more elaborate preparations, but I believe a trifling item or two in my car will serve our needs."

"Tell me what you want and I'll get it from the laboratory," she offered.

"No, the presence of both of us is essential. As it is, I regret the necessity of leaving you for even a few minutes. Be on guard, but I believe there is no immediate danger."

There would be no more attack from behind, she decided as she took a position in the corner. This time she kept her automatic ready. Frost locked the room when he went out. She concentrated on the other door in the rear of the room. Nervous apprehensions filled her, but nothing happened until Frost tapped on the door.

He brought a few things with him, and occupied himself for some minutes in various parts of the room. When he had finished, he again paused in front of the display case and scrutinized the little black demons. "What do you think of the beauties?"

Jean promptly retorted, "I suppose they're art, but if they're beautiful, I'm Venus. I'd hate to have them around."

"Beauty is more than a matter of superficial appearances. Which line of argument, if we carried it far enough, would bring us to the old metaphysical proposition of whether beauty is objective or subjective," Frost mused.

He gave the room a last survey. "Everything would appear to be in readiness. Before I turn the lights out, I would suggest that you take a position near the door to the adjoining room. I will——"

Footsteps tramped up the staircase to the accompaniment of a badly whistled popular song. Frost listened, frowning.

The footsteps continued up to the first landing and stopped at the entrance door. The whistle ceased. Then came a loud pounding.

"Who is it?" Frost called out.

"Telegram! Telegram for I. V. Frost!"

"Our friend Calyppi must have something on his mind," Frost murmured to his assistant. He walked to the door and opened it a crack, still frowning. There was no doubt of the authenticity of the messenger. He wore the regulation uniform, had the customary receipts, carried a couple of other telegrams, and bore the indefinable stamp which characterizes all telegram messengers.

"Telegram for I. V. Frost," he repeated. "Sign here."

Frost signed, watched him turn about and descend the stairs. He closed the door and started to open the message, still frowning. His face suddenly changed and he whirled about.

"Put 'em up and keep 'em up!"

For a minute, sick with self-criticism, Jean thought of taking a chance and turning around with the automatic that she still held. But Frost's hands were high, and he curtly told her, "Do as they say."

The automatic dropped. She faced about.

Two men stood in the rear doorway, with automatics trained on both Frost and his assistant. The heavier of the two stepped inside. His companion closed the door behind them.

The leader jeered, "Everybody falls for a trick some time or other. If you want to find out if anybody's home, send a telegram. Better still, wait on the fire escape and come through while they're busy with the telegram. Nice dodge, eh? Too bad you'll never have a chance to use it yourself."

Jean paled at the obvious implication. Frost seemed unperturbed. "Really?" he drawled. "Perhaps you flatter yourself."

"Shut up!" the leader snapped. "Both of you line up by the wall. Be quick about it, too."

Frost calmly moved to the side of his assistant.

The leader barked an order to his companion. "Get the thing. It's in the display case. The one that looks like an ape."

He kept the two covered while his partner walked over to the case. The second man opened the door and stooped to pick up the ninth primitive. He kept on stooping. He stooped all the way to the floor and lay there, still, inert.

The dark eyes behind the mask of the leader blazed savagely. "Some more of your damned tricks, Frost? All right. Take your own medicine. Go over and get me that statue."

"Anything to oblige," Frost replied. He strolled to the case, bent over, and lifted the little monster. "What would you like done with it?"

The burglar stared. The glitter in his eyes remained, but he was not so cocksure, now, not so boastful of his prowess. "Set it on the table. Then go back where you were."

Frost obeyed, leisurely. He did not go quite as far as the position he had previously occupied. He rocked on his heels. "May I offer a suggestion?" he asked in a mocking voice. "I would suggest that you start shooting at once."

The killer's glare held murder but he replied cunningly. "Oh, no you don't. I know something about you, Frost. It'd be just like you to fix up some way of striking back even after you're dead. I'll just make damned sure of a clear exit before I take care of you. Keep your hands up!"

He sidled over to the table and crooked his left arm around the carved primitive. He kept his automatic trained on Frost's head. He backed slowly toward the front door. His eyes burned in their sockets with a hard, deadly light. Jean read in every gesture and word the mark of the killer. He would shoot as he had shot before, from ambush, or without warning. He would shoot for any slight pretext, or for the sheer lust to kill. And if he was the hidden sniper who had picked off Connaugh Wilder, he was a lightninglike and accurate shot.

He backed all the way to the door and turned the knob.

Frost shifted his weight.

A great many things happened instantly. The killer's body convulsed. His limbs jerked and his muscles cramped. The contraction of his finger pulled the trigger of the gun. The contraction of his arm swung the automatic toward the ceiling. The powerful electric current which surged through him simultaneously exploded all seven shells in the clip of the automatic. The simultaneous firing of those bullets put a terrific strain on the weapon. It burst into bits, tearing the hand that held it and splashing its owner's face like shrapnel. The sudden flow of the house current into the door latch and knob, which Frost had accomplished by stepping on an open connection which he had left under the rug, blew the house fuses immediately after that momentary flow. The lights blotted out.

There was the sound of racing feet in the darkness, a scuffle near the door.

"Frost!" Jean cried out.

"Got him!" his cool voice clipped through the darkness. "I told him he should have started shooting earlier!"

X.

The prisoner snarled, "Maybe you'll succeed in sending me up for a stretch for burglary, but when I get out——"

Frost said softly, "For burglary, Gensel? For assault. For second-degree murder. For first-degree murder. And for kidnaping. You'll never get out, if you escape the electric chair."

Gensel openly scoffed. "You're crazy. Crazy as a bedbug." Blood dripped from cuts in his cheeks. The beam of the flashlight which Frost had given to his assistant played upon the captive. A handkerchief was knotted around his wrist, stemming the flow of blood into his injured right hand. His left hand was handcuffed to the hand of his companion who still slept from the gas he had inhaled upon opening the display case. The heavier man's vitality and strength proved amazing. He had already recovered from the shock that stunned him.

The professor fondled the grotesque little wood sculpture he had rescued. "Yes?" he drawled. "Perhaps you would like to be entertained by a story pending the arrival of the police?"

"Sure. Go on and spill a fairy tale. Spill any number of fairy tales. I've got nothing else to do but listen," the prisoner snapped. His eyes smoldered with a dark, evil blaze, and his white face strained with the effort to suppress the pain of his injuries.

Frost's eyes never wavered from their watch on the prisoner; and though Gensel was manacled, the professor kept his automatic trained upon him.

"The big-game hunter of modern times," he began indirectly, "is a far cry from the primitive hunter of old. He matches brain against brawn. He is favored by long-range rifles, the advantages of ambush, and all the resources which science and civilization supply. The sportsmanship of the game cannot be divorced from the kill, or the thrill of danger. The modern huntsman must steel himself against sympathetic emotions. To him, the charge of a wild-bull elephant, the spring of a tiger, and the flight of a gazelle are the same. The actions of animals may differ, but the huntsman's answer is always the same—a bullet without quarter. In that, lay your undoing.

"The minute that Connaugh Wilder was killed, I knew exactly what type of murderer to seek. A city gangster, or all but one in ten thousand of motivated or psychopathic killers, would use pistol or machine gun in preference to rifle or other methods. A rifle is a cumbersome weapon. It cannot be concealed. Its great accuracy is offset by its physical disadvantages.

"Connaugh Wilder was killed from a distance; not a great distance, but a matter of a hundred yards or more. No one could have known in advance that he was coming to me. Therefore, no one could have rented an apartment and set up an ambush in advance. Therefore, he must have been trailed by his killer. Shooting of such accuracy that a single bullet sufficed to pierce the neck and shatter the spinal cord would be phenomenal at that distance, considering the elements of motion and wind drift, if the marksman employed an automatic, and even if he were an expert shot. Therefore, the killer must have used a rifle, a long-range, high-powered rifle of great accuracy with whose use he was familiar.

"Therefore, he must have been at least familiar with distance shooting. Therefore, he was presumably at home in big-game hunting. Since he could not openly follow Wilder with a rifle, he must have been concealed. Since he was constantly in motion, his best recourse would be to a small, light truck. I have no doubt that the truck employed was built for the transportation of animals, with small barred windows that could be fully or partly closed by hinged panels."

Gensel stared at Frost out of narrowed lids. "Go on. Go on day-dreaming as long as you like," he jeered. A new note, a hunted look, had entered his eyes.

There was a glacial quality in Frost's response. "Suppose we shift the scene.

"An expedition winds its way through Africa. Between Rhodesia and Tanganyika, one of the members, Druo Wilder, let us say, disappears for a week. He returns with some film reels and some animal specimens, including an ape that whimpers. The ape is wounded. Gradually it recovers. The expedition proceeds. As the expedition reaches its embarkation port, Druo Wilder contracts malaria. He becomes delirious. He drops a hint that is overheard. Two members volunteer to remain with him and bring him back when the crisis has passed.

"In his fever, Druo Wilder babbles a precious secret; not all of it, but enough to inflame the conspirators. They attend every word of the sick man, but he keeps the important part of his secret. Convalescing, he returns to America. The conspirators wheedle, threaten, exhort, perhaps torture him, but he puts them off. They are mistaken. He has nothing and knows nothing. His possessions have been taken on ahead by the main party. Perhaps, after he reaches America, he can make a deal. It depends on what success he has. Whatever his answer, nothing can be done until after landing.

"But then the victim stalls. He professes ignorance. The plotters threaten to expose him. He laughs. They cannot expose him because they can produce nothing to support their contention. The man is shadowed. Still the plotters learn nothing. In a final effort one evening, when the victim resists, the main conspirator kills him. The murderer searches the house but discovers no clue to what he seeks, with the possible exception of the painting, over which he puzzles in vain. He becomes desperate."

Gensel moistened his lips. "A great yarn," he muttered, but his face was greenish.

With remorseless logic, Frost continued, "He deciphers the purpose of the painting, but not its meaning. He reasons that Druo Wilder, fearing for his life, may have telephoned his brother and released some inkling of the secret.

"One crook watches until Connaugh goes out alone. He telephones his partner, and either one then telephones Mrs. Wilder. Believing her husband has been injured, she rushes out. She is knocked out or doped, and abducted. Connaugh Wilder is then informed that the price of her release is the full secret of his brother.

"We now approach a remarkable problem in psychology," Frost suggested. Gensel's eyes had become glary. His bravado was melting away.

"Connaugh Wilder does not know his brother's secret, but he has the seal of death upon him in an incurable disease. His life is only a matter of months or weeks. He has an insurance policy with a suicide clause. He is devoted to his wife. Four motivations dominate him. He is doomed to death and knows it. His brother has been murdered and he wishes to avenge him. His wife has been kidnaped and he must release her. In order to accomplish one or all of these purposes, he must interpret the painting.

"He understands how Druo's mind worked, but his own mentality is insufficient to decipher the painting entirely. He goes as far as deciphering the significance of the apes, and kills the apes in his desperate anxiety to effect his wife's release. But meeting only failure on all sides, and seeing no way of extricating himself from complexities that his death may end and which his life will only confuse, he decides to use his last funds to have himself killed.

"That strange, pathetic request was in reality a simple and natural solution arrived at by a mind tortured with grief and the burdens of living. His death would probably mean the release of his wife. The insurance would keep her in modest comfort. He would be free from the pain of his illness. And if he could not avenge the murder of Druo, he at least would do nothing to help the murderers.

"But the conspirators have been shadowing Connaugh. When they see him come to me, they kill him. They think he has been on the right track. They think themselves safe because their identity was unknown to Connaugh. They think they can continue the trail where he left off. Through a dummy agent, they have already purchased the remaining apes from the Animal Import Co. And, as luck would have it, they have purchased the ape that was injured; imbedded in the fleshy posterior of the ape, where Druo's knowledge of anatomy and his possession of the medical outfit which jungle expeditions always carry enabled him to place it, they find, let us say—a piece of roughly carved ivory."

Gensel twitched. Walkner groaned. Gensel ran a tongue over dry lips.

Frost went on, "The piece of ivory baffles them. They cut it open, find nothing, perhaps throw it away in disgust."

Gensel's eyes almost popped, while the professor resumed his story, "You had trailed and killed Connaugh. Thereafter you went alone to Druo's home. You risked discovery but you had to go there immediately or it would be too late. You had to examine the painting again and try to unravel its meaning. You succeeded, partly by recalling the imbedded piece of ivory."

Deftly building his drama to its climax, Frost concluded, "The painting gave its own clue to the riddle. Human beings were in the trees but apes were on the ground. That was a reversal of reality. In other words, everything in the scene was to be taken at its opposite value. Instead of white baboons, black apes should be sought. Instead of being free, they should be sought for in captivity. The upper part of the ninth ape was exposed. Therefore, the object was imbedded in the buried half of its body.

"I was somewhat puzzled by the significance of the half-human, half-anthropoid ninth baboon, a point that my assistant was instrumental in elucidating. The symbolism then became plain. The ninth baboon was rooted to indicate immovability. A dead ape was out of the question. The answer must be either a stuffed ape or a statue of wood sculpture. Since the Ditzer Expedition brought back live animals, I chose the other alternative. Since human beings should normally have been on the ground in the painting, I naturally concluded that they were examining some sort of semianthropoid object. Since Druo was an artist, that object would most likely be in an art museum. Only an African primitive, as it is known in art circles, would answer all the requirements."

Frost twisted at the back of the sculpture. "The lumps of coal, with the flame above them, could have only one significance, for coal is carbon."

The statue opened, under a powerful twist of his fingers, and he removed a tightly wedged object, of a gray-brown hue, dull, like a stone. He surveyed it with appraising eyes, as he murmured, "And diamonds are carbon. This is a raw diamond, weighing at least 700 carats. If it is flawless; it will take its place among the great gems of the world. If its color is good, it will be worth about five hundred thousand dollars as it is, and will approximate three quarters of a million when cut and polished. There will be a tidy sum left for Mrs. Wilder, after I assist her in straightening out certain difficulties with the customs officials."

He looked at Gensel with a reproachful glance. "But this is nothing compared with the fortune you threw away. You should have been on the way to Africa now. You had the opportunity in your hand and you destroyed it in your search for a single diamond.

"On the instep of Druo Wilder's shoes, I found minute traces of a peculiar bluish earth. That piece of ivory could only have been the cleverly carved, topographical map of the route to the diamond soil which he had discovered during the week of his absence in Africa."

When the police took him away, Gensel was raving and screaming.

Frost had stopped smoking. A dullness, suggestive of ennui and disinterest, had begun to replace the glitter of his black pupils. Jean Moray tenderly felt her sore throat.

"I hope you're feeling better," he said as he helped her down the stairs.

That was all. She wished—but her wish would be futile.

DEATH DESCENDING

IT HAD BEEN a gay, bright evening except for the fog. It began with a good dinner, continued at the opening of a new play, then after-theater supper and dancing at a night club. The floor show, like the excellent champagne, sparkled. She felt exhilarated, a trifle reckless, and she looked her alluring best.

Jean Moray, endowed by nature with perfect health and body, lived by the principle that what nature bestows can be improved by art. A spirit of tantalizing deviltry, dwelt within her face. Her expression seemed constantly on the verge of sophistication, naïvete, aristocratic reserve and easy camaraderie.

Her escort accompanied her to the door of Number 11 State Street. She held out her hand. "A grand evening from start to finish."

He took the impersonal dismissal in good grace. "Sometimes I think you're made of ice. You don't have blood—just ice particles creeping along like the Northern glaciers. Maybe that's why we unfortunates fall for you—the mere fact that you're so far away."

"Isn't it always like that? Easy come, easy go," she answered lightly. "Don't most people appreciate things more the harder they have to fight for them? And isn't it true that we generally like some one else more than we are liked in return? Oh dear, we're getting terribly philosophical for two A.M. Call me up soon."

She watched his back retreat through the fog bank that had rolled in during the afternoon. Her glance passed to the house next door. A glimmer of light struggled feebly through the mists. That would be the laboratory window. What was Frost doing in his laboratory at this hour? Had something turned up while she was away, one of the infrequent bizarre cases that were as champagne and caviar to his existence?

It took her but a few minutes to slip into the house, wriggle out of the slinky lines of the pale-pistachio evening gown, that had so subtly and devastatingly emphasized her figure and set off the warm purity of her complexion and her honey-colored hair. She donned practical tweeds, and moments later had crossed to Number 13.

For any other bachelor in New York City, or anywhere else, the employment of an assistant as young and beautiful as Jean Moray would have called out the raised-eyebrow brigade, but Frost's reputation was, unfortunately, her own greatest protection. Jean didn't mind playing the part of a creature of ice, as cool as an Eskimo, but she found herself baffled by a glacier that would not melt.

It was only one of many contradictions in her character that she ignored the admirers she could have won, and reserved everything for the one man who didn't want her, apparently didn't give her a second thought, and had never shown the least sign of personal interest.

It wasn't fair, she decided, to a girl who was perfect, or practically perfect. Maybe if she threatened to resign she would get some action. No; Frost would probably shrug his shoulders and find another assistant, or else he'd raise her salary and let it go at that. Maybe the effect of her entrance would be more stunning if she'd kept on the shimmering gown, but still, Frost might be playing around with acids and chemicals and things by which dresses are likely to be ruined.

The fog eddied around her as her duplicate key admitted her.

She hesitated about knocking on the laboratory door and finally decided just to walk in. She paused on the threshold, closed the door softly behind her.

Professor I. V. Frost, at that hour, and in that place, looked like nothing of the modern world. Instead, he resembled some medieval sorcerer preparing a mysterious and poisonous brew.

Darkness obscured most of the laboratory. An overhead, shaded bulb threw a cone of light around Frost where he sat on a high stool at a table near one of the shuttered windows. He was half facing the door, his features shadowed except for his disheveled hair, the black eyebrows, and the predatory nose. His eyelids flickered up as she entered and she had a fleeting, sinister impression of eyes that burned with knowledge of esoteric secrets. The eyelids drooped, and his gaze returned to his work.

Blue flame flickered from a brazier in front of him. A tripod supported a small, vitreous alembic above the flame. Bottles and phials stood beside the brazier, and a miscellany of strange instruments and objects surrounded it.

Frost remarked idly: "It is pleasant to be admired."

"That's the most egotistic statement you ever made."

He withered her with a look of disgust. "I referred to the expression upon your face when you entered. It was unmistakably that of remembering the most flattering compliment that could be paid you."

Vexed at the rebound of her thoughtless assumption, she hastily changed the subject. "Am I intruding?"

"Of course," Frost admitted with disconcerting candor. "But watch if you like."

She walked to the worktable and observed in silence for a while until curiosity got the better of her. "Might I ask what you are doing?"

"Certainly, you may ask," he agreed, and lapsed into maddening silence.

In a beaker beside the brazier rested a mass of shredded stuff. She noticed a few spilled fibers on the table and picked them up. Some of the shreds were short, dark, and firm; others black, powdery; a few long and golden, fragrant as new-mown hay.

"Dehydrated tobacco," Frost explained. "A mixture of Latakia, Black Walnut, and Sweet Crop."

A colorless fluid simmered in the alembic. With tweezers, he dropped pieces of clove, cinnamon stick, and other spices into the boiling fluid. To the infusion he added a drop of attar of rose, essence of hyssop, and other exotic scents unfamiliar to her. The brew acquired an aromatic character both languorous and sharp, pungent and sweet. From an unmarked phial, he measured a quantity of white powder which he sifted into the beaker and shook vigorously until the tobacco and the powder were thoroughly mixed. He added a number of whole leaves to the liquid, dried leaves of a dark and peculiar plant which she could not identify. The infusion proceeded for five minutes, when he filtered it.

The resulting clear fluid, of a rich, wine color, he drew into an atomizer whose tip he fitted into the beaker. Alternately squeezing the bulb and shaking the beaker, he rehydrated the tobacco with the prepared fluid.

"Tobacco, as you doubtless know, is extremely sensitive to moisture, which it loses readily in dry atmosphere and regains promptly in moist air," he volunteered. "This mixture was dry as desert dust a minute ago. Within ten minutes, it will have completely absorbed the solution, and be ready for the bin." He nodded toward an odd little machine with a hinged receptable attached, a standard device for the home manufacture of cigarettes, with modifications of his own.

"And I had hoped," Jean mourned, "that it was a brand-new mystery that kept you awake at this hour. The perfect crime, maybe."

"If it were a perfect crime, it would never come to our attention. For that matter, there have been thousands of perfect crimes," he drawled.

She knit her brows. "Why wouldn't it be known? What makes you think there have been thousands of perfect crimes? How do you know there have been any, even one?"

The professor seemed surprised. "Isn't it obvious? If a perfect crime were committed, it would never come to our attention, or to any one's attention, for that very reason. Dozens of such crimes are undoubtedly perpetrated every year.

"There are many perfect crimes. Thousands of persons disappear in this city alone. Many are soon located. Some are not found for months or years. A few are never heard from or seen again, and their fate remains a matter for conjecture. They vanish as completely as though they had been transported to another planet. A few among these have doubtless been murdered and their bodies concealed so successfully that the truth is never known."

Jean argued: "How do you know that they haven't committed suicide in some hidden place? Or died a natural death under a different name in another part of the country or abroad?"

"I don't know," Frost admitted, while he watched long, white cylinders drop out of the machine. "No one except the murderer knows. That is the dilemma of the perfect crime: it does not exist except in imagination. It is never known or solved in real life, because it never comes to the attention of authorities. It does not exist in fiction because, if it is solved, it ceases to be a perfect crime, and if it is unsolved, it ceases to be fiction."

The doorbell rang insistently.

"That will be Miss Theresa Wilson," Frost announced. "She is rather late for her appointment."

Jean looked askance, but said nothing. Frost strolled after her into the reception room while she hurried to admit the visitor.

The three-o'clock caller proved to be a slender, smartly dressed young woman with "Junior Leaguer" stamped all over her. She had that peculiar type of bearing which makes society débutantes as characteristic and alike as so many fashion drawings by a given artist, the kind of smooth polish that comes from too much money, nothing to worry about, access to the best circles, and wishes quickly satisfied for the mere asking. But Terry Wilson was worried.

Jean introduced the visitor, who wasted not a second before plunging into the thick of her story. "Sorry I couldn't get here sooner, but after I phoned I decided to go back and see if the body was still scattered around or if it had vanished like the pieces of the statue and the ghost, but it, or I suppose you'd say they, were still there so I started off again and here I am." The amazing statement stumbled out in a breathless rush of words run together.

II.

Frost offered her a pack of cigarettes of a popular brand. She selected one and toyed with it nervously. For himself, he chose one of his own private manufacture. "We'll drive back with you at once." A gleam of interest brightened his eyes as he disappeared into the laboratory. Terry tapped a foot impatiently, gave Frost's assistant a quick appraisal. The professor returned with a valise into which he had hastily crammed some equipment.

"These may prove useful," he observed with cryptical nonchalance.

"But I haven't told you anything yet!" the visitor protested. "All I did was make an appointment!"

"Pardon me, but you told me a great deal the moment you arrived," he informed her. "Pray continue with this strange story."

The heavy fog closed in on them. "I couldn't drive very fast on account of the fog or I'd have been here much sooner," Terry apologized. Her features looked wan and drawn, bore the signs of fast living, but she walked with an athletic stride.

A long, powerful roadster of foreign make stood at the curb. The three climbed in. The fog hung everywhere, limiting visibility to the distance between lamp posts. The lights shone with a sickly glow. Terry threw the car into gear. It leaped ahead with a pur of power.

"The whole business began two nights ago," she explained. "I was driving in from the country and I got the scare of my life when I reached home. Our town house, I should explain, occupies a small block of its own facing the East River. There is a lawn and some shrubbery around the house, and all of it is inclosed by an iron fence. It was about two o'clock, and when I had practically reached home I saw something white in the road. It looked like a human head. Farther on was an arm, and other pieces lay around. I jammed on the brakes, feeling pretty sick, and then saw that a plaster cast had been smashed to bits less than half a block from our house. I decided the vandalism was none of my business and drove home. I kept thinking about the broken statue, and after putting the car up, I walked back to the spot.

"The fragments were gone. A car was roaring off, but I couldn't make out its license number. Only some white powder and a few tiny slivers of the statue remained.

"Why would anybody smash a statue in the middle of a street at night, and then go to all the trouble to pick up the pieces and carry them away?"

Frost listened with signs of increasing animation. "Go on."

"Last night I went to a theater party and got in early, for me. I didn't feel like sleeping, so I sat up reading. Around one-thirty I heard a crash outside. It sounded as if it were on our grounds. I went to the window and looked out. Another statue had been broken up and tossed over the fence. I watched for a while, but no one came. Then I saw something that puzzles me still. The statue was smashed into chunks, and above each separate piece hung a sort of ghost."

"A ghost?" Jean echoed.

"That's what it looked like. A misty ghost above every fragment of the limbs and torso. It was rather quiet, and I sat still, with a creepy sort of feeling. I got the impression that I was seeing things, or dreaming, and that everything would disappear if I waited long enough. Everything did disappear!"

Frost asked, "You mean that all the fragments vanished? While you were watching them?"

"Yes. I couldn't believe my eyes. Finally I dressed and went outside just to prove to myself I wasn't dreaming. I couldn't find a trace of the statue or a single fragment. It had been a fairly warm night. I thought maybe I had seen ice melt, but I know ice doesn't melt that fast. Besides, the ground was hard and not a bit damp, and anyway, why would any one want to throw a lot of ice in our property? I am positive that no one entered the grounds or left them all the while that I watched. I decided to treat the affair as an illusion resulting from a bad case of jitters. I'd seen the ghost of a statue, or the disappearing fragments of a ghost, whichever way you want to put it."

She took a deep breath and tossed the remainder of her cigarette out the window. Fog swirled in. The headlights were almost useless.

"To-day I had a busy schedule—luncheon engagement, cocktail party, dress fitting, dinner, and so on, and my last escort brought me home around midnight. We quarreled on the way, and after he left, I decided to take a run up the Drive. I got the car out and went as far as Van Cortlandt Park, thinking things over. It must have been close to two when I returned. I put the car up—the garage is built onto the house—and walked around to the front.

"The fog was so thick I couldn't see more than ten or fifteen feet. I heard a rush of air and a loud crack. It scared me but I walked on toward the front gate."

Terry Wilson bit a trembling lip. "I saw something lying there, whitish things scattered halfway between the house and the street. They—they were human, but the body had broken into as many pieces as the statue. It—it was awful. I'll never forget the sight of the—the head——" She clenched the wheel with hands whose knuckles stood out white.

"There was something horribly, horribly wrong about the corpse. I don't know what. It sickened me. It looked as if it had been dead a long time, and it didn't bleed. I turned and ran. I didn't go into the house. I got the car out again and drove off like mad. The fog stifled me. I guess I didn't have any clear idea for a while. I felt caught in a living nightmare. I knew I ought to call the police, but what if they came and didn't find anything, or suppose they did? I started to see our physician but first I feared he might tell me I'd had a breakdown, and then I was afraid it might prove real after all.

"Finally I called our attorney, and Mr. Vogel told me to get in touch with you immediately. So I did, but after I made the appointment I forced myself to drive back and see if the—the thing was still scattered around. It was. I suppose I should have stayed there and told you to come over, but I thought only of getting away as fast as possible."

Frost's brows knitted. His thoughts seemed elsewhere, though he asked a few perfunctory questions.

"You are not alone in the house?"

"Practically. My parents are traveling abroad. I returned early for the wedding of a friend and stayed to open the house. The servants are with the family. There's only the caretaker and my maid here."

"You were engaged?"

"Off and on for the past year," she admitted with candor. "To Fred Devore Allen. We quarrel a lot. He's the one I had the scrap with to-night and right now I guess the engagement's off again."

"I see." Frost's drawl was noncommittal. "He studied to be an engineer, did he not?"

"How did you know? What has that to do with all this?"

"Probably nothing whatever. Do you know of any one who would have real or fancied cause to threaten your life?"

Her face puckered. After a few moments: "No. I've never received any threats, if that's what you mean. I can't imagine why this should happen to me."

"I can," Frost said quietly.

Terry frowned. "You don't think it's just an accident?"

"Ridiculous! There are no limits to coincidence in life, but the laws of probability retain their validity. It is certainly not a coincidence that three similar distressing experiences have occurred in the same place at about the same time on three successive nights. As the Romans would have put it, *ex nihilo, nihil.* I might add that the mystery has only begun, though in progressive stages. Plaster cast—solid carbon dioxide—a corpse— You recognized nothing about the latter arrival?"

"Ugh!" Terry made a wordless grimace. "What I saw of it looked as if it had been buried for ages. What was the phrase you used? It sounded like a chemical."

"Solid carbon dioxide? That was your ghost of a corpse. Nothing else could so adequately answer your description. Commercially, it is known as dry ice. It is extremely cold, with a temperature of -40°C, and evaporates readily when exposed to air temperature."

"But the pieces looked like fragments of a corpse. Why would anybody scatter dry ice around? Or make it in the shape of a body to begin with?"

Frost said: "That is a question whose answer must be proved."

Jean noticed that he did not say "found," but "proved." Had his keen analytic faculties already raced through various alternatives and selected the true answer? His inscrutable features told nothing.

He remarked idly: "You have had other suitors, of course? Have you quarreled with any of them?"

"Suitors?" she repeated cynically. "Any girl nowadays who has good looks and money or money without good looks is swamped. I couldn't even tell you the names of a lot of fortune-hunters I've known."

"No matter. The motive will appear, eventually. In this case, and at this stage, the motive and the identity of our potential criminal are of less importance than the method. The method should lead us to his lair."

"Potential?" queried the driver. "Why do you say potential?"

"Because, if your descriptions are accurate, there has been no crime committed, yet. The crime is to come."

"No crime! Is it no crime to murder a man and dismember the body?"

Frost replied with a laconic paradox. "The fact that a corpse lies in pieces does not mean that it was dismembered. To mutilate and scatter a body that has died of natural causes does not constitute crime in the larger sense of the word. That which is already dead cannot be murdered."

From the blank wall of fog ahead an iron fence with hooked tops became vaguely discernible. Terry cut down her speed. "Here we are," she announced as the car drifted to the curb and stopped.

Through the heavy mist, shapes of men and feeble cones of light grew visible inside the grounds. Another car parked ahead of them could be dimly seen.

Frost frowned. "Did you call the police?"

Terry Wilson shook her head. "I'll question the servants, but I can't imagine why they would even come out on a night like this and I don't see how anybody could have noticed the thing from the sidewalk."

The professor crisply ordered: "Stay here. Better lock the car doors from the inside. Wait till one of us gives you further instructions."

And to Miss Moray: "I hope you won't need this but don it now." His voice sounded grim, imperative. Terry Wilson, accustomed to issue orders but not to receive them, seemed on the verge of rebellion, but for some unaccountable reason subsided meekly.

Jean Moray wriggled into the bulletproof cloak which had saved her life more than once, and followed Frost across the sidewalk. The black, glistening fabric swirled loosely around him. He looked like a bird of prey as he plunged through the fog, his valise in hand.

III.

As he opened the iron gate, a harsh voice growled: "Hold it! Right where you are!"

A flashlight swept up, poured a thin, weak light on them. An officer in uniform grew clearer from the gray obscurity. "Oh, it's you, Frost? How the heck do you get in on things so fast? And what's the idea of the fancy costume?"

Frost dropped over his face again the slitted hood that he had lifted. "Watch yourself," he warned. "Things, as you express it, haven't even begun to happen yet. Who notified the police?"

Sergeant Conway, whom Frost had met once or twice, answered grudgingly: "Nobody from here, that's a cinch. Some fellow phoned in, said we'd find a body here, hung up without leaving his name or address. Body—phew! I don't think they'll ever get it together again, let alone identify it." He pointed to the grisly fragments that had been collected. "Even the photographer can't do much against this fog."

"You've examined the ground?"

"Yeah, for all the good it did."

"Weren't there any astonishing circumstances?"

"Naw. Not even a footprint."

"That is the astonishing circumstance," said Frost.

The sergeant bristled. "Now look here, there wouldn't be any footprints because somebody threw the stuff over the fence, see? All we got to do is find out why somebody cut up a stiff and threw it here."

The professor stated calmly: "No one did." The sergeant opened his mouth but Frost went on: "Where was that chunk picked up?"

Sergeant Conway pointed to a spot forty feet from the fence.

"That is your answer," Frost observed. "It is the largest fragment and must weight between fifteen and twenty pounds. I suggest that you practice hurling a fifteen or twenty-pound weight and make a careful note of the distance you attain."

He bent low, examined the remains briefly.

"What d'you make of it?" asked the sergeant.

"Obviously it is, or was, a medical-school specimen, some unknown, unclaimed at the morgue."

"You mean some medic cut it up for anatomy and then junked it here as a practical joke?"

"Certainly not. This is in deadly earnest."

"Then what's it doing here?"

Frost answered with grim and ambiguous brevity. "Test. Try-out."

He abandoned his inspection and opened the valise. He moved across the lawn a few paces, like a dark wraith in the fog, and set up a compact apparatus. He adjusted its parts, set a mechanism in motion. It worked automatically. At regular intervals of a minute, then, a subdued click came from the black, squat mass.

"Don't touch it or interfere with it. Tell your men to leave it alone," he warned the sergeant.

Jean, long silent, her curiosity getting the better of her, demanded: "But what is it? It looks like a camera, like a lot of cameras."

"Horizon camera," he replied as though he was already occupied with other matters. "Unlike the ordinary camera, which takes pictures of only a section of the horizon, this one photographs the sky and entire horizon in all directions."

"And what good will it do?"

"Wait and see."

The sergeant scowled. "You can't take pictures in a fog."

"Can't you? I can."

The sergeant made a grunt of objection, said in a voice heavy with scorn: "I suppose next you'll be telling us the corpse fell down from the sky."

"Right!" came Frost's urbane retort. To his assistant: "Get into the house and go through every room and closet. Use Miss Wilson's keys."

Jean nodded silently and slipped off through the impenetrable fog. Frost turned aside on some mission of his own.

Without warning, the muffled sound of an exploding cartridge burst from the wall of mist. A bullet whined.

"Down!" Frost yelled, his voice partly checked by the hood. Another cartridge went off; the hidden marksman shot again, then a burst of firing raked the ground.

The volley seemed to issue from the south. The sergeant whirled and plunged toward his right, service revolver drawn. Elsewhere the shadows that were men blended with the ground. A slug slammed against Frost and flattened. It whirled him part way around. Jean gave a sudden little yelp as a bullet numbed her arm.

"Down! Get down on the ground!" Frost shouted.

Sergeant Conway ignored the warning. He fired blindly at the spot where flashes of fire briefly and faintly split the mist. Somewhere a window splintered, a bullet ricocheted from stone with a low whine.

Doggedly, Conway ran through the curtains of night and mist. Frost raced after him with a muttered curse. Suddenly the firing switched to the north, then it seemed to thunder from behind, from three sides, trapping them in a deadly, crisscross barrage.

Another slug whammed against Frost's bulletproof cloak. Sergeant Conway staggered, tripped again, kept stumbling sidewise. His gun arm hung useless. He clapped his left hand to his right shoulder, slid to the ground.

Either in obedience to Frost's cry of warning, or afraid of hitting their comrades in the darkness and confusion, the rest of the police withheld fire. Only Conway had answered that savage attack.

A burst of shots exploded simultaneously in a dozen places. Windows smashed, glass tinkled; the ugly whine of bullets ripped around them as though a dozen marksmen competed in rapid fire. But no stranger, no skulking forms, no hidden snipers made themselves even faintly visible through that thick curtain.

Frost and Jean raced for the stricken sergeant. A grimace twisted his features. He muttered shakily: "Naw, I'm not dead yet. Busted leg, shoulder, and one in the hip."

With swift, expert fingers, Frost and Jean stopped the flow of blood with strips torn from his shirt. An occasional bullet whined out of the murk, an occasional muffled explosion barked near by.

Sweat stood out on Conway's face. "Good night, how many of 'em are there? A million?"

"Easy," Frost cautioned him. "There's no one here but us."

Conway stared up with vague, puzzled eyes. "Nobody—here—but us? Corpse—from—sky. It's all—screwy—" His eyes closed.

An eerie silence descended, and the fog rolled heavily, ghostily, everywhere. Frost called into the gloom, "The danger's past—you can get up now." Figures detached themselves from the ground, rose from blobs to shadowy shapes.

Two burly policemen emerged from the sea of gray, lent willing hands to carry the limp weight of Conway.

"Close call. He'll live," Frost answered their unspoken question.

At the same time, a gruff voice ordered: "Search the grounds!"

Frost shook his head. "They won't find any one."

The two police stared at him searchingly, moved away in the direction of the radio prowl car. The fog swallowed them and their unconscious burden. Pounding feet sounded in the fog. Frost shouted: "Don't shoot at anything or you'll be killing each other! There was no one here besides ourselves!"

His words rang out with a weird, muffled quality. Jean felt a creeping of her scalp. The strange silence that had now descended, the fragments of a corrupting body, the phantom bombardment, and the interminable fog edged her nerves. What did Frost mean? Some one, if not several snipers, must have been hidden behind that pall for such rapid and indiscriminate shooting. And yet, now that the surprise attack had ended as abruptly as it had commenced, she felt bewildered. The shooting had seemed to originate on three sides. If that was the case, wouldn't the attackers be caught in their own cross fire? Or had the fog distorted sounds and directions? She recalled having heard of blind spots and curious effects that fogs give rise to.

"How could there be no one here?" she asked.

"The iron fence! See if Miss Wilson is staying in her car, then search along the base of the fence!"

She melted away into the gray density that maddeningly obscured objects and thwarted actions. Terry was still seated at the wheel of her car, nervously tapping her fingers. That she had obediently followed his command in spite of the shooting gave silent testimony to the power of Frost's stern order.

Drawn by the mysterious shots, two radio cars crawled into view, their headlights turned to a dull amber by the moisture-laden vapor.

Jean returned to the grounds, found the gaunt form of the professor kneeling by the fence left of the gate. He was furiously scooping out sod and dirt. For no reason that she could think of, his action and posture seemed more grotesque than anything that had yet happened.

Corpses might rain from the sky, a dozen men be ambushed in fog, and she would have accepted them as facts; but Frost on hands and knees, rooting around at the base of iron uprights, presented an illogical picture. She drew closer and dropped beside him to see what had attracted his attention.

"Ah!" came his low, pleased exclamation.

He had hammered and gouged out the hard topsoil with the butt of his automatic directly at the base of an upright. The iron railings stood embedded in a narrow flange of concrete that paralleled the sidewalk. Against this concrete base, and tilted diagonally upward at an angle of about thirty degrees, rested the shell of an exploded bullet. The soil was still warm and odorous of powder gases. A wire looped like an armature winding around and around the brass chamber, and wire and shell were hot. The wire continued in both directions along the concrete, buried an inch below ground level.

Frost pulled it up with his gloved hand, followed it to the next upright, and the next. At every other bar, one of the shells wrapped in the tight coil came out. Striding swiftly from rail to rail, he uprooted a line of shells extending to the corner post, and continuing along the side street. The wire and cartridges, after some fifty feet more, turned at right angle to the eighteenth upright, and led to a hedged-in arbor.

The arbor had been wired for electricity, apparently as an evening retreat for summer use. The underground cable that supplied it with current had been tapped; and the wire that Frost pulled up disappeared into a compact little box from whose opposite side another wire emerged and ended at the tapped cable.

"No need to look further," Frost commented softly. There was a biting, chilling edge to his voice.

The new arrivals from the prowl cars stamped through the fog, which had begun to take on a lighter hue from the approach of dawn, but which remained as impenetrable as the blackness of night. A pair of bluecoats loomed toward them.

Jean asked: "What's in the box?"

"Only one thing could be," he replied succinctly, without bothering to pry the box apart. "Remote control."

"How?"

"This contact mechanism must have been buried with an open switch that would close and tap the house current when radio signals on its specific wavelength were sent out by remote control. The cartridges were wound to act as resistance coils. When the current flowed through, they heated until the powder exploded. Differences in the amount of winding made the cartridges explode irregularly. A fiendish and cowardly ambush."

"But why? Why?" Jean cried out. It seemed monstrous, brutal. "How do you know the Wilsons didn't arrange this for their own defense in case of need?"

Frost drawled: "Easy to answer—ask Miss Wilson. I should say it would be protection of a most dubious kind, in view of the fact that the bullets along the front fence shot directly at the mansion."

"But it would take a day to prepare and lay down all this material here!"

"At least a day, if your assumption were true," he admitted. "But if you are implying that this was an inside job, completed while the Wilsons have been away, you are entering the realm of the incredible. To outward appearances, this must have been an inside job. It obviously points to planning or connivance on the part of some one in the household. The obvious and ready explanation is frequently the one most open to suspicion. In this case, the caretaker seems to be so inevitable a suspect that I have already dismissed him from consideration.

"Those cartridges, the wire, the contact-control box, were never assembled here. Prepared elsewhere, some one brought them here. The task of planting them could have been finished in an hour or two. I would suggest that you police question the caretaker. I rather imagine you will find that he was lured away, slugged, and robbed recently; or that he was attacked here and after freeing himself could not find evidence that the house had been burglarized, hence concluded that he had been the sole object of attack. On that occasion, probably a dark, misty, or rainy night, some one buried the phantom snipers."

One of the police growled: "You can't convince me that somebody inside didn't have a hand in it. Come on, Joe, let's find that caretaker."

Frost shrugged his shoulders in an indifferent fashion, as the blanket of gray swallowed their forms.

IV.

"We'll try the back of the house," Frost snapped, and strode off at a tangent from the disappearing police.

As his assistant hurried at a brisk trot to keep pace with his long strides, she inquired: "Who would go to such trouble to bury bullets? Why plan a mass murder?"

"No one did," he contradicted her. "There were seven persons including us in the line of fire, but only one was injured, and he will recover.

The angle and the spacing of the bullets made a fatal hit unlikely. No one who lay on the ground would be wounded unless he chose the base of the fence. You have just seen demonstrated the rarity of fatal injury in symmetric blind firing.

"Terror, not death, is the answer. Some one wanted to terrorize Miss Wilson; some one who didn't care whether she was killed or how many innocent bystanders got hit."

Jean felt chilly. What other menace had been prepared by that murderous unknown? She had an uneasy intuition that the fog might at any moment spawn death in strange and terrifying form.

"It's the worst fog I've ever seen," she remarked abruptly. "Whoever he is, he must have infinite patience if he got everything ready and then waited till a fog like this came along."

"He didn't. The fog is simply an unexpected blessing that nature has bestowed upon him, and an unfortunate hindrance that has been placed in our path. Miss Wilson is the object of his attack. He chose this time when she was separated from the rest of her family. A clear night would have helped us little, in spite of the fact that the fog is a disadvantage." Frost did not elaborate the paradox of his comments.

They skirted the north side of the mansion that loomed dark and mysterious in the fog. Shrubbery and bushes, occasional trees, swam vaguely out of the surrounding gray blanket. It was one of the worst and most persistent fogs that ever struck the Atlantic seaboard, an asparagus soup fog such as London might well have been proud to disclaim. At intervals, the mournful wail of tugboat whistles saddened the air from afar. River traffic had ceased, and the tugs sounded off solely in the melancholy hope of a breeze that would blow away the bank.

In the rear of the mansion lay small flower beds, bird baths, and more lawn. The Wilson mansion must be about the last of the private house-and-garden places left in Manhattan, she reflected; the sort of exclusive, limited estate which is common in the residential sections of cities throughout America, but which has virtually vanished from New York.

Frost interrupted her meditations with: "Try the base of a few uprights. If you don't find anything, look for me along the rear wall of the house."

With a nod of acquiescence, she faded into the dense mists.

Frost prowled along the shrubbery-bordered wall, his flashlight almost useless. Every blade of grass, every bud and twig, dripped with moisture. The dampness of the fog laid a sodden deposit on everything; its chill crept through clothing. Tiny rivulets ran down the sleek surface of his bulletproof cloak.

In spite of fog and careful concealment, he found something; and he was gingerly dismantling it when his assistant dropped beside him like a phantom materializing from the fog itself.

"Nothing," she reported. "What's that?"

Frost finished his work. "It, too, is nothing, now; originally an efficient little arrangement to crack the gas inlet, thus filling the house with gases which, when they reached sleeping occupants, or came in contact with a pilot light——" He shrugged in lieu of the unfinished thought.

Again Jean shivered. Menace and disaster hovered in the fog. Why? Why? It became increasingly evident that the Wilsons were a doomed family, or more specifically, Terry Wilson. What had she done to bring down upon her head this implacable vengeance?

Frost rose and continued to prowl across the lawn. Jean said: "You found one bomb, or whatever it is. Maybe there are more."

"The police can make a thorough search. The unknown counted upon their doing so. Therefore, he would not waste further time on instruments of death. In addition, he had only a limited period at his disposal, and the chances of being discovered or of the caretaker freeing himself multiplied greatly with every hour that he spent here."

"Then why look further?"

Frost quoted: "He who does not seek, does not find."

Silence and fog and graying, impalpable light. Silence, save for the dismal, infrequent hoot of tugs. Fog that clung like a shroud. Light that made the fog a shade less obscure but did not increase visibility. Jean hunted with Frost; for what, she did not know. Now and again she heard a low, muffled murmur of voices emanating from the police who prowled on their own missions.

Footsteps came from near by. The feeble arc of a flashlight swinging from side to side grew closer, and a bulky figure emerged.

Frost froze into position, tense, his head cocked in a listening attitude. Jean halted spontaneously. What had he heard? She strained her ears, thought she detected a sound as of a great bird in flight flapping—

Frost seized her in a powerful sweep of one arm and leaped backward. The sudden lunge caught her off balance, left her hanging over his arm, her back to the ground, her head facing the sky. Her eyes widened in horror and she slackened, on the verge of a faint. With a violent effort, she controlled her shaking nerves and struggled erect.

A faint, whistling rush of air had come from overhead. A dark figure hurtled earthward, a figure plunging head-first, with fantastically rigid body, arms stiffly at its sides, its wide-open eyes sightless and glaring in its frozen features.

Near the spot where she and Frost had been standing, the thing smashed on the ground. It landed with a sharp smack, and a noise of brittle crackle. Like a fallen icicle, it split into many parts. The body bounced shortly, sickeningly, as it splintered. Its head burst like some horrible egg and the pieces scattered. Arms and legs and torso shattered into queerly shaped wedges, fragments, and chunks with sharp fracture edges.

And no blood came.

In every other respect, those hideous remains seemed undeniably human; flesh and organs, veins, bones, muscles, lay in the appalling shards; and a red darkness as of blood underlay the marble pallor of skin. But not a drop of blood had splashed upon the ground. That which ought to have been gory pulp resembled, instead, the broken pieces of some wonderfully lifelike but mechanical model of a human body.

The policeman, looking sick, stooped toward the débris.

"Don't touch it!" Frost instantly commanded.

"Why not?"

"You'll burn yourself!"

A dull flush crept over the man's whitened face. "This is a hell of a time for jokes," he muttered in threatening tones, and forced himself to examine one of the gruesome hunks as if to convince himself that it could be no part of anything human.

He cried out, jerked his hand away as though fire had scorched it.

Frost simply repeated: "I warned you that you would burn yourself."

The policeman's eyes goggled. He rubbed his fingers on his coat. He showed no further inclination to investigate the remains, stared at Frost with as much awe as he had bestowed upon the broken body.

The professor bent over the ghastly relics and studied them, but avoided contact. A frightful cold emanated from the shattered thing. It was colder than ice, colder than solid carbon dioxide, colder than any subzero temperature that had ever been recorded in the polar regions. But as it lay there, broken and splintered, it began to adjust itself to air temperature; and slowly, terribly, tiny globules of blood commenced to ooze out like a dreadful sweat.

Though the head and skull had burst like the rest of that which had once been man, enough of the features retained shape to prove that the dead man had originally been dark, swarthy, with slightly slanting eyes— a Eurasian. The skin gradually lost its frosty appearance turned yellowish, then acquired the mottled color of a bruise. All his finger tips and teeth were missing, and not one specific peculiarity or clue to identity remained.

"In its way, a beautiful job," Frost drawled grimly. "Identification will be almost impossible, and even if made, it may never be possible to establish whether the man was murdered or died from natural causes."

"Why not?"

"He may have been killed by a blow that crushed his skull. But his skull was crushed by the impact of landing. He may have been killed by a stab in his heart. But the force with which he hit the ground split his heart. The fact that his finger tips and teeth are missing indicates that some one wished to hinder identification, but is no proof that the victim had not already died from natural causes before his descent."

The policeman muttered: "He fell from the sky. He must have been heaved out of an airplane!"

Frost shook his head in somber denial.

"They must have flown him so high he froze!" the policeman persisted. "I've read that it gets freezing cold the higher you go."

The professor said, with brooding eyes: "He did not fall nor was he thrown out of an airplane, a balloon, or any other sort of aircraft. It is true that extreme cold prevails in the stratosphere, but that cold is nowhere near the temperature to which this body has been subjected. I should like to believe that it came from beyond earth's atmospheric blanket, from the regions of outer space where the bitter cold of absolute zero prevails. Then we would be faced with an extraordinary mystery of truly cosmic horror, a riddle that might never be solved. But I am afraid we cannot have recourse to so tempting a hypothesis until all other possibilities have been exhausted."

The policeman objected strenuously. "Where else could he have come from? Why, damn it all, you saw it fall out of the sky."

"Yes, but it certainly did not get into the sky by itself, nor just happen to fall." He straightened, added briefly, "I'll send the rest of your men here. We've a great deal of work ahead of us, Miss Moray."

They vanished through the rolling fog without waiting for a reply. Frost sent the rest of the police scurrying for the rear of the house, then made his way to the horizon camera.

It was still functioning with a whir of automatic mechanism and a click that came regularly at the end of each minute. In spite of the men tramping around, it had not been kicked over; and it had escaped the fusillade of shots. Frost stopped its action and took it along with him, issuing instructions as he walked.

"I'll have Miss Wilson drive us back to State Street. I want you to stay with her, then, wherever she goes. Talk to her, obtain any information, however trivial, that may prove useful. I have all the factors needed to identify and capture the guilty, but anything you discover will shorten the time element.

"After daylight she will be safe, and subject to no more attacks until nightfall. Leave her at nine, but see to it that she has a police guard. Make an appointment with Mr. Fred Devore Allen and talk to him. Use any line of questioning you wish. Make sure that he also has police protection or a personal bodyguard. Next comes the longest and hardest task. First, you had better get in touch with Inspector Frick, and you'll probably save time and receive considerably faster action by using a headquarters phone. Call all chemical manufacturing companies and laboratories within a radius of twenty-five miles and obtain a complete list of names and addresses to which liquid air, liquid oxygen, or liquid nitrogen was delivered during the past three days in any quantity. Give a duplicate list to Inspector Frick."

"Why? He hasn't asked for it."

"And very probably he won't know what to do with it," Frost observed urbanely. "That will be his concern, not ours. Find out whether any of the orders represent new business and whether there has been a marked increase in the number of flasks delivered to a regular customer. When you have the complete list, bring it to me. I'll be in before two and after three."

"Where can I find you between two and three?"

"At the Regal Theater, when the first stage show goes on. There is an interesting act billed as 'Shot Before Your Eyes.' A good stunt act works wonders, you know. And I'll spend a little time at the offices of the Astroplane Research Society."

Jean gave him a critical appraisal, in some bewilderment as to whether he was serious or suffered from lack of sleep and too many cigarettes. While death hurtled down from the sky, he talked of idling time away in a Broadway motion-picture palace and at an interplanetary organization. She gave it up. His methods were peculiar to himself.

The fog, if anything, became denser. Its heavy pall enshrouded the city, reduced traffic to a crawling pace, made pedestrians look like shadowy and insubstantial phantoms. But Terry drove with a kind of second sight on the way back to 13 State Street, miraculously escaping half a dozen near accidents.

V.

I. V. Frost sat in a fog in the book-lined living room of his residence. The fog came from endless cigarettes whose butts littered every ash tray in the room. Though past noon, the room was in a half gloom, for he had not troubled to turn lights on, and outside, a wall of mist rolled through the city.

Frost's eyes glowed with a gleam as restless as the fitful rise and fall of fire in the ash; but only the bright smolder in his eyes belied the fierce repose of his features. They were thin, austere features, with sardonic lips and the brow of an ascetic, expressive of an inscrutable but relentless will and an acuteness of perception akin to the mystic's extrasensory powers. Even in rest, they preserved a suggestion of unlimited reserves of nervous energy ready to flash into action instantly upon demand; thus the paradox of explosive calm.

His abstraction persisted in spite of numerous interruptions. He tensed at each ring of the telephone; but the tautness disappeared as soon as the interruption ended. He was the key figure in a series of actions and investigations proceeding on an ever-expanding scale all over the city.

Jean Moray had called at eleven, reported: "Fred Devore Allen is missing. I've talked to his family. They say he's disappeared several times before after scraps with Terry. They aren't worried a bit. What he usually does is register under a different name at a small hotel for a day or two until he cools off. I tried to get a line on his movements after he left Terry last night, but all I found out was that he left his car in their regular garage. He walked into the fog and that's the last that's been seen of him."

"Abandon that line of investigation," Frost instantly ordered. Two minutes later, he was talking to Inspector Frick of the homicide bureau. Ten minutes later, a whole corps of detectives from the Missing Persons Bureau had quietly begun a search for the missing man.

At the morgue, experts in death attempted to reconstruct, against disheartening odds, two whole and recognizable bodies from almost shapeless fragments.

A fingerprint specialist was examining files at police headquarters for a clue to the identity of the first corpse. Another expert went through records of narcotic cases; still another studied thousands of photographs in the rogue's gallery. Investigators canvassed all pubic and private airports, landing fields, and airplanes over six States.

While the machinery went into motion, and exhaustive research pursued its laborious way, Inspector Frick paid the professor an unceremonious visit.

"I'm completely at sea," he admitted with his usual candor. "As far as we've learned, absolutely nobody made a flight in any sort of an airplane last night anywhere on the Eastern seaboard. There aren't any high buildings near the Wilson place. Nobody saw anybody heave the bodies over the fence. Neither of them's been identified. The caretaker sticks to his story that he was slugged, bound, and robbed a month ago, and it's down in the records—he reported it at the time. There isn't a trace of young Allen. I can't make head or tail of the mess. Why in Hades is your assistant sitting at my desk investigating shipments of chemicals? Have they got anything to do with the condition of the bodies?"

"Unquestionably," Frost replied. "Liquid nitrogen boils at -194° C, liquid oxygen at -181° C, and liquid air below -194° C."

"Did you say boils?"

"As water boils and passes into steam, so they boil and become gaseous again at the temperatures I mentioned. For that reason, I warned one of the policemen not to touch the fragments. He was burned by the contact with terrific cold, burned more severely than if he had touched a red-hot cinder."

"How much liquid air would be needed to freeze a corpse?"

Frost shook his head. "I cannot say with precision. The only way to find out would be to experiment. Unfortunately, I do not happen to have any spare corpses on hand. I should say at least six flasks, and probably more."

"Flasks?" repeat Frick with a puzzled expression.

The professor explained, patiently. "Liquid oxygen and liquid nitrogen are highly explosive and dangerous to handle. They are gases in an unnatural state, created through pressure and reduction in temperature. They cannot be kept in sealed receptacles, because they rapidly absorb heat, revert to gaseous form, attempt to expand, create their own pressure and explode. They are handled commercially in flasks that resemble very large thermos bottles, unstoppered. The evaporating gas escapes through the neck. Liquid oxygen completely evaporates or boils away in a day. It cannot be kept for any length of time. Not many concerns are equipped to manufacture it, and the demand is limited. For these reasons, especially since a considerable quantity would be needed to freeze a corpse to something like the temperature of liquid air, and since the liquid must by the necessity of its own nature be delivered well within twenty-four hours of being used, I set Miss Moray at her task."

Frick chewed his lip. "I see. Does the stuff make things very brittle?"

"Some of the hardest and toughest metals and alloys known will break like dry sticks after they have been exposed to liquid oxygen."

Frick was silent for an interval, while he reviewed in his mind the grotesque incidents. Then he said: "We're checking up thoroughly on the airplane angle, you know. Do you still think the corpses weren't dropped from a plane?"

"I do. In the first place, aviation ceiling is zero because of the fog. No one could pilot a plane over the city in such weather at a low altitude, and blind flying even at a high altitude would be foolhardy. In the second place, skilled marksmen find it almost impossible to score a direct hit upon a ground target of even large size. Under conditions that have prevailed since yesterday, a pilot could not possibly see a ground target, nor estimate within a wide margin of error how close to it he was. Yet the corpses fell less than one hundred feet apart. I repeat, they may have fallen from the sky, but they certainly did not descent from any flying machine of man's invention."

The inspector looked harassed. "For Heaven's sake, Ivy, stop talking riddles and nonsense. How else could the corpses possibly have got where they were?"

"That remains to be proved."

The inspector tried another track. "Why did you tip us off to look through the records of narcotic cases?"

"Because the second body was that of a man who smoked opium. He may have been arrested as a dope addict, or he may have been a dope peddler, or both. The Federal government has lately been making a determined drive against the illicit drug traffic."

"You think that the dope traffic is behind this?"

"Not necessarily."

Frick was fuming. "What the dickens do you think, Ivy? Is this a murder case, or isn't it?"

Frost answered: "What I think is of less importance than what I can prove. I think that the second man was murdered, but I cannot prove it. I think that he was killed by the application of liquid air above his heart, and that his heart immediately froze solid, causing instant death. The rest of his body was then exposed to liquid air. There is absolutely no possibility that you or I or anybody else except the murderer can ever prove that such was the case. It is an ingenious and fiendish crime. The man was dead before he fell. He was dead when frozen from head to foot. Whether he died of heart failure or was murdered by the method I outlined is beyond establishing on the basis of external evidence. Even the removal of the finger tips and teeth to delay identification is no proof of homicide. It is merely cause for suspicion. There is nothing more to say at present."

Frick lingered a few minutes longer, but Frost refused to be drawn into further discussion. The inspector returned to the fog of the outer world. Not long afterward, shortly before two, Frost also went out; but he returned by three, having seen the stage show at the Regal Theater and visited the offices of the Astroplane Research Society.

He resumed his earlier posture, and, looking like some strange, predatory, thin Buddha, remained in abstraction as the hours waned. He was almost as motionless as the bust of Socrates. Outside, the fog persisted, thick, soupy. Inside, the room gradually darkened, and still the professor sat cross-legged, while acrid, pungent fumes spiced the air around him.

It was late afternoon before his assistant hurried in. He glanced at her with a questioning lift of his eyebrows.

"Here's the list." She handed him several pages of typed names and addresses, rattled on breathlessly: "Gee, I'm tired and hungry! Didn't take time for lunch. I'd no idea there were so darned many peanut-sized laboratories in this neck of the woods that use liquid air and chemical companies that make it. My arm's absolutely dead from holding a receiver, so don't be surprised if it falls to the floor any minute now and I bet I hear a buzzing in my ear for the next century. This fog gets me down. What a swell time for a flock of murders! I imagine everybody I bump into is out to kill somebody else, and I can see all sorts of lovely little monsters creeping through the fog like the green man. I'll have an A Number One case of jitters if this goes on much longer.

"By the way, Terry is a peach. After we left you, we stopped and had a double chocolate malted and hashed life over pretty thoroughly. Her only trouble is too much money. She told me a lot about herself but nothing that would help any. We had a double Scotch and soda about seven—"

Frost groaned. "Malted milk and Scotch—at seven in the morning! That is the most disagreeable thought I have encountered in some time."

Jean looked surprised. Murder didn't faze him, but mention of malted milk and whisky did. Well, that was only a minor phenomenon in the paradoxes of his make-up. She rushed on: "The kid really doesn't remember the names of nine tenths of the people she's known. She's completely forgotten the names of a couple of men she almost got engaged to at different times, and she can't even recall what they did."

"How'd the pictures turn out?"

Frost answered, with a frown: "They didn't."

"What was the matter? Not enough light?"

"On the contrary, too much light." He handed her a batch of dry films which she glanced through. They were dense, badly overexposed, so black as to be practically worthless.

"I don't understand." She wrinkled her brow in mystification. "I don't understand how you expected to get even a faint picture in that fog and I don't understand where all the light came from that spoiled the pictures. I certainly didn't see it."

"Yes you did," Frost disagreed, "but it didn't register. There are various kinds of light and energy present at all times in the atmosphere. One of these is infra-red light, which reaches the human eye but which the human eye cannot see in the sense that it sees sunlight. But photographic emulsions and photo-electric cells sensitive only to infra-red light have been developed recently though they are not yet in general use. I used infra-red film, but unfortunately, our clever opponent realized that infra-red rays would pierce the fog and show us the manner in which the corpses fell and whence they came.

"He flooded the Wilson mansion with infra-red rays. They ruined the exposures in the same manner that ordinary film would be spoiled by pointing the camera directly at the sun. He could have done this in various ways, such as using reflectors to concentrate infra-red rays on the property, or sending an electric current through the iron fence which would case it to heat and give off the rays."

Jean mourned: "All that work for nothing."

"By no means!" Frost retorted. "To-night we shall trap him in his lair."

While talking, he had been studying the lists that his assistant had brought. He went through them twice with great care and then put them aside. She was unable to determine his reaction. The list may not have supplied the information he expected. It may have presented new factors not previously taken into account. It may have required a new interpretation to be placed upon preceding circumstances, or yielded the valuable information he sought. Whatever the list meant to him, he made no comment.

Jean, exhausted from the strain of thirty-two hours of continuous activity, waited in silence for Frost to speak, and suddenly passed into dreamless sleep in the chair where she had thrown herself.

She awakened just as abruptly to find the professor gently shaking her. With the quick recuperation of youth, she struggled out of slumber to alert readiness.

"Eight o'clock," he murmured. "Time for us to go."

He had evidently not slept a wink, and by the stale air in the room, and the immense accumulation of butts, and the bright fever in his eyes, she guessed that he had pursued his meditations undisturbed while she slept. He lived upon mysteries and enigmas.

He took a crammed valise with him as they went out.

VI.

The fog, damp, depressing, impenetrable, weighted them with a palpable sea. It penetrated clothing, chilled limbs, and settled in lungs. It became a load on the mind, and rolled with a slow and restless motion as though it had come to stay through all eternity. The whistles of river tugs sobbed now with a despairing and wistful infrequency. No liners had entered or left the harbor for two days. No airplanes had taken off or landed. No sign of a breeze had yet come to sweep away that throttling blanket.

The iron fence kept out the curious who came to peer at the Wilson mansion, and they could see nothing of the house. The fog at least served to keep their numbers down to a few stragglers. A police guard remained inside with Terry who had refused to take a hotel room for the night. Jean Moray and Professor I. V. Frost patrolled the grounds.

Once, on the way over, after munching through a couple of sandwiches hastily picked up, she had yawned, thinking of the long sleep that she would get in a cozy bed when the vigil was over. Here, all thought of sleep vanished. The chill of the night came not alone from the all-concealing fog, but from the invisible menace. Everything looked unreal, distorted like images of a dream.

The mansion loomed like an ogre's dwelling, vast and cavernous. The shrubs and trees became the transformed victim of an ancient and evil enchantment. The arbor seemed a nook of legendary twilight regions, and the flower beds lay under a dark and binding spell.

Inevitably, Jean's thoughts turned skyward. The blessed sky and the familiar stars had been absorbed in the persistent empire of fog. The remembered horror of a falling corpse stayed with her, and her thoughts again and again tried to soar beyond the veil. She shivered with each melancholy wail of a foghorn, every dismal honk of an automobile, the dripping of leaves, her own ghostly footsteps on the lawn.

The professor had spoken of the cold of outer space, the absolute zero whose congealing paralysis had never been equaled by man. Did he mean to imply, in spite of the liquid air of chemistry, that the bodies of the Eurasian and the other had descended from those far, unimaginable regions? Like most people, she had read articles on the gulfs between the planets, and separating the stars. She possessed a smattering of information about cosmic laws and astronomical distances. Those tremendous thoughts kept recurring to her, for Frost had insisted that the corpses had not been hurled over the fence, thrown out of the mansion, or dropped from an airplane.

Where else could they have come from except the outer atmosphere, the plaything of little-known forces that swept them away long ago and returned them at random? Though Frost had also said he would consider the outré hypothesis only when all other alternatives had been exhausted, suppose he had already exhausted them?

She prowled around to keep warm, but she seldom drifted far from the professor. He had again set up the horizon camera, and now it clicked, not at the minute intervals of last night, but every ten seconds.

"What good will it do?" she asked, puzzled. "If it failed before, won't it fail again?"

"I've added an infra-red filter to the lens," he explained shortly. "The sun can be photographed with an ordinary camera by use of the proper filter. Same principle as wearing smoked glasses to look directly at the sun. The infra-red filter screens out fifty per cent of the infra-red rays. That, together with a reduction in the length of exposure, should obtain fair results."

He proceeded to arrange additional apparatus, chiefly a black box with a series of what looked like four oversized ear trumpets mounted on its top. He pressed a button and the four horns revolved slowly, steadily, making a complete revolution in a minute.

"What's that?" she inquired.

"Form of sonometer—sound detector and amplifier." Frost picked up a pair of receivers and clamped them over his ears. A wire led from them into the black box. He crouched with an expression of intent concentration. She watched him for a while, then moved around.

Time dragged yet flew in a curious, dual fashion. Each minute lagged with the restless burden of waiting, the everlasting chill of the fog; yet each minute flew with the hush of expectancy, the thrill of imminent danger and death that the fog might spew at any moment. Her own tension mounted as time passed; and for once she experienced a mood of unreasoning irritation against Frost for his calm and stony immobility.

The camera mechanism clicked with unvarying regularity, a monotonous sound as exasperating as the tick of a clock. The four horns revolved in a manner as inevitable as the spinning of earth on its axis.

Ten o'clock went by, ten thirty, eleven, and finally midnight slipped behind. She felt cold and weary and on edge; but Frost stayed by the box. Neither time nor fog nor cramp seemed to have a place in the ascetic discipline of his will.

At some period beyond midnight, when the fog hung like an almost physical entity around them, and when her jumpy nerves had begun to create a threatening monster out of every tree and bush, she was walking a few yards from Frost and sensed rather than saw him tauten. His hands darted to the black box, and the horns ceased revolving. She hurried to his side.

Then, even to her unaided ears, there rose from afar in the fog a strange, raucous, and harshly roaring clamor as weird as the wail of a banshee. It died out, to be replaced almost immediately by a dull blast that boomed through the fog. As the sound faded, a sharp crack issued from somewhere near the top of the mansion. She spun around and darted toward the house in a spontaneous impulse.

Fred Devore Allen returned from the missing. He made his appearance in broken sections that showered the foundation of the mansion. Shocked into rigidity, she saw his body fall in six fragments—arms, legs, torso, and head. The grisly and whitely pallid parts split further upon impact, severed horribly into still lesser chunks. The fog blanketed them with cold vapor, but they were colder than any fog. She bit her clinched hand to stifle a scream, whirled and ran toward Frost.

The professor had stopped the camera and removed its film holder. He was already feeding the film into a metallic container.

"Ivy!" she gasped. "There's another—"

Frost cut her short. "Stay here. Watch this." He caught up a large carton and raced toward the rear of the house, his face hard, his eyes slitted and flaming like twin, black coals. He carried a pair of tongs with which he collected the fragments of the body and deposited them in the already half-filled carton. One of the tong ends snapped from the terrific cold, the other followed. He continued with the remaining stubs until all the chunks lay upon the solid carbon dioxide in the carton. At -40° C, the dry ice would prevent the shattered body from softening for hours.

He dashed inside the house, put through a call to Frick, and returned to his assistant. He opened the metallic receptacle and lifted out the roll of developed, dripping film. He held it up, his flashlight behind it, and studied it against that illumination.

A minute later, the engine of his car turned over and he swiftly picked up speed toward the Queensboro Bridge.

He must have read his assistant's thoughts. Before she framed the question, he drawled: "You really ought to see the act called 'Shot Before Your Eyes.' It is a most enlightening performance. Picture the stage, the preliminary announcement, the soft background of the orchestra playing. A gentleman in tights inserts himself in the mouth of a cannon. A beautiful girl walks to the breech. Breathless suspense. Only the head of the gentleman protrudes from the cannon. The beautiful girl lights a fuse. There is a concussion, a cloud of smoke, and the gentleman sails forth from the cannon. He describes a perfect parabola and lands on the opposite side of the stage."

Light dawned upon her. "Of course! I saw it done years ago. The man is shot out of a cannon."

"Is he?" Frost inquired.

"Well, isn't he? Didn't you just say so?"

Frost said: "Let us consider the matter more carefully. There is a concussion which the audience assumes to have come from an explosion in the cannon. But the sound may have come from a synchronized, harmless explosion off stage. There is smoke, assumed to be powder gases. On the other hand, it may emanate from smoke-producing chemicals. The man emerges from the cannon, but in spite of the evidence that the audience has seen and heard, the man is not shot out of the cannon."

The lights of the bridge faded behind them, and Frost turned right twice. He now drove toward the seamy factory and manufacturing district that fronted the river. In spite of the fog, he drove as if brilliant sunshine favored him. The car sped through gloomy streets, halted at last in front of a dark and decrepit building.

The dank, miasmal odor of the river assailed their nostrils. They saw no one. The fog swirled around them and hid the upper part of the building. The old edifice stood sandwiched between other grimy structures. A legend on the display window spelled: Suntan Face Powder Co.

"Of all the incredible gall!" Frost exclaimed. He did not stop to elaborate his odd comment.

Two doors made a right angle in the narrow entrance to the building. The door on the right led to the Suntan's offices. The door facing them bore no signs. Solid stone wall rose on their left.

The unmarked door proved locked. Frost took a steel instrument from his pocket and snapped the lock with a sudden, powerful twist. His flashlight probed a worn flight of stairs which he raced up three steps at a time. The second floor was empty save for some cartons stacked in a storage room. Frost kept on climbing past the deserted upper floors, Jean hard at his heels.

An iron ladder led from the sixth-floor landing to the roof. Frost went up it and heaved the hatch cover aside. His assistant followed him out on the flat, dirt-covered roof.

The fog hung even thicker here than at ground level, but not thick enough to cloak the shambles. Blood spattered the roof—fresh blood, in wet, crimson drops and streaked splashes. All around lay bits of gleaming metal, and scattered inextricably among them were the torn and shredded fragments of what had once been human.

VII.

Frost examined the remains of man and metal, strode from piece to piece, bent low over them in the quick glance that sufficed for his keen perceptions. The only information they conveyed to Jean was that someone had been blown to bits here, recently, along with the metal of the bomb or machine.

He finally returned with a brooding and far-away expression. He peered into the fog whose dense concealment seemed to Jean no more obscure than the riddle of corpses that plunged from the sky or that exploded into shreds. A note of cold anger harshened the professor's voice. "From here, the body of Fred Devore Allen went hurtling across to the Wilson estate; and here lies all that is left of the man who launched it on its way."

She wondered at his tone. He had solved the mystery. Then why feel annoyed? "It is the end of the trail?"

"It is not. That is what we and the police were supposed to believe, when we were expected to discover this days hence. It seems incredible," he burst out, "that the liquid oxygen could have been shipped from some distant point. It could not be transported at all by air express, and even the fastest trains take hours. So much of the stuff would boil away that he would have needed to order great quantities. Yet there is nothing unusual about any of the orders in the list you made up. Are you quite sure that you covered every possible local source?"

Jean insisted: "There is no error. But maybe it wouldn't be possible to locate the source of the liquid air. Suppose that somebody in charge of manufacturing it for some company or research laboratory is the man you're after. He could make more than the orders called for, and store the rest right in his laboratory. It wouldn't show on the sales records, and no one would know if he used it himself at night, because it would have boiled away by morning anyway. Why, I might even have talked to him this afternoon, and he may be laughing up his sleeve at us now because he could truthfully give me the records of sales and—"

Frost seized her and propelled her with such violence toward the open hatch that she almost tripped down it. The hunt was on again; she knew it by the glow in his eyes and the zest in his features. "Miss Moray, if you have only one deduction as inspired as that for every three months that you work, you may consider yourself indispensable."

"Well," she said plaintively as she steadied herself, "you don't need to practically throw me through an open hatch to prove I'm indispensable."

At the second floor, Frost halted just long enough to tear open one of the cartons and pocket a box of face powder. His assistant, breathless from the rapid descent, and perplexed, stifled her curiosity until they were outside. What in the world did Frost want with a box of cosmetics? Back in his car and before starting off, he took out the list of names and addresses, studied them anew with the aid of a pocket map of the city spread open beside them.

A moment later, the car hummed along the route they had recently traversed. Jean could suppress her curiosity no longer. "What happened back there on the roof?"

"Do you remember hearing a raucous noise followed by a muffled boom just before the body of Allen descended? Upon that roof was mounted a short-muzzle light-weight cannon, based upon rocket principles. Some one placed the frozen body in the muzzle. A chamber in the gun contained liquid nitrogen. He poured liquid oxygen into a connecting chamber. The two together have an explosive force many times as powerful as nitroglycerin. The pressure built up to a point where the metal wad upon which the body rested could no longer resist. The body hurtled in an arc to the Wilson house and the wad dropped into the river between. But another chamber had been built into the gun, a chamber that had no safety exhaust and that closed tight the moment the liquid air had been poured. The gas expanded there until the gun exploded from the pressure."

Penciled lines appeared on Jean's forehead. "You mean he committed suicide after killing Allen?"

Frost shook his head. "It looks like an accident. It could have been suicide. It was murder—cold-blooded murder of an underling by a criminal yet to be caught."

"Did all the bodies and dummies come from there?"

"No. The statue and the carbon dioxide mass were shot out as tests from two different places, to determine the accuracy of range. We have just left one of the sources. We will shortly reach the other source, and the final solution."

"Why did you take the box of face powder?"

Driving with one hand at a thirty-mile clip through the fog, Frost took out the box of powder with his free hand and pried the lid off. He poked among the scented talc, drew forth a thin, flat packet whose corner he tore. It contained a white powder.

"Cocaine."

He twisted through fog-hidden streets past fog-shrouded buildings to another district of grimy factories and warehouses fronting the river. He halted in front of one that bore the legend engraved on stone: Chemical and Pharmaceutical Products Co. It covered an eighth of a city block, and though the mist concealed its higher floors, a halo of light shone up there.

Frost rummaged in the valise, took out some things that he dropped in his pockets. His face had grown grim, his attitude as deceptively restrained as an eagle poised to strike. The doors of the building were locked, but a night light burned in the entrance hallway, and Frost rang the watchman's bell.

Less than half a minute passed before a semibald, husky Scandinavian with blue eyes, tanned face, and a prominent gun made his appearance. He looked at the strange pair with a question in his eyes.

Frost said: "We're on police business. There are lights on the top floor—"

"That bane yust Mr. Arthris. He works by night."

"He's the man we want to see." Frost pushed his way in, said something in a low voice to the Swede which Jean missed; but the big watchman nodded and they passed. It was not the first time she had seen him enter without question where almost any one else would have found himself blocked.

They chose the stairs in preference to the elevator; and on the top floor, Frost directed her to await in shadows until he returned. He vanished toward the roof, but was back before she had occasion to feel worried. Off the corridor loomed various doors, dark and locked, and one large double door behind which a light showed.

The professor kept one hand in his pocket, twisted the door handle and pushed his way in with the other.

A long, broad laboratory stretched before them, a room scrupulously clean but filled with tables and equipment, racks of bottles, measuring implements and scientific tools of infinite variety, heavy mechanisms and delicate precision instruments, microscopes and electric furnaces and fantastically shaped devices of conjectural purpose. Jean took them in as a general impression, at the same time that she noticed the dark little man with the thin mouth and crooked nose who, from the table where he worked, glanced toward them in mild surprise.

"May I ask the meaning of this unwarranted intrusion? There are standing orders that I am not to be disturbed," he complained.

"Let this be the first and last. I can safely promise you that you will never again be disturbed—here." Frost said.

"Go away!" said the dark man, and his eyes glittered behind the thick lenses of his spectacles. "I don't care who you are or what you want. Go away. I am performing a delicate experiment and I cannot be disturbed."

He started to turn back to his work, and Frost's voice came with a slurring lash, "Oh, yes you can. Gaino Arthris, you are guilty of the murders of Fred Devore Allen and two other men, to name the more vicious of your crimes."

"But you must be mad! That is ridiculous. I never heard of the man, and why should I want to kill any one?" protested the stranger.

VIII.

"Shall I refresh your memory?" Frost snapped.

"Refresh my memory? Now I know you must be mad. How can you refresh my memory about something of which I have no knowledge! Go away at once or I will ring for the watchman. I have no time for fairy tales."

Jean felt resentment mount within her, for no reason except the nasty and disagreeable attitude of the obstinate little man, together with an offensive egotism that oozed out of him.

"We have no intention of leaving," Frost drawled, "except with you. Let me implant upon your mind some facts of which it seems to be blank. Possibly you would appreciate it the more in the guise of a fairy tale."

His imperturbable manner, icy, incisive, obviously began to get on Arthris' nerves. He shot Frost a look of venom and opened his mouth, but the professor forestalled him with: "Once upon a time, there lived in the fabulous city a chemical engineer. He was exceptionally clever, but emotionally unbalanced, unprepossessing in appearance, and with a quirk to his mind. Because he proved himself a good chemist, he found his shortcomings overlooked. He obtained a responsible position with a concern of manufacturing chemists.

"Because of his nature and abnormal sensitivity, he lived an essentially solitary life, and in a world largely of his own imagination. He preferred to work alone and at night; and because he had made his services valuable, his wishes were granted.

"Now, in the darkness and silence of night, and as he lived in his distorted world of imagination, he began to acquire delusions of grandeur. He would lead a second life. He would derive from another rôle the thrills and excitement that he visualized. He held a most strategic position for a double life. He could cloak himself behind his position of responsibility and trust. He attached himself to drugs, which he requisitioned from his own company's supplies for legitimate research, but the larger part of which he diverted to his own needs. His ideas expanded. There were profits—enormous profits—to be made in the smuggling and illegal bootlegging of narcotics. He began to inhabit doubtful places in the late hours, after he had finished his work. Since the keen-eyed recognized him as an addict, he had no difficulty making contacts."

The beady eyes behind the spectacles stared at Frost unblinkingly, and Frost returned a gaze of even more hypnotic intensity. "Eventually, proceeding with extreme caution, he had a smuggler and a peddler under him, one of whom was a Eurasian. His double life, his vicarious thrills, progressed rapidly.

"During one of his infrequent attempts at normal, social activities, he met the princess, let us say Miss Theresa Wilson. She became mildly interested in this individual who differed so from the men of her class whom she usually met, but she quickly returned to her customary type.

"The chemist, unfamiliar with emotions, conventions, and the easy-going familiarities of contemporary life, mistook the princess' casual friendship for something more. He felt bitterly resentful. He compensated for his uninspiring personality by developing a hatred for those more fortunate than he. He determined upon revenge for the princess' slight. In the brooding darkness of night and the long hours of seclusion, he decided further that if he could not have her, then neither could any one else."

Arthris stirred restlessly as if to interrupt, but Frost gave him no chance. "His morbid imagination, whetted by injured feelings and rejected attentions, whetted further by knowledge that he meant so little to her that she could not even remember his name, stimulated by drugs and drug hallucinations, and by the announcement that she had become engaged to another, received greater impetus from the growing Federal drive against the narcotic traffic. The fear of discovery sank into his twisted brain, even though his agents did not know his true identity. With discovery, his dual life, his delusions of grandeur, his revenge, his everything would come to an ignominious end.

"There must be a way out. He evolved a plan of fiendish, brutal ingenuity. He would use his two agents for vengeance upon Miss Wilson. He would destroy her fiancé through them, and destroy them afterward, through the resources of modern science and chemistry to which he had access. He would destroy them in a spectacular fashion that would baffle the police, terrorize the princess, and cause the murders to be charged to his own victims. Behind his mask of position, he would revel in the sensational mystery he had launched.

"He planned thoughtfully, with every attention to detail. When his phantom ambush and bomb were planted, he had only to await Miss Wilson's return; for though she might marry and live elsewhere, thus avoiding the buried bullets, his death from the sky could be calculated within a small margin of error to descent upon any site he chose within the city."

Arthris' mouth twitched; his eyes seemed pin points; he found voice at last in shrill, sullen rage. "Haven't I told you you're spoiling an experiment? Get out! Go to the police with your nonsense! I won't listen to any more!"

Frost continued: "Next he built two apparently identical guns; but one was a simple spring catapult of variable tension and recoil, and one worked by the propulsive force of liquid nitrogen and liquid oxygen. He placed the first upon the roof of the laboratory where he worked. Because he could use the freight elevator and delivery entrance to which he had keys, he was able to come and go from the laboratory without the knowledge of the night watchman. The parts of the second gun he carried to the roof of the Suntan Face Powder Co., the building which served as a blind for his traffic in narcotics.

"On successive nights, he checked the accuracy of his calculations by a plaster cast hurled from one cannon and a mass of solid carbon dioxide from the other. He even collected the fragments of the statue to find out in what way and to what degree it shattered.

"He then sent a true body weight, a corpse, after the trial dummies. The origin of the corpse is a minor point—it may have been a medical-school cadaver which he had shipped to him personally at the laboratory, or it may have been filched from a potter's grave by his agents.

"In his grandiose conceptions, nothing could go wrong. The wilder his schemes, the more they appealed to his warped understanding; the deeper he went, the farther he had to go in order to rid himself of all loose ends."

Frost's words echoed hollowly through the long spaces of the laboratory. Arthris licked his dry lips with a small, pink tongue. His forehead had begun to wrinkle.

"Shall I go on with the fairy tale?" Frost asked with a curt, accusing inflection. "I could tell how he arranged to let one of his dupes in through the delivery entrance of the laboratory, where he killed him and sent the chemically refrigerated body upon its last journey. Would you like to hear how, in his crazed jealousy, he trailed Allen, slugged him, and kidnaped him in the fog? Perhaps your conveniently elastic memory would be interested to hear how an appointment was made with your remaining partner in crime at the Suntan Face Powder Co., where he, too, was killed. Then the chemist poured liquid oxygen over the body of Allen, and hurled him upon his way, announced by the noise of the exhaust gases.

"Our chemist immediately left the scene; and he had hardly gotten away from the building before the strange cannon exploded, blasting the dead or unconscious body to bits. It might not be found for days. Investigation would uncover the drug packets in the powder boxes. The crimes would be ascribed to a vice feud, with a verdict of murder and suicide or accidental death by a person unknown. Then, by remote control the chemist would release the bomb that would destroy the princess; but the chemist did not know that the bomb had been discovered and dismantled; and he sat in his laboratory vainly waiting for the sound of the explosion and the fire that would mark her passing.

"He thought himself beyond suspicion, because of the difficulty of establishing a motive, the absence of clues. He did not realize that he left an accurate picture of himself in the way he worked, and that his own methods would inevitably expose the trail to his hiding place. He had never in his worst apprehensions believed that he could possibly be under suspicion before he had time to destroy the last evidence; with the result that, when trapped, he was convicted by his catapult which still stood upon the roof of the building where he worked."

Gaino Arthris shifted his position, and the room plunged into blackness.

Frost's voice bit through the darkness; "Take the roof, Miss Moray."

She whirled, stumbled to the door, but twisted its handle and pushed without result. Arthris had shut them in by some automatic or electric mechanism when he turned the lights out. They themselves were trapped—locked in with a drug-crazed introvert, a madman, who had at his finger tips every chemical, gas, drug, and deadly weapon known to science.

IX.

She stood, silent, motionless, straining each nerve in the effort to see by ear and to avoid giving her position away. Her heart beat faster, with a *thump that sounded as loud as a trip hammer to her own hearing. She* tried, hopelessly, to see. Nothing could be discerned in that inky blackness, with the heavy wall of fog pressing against the windows and blotting out even the faint light from stars.

She heard what sounded like softly running feet. There came a rustle from the vicinity of Frost, a thud as if he had tossed something, a flicker of light, then a flood of blue-white sizzling incandescence from the calcium flare. It brought even the far corners of the room into brilliance that only sunlight could have exceeded.

Crouching behind a table yards distant, Arthris was swinging an arm up over his head, and an ovoid object sailed through the air, an object vaguely like a Mills grenade. The little man whirled, sprang toward a high stool a dozen feet away, leaped upon it like a rabbit, with a hooked and cross-barred pole in his hands. He swung the pole through a skylight opening, caught its hook end upon the roof, and climbed up the cross bars.

In that first blur of events, Jean's senses could only register what she saw. She had to comprehend them before she could act. But as the ovoid hurtled toward them, Frost's right hand swung up, and in it nestled a curious weapon with a long, heavy barrel. He fired once, and there came a whang of metal as the powerful, armor-piercing bullet ripped into the ovoid. It stopped, spun backward from the force of impact. A shrill, hissing roar issued from it, and like a thing tortured, it shot around at crazy tangents and unpredictable angles.

The shot broke the spell that had frozen her, and her automatic leaped into her hand. She aimed at the top of the pole up which Arthris was scrambling and emptied the clip. She scored two hits, shot away half the thickness of the pole, and the lower part fell from Arthris' own weight. Like a flash he rolled aside and darted behind the protection of other tables and machines, his face a mask of rage and insane fury.

"Nice shooting!" Frost's cool voice reassured her. "Watch out for that leaping grenade. It could give you a nasty crack but the liquid oxygen that's boiling away and heaving it around is the worst part of it."

The ovoid hopped toward them, hit a chair, sizzled off in another direction, skipped to a table and smashed a microscope. It took another bounce and flew past the man who had hurled it. Again it whirled in its erratic flight and streaked across the floor toward Jean. She jumped. The grenade flew under foot, caromed, and bounded into a jar that it shattered. A bitter odor rose as the fluid spilled over and ran to the floor.

"Keep away from it," Frost warned. "Hydrochloric acid."

A hum swept up, and a drone, a crackle. A huge machine pointing toward them flickered with light. Frost aimed, fired. A wire twanged with a sudden flash of sputtering radiance and the hum died away.

"Pretty little thing," Frost drawled. "A little more of that and we'd have carried scar tissue or cancer for life. High-voltage X-ray, but short-circuited now."

From Arthris' hiding place sailed a small object that Frost did not attempt to hit. While Jean frantically reloaded, the object curved into Frost's hands. He caught it, heaved it away so that its motion did not cease for an instant. It crashed through a window, and exploded as it crashed. A volume of white smoke poured out and mingled with the fog.

Frost said grimly: "This has gone far enough. Tear gas now. Heaven knows what next. He's lost his head and is ready to turn anything loose, whether it hurts him or not in the process."

Arthris' hand shot up again but Frost fired and the missile plowed through table and zinc sheathing. A cloud of choking fumes rolled around the bullet hole.

"Get behind something," Frost curtly ordered, and dropped behind the nearest protection.

Arthris, stooping, dodged between tables toward a rack of tall, glistening containers that resembled thermos jugs. Whether he ran purposely or accidentally toward them, he fumbled with something he carried. He stumbled blindly, his face hideous with ungovernable frenzy. Blood ran down his chin, his hand. He coughed and rubbed his streaming eyes.

The flying ovoid smacked into the rack of containers and one tipped over. A bubbling, colorless, steaming fluid poured out. Arthris did not, could not, see it. He tripped over the fallen container, and clutched wildly to break his fall. The container whose neck he grasped toppled, and the contents splashed over him.

He did not scream, nor cry. Only a sudden gasp clogged his throat as the liquid air froze his head. Death, painless, almost instantaneous, reached for him with fingers as cold as the spaces between the stars.

Frost made a spontaneous movement toward one pocket, extracted the case of his peculiar cigarettes. He opened it, closed it, and returned it to his pocket intact. By that gesture, Jean knew that the mystery had begun to lose interest for him.

His face all at once looked tired, gaunt. The extraordinary brightness in his eyes had started to dim. "If you wish, you can remain here and explain to Inspector Frick, whom I will notify, what happened. But there is nothing to say that cannot equally well be said in the morning. Let's go."

He turned wearily toward the door, had it open in less than half a minute. The watchman was racing down the hall toward them as they emerged. They left him goggling at the fantastically lighted laboratory, with its now dying calcium flare ebbing its radiance upon the débris and an infinitely cold body.

IMPOSSIBLE

"IT ALL BEGAN a little over two weeks ago," said the dark man, shifting his beady bright eyes from Ivy Frost to Jean Moray as if he really didn't expect to be believed. He was not small, but seemed so, in contrast with the lean and towering figure of the professor.

"That was when the advertisement appeared. Frankly, I don't know who my employer is. I don't know where I work. I don't know what I'm doing half the time. Copying Chinese script one day—I don't know Chinese. Talking aloud for hours the next day with nobody anywhere near me. The strange cry like the wail of a banshee. Then the time I had to strip naked and walk up and down the bare room for hours. I'll go crazy if I don't get help soon. I went to the police but they just laughed when I couldn't even tell them the license number of the car. They said I was drunk. When I tried to tell them more, they threatened to put me in the psychopathic ward at Bellevue."

"Start at the beginning," Frost quietly commanded, and his cold, logical approach to the visitor's jumble of words served to calm that jittery caller.

He had come, without warning and without appointment, to the private mansion at 13 State Street where Prof. I. V. Frost preserved a state of chronic boredom until some queer or fantastic crime lured him into winding labyrinths.

Frost held degrees in science, literature, and law. He had taught for a period, and pursued researches into chemistry, physics, biology, and physiology for some years. When he tired of accumulating knowledge, he had turned to utilizing that knowledge and the resources of modern science for the detection and apprehension of criminals.

Private investments—income from several inventions and from publications—plus the occasional large fees that he received enabled him to pick his cases. There were types of investigation which he flatly refused to handle at any fee—divorce cases, political skullduggery, mere swindles and confidence games, fraudulent financial transactions, and so on. Routine work and the messes into which human beings have a genius for miring themselves held no appeal for him. The police could handle such matters in competent fashion.

He specialized in crimes extraordinary, bizarre, and subtle. The case of a "Green Man Creeping," or an "Artist of Death," or a murderer who used such novel instruments of death as solid carbon dioxide and liquid nitrogen, would absorb the whole of his thought, life, and resources until he had solved the puzzle.

His only assistant was Jean Moray, and the two made a partnership as queer as any case they had encountered. Frost, extraordinarily tall and thin, stood six feet four, with gaunt, ascetic features, black eyes, a predatory nose, irresistible will and reserves of nervous energy that seemed never to be exhausted. His hands and fingers, of long, slim beauty, would have been more appropriate to Jean, who was young, lovely in an exotic way, and restlessly full of the devil.

She had a face and figure men stared at—one reason why he employed her. Many a time that sensuous appeal of hers had focused attention, leaving Frost free for priceless seconds of swift action. She was a creature of chameleon moods, provocative or sophisticated; in turn the hoyden, or his gifted understudy. She had courage enough in an emergency, but she was driven more by a reckless thirst for excitement and adventure. She flirted outrageously with most men and then left them for the best of all reasons—no reason. She couldn't make a dent in the impregnable fortress that was Frost, and therein lay the pique of their relationship, a perfect stalemate—the irresistible force and the immovable object. She owned a quick, alert mind, when she wasn't trying to improve her natural beauty, and had proved herself an excellent aid when she wanted to.

She listened now with frank curiosity and skepticism to the statements of one Nick Valmo, who brought a strange tale. She shook her head slightly, rippling hair as warm and golden-brown as ripe wheat, and her full lips pursed. A quick glance at Frost showed him to be lighting a very long and decidedly pungent cigarette. That settled matters. When Frost began to poison himself with those abominations, it was an unfailing sign of his interest.

The dark man said, "Well, a little over three weeks ago, I noticed an ad in the personal columns. I was out of a job and down to my last dollar. It looked made to order for me. Here it is."

He fished a small, crumpled newspaper clipping from a pocket and handed it to Frost, who passed it to Jean. It read:

> Wanted: man, single, 5 ft. 9 1/2", 140-150 pounds, age 26-30, brown eyes, black hair, Latin type, perfect teeth, no physical disabilities, for interesting experimental and research work. Must be prepared to spend days out of town. Good salary to right party. Call in person, Room 1421, Lawyers Bldg., Tuesday after 9:30 A.M.

The visitor continued, "I got there at nine. I thought I'd come early and be one of the first in. About a million other men had the same idea. I never saw such a mob in all my life, and they all looked pretty much alike, because they were all about the same height, age, weight, and color. That was my first general impression. Studying them closer, I could see differences of course. There were silky black-haired ones, coarse brown-haired, and all shades between.

"It was ten before my turn came, even with a constant stream going in the door and coming out a different one farther down the hall. A lot of them must have been rejected on sight. I finally got into the office. A little, leathery-looking, middle-aged chap sat behind a desk. He had shrewd eyes, a half-bald head, and two of his upper front teeth stuck out. It gave him a sort of mousy appearance that I didn't like. He asked me the usual questions about my age, health, background, and so on. I could tell he was definitely interested, though I couldn't tell why. He finally said he thought I might be just the man he was looking for. He wouldn't tell me any more about the job, except that it would involve some very peculiar duties."

Nick Valmo paused to grunt through his nose. "Peculiar! they're about as cockeyed as any I ever heard of. This lawyer, Simon Mord, told me to buy a white gardenia, go to West End Avenue and Ninety-fifth Street, and stand on the northwest corner from two to two-thirty that afternoon. It sounded ridiculous and I told him so. He looked at me very coldly and simply said that if I wanted the job I'd have to follow instructions. He also told me to report back at his office at four and he'd let me know if I had the job.

"So I went through with it, and nothing happened. I bought the gardenia, and I stood at West End and Ninety-fifth from two to two-thirty. I felt pretty silly, just standing there, staring at the few people who passed me and being stared at by them. At two-thirty, I decided to walk downtown a way since I didn't have to be back at the office until four. Well, I started walking down West End Avenue, and darned if I didn't pass five other guys in five blocks, all much the same type, and all wearing different flowers in their lapels, a bachelor's-button, carnation, daisy, and I forget what the other two were.

"I got back to Mord's office at four. Mord told me the job was mine, and that he had been retained by a well-known sociologist or psychiatrist, I forget which. It would be a queer sort of job, lasting two weeks, and paying a hundred a week. If I followed instructions, and tested well, there might be more work at the same salary. Who wouldn't take a plum like that in times like these?"

Again Valmo stopped to shake his head. "I wouldn't blame you if you think I'm daydreaming, but here's what happened.

"The next morning, I followed the instructions that the lawyer, Mord, gave me and went to the corner of Central Park West and Sixtieth Street. At eight A.M. a small truck like an ambulance stopped. The driver told me to hop in the back and I did. Another man was sitting inside. He closed the rear doors. He had black hair, a sandy-colored mustache, and his eyes were a sort of mottled hazel color. He spoke in a drawl. His finger nails were down to the quick from picking them. He said his name was Gordon. He was heavy-set but not very tall.

"Well, he gave me a pencil and pad, and told me to write down from time to time how far I thought we'd gone and how much time had elapsed. I was to do this without taking my watch out. Naturally, since the car was completely inclosed, I had nothing to go on, except the sound of the motor. I couldn't tell when we were doing twenty or fifty, or whatever the speed was. I tried counting but I couldn't tell if ten minutes passed or an hour. My perspective went haywire under those conditions.

"I do know that we rode for a long time. It grew stuffy inside, and I had covered pages with meaningless notations about miles and minutes. Finally the car stopped, and the driver came around to open the rear door. Gordon and I got out.

"We were in front of an old brick house, completely surrounded by woods. The woods came to within a hundred feet of the house. A private dirt road evidently looped off the main road, which must have been some distance away because I couldn't hear any sounds of traffic.

"We entered the house but they didn't show me through it. Instead, we walked into a central hallway and immediately turned left into a large, almost bare room. There was only a desk and a chair in it. I was beginning by this time to wonder what sort of mess I'd let myself in for but there wasn't anything I could do about it, so I kept still. Anyway, curiosity was eating me up.

"Gordon took away the pad with the stuff I'd scribbled on it. He told me to sit at the desk and copy what I found there. Then he turned around and shut the door. I walked over to the desk. A thin book of what looked like Chinese printed on a strange, brownish sort of paper lay there, with some typewriter paper, and pencils."

Valmo took a deep breath. "Then I looked around the room. It had three windows, all of heavy plate glass that you couldn't see through. The windows were spiked shut. A door in another wall had a section of thick glass. I tried the door I had come through. It was locked.

"The only other openings were two small ventilator grilles, one in the ceiling and one in the floor. Finally I went to the table and started work. I tried to copy the stuff in the book and it just about drove me crazy. I had the devil of a time imitating those queer characters with their funny little strokes and lines. I hadn't the slightest idea what they meant, and I didn't know whether they read backward or forward, upward or down. For all I knew, I might be copying the book wrong end first.

"Then I got goose-chills. I can't explain it. I had the feeling that I was being watched, studied like a fly on a pin, and it made me squirm, only I couldn't see anybody and there was no one in the room."

Valmo looked unhappy. The mere recital reminded him too vividly of those queasy sensations. "I suppose I worked about an hour. Then Gordon opened the door, gave me a plate with a couple of sandwiches, declined to answer my questions, and went out again. I worked about an hour more. Then he came back and said we were returning to town. We made the trip in the same manner as before. Gordon told me I'd done well so far. He opened up a little, and said that a noted psychologist was doing some testing, and it had to be done without the subject knowing what it was all about, in order to get natural reactions. He asked me if everything was satisfactory, promised my first week's salary in five days, and gave me more instructions.

"Every day since, I've gone through the same experience. They always pick me up at a different place, sometimes in Manhattan, sometimes in the Bronx. As soon as I'm inside, I get busy with the paper and pad. I know from the different sounds I can hear that we've gone through tunnels, and over bridges, but I don't know whether they're the Queensboro Bridge, George Washington, Brooklyn, Manhattan, or what. Sometimes we've used ferries, but from where to where I don't know. Maybe it's just what they tell me it is. They gave me a hundred dollars a week ago. They gave it to me again yesterday.

"All I know about the brick house is that it takes three hours to get there. We leave at eight and it's around eleven when we arrive."

Valmo paused to fish a pack of cigarettes from his pocket and light one. Frost waited in silence until he resumed his narrative.

"The second day there, I was asked to walk up and down, talking aloud about anything I wished, who I was, what I'd read, what I thought about the New Deal and Communism, just anything that entered my head. They were going to time me, and at the end of a definite interval they would return and test me for various reactions. I rambled on for exactly two hours. Then they came back, Gordon and the driver whom I knew only as Al, and gave me some psychological tests. They followed their employer's instructions, and didn't pretend to understand it themselves.

"The third day, I was told to strip, and walk back and forth, keeping a measured pace to a ticking pendulum.

"The fourth day, I sat alone, the hardest experience of all. I did nothing but sit still. It got on my nerves so after awhile that I could have screamed. I knew somebody watched me, but there was no one around and no way that any one could see me. I just sat there with a bad case of jitters, expecting something to happen, wondering about the location of the place, trying to figure out who and what was behind it all.

"Then I heard something. It came without warning, and it scared me out of a year's growth; a sudden cry, a mournful rising and falling wail, full of agony, that kept on for about a minute. I was covered with sweat when the sound died away. I know that that scream was some one's death cry. But I can't prove it, and I don't know who that some one was."

Valmo's forehead beaded with sweat at the memory, his hands shook. He lived again the tension and terror of that moment.

"Gordon came in, after an hour or so, and told me to write down an exact description of anything that I had heard, and guess what caused it. He told me to write in detail. He said he felt sorry he couldn't warn me, but they were testing my memory and power of observation by sounds. Naturally I didn't write what I really thought.

"That's about all I know. Every day I've gone through the same sort of rigmarole. Oh, they've treated me decently enough, but it's the confounded mystery of it all that's got on my nerves. Copying Chinese, talking aloud to myself by the hour, walking up and down as naked as the day I was born. Why? Why?

"Two days ago I heard another cry that ended suddenly; it prickled my scalp. I've never seen anybody die, but only a person dying by violence would shriek like that. I almost went to the police a second time but I was afraid I really would be sent to a psychopathic ward. Yesterday they paid me another hundred dollars, and told me I'd receive new instructions in a day or two. I haven't heard from them yet, and I'm convinced now that I never will hear from them again."

The puzzled, plaintive voice ceased. Valmo looked expectantly at Frost. Jean Moray studied the visitor with sympathetic eyes. He may have been unduly credulous, but she visualized herself in his place. For curiosity's sake she would have done much the same thing, with the same bewildered reaction.

Frost said, "Give me your shoes."

Nick Valmo jumped angrily to his feet. "What the hell!' he exploded. "I get in a jam and you want my shoes! I won't——"

Frost stopped him short, "Sit down! Give me your shoes!"

Valmo opened his mouth, closed it without speaking. He took a look at Frost's suddenly glittering eyes and stern features. He sat down and removed his shoes. Frost left the room with them. Valmo squirmed uncomfortably and tried to hide the holes in his socks. Jean said nothing in that awkward interval.

Frost returned in a few minutes and gave the shoes to their owner. "I will take the case."

He walked with Valmo to the door. "If they communicate with you, call me instantly. Keep to your room and be on guard. Have you a gun and permit to carry it?"

"Yes. Now, about your fee——"

"Forget it," said Frost. "If you were wealthy, I would write my own check. As it is, you bring me a riddle with some peculiar and rather fascinating angles. My mind won't be satisfied until I know the answer. It is like a mathematical problem, or a puzzle, which I will solve for the sheer pleasure of it. You, as a person, do not interest me in the slightest. As one piece of a problem, you are highly interesting.

"However, there is nothing that I can do as yet. You think that one or two persons have been murdered. Proof is lacking. I will make routine investigations, but what I count on most is your notifying me immediately if Al and Gordon communicate with you again. Only then can I act."

II.

"And what," Frost asked, "do you make of Valmo's adventure?"

Jean Moray answered, "I really don't know. Why would any one want to put on such a mystifying show for somebody as unimportant as Nick Valmo? I'd hate to be in his shoes, though. The poor man is so gullible he's likely to get himself killed before he realizes what's happening."

"Are you telling me that you swallowed his story?" Frost asked in a dry and slightly disgusted tone.

The question startled her. "Well, isn't it true?"

"In almost every detail, yes."

"Then why do you throw doubt on it?"

"Because it happened to Nick Valmo."

Jean's eyes glinted. She felt a surge of exasperation over Frost's curious remarks that seemed to progress in circles. "For goodness sakes, what are you driving at? It's true and it's false; it happened to Nick Valmo so you don't believe in it—why?"

Frost drawled, "The experiences, I have no doubt, did occur to Nick Valmo. But that was not Nick Valmo!"

"Not Nick Valmo! Do you know somebody by that name?"

"I have never before encountered the name anywhere."

She stared at him in open astonishment. "If you don't know the real Nick Valmo, how in the world could you possibly guess that the man who came to us was not what he pretended to be?"

"I did not guess," Frost retorted. "I deduced an obvious truth from factual evidence."

"Well," she hesitated, "if he isn't Valmo, he's a convincing actor. He positively trembled with fear at one point."

"Not for the reasons he gave. In his narrative and appearance, however, there are nine separate indications that he is not Nick Valmo, among which three of the more apparent are his nose, his hands, and his feet. He seemed to have scraped his nose, but if you observed it accurately, you would have noticed a faint scar-line. A similar minute line encircles the first joint of all his fingers. His shoes are well-worn, yet his feet bulge the vamp noticeably, and the shoes are much too long. Furthermore, the hardest wear has occurred in parts where his own feet could not have been responsible. Therefore, he is wearing Nick Valmo's shoes. Therefore, his face and fingers have been altered to resemble Nick Valmo."

"Then why did you tell him you would take the case? Why did you say you wouldn't investigate it until you heard from him again?"

"Because he is a murderer," Frost answered coldly, "and because he was hoping for precisely that reaction. His story is improbable; he offers little evidence, and there is only his belief that a crime was committed. No detective or private investigator would be inclined to take much stock in it, or to investigate it unless there were further developments. Yet he told us how Nick Valmo died, and told it in such a fashion as to make it virtually impossible to locate either the scene of the crime or the body.

"He has lost his identity and stepped into his new rôle of Nick Valmo. He wears Valmo's clothing. Who he is and what compelling motive has driven him to drastic actions are only two of several problems that must be solved immediately."

Jean put on a slight frown. "And just how do you propose to accomplish the impossible, starting with practically nothing?"

Instead of answering, Frost lifted the receiver and phoned for Inspector Frick of the Homicide Bureau. "I. V. Frost speaking. Ask all patrolmen and squad cars to keep a special watch on vacant lots, parks, cemeteries, and isolated spots for the body of a well-dressed man who has a professional appearance and does not look like a criminal. He will be—"

"For heaven's sake, Ivy, what kind of a wizard are you?" came Frick's startled voice. "A body fitting that description was found in Oakview Cemetery less than an hour ago. They've finished the field work and it's on its way to the morgue. Clear case of murder. Fingerprints on the man's collar ought to send some one to the chair."

"Identification?"

"Tentative as C. D. Styker, the wealthy business man who disappeared about a month ago. Member of the family coming down to make identification positive. Want to see the corpse?"

"Not now," Frost replied. "I am going out to read the tombstones in Oakview Cemetery."

Frick's voice seemed to explode. "Going out to read—tombstones by night—say, what sort of a gag is this?"

Frost drawled, "Do you keep fingerprint cards on file after the subject is dead?"

"Why, yes, for a while." The inspector's tone became puzzled. "They sometimes prove useful even a year or two later. After five years, we generally weed out the old ones. Why do you ask?"

"You stated that fingerprints were found on the dead man's collar. I would suggest that you first run through the file of persons who have met death within the past two years."

"Now listen, Ivy, that's ridiculous—"

"I have no time to discuss the matter now. I will get in touch with you again later."

Frost clicked the receiver and turned to his assistant. "Miss Moray, I will be gone all night. I want you to stay behind and sleep. Get all the rest you can. Be ready for a summons at any instant between eight and nine in the morning. It is highly important that you look your best and function most efficiently."

With that he disappeared into his laboratory, for what reason she could only guess. Its seemingly inexhaustible diversity of equipment and supplies had never failed to provide him with exactly what he wanted and precisely when he wanted it. His absence lasted scarcely a minute. He came out with an expression of abstract speculation and did not appear to be aware of her existence, or, for that matter, to be conscious of anything except his own thoughts; and those he kept to himself. He was smoking another of the long, suspicious cigarettes that he manufactured himself. The pungent fumes, sharply aromatic, eddied in his wake.

He took the Demon, as his assistant had nicknamed it. The Demon was an automobile which he had assembled from standard parts and parts built to his own specifications. Jean had given it its name on the ground that only a demon could handle it at its top speed of 135 m.p.h. It looked like a cross between a sedan and a limousine, and replaced a similar car that had been demolished by explosives in one of Frost's first cases. The second Demon, like the first, had everything—bulletproof glass, armor-protected engine and fuel tank, heavy-tread tires filled with a composition that automatically repaired blowouts and punctures, smoke-screen equipment, racks and compartments for a wide variety of ammunition and accessories, and secret features that came to light only with Frost's need for them.

He ambled along at 35 and 40 most of the way. His air of profound reflection did not change. He looked oblivious to traffic and traffic lights, to pedestrians and crossings. The frequent almost-accidents never became catastrophes. Jean had once said that Frost was at least two persons and probably more—a Protean intellect detached from a physical body with which it frequently coöperated.

The caretaker at Oakview Cemetery said gruffly, "Sorry, but no visitors are permitted after sundown." He stood in front of a small stone structure just inside the entrance.

Frost said, "I know. I would appreciate your keeping an eye on my car. It will not take me long to read the inscriptions. Are there many crypts and mausoleums?"

"No, and they're all grouped around that monument—you can just see it over there. If you'll return—"

"Thank you," the professor nodded as he strode past the caretaker, who stared dubiously at the figure retreating into the darkness that enshrouded the grounds.

The beam of Frost's flashlight winked upon inscription after inscription. Thousands of headstones rose above graves, but crypts and vaults were few. He paused an instant at each of these, until he came to one which stopped him. The beam remained steady, but an oddly shaped tool in Frost's right hand made twisting sounds in the keyhole.

The caretaker sauntered toward him, then ran. "Stop! You can't break into a vault!"

"I already have," Frost stated calmly as the door opened.

The man protested, "Permission from the family and the police are required to open a tomb. I will summon the police—"

"Excellent! I believe they would find it eminently to their advantage to follow me," Frost assented as he led the way to a small crypt. In the crypt lay a coffin, whose name plate had begun to tarnish. It bore the simple legend: Sam Trogg, 1904-1933.

While the caretaker watched him with an air of uncertainty and anxiety, Frost pried up the lid of the casket.

The cadaver of Sam Trogg had not improved with age. His finger nails, through the mysterious alchemy of the grave, had kept on growing. They were long, gnarled, and of a hideous yellowish-gray hue. His hair had matted and twisted beneath his head. His features had gradually shrunk until the bony configurations of the skull showed through the withered skin.

A faint mold had developed unevenly upon the cadaver. It adhered at its thickest to the features, and at its slightest, on the hands. Frost studied the mold with a jeweler's eyepiece. He likewise examined some microscopic granules on the cerements.

"What are you looking for?" asked the caretaker.

Frost led the way out after an ambiguous reply. "Tales told by dead men." He used the same odd instrument to relock the door, and handed the caretaker his card. "In case you wish to consult the police, or if the incident brings further discussion," he finished dryly.

He took long strides to his car. The Demon lived up to its name. Twenty minutes later, just before nine, he stopped at the municipal morgue, and asked to view the body found in Oakview Cemetery. Relatives of the dead man, he learned, had already furnished positive identification that he was C. D. Styker.

Frost scarcely glanced at the corpse. He devoted a few moments to scrutiny of three fingerprints in a smear of dust upon the dead man's shirt tabs. When he left, his abstract expression remained, but to it was added the ghost of a sardonic smile.

III.

Inspector Frick glowered at his desk in police headquarters. The inspector, a wiry, slender, medium-sized individual of ruddy countenance, had a stiff carriage and walked with a crispness that resulted from his years of military service as a major. More persistent and tenacious than keen in his abilities, he nevertheless had been successful in cracking a number of tough homicide cases. His name carried prestige and considerable influence in police circles.

He was Frost's strongest friend on the force. The rivalry that frequently prevails between police and private investigators simply did not exist in their case. Frost got along with the officials better than most private operatives because he ignored fame, cared nothing about publicity, and had often handed to the force a criminal or corpse with air-tight evidence.

Frick frowned up at Mason, a fingerprint expert. "You're positive that there is no mistake? You're certain there hasn't been a slip?"

"Absolutely."

Frick continued to glower at the objects before him. He had ample reason. The enlargement of a photograph showed three clear fingerprints on the collar of a dead man. The other item was the file card of Sam Trogg, with the notation, "Electrocuted at Sing-Sing, Aug. 21, 1933."

The briefest comparison proved beyond question that prints of a man executed in 1933 and prints left by a killer in 1935 were identical!

Frick said, "Do you realize what this means if it gets out?"

Mason nodded. "Fingerprints are an infallible means of identification because no two prints have ever been alike. I've seen apparent exceptions, but they were only partial prints or poorly done, and clear prints later showed the distinctions. Even identic twins show difference in their fingerprints. Yet these three prints are exactly like Trogg's. If this gets out, it means that every criminal lawyer in America will be filing writs for the release of criminals who were convicted by fingerprint evidence. It means a blow to a system of identification built up for half a century."

"Right!" Frick agreed, scowling, "I wish to heavens we'd smeared those damn prints up ourselves. I wish we'd never found Trogg's file card. For once I wish Frost had kept his mouth shut."

"What are you going to do about it?"

"What is there to do? If we publish this, the shysters will spring a bunch of convicts. Not only that, it'll be harder than ever to get convictions against new killers. Maybe we'd better destroy these fingerprints and forget we ever saw them."

Mason said, "It might be a good idea to look into the Trogg angle. I don't remember the case but maybe he escaped or got a pardon and our records are wrong."

Frick phoned Sing-Sing, scowled some more. He called a New York undertaker, and his scowl deepened.

"It's all screwy," he announced irritably. "Trogg was electrocuted all right, and buried—in Oakview Cemetery. Undertaker claims the body was embalmed but we'll have to check. Maybe the guy came to life again by some fluke and let himself out. It seems he had plenty of dough and they put him away in one of those crypts where he could get out by himself. I'm going to get a court order—"

The door opened unceremoniously.

"Frost!" the inspector exclaimed. "I want a talk with you. Something about this Styker bump-off smells. We're going to open the grave of Sam Trogg and—"

"Save yourself the bother. I just came from there."

Frick gaped at him. "You've just come—say, what is this? How the hell did you get in so fast? Damn it, Ivy, we didn't even identify Trogg's prints till fifteen minutes ago and you say you've already been out to the cemetery!"

"And examined the *corpus delicti*. If it will interest you, some one else recently opened the grave and took wax impressions of the fingers, from which a cast was subsequently made."

"Can you prove that?"

"I found particles of wax and the mold is gone from the finger tips."

"But cadavers decay—"

Frost cut in, "A well-embalmed body frequently will show little sign of deterioration for years. Take another look at the fingerprints on Styker's collar. They contain none of the waxy and fatty skin excretions which are always found in genuine fingerprints. They could not have been left by human hands."

Frick's scowl did not noticeably lessen. "So now the fingerprint clue is a dud and we haven't anything to work on. Phooey! What a case!" He ended in disgust. "What are you going to do about it, Frost?"

"I may go walking on the bottom of a lake."

"Oh, sure, sure, that's a hot idea. Guess I'll take another route and go walking through the stratosphere," the inspector said sourly. Nevertheless he eyed Frost with a shrewd appraisal. The professor's unexpected statements had a way of developing into fact.

"My primary purpose in coming here," Frost replied, "was to ask whether the police are particularly anxious to arrest a man with a bulbous nose."

"Oh, nuts," Frick sighed wearily. "Not any more than they are to catch a man with big teeth or one with a full beard."

Frost said curtly, "I am serious."

The inspector shook his head gently, but opened a drawer. "Here's one that came in a month ago—swindler named Coleman wanted in several States." He handed a poster to Frost and dug out a few others. "You'll find plenty of other guys with bulbous noses in the Gallery if you want to run through it."

"These will do." He glanced at the faces, returned the sheaf to the inspector, and departed before Frick could ask more questions.

John Vogel, senior partner in the law firm of Vogel, Vogel, and Brant, slowly turned the pages of a book he was reading. Many important legal matters had occupied his attention all day, and he had spent the evening preparing an important brief. Now, before retiring, he allowed himself an hour of relaxation, with pipe and text, in his library. The hour was ten. Light from the shaded lamp slanted across his jovial, rather cherubic face. Jovial, except for his eyes, which were astonishingly owl-like and shrewd. The large octavo he read bore the title, "The Toxicology of Mushrooms, Toadstools, and Fungi," by Prof. I. V. Frost. He was both an old friend and legal representative of Frost.

John Vogel, white-haired and past fifty, read with relish. Full-page plates in color illustrated various poisonous mushrooms in their native state. A salty style of writing and a wealth of historical and miscellaneous background material enlivened what easily could have been a dry, scientific treatise.

"The *Amanita Phalloides*," he read, "has long and rightly been regarded as one of the most highly toxic of North American mushrooms; yet a nation that thrives upon bird's-nest soup makes of this mushroom a quaint and somewhat sinister delicacy. The Chinese employ a process of repeated boiling with native herbs to extract most of the phallin, the characteristic poison of the *Amanita* group. The water in which these mushrooms have boiled is then distilled to yield——"

A buzzer interrupted him. He closed the book, rose and crossed to the telephone stand. He lifted the receiver, listened. Then: "It is weeks since I heard from you, Ivy," John Vogel complained with a smile.

"When I have completed a case that I am investigating, I will pay you a social visit for a change," Frost promised. "J. V., I want some information. I want it fast. Can you tell me anything about a lawyer named Simon Mord?"

A dozen bits of knowledge slipped through John Vogel's mind in a flash: The times he had clashed with Mord as opposing counsel in court; Mord, who defended the sour cream of the underworld in murder cases; Mord, whose brilliantly shady career had never got him disbarred, and against whom two indictments had been quashed; Mord, who used every resource of law to protect the worst leeches of society; Mord, whom even the powerful bar associations had not been able to dislodge.

Could John Vogel give Frost details about Simon Mord? J. V. could—and did.

The prim young woman who wore glasses and had a schoolmarm appearance glanced at the clock and yawned. In fifteen minutes she could close the newspaper reading room and go home. It would be pleasant to leave the musty air of the library, and its inevitable odor of unwashed humanity. She hated her job and she hated the people who used the room.

All the bums and loafers, the ragged-clothed men with unshaven faces, the idle poor who had nothing else to do seemed to concentrate upon the newspaper room. They came and they stayed for hours until the air reeked of their presence. They read to-day's tabloids. And many of them who knew little English buried themselves in queer periodicals of a Hebraic, Russian, Polish, or Italian nature.

"Sorry, but the *Volkszeitung* is in use now . . . No, we don't carry the Fresno *Bee* . . . Tuesday's issue of *Avant*? Sorry, but it hasn't come in yet. It should arrive to-morrow . . . Here is *La Semana*—"

She attended to her duties efficiently, keeping pace with requests and the delivery of papers previously asked for. The demand was now rapidly falling off as closing time drew near.

She opened a drawer to get at her purse. A voice, incisive, crisp, halted her. "I want a complete file of the *Courier* and the *Press* for the past month."

The request was absurd. At this hour—why, it would take till long past closing time for any one to go through those files. She glanced up with a frown of annoyance. An incredibly tall, towering, and determined individual faced her. He didn't frighten her and he didn't attract her. He simply registered power, driving power that would ruthlessly trample her aside if necessary for his ends. Her heart gave a flip-flop, but she said meekly, "I will have them for you in a minute."

Then she was angry with herself for having yielded to his unreasonable request. Her anger, however, did not find words. The rangy man leaned upon the desk, with a faraway look in his eyes. When the files arrived, he took them to the nearest table.

She watched him. The room gradually emptied. He went through the first file with a speed that surprised her. He stopped three times, and copied items. He must have used shorthand, because he halted for seconds only.

Closing time came. All the other visitors had left. For some reason, she dallied about the last details of closing up for the night. The rangy man flipped through pages of the second file as if each page were only a single picture.

"Thank you," he said briefly when he left, and her eyes followed him out the door before she saw the ten-dollar bill on the desk. She looked at his call slip, which was signed, "I. V. Frost."

Though most other offices in the Federal Building were darkened, light showed through the windows of the Topographic Survey. Two clerks toiled, getting out maps, diagrams, and charts, for the benefit of an active man in his middle thirties, who looked exceedingly business-like and practical. It was almost midnight, and the clerks hoped that they would be able to finish their work soon and give to their superior the specific items he was seeking.

They looked up in surprise when an imperious knocking sounded upon the locked door. They glanced uncertainly to the third man, who walked over to the door, stood aside, and opened it, wary caution in every move he made.

Suddenly he opened the door wide. "Frost! What on earth brings you here at this hour?"

"I myself might ask," Frost observed with a smile, "what brings you here at this hour. The division of investigation of the Department of Justice would hardly send its local chief of staff to aid the Topographic Bureau in making surveys. I have a list here of certain soil particles, and I want to know where, within a radius of fifty miles, such soil can be found. I have a special interest in the wilds of northern New Jersey."

For half an hour, Frost pored over files, maps, and geological surveys. When he left, his face was grimmer than when he arrived, and a brooding aspect had entered his eyes. He smoked incessantly his long, self-made, mordant cigarettes. There was a hint of neuroticism in that habit, and in the slender hands, feminine in their beauty, that made so striking a contrast to his lankness and odd appearance.

"Shut-eye" Dade was plastered. He knew he was plastered and guessed he ought to be staggering home. He'd dropped over to "Stiffy" Litescu's shack and a couple of the boys were there, so they opened up a jug. They ran illicit stills in an out-of-the-way part of the northern New Jersey wilds. They all grew roaring drunk on their own stuff, but Vic, who got his nickname from a trick of keeping his eyes half closed and of frequently going by-by from soaking up unbelievable quantities of his own beverage, saw a fight brewing. He didn't feel like a fight.

Shut-eye fell only a couple of times as he headed for the woods in a sort of looping zigzag about 2 A.M. There was a road, but a bad one. He seldom used his car for his social affairs, because shortcuts through the woods and over the hills got him there before a car could creep over the much longer route by road.

Nevertheless, Shut-eye's method of getting home was somewhat circumspect. The trees were particularly nasty. They reached out and bit him several times. Once a tree trunk gave him a biff on the nose and he skinned his knuckles giving it a good hard biff in return, before he discovered that the dastardly assailant was a tree. At another point, a boulder cunningly rose up and pulled him down to earth, so Shut-eye put a few bullets into it to teach it a lesson.

Woozy things kept popping into his head, and sometimes he wasn't sure but what woozy things with peculiar tails and the most extraordinary colors and shapes weren't popping up and down in the woods. He pursued a pair of nine-legged ostriches with heads at each end but he didn't succeed in catching either of those marvelous birds. They somehow got away from him.

Shut-eye reeled blithely on his homeward way. He did not look like a person to be thought of in terms of blithesomeness and conviviality, but gay he seemed and plastered he was. A good five feet eleven, he looked smaller because he walked with a stoop. A young crop of whiskers sprouted hither and yon upon his face, whose other main characteristic was a distinctly glowing nose pushed to the fore by cadaverous cheeks. The entirety of this exquisite person finally arrived, after a series of further minor encounters with recalcitrant nature, in the general vicinity of his farm house.

He managed to get onto the dirt road that straggled toward it, and after a few hundred paces came in sight of his home. The old shack, as he called it, seemed a bit on its uppers, for it did a rather fancy jig in his honor. Then, too, a boulder that he hadn't noticed before seemed possessed of a strange determination to walk like a man.

To Shut-eye's great consternation, the boulder succeeded. It rose to towering proportions. It somehow acquired a pair of glittering black eyes and the beak of a predatory bird. Its profile was etched in sharp and ruthless severity against the sky.

With a yell of pure fright, Shut-eye popped his eyes wide open for the first time in years and sprinted for the house with such determination that he knocked himself cold when the doorknob leaped out and socked him on the cranium.

Prof. I. V. Frost, having watched the stranger's eccentric progress with a glint of interest, shrugged. He ceased his examination of the soil and melted into the darkness.

IV.

When Jean Moray, fresh as a grape from the vine, emerged from 11 and tripped over to 13 State Street at 7:30 A.M., she found Ivy Frost ruining himself with cigarettes and black coffee. Since he was perfectly content, she insisted upon preparing a breakfast of orange juice, toasted English muffins, bacon and eggs. Frost continued to saturate his system with cigarettes and coffee. Exasperated, she ate what she could and consigned the rest to oblivion.

"What do you make of these?" He read aloud to her the shorthand transcriptions he had made of three newspaper items.

> Chicago, Ill., Aug. 2— Police announced to-day that recent victims of confidence games had failed to identify a suspect using the name Harry Peters as the sought-for swindler. Charges against Peters will be dropped.

Peters at first was thought to be the most notorious and elusive con man ever hunted in this country. His real name and history are unknown, though he is generally listed as Stanley V. Coleman, his first alias. He has never been arrested, nor is his photograph on file. However, victims have supplied police with an accurate description of him, and a full set of his fingerprints has been collected. It was these fingerprints, rushed here from Washington, that furnished final positive proof that Peters was not the wanted fugitive.

The swindler has used a different alias for each of his schemes, and has operated in all parts of the country. He is known to have collected more than a million dollars from fraudulent schemes in the past five years. His actual "take" is believed to be considerably larger, since wealthy and prominent persons frequently do not prefer charges for fear of newspaper publicity.

Albany, N. Y., Aug. 9—Chief of Police Dan Q. O'Reilly to-day announced acquisition of a photograph of Stanley V. Coleman, a fugitive swindler for whom a nation-wide search has been in progress. Coleman has used more than a dozen aliases.

The picture came into the hands of police by accident. A newsreel taken here and showing only at local theaters was responsible for the photograph. The newsreel depicts a shot of the large crowd which gathered to witness the spectacular fire on the water front several days ago. A man in the audience, whose name police withheld by request, positively identified a man in the crowd as the notorious confidence man who swindled him out of a large sum of money at a southern resort two years ago.

Police attach great importance to the photograph. Thousands of copies are being distributed all over the country. From the way the fugitive covered his face immediately after the camera was turned toward the crowd, police believe he knew he would eventually be identified. While a close check-up is in progress, police are certain that he has already departed from this vicinity.

Cleveland, O., Aug. 25—Positive identification of a victim of amnesia found wandering on the streets yesterday as W. O. Byrnes, missing business man of Toledo, was made by relatives to-day, according to police announcement.

Byrnes at first was thought to be C. D. Styker, missing director of the Park Avenue Bank, of New York, for whom an intensive search is in progress. Styker disappeared under mysterious circumstances on August 11. He was last seen in the late afternoon, driving his car toward the George Washington Bridge. The car was found abandoned in Albany on Aug. 12. There were no signs of violence.

The former physician who retired at 30 to devote all his time to the directorships he holds in several companies, is thought to have been a victim of amnesia. He is now 41. A strange circumstance of his disappearance is the fact that, on August 5, a week before he vanished, he withdrew $100,000 in cash from his personal account. No trace of the sum has been found, nor did he give a hint to any of his associates concerning his purpose in withdrawing so large an amount. All his affairs were found to be in order.

The moment he ceased reading, Jean said, "At this stage, I wouldn't even try to guess what it's all about. If you mean to suggest that the three clippings are related to each other and have some tie-up with the fake Nick Valmo, then it's just a fancy mess. Instead of having one puzzle to solve, it looks as if about every kind of crime there is is mixed up in this somewhere."

Frost gave her a thoughtful appraisal. "Your comments, though slangy, are rather apt. And yet, I think one or two small deductions may be made. Arrange the incidents in order of their time.

"August 2: Police are seeking an operator of confidence games; 5: Styker withdraws $100,000 in cash, in New York; 9: Coleman is photographed in Albany; 11: Styker disappears while driving out of New York; 12: Styker's abandoned car is found in Albany; 12: A strange advertisement appears in a New York paper; 13 to 27: Nick Valmo answers the advertisement, and receives a job whose duties are, to say the least, remarkable; 28: Some one claiming to be Nick Valmo comes to us with a story.

"Into the picture, also, must be fitted two gentlemen known as Gordon and Al, and a brick house, location known. From particles of soil adhering to Valmo's shoes, I discovered the nature of the ground surrounding the house, and from U. S. government surveys, I have located the district in northern New Jersey."

Frost glanced at the clock. "I talked to a bank official and found that no record of the serial numbers on the bills withdrawn by Styker had been kept. I visited his residence and discovered several sheets of paper covered with figures, but giving no clue as to their purpose. They are the serial numbers of the missing currency. Come into the laboratory."

He led her to a row of items on a table. Swiftly he went to work upon her hands, incasing them in tight-fitting gloves of a black sheen that reached well past her wrists. Over the back of each hand he affixed a glass phial, swathed it in cotton, and bandaged it securely. "You many need these. Go to Valmo's address, 119 Kaye Street. Use the coupé. Stay in the car and keep low. When Valmo emerges, follow him. Follow him wherever he goes, and remember that you will be in constant danger. Start now; you should reach Valmo's address by nine o'clock."

She had chosen to wear riding breeches, boots, and tuck-in silk blouse. As she passed out of the room, she looked like anything but a student of criminology. She seemed, instead, the loveliest young woman east of the Mississippi, a beauty winner out for a walk, or a star off for a ride.

Frost returned to the library and idled with cigarettes and coffee until nine o'clock. On the hour, he phoned the office of Simon Mord. A secretary answered.

"Tell Mord that I. V. Frost will meet him at his office at 10 A.M. to-morrow for an important conference concerning Nick Valmo."

He repeated the statement. He declined to elaborate or wait for the secretary to consult the attorney. He dropped the receiver in its cradle.

A loaded valise stood on the floor of his laboratory. He took it with him when he rolled out in the Demon. It began to live up to its name immediately as he sped downtown.

V.

Jean Moray kept her head below the level of the dashboard, and flush against the left front door of the coupé. That was one of Frost's ingenious ideas. She could see the mirror above the steering wheel. It reflected another mirror in the back of the car. The rear mirror reflected the street ahead. Thus she could see, without being seen, unless some passer-by came up to the auto and deliberately peered inside.

The position cramped her, but she wriggled around a little. She craved a cigarette, but did not dare smoke. She glued her vision to 119 Kaye Street. She squirmed from time to time, easing herself into a more comfortable position. Two hours of this slow and tedious waiting passed. Her black-incased hands drew her attention at intervals. Judging from the swellings, any one who looked at them would have said she had broken them.

At 9:15, Nick Valmo came out. He walked swiftly to the corner and turned it. Jean threw the car into gear and followed. She kept about a block behind him. He walked for two more blocks and came to a closed but unlettered truck of the kind that laundries use. He climbed in the front seat. A few seconds later, the truck rolled off.

Then began a long and, at times, difficult pursuit. The truck headed toward lower Manhattan and entered the Holland Tunnel. She almost lost it in Jersey City. For forty miles, sometimes only a block behind when passing through towns, but occasionally dropping as far as half a mile to the rear on the open highway, she kept the car in sight.

She became hungry about 10:30, and contented herself with a bar of chocolate.

Then the vehicle ahead turned on to a macadam side road. Signs of habitation became increasingly rare, and she found herself in a hilly region of second-growth wilderness, a tangle of thick underbrush through which young trees struggled.

By sighting ahead from the crests of hills, she was able to tail the car but remain well behind. Ten miles of this, and the lead car again turned off on what was little more than a dirt road, wide enough for two autos to pass with difficulty, and seldom used. She had encountered other automobiles on the macadam road, but here there was none. The silence of the place made her uneasy. She dropped even farther behind, though the coupé made as little noise as any car can.

The dirt road rambled and twisted. She followed it for perhaps three miles, without coming to another road, when she swung around a curve.

There stood the truck, parked at the edge of the road. She let her coupé drift past it, saw that it had been deserted. She stopped around the next turn, and hiked back to the truck. She cut between it and the trees.

"Just a moment," drawled a voice, preceded by a flat automatic.

The door at the rear of the truck opened, and a man dropped to the ground. Although he had no mustache, his appearance otherwise fitted the description that Valmo had given of Gordon.

"Keep your hands high."

He lifted the automatic from her hip pocket, and prodded her ahead of him.

"In," he ordered curtly, nodding to the woods.

A faint trail led through the wild tangle of young growth and trees. Nine people out of ten would never have seen the trail, but Jean had spent so much time on summer canoe trips through forests and streams of the Great Lakes district that she could read nature almost as well as a crack woodsman.

She walked a quarter of a mile and came out on the edge of a lake perhaps a half-mile wide. Al and Nick Valmo stood beside a beached canoe.

Valmo looked at her with a cold and impersonal stare. "Give her the works," he ordered, showing no sign of emotion.

From behind her came Gordon's voice, a slow and stubborn drawl. "Not me. She's too damn good-looking. I always had a weakness for dames. This one's tops. There aren't many like her. Let's take her along."

Valmo said evenly, "That's impossible. The whole scheme has gone wrong as it is. If we keep her, chances are that Frost will come around with some of his poison."

"What more d'you want? You're boss of the show, but we'll be just that much stronger if he does turn up. He won't try anything if he knows we've got the girl."

"I've never heard of that stopping him," Valmo insisted. "If he ever does find her, we'll be so far away that we'll be safe. We can't take her with us for very long, anyway."

"Look at her hands. They're sprained or busted. She hasn't got a chance."

Valmo said, "Give her the works."

Jean's heart did a flip-flop. There was no possible reprieve, judging by his calm insistence. Pride would not let her plead for her life.

"While you gentlemen are trying to decide what to do about my very valuable body, let me change my make-up and fix my hair," she suddenly requested.

They stared at her in momentary astonishment as she patted, arranged, and smoothed her hair. Her right hand flashed out with a trim little automatic. The one shot she fired skimmed above Valmo's head. It went wild when Gordon came up fast from behind with a blow that knocked the pistol out of her hand.

Instantly occurred an action that provided the brief paralysis of surprise. As Gordon ran up, and knocked the gun away, her arms twined behind her and she bent forward. He sailed over her head. It was a defense trick she had practiced upon try-out subjects.

There was no unusual force in her action, but it was an action totally unexpected from a woman. She had a glimpse of Gordon, as though poised sprawled in mid-air, in front of her and facing her, yet falling away. She had a desire to laugh. She noted in the same tense moment that sheer surprise had caused Valmo and Al to lower their guns.

Gordon hit the earth with a thud.

Jean straightened, and remained motionless, her arms hanging free. She made no attempt to run or to dive for a gun. She stood like a statue as though nothing of consequence had occurred.

Gordon scrambled to his feet. The guns of the two others covered her again, but she simply stared at them as though nothing had occurred.

"Crazy—she's crazy as a loon," Gordon muttered.

"Busted hands!" Valmo snarled and walked toward her.

She uttered no protest when he cracked the butt of his weapon against each hump. There were splintering sounds. He brought out a pocketknife and slit the bandage. The acid spurted and a drop touched him. He let out a yelp of pain.

Valmo sniffed the fumes, and gradually a queer, taut determination settled on his face.

"I get it," he breathed. "Just in case we felt sentimental and tied her up, she'd rub her hands back to back and the acid would eat away at the rope. Swell idea. Now that the acid's gone, that's just what we'll do."

Jean fought and twisted like a cat. Terror produced a strength far beyond her sex and years. The odds were hopeless. They tied her hands behind her back. They knotted her ankles, drew them up tight, and lashed them to her hands. To this they fastened a rope around her neck.

"Now," said Nick Valmo, "you may have the pleasure of signing your own death warrant. Just lie quiet, until you start aching. Then move a little, and garrot yourself. Yell all you want to. So long, sister."

He blew her an ironic kiss. Al and Gordon turned back on the trail and headed for the two cars. Valmo shoved off in the canoe. She could barely see him through the tall reeds that grew thickly along the shore. The canoe faded across the lake.

For a minute, she clung to a desperate hope that they were merely torturing her and would return. The canoe continued on its straight course. She heard the noise of motors starting, and the mesh of gears as Al and Gordon drove the cars away. Then, for a brief interval, sheer panic swept her. She made an inadvertent motion, and the rope tightened inexorably on her throat. She held herself rigid because she had to. If she began to relax, or tried to straighten her already aching limbs, she would garrot herself.

She hoped, half-expected, that Frost would suddenly pop out of nowhere. He had a habit of turning up when the need was greatest. But this time, he could not help her. He had foreseen what might happen, but her own ill-taken action had deprived her of the safeguard.

She had made no plea to Valmo and she uttered no cry now.

Slowly, with infinite pains, she twisted her hands, but the slightest motion tightened relentlessly the rope around her throat. Whatever she did, however she moved, would only result in strangling her. She became acutely conscious of each sound, from the chirp of a cricket and a squirrel's chatter to the song of a meadow lark. Oddly intermingled with these was a far drumming which she recognized, in sudden despair, as a roaring in her own ears. It was the end, the pulse of doom. Since she could not help herself, quick oblivion would be preferable to the delayed agony of fiery gasping for breath. She tautened her body.

VI.

There was a swish of branches and crackle of dead leaves. She felt something pounce upon her hands from behind, and all at once, miraculously, she could breathe.

"Take it easy," drawled a cool, confidence-restoring voice. The swimming haze cleared away from her eyes, and she struggled upright to look at the professor.

"Ivy! You came!" she gasped.

"I dislike platitudes and I did nothing of the sort," he snapped. "I have been here all along. I watched the entire proceeding."

Anger flooded her face. "You've been here? You watched?" she blazed in incredulous fury. "You let them do that to me, almost kill me, before you could be bothered about saving my life? You aren't even human! You're a ghoul! You're—"

"Stop it," Frost interrupted in a brusque but insistent tone. "You have not been in any real danger. I deliberately initiated the steps leading to this occurrence. It was necessary in order to force the hand, so to speak, of the murderers and compel them to expose their plot. The inconvenience to you could not be avoided because I wished to give them ample opportunity to depart well out of hearing distance.

"The brick house is on the opposite shore. We shall raid it shortly. Meanwhile, I am going to walk across the lake. I would suggest that you encircle it. Proceed with caution, as you approach the other side. I will meet you by that boulder some two hundred yards to the right of the canoe. Take the valise with you."

He returned to the thicket from which he had emerged. Inside it, he opened his valise and donned more clothing. The suit was a self-sustaining diver's outfit, with oxygen tank, weighted shoes, and a small but powerful lamp in the helmet.

Jean watched him walk into the water until it closed above his head. She rested for several minutes, recovering from the shock of her experience. She looked at the long way around the uneven shore of the lake, and the short, inviting, direct way.

She brought the valise from its hiding place, and found that it was light enough to float. She laid her clothing inside it and struck out across the lake, pushing the valise ahead of her. She leisurely dawdled along, luxuriating in the cool pleasure of the water. It helped to calm her and steady her perspective.

On the other side, she dried herself in the sun.

When Frost strode into the lake, he stopped, as his head went under. He checked every part of the outfit. It was in perfect working condition.

The water proved to be fairly clear. The bottom, sandy and pebble-covered near shore, became rocky farther out. A dozen yards from shore, he could still touch the surface with his hand. A thick patch of weeds grew here. A school of sunfish and a bass swam away. Then the going became rougher, with steep descents and drop-offs. A hundred yards out, the bottom leveled off at about forty feet. Here there were occasional patches of mud and sand among the rocks. Silt eddied up slowly in his wake. Little light filtered down to this depth. He could have discerned nothing in that darkness except for the strong beam from his helmet. He kept swinging his head from side to side, so that the beam cut a semicircle. Even so, visibility stopped at about ten feet.

The water, lukewarm near shore, grew chilly in its deeper places. The pressure was noticeable, but not seriously uncomfortable. His ordinarily swift, decisive movements acquired that peculiar lag which the very nature of under-water work entails.

He passed occasional sink holes. He circled one mud patch which an exploratory test proved treacherous. The bottom remained roughly level. In that strange, soundless, lightless, windless darkness, he prowled like a figure in a picture run off at slow motion. He discovered none of the usual array of tin cans, broken bottles, rusty wheels, and similar junk that lakes have a habit of collecting.

A full half hour went by. He turned toward his right and walked exactly ten paces. He swung around and in doing so the beam of light diffused a ghostly aura upon an object sufficiently grisly of itself.

The object was a human leg. It stood upright. It would have floated to the surface except for the rope around its ankle. A chunk of rusty iron securely anchored the rope.

Frost moved toward it, and the leg swayed gently, with a slow and horrible motion, as though the leg was trying to escape. Then, beyond it, he discovered a second leg, similarly fastened. Near them drifted a pair of arms, socket up, fingers spread wide around the rope as if to clutch it, an arrested motion that would never be completed.

These four gruesome objects were a heavy drag. He walked slowly toward shore, carrying two weights in each hand. A weird figure in the diving suit, he looked like some creature of nightmare, with the extra arms and legs trailing behind him.

Jean Moray, scared speechless, fled into the woods when parts of a corpse suddenly popped to the surface a dozen yards out. She dressed hurriedly and saw the professor deposit his burden. He returned to the lake.

A stream of tiny bubbles marked his under-water trail. Arms and legs as a rule do not mature without a head and torso.

In another half hour, Frost emerged with the remainder of the corpse. He rid himself of the diving suit.

"Some day," he warned, "you will invite death once too often. Against the grays and browns of the soil, the greens and shadows of the woods, your whiteness made a perfect target when you sunned yourself."

"But didn't you think I had a perfect figure?" she asked, instead of showing confusion.

Frost snorted. "Now that I have assembled Nick Valmo let us add the elusive Stanley V. Coleman to our collection."

She looked at the sickening fragments of the dead man. How Frost proposed to identify him she did not venture to guess. The remains had begun to bloat. The hands had been burned so severely that no fingerprints could be obtained. Only a charred semblance of a face was left.

Frost handed her a long-barreled pistol and extra ammunition. "When we reach the house, watch the rear. I'll skirt around to the front and find out if it is occupied. Stop any one, alive if possible, but shoot to kill if necessary."

He led the way to a faint path that wound away from the lake. A couple of hundred yards at a slight upward slope brought them to the house in the clearing. There, the small truck and coupé were parked.

He separated from his assistant.

Keeping far enough away to be concealed in the underbrush, and moving slowly to avoid making sounds, Frost circled to the front of the house. Lying on the ground, at the edge of the clearing, he slipped a glass projectile into a peculiar gun. Then, aiming carefully at one of the lower windows, he fired. The projectile smashed through the window, and a volume of white smoke rolled up. Loading and firing rapidly, Frost put one of the tear-gas bombs through every window in front.

Suddenly, part of a figure appeared at an upstairs window, and the coughing stutter of a submachine gun chattered through the air. Leaves began slanting from the young trees, spouts of dirt kicked up from the ground, and the whine of bullets was answered by smack upon wood. The swinging gun sprayed the whole front for perhaps fifteen seconds. Then the white smoke eddied around the figure and it stumbled back.

At the same time, the front door opened with a jerk. A man, gun in hand, crossed the porch in a single leap that carried him to the protection of the truck. Frost shouted, "Stop or I shoot to kill!"

He leisurely brought out a duplicate of the revolver he had given his assistant, and sighted accurate. There was a sudden roar as the motor turned over, and the car leaped away in second gear. The professor fired. A trickle of fluid splashed down the hood of the car and a burst of flame roared up. A hand poked through the window and its gun spat flashes. Frost shot once more and the hand went limp. The car slowed down, and rambled erratically, and finally stopped, enveloped in flames.

From the rear of the house came the splutter of the submachine gun, briefly. A single shot ended it. A moment of silence, a savage curse, then the gun coughed again and was answered by the pistol.

The sounds of the shooting died away. The acrid fumes of burned powder mingled with the smell of burning gasoline and paint, the odor of tear-gas. No one else appeared. Silence settled again, save for the crackle from the truck. Frost walked around to the rear of the house, found Jean looking at a sprawled form.

"It's Gordon. He ran out of the house. I ordered him to stop but he began shooting. I hit his leg and he fell. He got up shooting. The second shot I fired went through his heart."

"And Al is dead in front. That leaves Coleman," Frost drawled. "Good work. I would have preferred them alive, but they knew the chair was ready."

They turned toward the house, and entered, protected by temporary masks that Frost had fished from a side pocket of his coat. They found a room, exactly as Nick Valmo described it, almost bare, its window broken from the tear-gas projectile.

Frost pointed to a panel of heavy glass in a door opposite the window. "That is how he was spied upon."

She walked over to study the section and turned around puzzled. "I don't see anything strange about it."

He led the way into the hall, and into the adjoining room. Jean looked through the glass into the room they had just left. She exclaimed, "Why, from this side I can see—"

"Precisely—one-way glass. You can look through it from one side only. It is a recent discovery of science that is just beginning to find commercial use."

They entered a room across the hall.

Jean gasped, "Nick Valmo!"

"Stanley V. Coleman," Frost corrected her.

The man, however, paid no attention to them. It is difficult to speak when you have a bullet in your brain, and are lying face up on a stretcher.

The restless glitter of speculation reëntered Frost's eyes. He knelt beside the body. The dead man's hand still clutched an automatic. Instead of examining it, however, Frost made an unexpected move. He left the room, and came back later with a small box. From the box he took chemical solutions, and from the pocket of the dead man he took a handkerchief. He treated the handkerchief with the chemicals.

Death had woven strange patterns around this house. A gaunt scientist, working in silence, and accompanied by a bright young woman radiating beauty, proceeded to extract its secrets.

VII.

He was a leathery, middle-aged man, semibald, and two of his upper front teeth protruded. They lent him a mousey appearance. He had high cheek bones with pale-yellow skin. He sat with a woman many years his junior, and uncommonly attractive in an obvious fashion. She was a medium blonde, with hair like red mahogany, and of an appearance that suggested the good-looking, well-paid private secretary.

Simon Mord had a curious hold over women. Unattractive physically, he possessed a sharp and nimble mind. He was not only astute; he emanated a sinister influence beneath the smooth conviction of his speech. He had an important if not admirable reputation, and he spent with a free hand. Generally he got what he wanted, and paid for it.

Now, his fingers tapped lightly upon the table and he wore a preoccupied look. The woman sipped an after-dinner cordial, but he barely touched his. Fastidiously dressed, in a manner that never failed to impress juries, he toyed with a gold ring on his left hand.

"You haven't been saying much to-night," she complained. "Is anything wrong?"

"Lawyers always have cases and clients to worry about, among other matters of importance. I will need to return to the office this evening."

"Shall I come with you?"

"You would only distract me."

The woman smiled slightly. "Are you seeing me later?"

"I expect to be through by eleven or twelve."

Simon Mord had a habit of giving indirect answers to questions. A few minutes later, he saw his companion to the door, and into a cab. He watched it roll away from the restaurant, before turning his steps in another direction.

The Lawyers Building was several blocks away. He walked the distance in order to remove some of his after-dinner sluggishness. His face, which usually masked his emotions, showed a certain complacency.

He fumbled for a moment with the key before he managed to open the door to his suite. He pushed a light switch and took a drink from the water cooler after crossing the room. There were two doors to Simon Mord's office—a private one to the hall corridor, and another to the rest of the suite. The arrangement had advantages.

Leaving the reception room, Simon Mord walked past two rooms of file records and desks before he reached his own office. This door was also locked, and it took him a few seconds to enter. He pushed the light switch.

A tall man was seated at Simon Mord's own desk—a stranger of forbidding appearance. He looked at the lawyer without speaking, and the lawyer suddenly felt apprehensive. Could his plans—but no, it was impossible. He stated, in a thin, even voice, "Unless you give me a satisfactory explanation at once of this burglarious entry, I shall summon the police."

"Sit down. The *argumentum ad hominem* is utterly worthless here."

"Since you prefer the police—"

"Sit down! And allow me to introduce myself. Prof. I. V. Frost."

Frost did not rise. Yet Simon Mord, who knew the psychological advantage that a standing person has over one seated, discovered that he was in the presence of a noteworthy exception to the rule. He stepped forward with a slight show of irritation and took the chair facing the desk.

Mord said, "Our appointment was for to-morrow."

The professor's glance flicked over the attorney from head to foot for an instant. The glittering eyes then stared into Mord's with an almost hypnotic intensity. "Many times," he began, "convicts and individuals of more or less evil repute have sat in the chair that you now occupy and have listened to your advice. Now, I believe that you will find it a matter of wisdom to listen carefully yourself, with due attention to details.

"A murder, or a crime, known only to the murderer or criminal, is the only crime that cannot be solved. The moment a crime is discovered, or a dead body found, solution is inevitable and identification of the guilty certain, provided only that the investigator possesses accurate powers of observation, analysis, scientific equipment both mental and mechanical, and patience.

"If the criminal himself admits any one else to his secret, or connives with any one else, that very knowledge is not only one more link against him, but also a powerful motivation for further criminal activity.

"Crime begets crime. Those who harbor knowledge of murder are in as dangerous a position as those who have murdered. They may kill, in order to avoid being killed. A murder case in which a single death occurs is of extreme rarity. Death waits on the gallows or in the electric chair for the killer; and before caught, he frequently kills and kills again—policemen, innocent bystanders, witnesses to his crime, confederates whom he fears may squeal."

"What has all this to do with me?" Mord inquired.

"It is the introduction to a tangle of circumstances in which your part will emerge. It is a complex tangle that began from a simple, single source, but which developed along devious ways until it involved the lives of many people. I entered the snarl in its middle and worked forward to the end and backward to the beginning, but I believe that you, since you are a lawyer, will prefer a straightforward narration of the facts.

"The facts began on August fifth, when C. D. Styker withdrew $100,000 in cash from his personal account. He withdrew that large sum because he had succumbed to the confidence wiles of a swindler called Stanley V. Coleman. He intrusted that money to Coleman, who promptly disappeared.

"Coleman got as far as Albany, where a news-reel photographer took a picture of a crowd in which he stood watching a fire. The picture was identified by an earlier victim of his schemes. Coleman's years of cunning immediately became nullified. With his picture broadcast and the police familiar with his face, he could never operate as successfully as in the past. He was through, unless he in turn could nullify the value of the picture.

"Like other crooks, he decided to alter his appearance, and go through a face-lifting. Unlike the others, he was more thorough in his plans, and more ingenious in their execution. He would not only lose his previous identity. He would become a person already in existence. In order to do this, he must study that person, dispose of his body in a place unlikely to be found, and resume that person's existence in a manner not likely to rouse undue suspicion.

"Coleman first of all got in touch with his latest victim, Styker, told him that the deal had fallen through, and that he would return the sum or look around for some other proposition. Styker had not yet reported the matter to police, partly from fear of newspaper publicity, and partly from fear of a libel and slander suit in case Coleman proved authentic upon investigation. Styker sized at the chance and drove out to meet him.

"Coleman, meanwhile, had been hiding out with Al and Gordon, two of his friends. When Coleman met Styker, he drew a gun and forced him to switch to the truck which Al drove to the brick house, while Gordon ran Styker's car to Albany in order to throw any pursuit off the trail."

Mord said dryly, "A story is always better when backed by proof."

"It grows better. It is backed by physical proofs and that strongest of all evidence, circumstantial evidence," Frost retorted.

"Coleman now had the $100,000 and Styker. Styker had gone willingly across a state line, by himself, but actually it was a clear case of kidnaping. Coleman now promised Styker the return of his money if he would perform an operation. That was the real motive for the abduction of Styker. Coleman remembered that Styker had been a surgeon before he gave up his practice in order to manage his financial affairs. Styker consented for two reasons. He wanted his funds, and he knew he would be killed if he did not obey.

"The swindler next communicated with his lawyer. The lawyer objected to his request but Coleman remained adamant. The penalty of being a lawyer for the underworld is that the underworld itself can doom the lawyer. Coleman had had transactions with Mord before. Thus there appeared the advertisement for a man of Coleman's general appearance, height, and weight. Out of the thousands of applicants, it was easy to pick a half dozen who bore a superficial resemblance to him. They stood upon different corners, and Coleman drove by to examine them. He picked out the most suitable victim and identified him by the flower in his lapel. Thus Nick Valmo received his fatal job."

Mord leaned back in his chair. "I have a great deal of work to do. Your tale is interesting because of its absurdity. My time demands more serious matters. Unless you quickly—"

Frost continued, "Nick Valmo, down and out, with no relatives and few acquaintances, proved an ideal victim. He was Coleman in height, weight, and general appearance. Like Coleman, he possessed a perfect set of teeth, hence could never be identified by dental work if his body should be found. Fingerprints and facial characteristics would be attended to by Styker under Coleman's guidance.

"For two weeks, then, Nick Valmo was under observation. The method of bringing him to the brick house was designed to confuse him about the location of the house, and his own jotted notes proved his ignorance. The method had one drawback. It may convince a man that a goal is farther away than it actually is, but can never convince him that it is closer than it is. The method, the copying of Chinese, and so on, was also a safety factor for the conspirators, for no one would believe Valmo if he carried his tale to the authorities.

"Coleman thus was able to study Valmo's walk, his gestures, his voice, and handwriting. He found out that Valmo had no body scars. He found out from Valmo's monologues all he needed to know about the victim's life and habits. Coleman had to be a good actor in order to be a convincing swindler. He could easily step into his new rôle.

"It is easier to modify a face than to enlarge it. Styker's task was comparatively simple. He removed the rounded tip of Coleman's nose, and some of the facial tissue, until he sufficiently resembled Valmo to pass examination. The cries that Valmo heard were part of necessary pain; for Styker had lost some of his skill through neglect of his practice.

"As soon as Valmo's usefulness ended, he was drugged, and his finger tips transferred to Coleman. Then Valmo was killed, and his face and hands burned with a blowtorch. To the bottom of the lake went his dismembered body.

"Styker, because of discredit to himself for his own part in it, might not have exposed the plot, but he had to be killed since he knew too much. No one would suspect the real motive behind the murder of a well-to-do business man. Coleman, in addition, had prepared a red herring for the police."

Simon Mord's palms grew damp. He lighted an expensive cigar, and moistened his lips. His mind schemed ahead.

Relentlessly, Frost went on. "Coleman had strolled through cemeteries in search of the red herring. He wanted fingerprints from a cadaver.

The grave of Sam Trogg gave him precisely that. It was a crypt, easy of entrance. He intended to clear himself of any possibility of a murder charge in connection with Styker's death. He never expected that the fingerprints would be traced down; but if they were traced down, they could not be connected with him.

"He did not know that fingerprints are made by waxy and fatty body secretions. The casts left fingerprints upon Styker's throat, but there was no such fatty secretion in those prints. The prints could not have been made by human fingers. Therefore, I knew that Sam Trogg's fingerprints had not been duplicated in another, a living human being.

"Coleman now stepped into his new rôle of Nick Valmo, and he stepped straight into death. For under an alias, he had deposited his funds through a power of attorney held by Simon Mord. Part of his latest haul went to Al and Gordon, but $75,000 was turned over to Mord for deposit. Mord, however, kept the money in his safe, pending certification that the numbers of the bills had not been kept. Mord had two powerful incentives to dispose of Coleman. Through the power of attorney, he could appropriate all the funds that Coleman had accumulated, amounting to over $500,000. He had feared Coleman, because if Coleman was caught, his testimony could disbar Mord and send him to the chair for complicity in murder."

Frost regarded the attorney with a brooding eye. "When Coleman, in his new rôle of Valmo, came to me, his story should have proved his greatest protection. In most cases, investigation would have ceased for lack of evidence. Coleman would be sought in connection with Styker's withdrawal of money, his disappearance, and his death. But Coleman had become Valmo and there was nothing to connect Valmo with Styker.

"Coleman's plan was really brilliant; for if, by any chance, the body of Valmo should be taken from the lake before it decomposed, Coleman would claim that it was actually the body of Coleman, who must have died under the knife just as Valmo's fingertips were about to be transferred. Coleman would insist that he was Valmo, and that the conspirators had abandoned the plan just when they had made the primary incision around his fingers. If Al and Gordon were picked up, he would not identify them. If faced with the body of Styker, he would assert that he never saw the man. In other words he would testify to his own death, and no one could prove that he was not Nick Valmo.

"I reasoned that Coleman was acting solely to protect himself, for if he had taken you into his confidence, you as a lawyer would have counseled him against coming to me. Coleman, Gordon and Al would not return to the brick house. Since there was no motive for further action, I supplied that motive by phoning your secretary this morning and making the appointment for to-morrow. I had no intention of keeping that appointment. I knew that you would immediately get in touch with Coleman and dispose of him because he could expose you and send you to the chair for murder conspiracy.

"Therefore after I left my message, you promptly called Coleman and summoned him to come at once to the red brick house, on the logical pretext that you, as an attorney, could certify whether all evidence of the murder had been destroyed. What you could foresee was that Coleman went off on a tangent. He in turn called Al and Gordon to take him there in a small truck. As it happened, Coleman rowed across the lake and reached the house before Al and Gordon.

"There you, first of all, handed over a new pistol to Coleman, and asked for his in exchange so that Coleman could never be identified by bullet grooves. You shot Coleman with his own gun at such close range that there were powder burns. You then wiped the gun and replaced it in Coleman's hand so that it would look like suicide.

"When Al and Gordon reached the house, they found Coleman's body. They had it laid out and were ready to dump it in the lake beside Valmo when I and my assistant interrupted the proceedings."

Mord's hands were sweating. He rose and went to the window and stood in the light breeze to cool off. He walked back to the desk and said, in thin tones, "Only proof and evidence back up any story."

Frost answered grimly, "I have the proof and evidence to support every phase of the story, from the serial numbers on the bills that Styker took out of the bank, to your murder of Coleman. The participants in the chain of crime are dead, save you, who will join them shortly, but the facts remain.

"I can identify Coleman and Valmo by the unburned hairs on Valmo's head, fingerprints, and palm prints in Valmo's room and in the brick house.

"The evidence that damns you, Simon Mord, is complete and final. You did not know that science can now bring out fingerprints not only from polished surfaces, but from paper, cloth and other substances. You wiped Coleman's pistol with his own handkerchief, and I found your fingerprints upon it, together with dust and oil from the pistol. More damning still is the packet of bills, amounting to $75,000, which I found in your safe half an hour ago. Those bills are new. They had few fingerprints, because bank tellers use finger guards. But Styker had handled each bill, in copying down the serial numbers. Coleman had handled the bills in counting them. And you had handled the bills when accepting them from Coleman. Upon those bills alone, is the silent testimony that will send you to the chair."

The professor ceased speaking and laid two objects on the desk. A sudden quiet, and electric tension developed in the room. It was broken by a faint sound, the soft pat of footsteps. A rush of air swept from the window as Simon Mord's body hurtled to the ground.

Simon Mord had committed suicide because of a handkerchief that did not belong to him and a $100 bill intrusted to his keeping.

Frost's face remained impassive. The black glitter in his eyes had already begun to fade as he rose from the desk.

MERRY-GO-ROUND

THE DAY'S HEAT and the high humidity had driven hundreds of thousands of people away from the city and out to near-by beaches. They sought relief in the surf of Jones Beach, cooled off at the Rockaways, swarmed to Coney Island.

Until nightfall, the waters off Coney Island were dotted with bathers, the beach thick with massed humanity.

But with the approach of midnight, the exodus proceeded at full force.

The last dribble of visitors departed from the playlands. Lights winked out. Attendants locked the different premises. The sweepers and cleaning crews finished their work of preparing for the next day's crowds.

Like the other playlands, Platinum Park was deserted, its amusement devices stopped for the night. The turnstiles had been locked; and now, long after three A.M., a deep and desolate hush hung over the park. Its vast interior looked gloomy. Only the vague blurs of revolving tunnels, slides, the whip, and other attractions could be made out against the darkness.

The night watchman dozed. He made the rounds of the park every hour, and between times napped in a chair tilted against a wall of the dance floor.

Nothing had yet happened when he made his tours of inspection. There was no reason why anything should happen. The large sums taken in at the ticket booth were invariably placed by the cashier in the night depository of the nearest bank. The only money kept in the safe was several hundred dollars' worth of change in cumbersome coins. The park contained no readily portable objects of value, hence had little lure for burglars. A night watchman seemed like an unnecessary luxury indulged in by the operators.

The middle-aged, semibald, sleepy-faced watchman, Sam Variss, went methodically about his duties. He could have passed for a business man or a merchant, and gave the impression of having a temper slow to be roused but of bull-dog persistence. His pug nose looked inadequate for his square chin.

He swung his flashlight in arcs around the turnstile. The cone of light traveled across the ticket seller's booth, the wire fence inclosing the park, and the inside entrance to the dance floor. Nothing was wrong. Nothing had ever happened, and probably nothing ever would occur that was out of the ordinary.

He turned away from the entrance and followed the path that ran along the front of Platinum Park. Other paths branched off to open-air attractions like the ferris wheel and roller coaster.

In his ears was the sound of surf, the noise of the hourly surface car, the exhaust of an occasional automobile, but the quiet seemed tomb-like by comparison with the day's racket. Grass and bushes that his beam passed over dripped from the saturated air. The amusement stands loomed dark and vague.

As Variss walked on, flashing the light around in his usual routine, a merry-go-round began playing.

That was unusual; not only unusual, but almost unbelievable at this hour. The music, slow and faint at first, swept up louder and faster as the carrousel swung into its full speed. There were four of these devices in Platinum Park. The darkness and muggy atmosphere made it difficult to tell from which direction the sound came, or even whether it originated within the playland.

Variss listened intently. The strains of music blared forth with a startling, eerie quality. He ran along the path to the nearest carrousel. It was at rest. The tinny tune kept on.

The sound began to jangle his nerves. Some drunk must have got into the park through one of the other entrances and started the merry-go-round for a lark. Maybe a party had started out for a midnight spree.

Yet Variss didn't hear shouts or the sounds that even one man would make; and any one running the instrument at this hour ought to be singing at the top of his lungs. The absence of other noises made the clangy tune stranger still.

Variss ran toward the main building which housed two of the carrousels, but as he drew nearer, he heard better, and it became evident that the sound proceeded from the fourth one, on the opposite side of the grounds.

The music, weirdly ominous and out of place, would have made any one's nerves jumpy. He ran along the paths, his flashlight picking a way past attractions whose shapes were queer enough by day, and as unpleasantly real in darkness as the creatures of nightmare.

He hurried through the middle of the park. The music grew louder and closer and monotonously disturbing. He could see the blurry, revolving platform of the merry-go-round now, its triple bank of movable mounts surging upward and forward, downward and backward, while the platform repeated its endless cycle.

The watchman flashed his beam over the control switch. No one was there.

Into the cone of light rode animal steeds—lions, tigers, zebras, camels; and fantastic steeds—unicorns, centaurs, sea horses, griffins. Rising and falling, they mounted into light to the strains of a popular waltz, and without riders. It looked like some one's idle prank, or the mischief of an invisible watcher.

Then, into the diffused glow of the flashlight, bobbed a griffin with a rider, a white rider, gleaming and terrible. The skeleton rose with its steed, and its vacant eye sockets stared at Variss, and it grinned a fixed, tooth-champed grin.

The prickles rose on the back of Variss' scalp. The skeleton's fleshless arms clutched the mane of the griffin, as though urging the steed faster. The bony feet were thrust in the stirrups. The mount and its white rider reached the top of their rise and passed from view.

Variss hastily swept his flashlight around the entire vicinity. He saw no one lurking in the shadows, no figure running off, no sign that anything else had been disturbed.

The beam returned to the merry-go-round and picked out that fleshless rider, rising and falling, advancing and retreating with the griffin in the endless circle of death. The skeleton had slumped lower from the motions of its steed, and seemed to be telling a macabre tale to the griffin, a tale whispered secretly below the metallic din of the music.

Variss walked forward. He didn't feel like hurrying. The flashlight wavered a little. He had advanced almost to the edge of the platform when the skeleton slid off its mount with a horrible crackling clatter; but its right foot caught in the stirrup, and the bones clicked and scraped as the steed progressed through the slow cycle of its motions.

The watchman jumped on the platform and worked his way to the rigid center part. He pulled the control stick, and the merry-go-round began to lag. Its musical accompaniment slowed down, became fainter. Finally the sound and motion ceased, but the skeleton rider still had one foot in a stirrup. Cavernous eye sockets stared up, and its jaws retained their hideous grin.

Variss did not disturb the skeleton or go within several feet of it.

His face was clammy when he called the police. "Listen," he blurted, "there's a skeleton riding a griffin around Coney Island—"

"How are the pink elephants doing?" sighed a weary voice from headquarters. "Brother, cut out that stuff and try sleeping it off."

"But I tell you a skeleton on a griffin—" He was talking into a dead mouthpiece. He hesitated for a few seconds, then looked into the Manhattan directory and dialed another number. He received an answer almost immediately.

"I'd like to speak to Professor I. V. Frost."

"You are," came the crisp reply.

"This is the night watchman calling from Platinum Park at Coney Island. You don't know me but I've read about your work on different cases. A queer thing just happened here and when I called the police, they didn't believe me. I found a skeleton riding around on a griffin—"

"I will be there within thirty minutes," Frost cut him short.

Variss, after making allowances for swift dressing and speedy driving from 13 State Street in Manhattan to Platinum Park in Coney Island, didn't see how Frost could make it. If the professor took time to notify his assistant and wait for her, the feat would be impossible.

The night watchman hung around the manager's office for several minutes, wondering whether to summon the police again, and how to phrase a report. He made a second effort. By giving additional details and speaking more calmly, he convinced headquarters that he was not a victim of hallucinations or *delirium tremens*.

II.

In the lessening darkness that is prelude to dawn, the two patrolmen from a radio car looked down at the skeleton.

"This is just about the limit in crazy publicity stunts," announced Kerrigan, the bigger and more skeptical of the two. "It beats all the bonehead gags I ever heard of. The management has the watchman fix the set-up, then he pretends to find it. It's so goofy the papers will eat it up. Everybody that comes here to-day will try to get in the park just to see where they found the skeleton. It will make the front pages all over the country, a million bucks' worth of free publicity. You'll need fifty extras to keep things moving."

Variss looked disgusted. "Speaking of dumbness, I had to phone twice before I got any attention."

The third man, Rian, gave him a scowl. "All right, wise guy, why would anybody want to go to all the bother of lugging a skeleton in here and propping it up on a merry-go-round, and start it going? If it ain't a publicity gag, it don't make sense."

"That's your funeral, not mine."

Rian and Kerrigan both started to talk when the drone of a powerful car traveling at high velocity sounded in the distance. The two turned simultaneously toward Ocean Avenue. Headlights shot toward them like twin bullets. Variss glanced at his wrist watch. It was twenty-eight minutes since he had called Frost.

"That guy ought to get about three tickets in a bunch," said Rian, then added grudgingly, "if you could catch him."

A lean, towering figure—at least six feet four—unfolded from the driver's seat as the car stopped. After him came a young woman who had to trot to keep up with his long stride.

Kerrigan momentarily forgot about the skeleton. He watched the approach of the paradoxical pair that he had heard much about but never seen. Frost wore corduroy trousers, a military shirt without tie, and old, chemical-stained, leather jacket; yet they seemed oddly appropriate to him. His thin, ascetic features looked eager. His black eyes smoldered with an almost neurotic tension. A cigarette glowed between two slender fingers.

His assistant, Jean Moray, had an equally arresting individuality. She had come to him a year ago with a bizarre problem which he had solved. Then she had accepted his offer to remain as his understudy.

Her five feet seven was overshadowed by Frost's height, but in contrast with the singularity of his appearance, her matchless figure and the loveliness in her wise young face stood out the more.

Frost, always imperturbable, was the coldly impersonal analyst as completely as any human being could be, while Jean changed her moods as frequently as her wardrobe. She had high cheek bones, a flawless skin, and a beautiful mouth that belied her wide-set, hazel-green eyes. Hers was an exotic face that did not come under any standard type, and that expressed her own distinctive personality.

Frost drooped over the skeleton. For a full minute, he knelt beside it, examining it in minute detail. His eyes glittered, but he showed no more emotion than if he had been glancing at a sack of potatoes. When he stood up, he drawled, "Interesting. A very pretty object for logical analysis."

Jean looked at the thing critically, and with distaste. "I certainly don't think it's very pretty. I'd even go so far as to say I don't ever expect to see an attractive skeleton."

"Yet, to the observing mind, it affords matter for some nice distinctions."

"I wouldn't like it, no matter how nice it was. I don't think I care for skeletons."

"My dear Miss Moray," Frost said acidly, "your attitude may be excellent as personal philosophy, but it hardly serves to advance the reconstruction of a rather mystifying crime, its solution, and detection of its perpetrator."

"Crime?" echoed Kerrigan, scoffing. "Guess again. Look close enough and you can see the wire supports. It's a museum piece. We'll likely get a report to-day that somebody's pet skeleton was swiped."

"Look closely enough," Frost retorted, "and you will see that the supports are crudely fashioned and not skillfully placed. A novice performed the work."

"I suppose next you'll be telling us the same guy bumped him off."

"Precisely."

Now hostile, Kerrigan gibed, "You wouldn't mind telling us how the guy got bumped off?"

"Not at all," Frost replied with a faint, sardonic smile. "A bullet, probably a .38 or .45 fired from close range, killed him."

The watchman looked at the professor in open astonishment. Rian didn't know what to make of him. Even Jean, accustomed to his feats of pure deduction, watched him with an air of some doubt.

Kerrigan hammered away. "While you're at it, you might as well let us know just about when he got the works."

"I will gladly do better than that," Frost offered. "He got the works, as you picturesquely phrase it, exactly nineteen days ago."

Kerrigan's impatience reached its limit. "Are you trying to kid us? I've seen enough stiffs to know that it just couldn't be as far gone as this in a climate like this inside of three weeks. That's impossible. Nature don't work that fast."

"Right," Frost observed blandly. "The processes of nature can be artificially accelerated, however."

Kerrigan snorted, "By the way, you didn't mention who the guy was whose skeleton is here."

The professor tapped a cigarette and lighted it. He exhaled a cloud of acrid fumes with keen enjoyment. "I was coming to that point. The man's name happened to be Werner G. Reisenham, one of the owners of Platinum Park."

The night watchman's jaw fell. He looked pop-eyed. Kerrigan opened his mouth to blurt out some comment. Jean said nothing, but her thoughtful glance passed back and forth between the professor and the sprawled bones.

Rian broke that moment of tense silence. "Haw haw haw!" he exploded in a sudden burst of laughter. "That's the funniest thing I've heard in years!" He gasped. "Sherlock Holmes was a piker compared to this guy! They ought to can the G men and make him the whole works! He just comes along and looks at a skeleton. Then he announces that the guy was murdered, how he got bumped off, when, and who he was! Haw haw haw! I never heard anything like it! I bet it's the first time in history that anybody looks at a pile of bones and guesses everything and even deduces the name of the guy they came from!"

Frost regarded Rian with a calm, freezing intentness, the black pupils of his eyes grown larger and brighter. Rian stopped laughing. Frost continued to scrutinize him, as though he were a fly stuck on a pin. Rian began to squirm and fidget, unable to turn away from the professor's hypnotic gaze.

"The bones of skeletons in museums and medical schools," Frost stated in a matter-of-fact tone, "are dry if not brittle with age. So also are bones that have weathered, such as the three-year-old skeletons recently found in Vermont. Bones bleach in the sun. This skeleton is unbleached, fresh, the bones moist and far from brittle. The bones very recently were surrounded by flesh. This is deduction of the most obvious kind.

"The fact that the skeleton is wired indicates that some one wanted the police to believe it a laboratory specimen left here as a practical joke or a publicity stunt; which in turn creates suspicion that murder is involved.

"Further examination of the skeleton discloses that the third rib is wired, and the spinal column at the second vertebra. A section is missing from the rib, a larger fraction from the spinal column. The skeleton otherwise is complete, and has been handled with care.

The bullet of a large-caliber cartridge, fired at close range from the front, would leave just such evidence in shattering the rib and emerging through the spinal column. Since there would be no purpose in firing such a shot after death, it is evident that the shot was the cause of death.

"Studying the skeleton for peculiarities, I note first of all that it contains a perfect set of teeth. The man never had to visit a dentist.

Secondly, a small, triangular piece has been cut from the base of the skull, replaced, and allowed to knit, obviously the result of a brain operation. Thirdly, the bones of the feet are excessively long and narrow, and the arches have fallen. Fourthly, the right thumb is misshapen, and the forefinger broken and healed at the second joint. Fifthly, the man must have been between five feet ten and one half inches and five feet eleven inches tall. There are other peculiarities which I need not elaborate.

"Briefly, none of them is of special value; but taken together, they constitute a set of peculiarities that could belong to only one individual, and they identify him as Werner G. Reisenham who disappeared nineteen days ago, and who possessed exactly these characteristics."

Rian and Kerrigan looked stupefied. Variss listened intently. Jean objected, "But that still doesn't explain everything. If Reisenham disappeared only nineteen days ago, he wouldn't have turned into a skeleton by—"

"The stripping of flesh from bones is a little-known and macabre subject upon which it is unnecessary to elaborate," Frost commented dryly. "The process of decomposition can be accelerated by various methods. For instance, many other substances than food have been boiled for specific purposes."

III.

Rian and Kerrigan exchanged glances.

"I would suggest that you summon the homicide detail," Frost urged impatiently. "Whether you believe it or not, this is a murder case. Tell headquarters to notify Inspector Frick that I am here."

"Get to a phone," Kerrigan ordered the junior member, and as Rian swung off, he turned threateningly toward the night watchman. "You're on a spot, fella. Come clean. You done it, didn't you?"

Variss growled in disgust, "You cops are a pain in the neck. While you stand here jawing, the killer gets farther away. Pick on the nearest guy and give him the works seems to be a police habit."

"You were here, weren't you? You could 'a' done it. How come you're the watchman and didn't see nothing?"

"Listen: I'll probably get sacked because this happened. I might as well kiss my job good-by right now. Even in daylight, you can't see this part of the park from where I was. It's no trick at all for anybody to climb over the turnstile, and they'd have three quarters of an hour to work in between my rounds. It wouldn't take five minutes to fasten a skeleton to the merry-go-round loosely, throw the control lever, and beat it. So far as that goes, sure I could've done it, and had a darn good reason, if that's Reisenham. I hated the guy, and so did everybody else around here."

Frost interrupted with: "How long have you been on night duty here, Variss?"

"About a month. Why?"

"Where were you before that?"

"I was day guard at the Werner Turner—that's the new attraction they just installed this year that's been such a big hit."

"What happened to the night watchman before you?"

"Jepson? Search me. He got canned, I guess. I haven't seen him around since."

Frost drawled to Kerrigan: "Many a man before this has committed murder over labor trouble. Have Jepson picked up for questioning. He had a motive, knowledge of the park, and familiarity with the watchman's duties which would enable him to carry off this coup."

The patrolman admitted, a note of grudging approval beginning to show in his attitude: "You know how to get the answers."

Frost continued: "Also, notify the other two partners of the Platinum Park Corporation. Rout them out of bed, use pressure if necessary, and get them here before the remains are removed."

"What's the point of that?"

"Corroborative identification for one thing. I have other reasons that I do not at the moment care to divulge. The two men are named Leo F. Barburg and Milton Moss."

Frost, who had been speaking in a somewhat mechanical fashion as though his thoughts were elsewhere, walked toward the center of the merry-go-round. The operator's stand and the control lever were situated upon it. This latter object appeared to interest him.

The control, a metal handle that projected about a yard from the floor, worked in a slot a foot long. He stooped and examined the groove, then tested the lever. It took considerable pressure to force it from the stop position at an acute angle to neutral at a right angle.

Then the lever made contact, slid easily the rest of its distance to full speed at an obtuse angle. The platform began to revolve. Frost at once jerked the bar back, stopping the motion and the rising strains of music as Kerrigan yelled a protest. The platform revolved slowly for a few yards upon momentum.

A second lever, parallel with the first, proved to be a safety brake. Its only function was to halt the carrousel in case the first handle jammed while the unit was operating.

"What's the sense of that?" demanded Kerrigan truculently.

"Pure curiosity. I wanted to see how it worked," Frost explained. "And now it might be worthwhile to retrace the route which the watchman would have told you he had followed, if you had thought to ask him about it."

For an instant, Kerrigan looked uncertain. He couldn't be sure if he was on the receiving end of an indirect thrust. "You trying to get us away from this spot? Didn't I see you pick something up?"

"I believe you did," Frost answered with disconcerting candor. He opened his right fist and exhibited a small cylinder of nickel-plated metal. "I was testing the lever to find out whether any one could manipulate it readily. It has been deliberately tightened so that, if left unguarded for any reason, no children and few adults would be able to operate the carrousel. During my inspection, I found this object wedged in the groove."

"What the dickens is it?" asked the puzzled patrolman after turning it over several times.

"A simple timing device. It works by a combination of compressed air and a spring, and consists of a rigid shell with a movable piston inside. Compress the piston and it is caught within the shell. The spring forces a disk against the compressed air, which escapes through a tiny pin point in the shell, and when the air has leaked out, the spring releases the catch which in turn causes the piston to plunge out.

"The complete action requires five minutes. This device explains why Variss did not find any one at the carrousel. Whoever put the skeleton on the griffin also set the control lever upright and slipped the timer into the slot. He then had five minutes to leave the park and be far away, before the piston sprang out and pushed the lever sufficiently to operate the carrousel."

"I thought you said it took a lot of effort to move the lever?"

"I did." Frost frowned impatiently. "And it does, up to the point where the lever is in vertical position. At the instant of contact, the lever slides easily and smoothly, and would respond to even less pressure than the timer exerts."

Variss, who had been on the fringe of the group, staring at the skeleton in fascination, paying little attention to the others, caught the last few sentences. He turned around, said with abrupt interest, "Let me see that gadget."

Kerrigan handed it over, and the watchman studied it briefly. "It's just like mine," he volunteered, and fished an identical timer out of a pocket.

"Well, I'll be damned!" the surprised patrolman burst out. "Where the dickens did you get that? How many of these things are there around here?"

"Plenty," was Variss' terse reply. He added: "I got mine when I was doing duty on the Werner Turner. There's a concession just inside the park, where the suckers toss rings for prizes. A lot of the prizes are timers, which aren't much use to most people, but they're something to play with. Besides that, all the operators of the power attractions have—"

"The which?"

Frost answered for Variss: "The power attractions are those such as the whip, the scooter, the carrousel, the caterpillar, and all those which operate by electrical power, as distinguished from the fixed attractions like the slides, magic chamber, dance floor, and dolls' palace."

"That's right," Variss agreed. "As I was saying, the operators all have these timers. Every now and then, some one falls off and gets hurt. Instead of stopping the attraction, which would let a crowd gather, the operator slips a timer in the lever control and goes over to help. He and the starter put the person on his feet, if he's all right, or carry him away, if he's really hurt. That way, the unit keeps moving, a mob doesn't collect, and the timer automatically shuts off power if the operator is away very long.

"The gadget is used regularly on the scooter because the cars are always jamming and it takes two men to pull them apart and keep them going. So the scooter operator generally slips a timer into the groove and then goes to help out on the floor work."

Kerrigan asked: "How many power attractions are there?"

"Twenty-eight out of the forty-one amusements here," Variss replied.

"Twenty-eight! Plus the two or three we got already only gives us about thirty suspects to work on." He had an inspiration. "We ain't getting anywhere. Supposing you start out and show us the route you followed just before you found the skeleton. Rian, you stay here and wait for the homicide squad."

Frost wore an air of slightly ironic mirth as Kerrigan marched off with the watchman. After several paces, the patrolman looked back in some doubt and called, "Coming along?"

"No."

Kerrigan hesitated, decided to go through with the survey, and disappeared with Variss toward the front of the park.

"Let us try the rear half," Frost told his assistant.

Dawn was approaching; the gray light grew steadily clearer, and tints of orange had crept up in the eastern sky. The air remained sticky and warm, prophetic of another torrid, intolerably humid day.

The professor remarked: "Survey the northern part of the premises while I investigate the southern. Don't bother about footprints. The atmosphere is so saturated that any prints would have filled in long before we arrived, even if the police had not trampled around."

Jean said: "I can't imagine why any one would want to go to all this trouble about a skeleton. There's not only the risk of discovery but just the plain, nasty nature of the thing. Why bring it here? A dozen other places would be better, and with less chance of being caught."

"On the contrary, this is one of the most adroitly prepared crimes that has yet come to my attention. There are no tangible, specific clues. There are innumerable suspects. And in the ordinary course of investigation, the affair would have been dismissed as a prank, with the identity of the victim never known or sought for, and consequently the murder never discovered or search for the murderer launched.

"Yet deductive logic affords us a number of more than tenuous aids. There must have been excellent reason for placing the skeleton upon a carrousel. So many other parts of the grounds would be more accessible that we may assume a particular reason; and it is further significant that the skeleton rode a griffin.

"Reisenham's full name was Werner Grifon Reisenham. Any observer should at once note the similarity between Grifon and griffin. We may deduce another connection between the carrousel and the skeleton. Other attractions were closer to the entrances, yet the merry-go-round was selected. Why? Partly because it was hidden from the streets, and offered greater protection against chance discovery; but, also, the merry-go-round is a symbol for the run-around. We have an additional as yet unexplained connection with Reisenham's name, the new amusement called the Werner Turner.

"Besides these leads, there are four definite suspects with motives, twenty-eight others in reserve, so to speak, and more yet to be found. The problem has subtle and difficult aspects. The murderer may escape by the magnificent ingenuity with which he has involved so large a number of persons."

Jean frowned. "But why Coney Island? Wasn't he taking a long chance?"

"Quite the opposite. He could hardly have picked a safer spot. Among the vast numbers of visitors here, a man could be stabbed and half carried, half supported to a place of concealment without attracting attention. People are constantly bruising and cutting themselves upon the more tough-and-tumble devices, or suffering nose bleeds. Blood spots are so common that no one attaches special significance to them. Again, it would be a simple matter to bring the skeleton in wrapped as a bundle and leave it at the check room. The murderer, if caught while attempting to enter the premises at night, would probably be set free as a mere intruder. In case of a murder actually committed here, there is almost no likelihood that a helpful clue will be found, because the huge numbers of passers-by would destroy any evidence within seconds simply by trampling it."

At the western end of Platinum Park, Frost separated from Jean. Obedient to his instructions, she began a canvass of the northern side. Frost covered ground even faster than his assistant. His trained eyes seemed to have a photographic quality, to register instantly everything that came within range of vision.

A swirl of faintly aromatic, pungent smoke from the long cigarettes of his own manufacture swirled behind him. He prowled around the different units, peered under the platforms of such as were elevated from the ground, scrutinized the grass and shrubbery, the paths and walks.

Toward the south-central portion of the inclosure, he saw a small, one-story stone shed. The door was locked, but with the aid of an instrument that had a predilection for locks, he entered in short order.

A dynamo stood at one end of the room, and a variety of garden tools, lumber, odds and ends of metal. He descended a stone flight of stairs, and found himself in a much larger room, a workshop with benches, lathes, and other common carpenters' and machinists' equipment. Well-stocked drawers contained electrical supplies, hardware, and spare metal parts in a wide assortment. Portions of scooters, ferris-wheel boats, and caterpillar cars indicated that the shop was used for quick repair of damaged and broken devices.

At the far end of the room, resting upon a series of burners, stood a large and battered copper boiler. It had served many purposes in its day, and was discolored by verdigris, streaks of paint and turpentine, oil smudges, patches of dried tar. A drain lay near it at the bottom of a circular depression in the floor. Not far from the drain a splotch of tar had hardened on the cement. In a basket of junk, he found a silver circlet hammered flat, and the battered pieces of a watch. These he pocketed, and borrowed a trowel with a long, narrow, V-shaped blade.

Emerging from the shed, Frost saw no one in the vicinity, though he heard voices from other points. It had now grown fairly light. He walked slowly along the path, eyes intent upon its surface. He proceeded for ten paces before he stopped and knelt on the cinders. To the average onlooker, there would have seemed no reason why he should stop at that particular spot, for it did not show any apparent difference from the rest of the path. Yet something caught his eye and he went to work without hesitation.

He forced the long, thin blade of the trowel to its full depth and lifted out a scoop of soil. With swift movements, he hollowed a cone two feet deep. A few more efforts and Frost uncovered what he was after.

The trowel struck softer stuff, which happened to be the rest of Mr. Reisenham, in a horrible state.

IV.

Frost replaced the soil and smoothed over the cinder surface. He returned the trowel and locked the door of the shed. He heard a car arrive, the sounds of several men. A babel of voices came from the merry-go-round as the homicide squad went to work.

Frost continued his search. The southern boundary of Platinum Park was the wall of a building that ran clear through from street to street. The park property was open in many places, but toward the front, the dance floor and magic-chamber units were inclosed and adjacent to the dividing wall.

He saw a door on the side of the magic-chamber attraction, a half-hidden, little-used door that swung inward. He entered and found a narrow passage between the wall and the magic chamber. The left side was lined for part of its distance with glass, but pressure caused a panel to swing and he looked directly into the chamber. The mirrors were double-faced and pivoted. At one time, the passageway had served as an exit.

Frost closed the opening and searched on, his flashlight cutting the total darkness. Halfway along the corridor, he saw another door in the wall to his right. Finding it unlocked, he went through.

The step brought him face to face with a gorilla, a spectacle that might have proved a trifle distressing if the animal had not been stuffed. He stood in the dimly lighted interior of a side show. The gorilla was mounted on a pedestal in a kind of alcove nine feet long, which opened directly on the main floor. To his left was a stand, now curtained, bearing the legend: HERMES THE MAGICIAN. The stand to his right screamed: MADAME SERPA.

Investigating the magician's stall, he found a miscellany of crystal globes, wands, turbans, cards, silken scarfs, hollow white balls, and similar paraphernalia, as well as scissors, swords, daggers, and a blank-cartridge pistol.

He entered the neighboring stand and surprised a somewhat plump but decidedly personable woman who wore a spangled blouse, a grass skirt, anklets, a head circlet of artificial flowers, and an eight-foot-long python which twined affectionately around her throat and left arm. She had a bold, blond face, voluptuous rather than coarse. Her tawny, golden hair was cut extremely short, and her head festooned with little curls that looked rather silly.

"What's the big idea?" she blurted.

Frost didn't bat an eyelash or show the least surprise. He asked casually, "Why do you hate Reisenham?"

"Because he's a cheap skate, a dirty, four-flushing—" She stopped in mid-sentence. "What's it to you?"

"Suppose you tell me about it."

"Why should I?"

"Because it will do you more good to talk to me now before facing the police later." Frost's flat statement had the force of an inflexible dictum. "Reisenham has been murdered."

Madame Serpa shed nary a tear. "The big slob made a play for me once, but I gave him the gate."

"What about Hermes?"

She hesitated, admitted: "He hasn't any use for Reisenham, either. That's partly because he and I are good pals. Maybe we'll get hitched one of these days. So Reinsenham's dead. How'd it happen?"

Frost suggested, "There doesn't seem to be much love wasted on Reisenham among the side-show community."

"There ain't," she snapped. "Reisenham and his two pals tried to buy us out, but Markey—he's the guy that owns the joint—won't sell, and we're all for Markey. There's been trouble ever since the fire here early this spring that almost put us out of business. They never did find out how it got started, but we've had our own suspicions."

"If the two organizations are such rivals, isn't it unusual that the doors between them are not kept locked?"

"Not particularly. Years ago, both outfits were under the same management. After the owners sold out, and a new gang took over the Platinum Park Corporation, the doors were supposed to be locked. They generally aren't . When any of us want to have some fun, we just walk into the park. When any of their operators want to see the side show, they come in through the doors. It's a sort of friendly arrangement we have. The big feud is against the owners. All the park people are poorly paid for long hours and hard work."

Frost looked at a row of daggers.

"I do several numbers," she explained. "Knife-throwing, snake-charming, and the shakes. Some call it dancing, but don't let 'em kid you."

"Thanks for the elucidation," said Frost dryly. "How do you happen to be practicing at this hour?"

"I often get up at dawn. My number is the first one finished at night so I generally hit the hay before any of the others."

"I don't suppose Hermes or Markey would be up yet?"

"Why, yes, they are. Hermes, his real name is Harry Guger, sprained a thumb yesterday and he didn't sleep a wink so he got up. He's been around for the past hour. Markey came down to look over the joint. He's thinking of shifting things around, kind of, and maybe adding a couple of new acts. It's hopeless trying to do any work around here in the day or evening. Crowds are too big. They get in your way."

"Do you live here?"

"Sure. Most of us do. There's a flock of rooms and apartments on the second floor. They're handy and good enough."

Frost left. The snake slid down Madame Serpa's arm and gazed beadily at the departing figure.

The professor, however, made no attempt to question Markey or Hermes. He surveyed the premises with a quick glance. Toward the front, a tall, sallow man with a little mustache and long, black hair was looking at the street. On the opposite end, a plump, shorter man in an eloquent brown suit was fussing around some booths.

Frost returned to Platinum Park.

The merry-go-round swarmed with police. Even Inspector Frick had routed himself out of bed. The inspector, a gray-haired man whose crisp bearing was a hallmark from his years of army service, was an old friend of the professor, and his most influential supporter in the department. He detached himself from the cluster when he saw Frost approaching.

"Look here, Ivy, what's this business about identifying a skeleton just by looking at the bones?" he asked, a bit worried.

"There is nothing mysterious about it. I don't know why your men are making such a fuss over a simple analysis." Frost repeated his earlier observations. "I have three more suspects for you, all with excellent reason and opportunity to have committed the murder," he added, mentioning Hermes, Madame Serpa, and Markey.

Frick was nonplused. "We'll have to have experts check up to make sure the bones are those of Reisenham—"

"Save yourself the bother. Here are his ring and watch. The numbers have been hammered and filed, but acid treatment will bring them out again. It was an expensive watch, and the jeweler who sold it undoubtedly kept a record of its serial number. If you require further proof, you need only dig up the rest of Reisenham. What is left of his more perishable parts lies thirty feet east of the stone shed. He has deteriorated sadly."

The inspector issued prompt orders. "This is going to be one fine mess. Moss left his home at midnight and hasn't returned yet. No one answers the phone at Barburg's apartment. Jepson moved out of his furnished room a week ago and didn't leave a new address. Well, we can start questioning those three birds in the side show, anyway. Ivy, we'll need your help on this. I'll be glad to get anything you pick up or figure out."

"As a matter of record," Frost meditated, "this really is not one of my cases. While Variss notified me because of police inaction, there was no direct commission, and this is strictly a subject for the customary police procedure."

"I know it, but I'll O. K. anything you do even if it does get under somebody's skin at headquarters. This is a weird one, and the way it's breaking, we'll never hang it on the murderers."

"It is not without some tantalizing features," Frost conceded. "Be here at three o'clock. In the meantime, there are a few slight inquiries of my own to be made."

"What's coming off at three?"

"I intend to enjoy the park's excellent facilities for amusement. I will take keen pleasure in riding the roller coaster, for instance."

The professor collected his assistant, whose search had gone unrewarded, and brought her up to date on developments. As they drove away, he explained: "The Missing Persons Bureau sent out an alarm on Reisenham when he disappeared. His wife is in Europe. His partners notified the police. An investigation was launched, but it elicited very little of importance. Reisenham had not received threats, so far as is known, though he appears to have been a disagreeable person whose methods and attitude antagonized almost every one with whom he came in contact. He was last seen in early evening on the night he vanished, when leaving a Manhattan restaurant where he had dined alone. He was believed to have been a victim of amnesia.

"In addition to the bizarre circumstances under which his skeleton came to light, we have several other puzzling questions to answer. Reisenham was killed in Platinum Park. When and how did he get into the park without being recognized, and for what purpose? Thus far, each individual concerned has proved to have a reason and opportunity for murdering him, but the deeper motive has not yet emerged. The murderer has shown remarkable intelligence and subtlety. Instead of trying to protect himself with an alibi, or to cover his tracks, he operated at a time and place, and under circumstances, that cast equal suspicion upon a large number of suspects, most of whom will have great difficulty in establishing even the flimsiest alibi. That will be their main protection and the murderer's immense advantage. There is no conclusive evidence pointing to a specific person. There are no conflicting stories that would enable us to select truth from falsehood."

"Gee!" exclaimed Jean, with wide-eyed interest. "It's a honey! It sounds like he'll get away with it if they ever do suspect who he is!"

"That doesn't sound like you. Your terms are both slangy and not altogether accurate. I know the motive and the identity of the killer. Deductive logic is, however, insufficient evidence. Therefore, I will set a trap for him, and then supply him with motivation to spring the trap."

"How?"

"You will see when the time comes. There is some preliminary work to be done. You possess a rare beauty, Miss Moray, a beauty that immediately arrests the attention of all who see you."

A thrill of pleasure over his unexpected compliment raced through her. It was the first time since she had been associated with him that he showed a personal interest in her.

"Exactly at three o'clock," Frost continued, "I want you at your ravishing best to stand in front of the Magic Hall and watch the loading platform of the Whirlwind which will be easily visible."

Jean could cheerfully have kicked his shins at this dash of cold water upon her secret hopes. Frost simply didn't fall, but the more he remained dispassionate and aloof, the more piqued she became, and the more determined to employ every wile she had. She flattered herself that she was full of wiles. Only, she thought ruefully, it doesn't help a girl much to be full of wiles and lure and charm and beauty and brains and things if they run smack against an inhuman monster who is mainly interested in logic.

She was brought back to earth with a rude jolt when Frost said abruptly, "You shouldn't waste time on such idle speculations."

V.

When the professor stopped at headquarters shortly before noon, he found Inspector Frick in an irritable mood. The inspector had just come out of his office. "Ivy! I want a few words with you about this Reisenham mess. Have you seen the papers? The news photographers got there just after you left. I tried to hold them down, said the skeleton was only somebody's prank, but it was such a crazy stunt it made the front pages anyway.

"I'll admit it's a hell of a weird picture, probably the sort of stuff the public laps up, but it's putting us on the spot. You were right about the identification. Our experts corroborated it after examining the rest of the remains and bringing out the watch number. Coney Island will be mobbed to-day. There'll be half a million extra people out there just to get a look at the merry-go-round. There'll probably wreck the thing trying to get souvenirs."

"What about Jepson?" Frost asked.

"He was picked up this morning staggering home to a Bowery dump. Admitted he'd been wandering around Coney Island, claims he doesn't remember much of anything that happened. He's sobering off now. Admitted being sore about losing his job, called Reisenham plenty of names before we told him about the murder. That cooled him off, but I don't think we'll get much out of him because he was too drunk to remember what he'd been up to."

"Did you find Moss and Barburg?"

"They're in my office now. Can you beat it? Barburg claims he was in bed all night, and just didn't bother to answer the phone until he finally got up about nine. He lives alone. Moss is a slippery eel, admits he wasn't home all night, but says it's none of our business where he was.

"What gets me is that both Moss and Barburg admit having been at Platinum Park practically all night the evening Reisenham vanished. It seems they wanted to look over the property to see about repairs and improvements, and couldn't do it in the daytime on account of the crowds.

"But they didn't stay together, and they told Variss to take the night off. On two different occasions, one of which lasted for more than an hour, they were separated. On the night after Reisenham disappeared, a crew of workmen did several jobs around the place, and dug up a depression in the path to fill it with a sand base; they left the excavation for an hour and a half to work elsewhere; and that filled-in patch is where we found the rest of the body.

"We got the same sort of answers from Markey, Hermes, and Madame Serpa. We've questioned half the park's employees, and discovered that they were all underpaid and overworked and down on the management. Any one of these people could be guilty, and not one of them has an iron-clad alibi.

"You'd think"—Frick clipped the words bitterly—"that one, just one of those twenty-eight power operators would have gone straight home after work, or strung along with some one else; but no, they drop in at different places for a couple of beers, so they say, or their car breaks down, or they get a sandwich somewhere, or they decide to walk home at their own sweet time, or they had rooms by themselves, and there's a lost hour somewhere in all their stories.

"The one thing I don't want is another suspect. I'm sick of 'em! I'd like to find just one person involved who offered an air-tight alibi and I'd clap him in jail so fast that he'd see double!"

"And if you found an air-tight alibi, you would have the murderer." Frost soothed the fiery little inspector. Frick had never before been so wrought up over a murder case. The professor continued: "One of these suspects is the murderer. He knew the circumstances well—but so did they all. He had a motive—but so did all the suspects. He had the opportunity—like the others involved. And he had the brilliant audacity to deprive himself of an alibi—because none of the others could produce witnesses to account for all their time.

"I'd like to ask Moss and Barburg a couple of questions."

They entered Frick's office. The remaining partners of the Platinum Park Corporation were a sinister pair. Barburg, thin and cadaverous, with hands like claws, resembled a scarecrow. His skin was worm-white, his eyes snaky, his nose as thin as his lips were cruel.

Moss, fat and oily, had Slavic features. His flattened nose went with his moon face. Everything about him seemed round and greasy, from black hair drowned in pomade to fingers like so many plump grubs, and a pudgy figure in a snuff-colored suit.

The professor, raking each with a glance, addressed Barburg. "What did the Platinum Park owners stand to gain by Reisenham's death?"

Barburg peered at his fellow partner with an air of melancholy aloofness. His ophidian gaze returned to the professor, and his voice dripped with self-pity. "A very sad blow. It will cost us money. That it should come at a time like this—"

"Is all to the good," Frost snapped. "The publicity is worth a million. What understanding did you have among yourselves?"

"We? Why should we—"

"Talk," Frost ordered. "The partnership agreement."

Barburg changed his mind and his tactics. Frost's eyes were glittering with a restless, unpredictable, but irresistible purpose.

Barburg talked. "When we bought the park, we put $50,000 apiece into it. The one-third interest was nontransferable. If a partner died or got out, his interest would be purchased at cost and divided between the other two."

"A one-third interest in Platinum Park would sell in the open market to-day for more than a third of a million," Frost drawled. "By Reisenham's death, you divide between you an equity valued at approximately $350,000 for which you pay only $50,000."

Barburg nodded uneasily. "But that—"

"Yeah," Frick interrupted him wearily, "but you were all one big happy family, weren't you?"

Frost turned to Moss. "What is a universal joint?"

The round one looked puzzled. "Should I know? Should I know? I'm asking you," he chirped in an emotional voice.

Barburg answered for him, "It sounds like a place that anybody can get into."

Frost asked, "Why do you keep a night watchman at Platinum Park?"

Barburg replied with reluctance: "There was some trouble early this year. I believe an unfortunate fire damaged the side show. I don't know why we were held to blame. We heard rumors and threats that the park would burn up. So we installed a night watchman."

Frost beckoned the inspector to walk out with him. In the corridor he stated: "There isn't enough evidence to hold any of the seven immediate suspects. Turn them loose, but keep track of them, and see that they all are at the Whirlwind in Platinum Park at three o'clock. However, do not let them know where they are being taken or for what purpose."

"Easy enough, since I myself don't know," the inspector tartly replied. "What did you have in mind by that question about universal joint?"

Frost was already on the way out. His long stride kept him a jump ahead of the pungent fumes that trailed him.

VI.

Coney Island expected a huge turn-out on this, one of the final Saturdays of the season. The concessionaires revised their estimates upward when the day broke hot and sticky with a humidity almost at the saturation point. But their most lavish hopes fell short of reality when the metropolitan dailies carried pictures and lurid accounts of the skeleton rider.

The spectacular nature of the occurrence, the wide publicity given it, and the natural drawing power of Coney Island combined with the discomfort of the heat wave to lure one of the greatest throngs within memory to that popular resort.

From early morning, the subways were jammed. By noon, more than five hundred thousand human beings had flocked around the beach, board walk, and amusement centers. By mid-afternoon, it was clear that between 1,500,000 and 2,000,000 visitors would swamp all facilities.

The figures in the waxwork museums looked as though they would melt from the heat. Barkers grew hoarse shouting their cause and trying to outshout rivals. Every time a hula dancer or a strong man, a midget or a leopard woman appeared in front of a side show, a dense mass of humanity washed around the bait.

The swirl of energy centered around Platinum Park. It was experiencing the largest single day's take in its existence. Hundreds and thousands waited in line at each of its forty-one attractions. It took strength and patience to get anywhere near the merry-go-round, until special guards had to be called out to keep the line moving and preserve order of a sort.

Just before three o'clock, a most alluring young woman suddenly appeared in front of the Magic Hall.

There was a cluster of people around the Whirlwind which, like all the others in Coney Island, claimed to be the highest and fastest roller coaster in the world.

Inspector Frick and his plain-clothes detectives had done their work well. They had quietly rounded up Barburg, Moss, Variss, Jepson, Markey, Madame Serpa, and Hermes, all of whom watched with various reactions as Professor I. V. Frost calmly climbed into the front seat of the coaster car, with a package in his lap. No one else rode with him. Not long before he took his seat, he vanished beneath the supporting framework of the roller coaster with another package, which was missing when he returned.

As he sat down and the operator started to push the control stick, Moss broke from the group and waddled toward him. "Why do you waste our time?" he complained. "All these people waiting, with cash tickets already. Maybe I go with you, yes?"

"No."

"Is there something wrong in my wanting to go with you? I'll go along for fun, yes? Such a business!"

The professor squelched him. "I ride alone."

Frick, who had jumped after Moss in an effort to head him off, tried to act now as peacemaker. "It's his affair after all, Ivy. If he insists on going along, I don't see that we have much right to stop him."

"If he wishes to take the risk and responsibility, that is his funeral, not mine," Frost retorted. "Operator—contact!"

Moss seemed undecided over the professor's cryptic comment, and while he wavered, the coaster car gathered momentum, slid down the preliminary dip, caught in the grooves of the endless belt for the first high climb that would launch it on its way. The slightly baffled watchers saw it creep to the top of the incline and poise, heard it thunder down the first cliff.

It shot to the next crest, slowed with the drag of the safety brakes, hurtled on another giddy dive. The roar and rolling clatter, one car shooting with one occupant only, developed an uneasy tension in the group who watched. They waited for something to happen, and nothing happened. Or they seemed amused, but only Frost genuinely enjoyed the episode. Or they looked bored, anxious to leave.

The car thundered down the last, long decline and curved into view again. Frost's hair whipped in the breeze. His features expressed a keen relish. He leaned forward enthusiastically, an almost happy gleam in his eyes. Frick felt disappointed. It just wasn't in character for the professor to amuse himself at the expense of others. This was child's play, when murder had to be solved.

Frost made no move to climb out. "Great! I'm going around again!" he exclaimed.

The car got under way. Moss, fidgeting nervously, suddenly bounded across the platform and leaped into a rear seat as the coaster car slid off. Inspector Frick made a vain dash after him, shouted angrily. Moss looked back, grinning.

Frost turned around and spoke curtly, but whatever he said did not reach Frick above the clatter of the mechanism. The car went up the steep haul. Moss faced the professor, then clambered over the intervening seats until he sat beside Frost.

As the coaster car reached the crest, Frick thought he saw a smolder in Frost's aspect, a glance that was tenseness, command, and anticipation. Moss waved his pudgy arms in expostulation. The car plunged from view with a crescendo velocity.

The deep bass note of its highest speed at the lowest depression began to rise as the car shot up the next ascent. It flashed into sight again on the second mount, hurtled toward the brow. Frost was leaning forward against the power of momentum, his hands gripping the crossbar. He had turned his head slightly, and seemed to be issuing orders to Moss, but his gaze remained intent upon the track.

Suddenly Moss stood up. The car leaped to the peak of the ascent. There was no drag of safety brakes. It did not pause in its wild rush. It rocketed from the tracks and its own momentum hurled it a dozen feet skyward. It crashed clear of the wooden railing.

The mysterious awareness of tragedy brought a hush over the crowd, a silence of magnetic tension. Frost, rising like a predatory bird from the car, made a futile grab for Moss. Moss, crazed with fear, fought him and leaped for the torn railing. He resembled a huge beetle as he sprawled for a moment with arms and legs threshing. He missed his aim by a wide margin, hurtled earthward beyond the scaffolding.

To Frick's horrified gaze, the body of Frost plummeted after Moss, in the wake of the plunging car. There came a terrific crash; and with that fatal sound, the tension broke; a murmur surged up from the crowds; then the scuffle and scrape of countless running feet, as thousands upon thousands swarmed toward the scene of the crash.

VII.

As Jean Moray watched Ivy Frost prepare to enter a coaster car of the Whirlwind, resentment that she had felt earlier began to boil inside her. Frost was only using her as a tool, a means to an end, as he had done numerous times before. She might be an efficient aid, gifted in many ways, but still he treated her as an assistant only. He did the thinking, and she followed orders. And now, as always, he had set the stage. Perhaps she also served who only stood and waited, but Jean grew quite unreasonably rebellious as she thought about it, and worked herself into an angry mood.

Why should she merely follow orders? Why not act on her own initiative for once? Frost had specified the Magic Hall, therefore it must possess special significance. It was time she threw off this high-handed domination.

All at once, she knew that she was *not* going to stand in the background and watch Frost put on a show. Her expression altered with the spirit of mischief and determination.

She deliberately turned and started for the door to the Magic Hall.

"Hey, lady, get in line. There's lots of folks ahead of you," the ticket collector protested.

"There were," she corrected with and impudent smile. "I'm Miss Moray, Frost's assistant, on special duty about the murder."

"Oh. Well, you'll have to wait a minute anyway. There's somebody inside now."

"How does it happen that only one person at a time is admitted?"

"Well, it's like this: When the Magic Hall first opened, we used to let folks in by the dozen, but they got all mixed up, bumped into each other, busted the mirrors, and raised a general rumpus. It's a tricky place. You've got to watch yourself. So the owners finally made it a rule that only one person or one couple could go through at a time."

A bell rang. The ticket man asked: "How much time do you want?"

"Just a minute or two."

She walked through, but dallied in the entrance hall. A series of six preliminary mirrors lined one side of the corridor to the Magic Hall. She looked at her reflection in the first one. The glass, warped to height, showed her incredibly tall and thin. "Good gracious! Is that I?" she exclaimed to herself. She hastily passed on.

In the next panel, with horizontal concave and convex curves, she saw her figure weirdly distorted. She pouted wryly at this monstrosity.

The fourth mirror brought new disillusion to the figure of which she was proud. It was a convex glass in which she saw a caricature whose beadlike head and feet expanded at obtuse angles toward a waist line that was yards broad.

The next panel reversed the preceding image. She wrinkled her nose. "I don't like you. I haven't liked any of you so far," she declared emphatically, pointing a finger straight at her reflection.

The passage now made a right angle turn. Following it, she entered the Magic Hall and halted, amazed and fascinated by an optical illusion of extraordinary imaginative effect.

The room itself, while scarcely more than eight feet in height, covered a fairly large area, whose original size proved difficult to estimate accurately, because of the mirrors and the room's odd shape. Aside from the floor and ceiling, the room was a dodecahedron, each of its twelve sides a mirror, and each mirror faced by an opposite.

Jean's true image, caught in one mirror and reflected to the mirror opposite, bounced back again; and thus tossed between mirrors, multiplied to infinity and diminishing to infinity in all directions, presented her with her receding counterpart in countless hundreds and thousands whichever way she looked. And with the illusion of multiple identity came the illusion of tremendous vistas and immeasurable distance; for the mirror walls reflected themselves and flung each other into ever departing remoteness.

She realized with apprehension that she had lost the true location of the exit.

She took a step forward, and all the thousands of her counterparts in all the thousands of receding chambers took the same step, creating another fantastic panorama. She watched throngs of identical Jeans walk among throngs of identical halls; but in all that repeated and multiplied movement, sound was absent. The comparative silence intensified the phantasmal, eerie nature of the experience. She looked at ghosts. Her eyes ached and her senses lost awareness of actuality.

A portal began to open, a thousand portals. Quick unease came over her, when she tried in vain to fix the precise location of the mirror that was pivoting. Perfect indirect lighting did away with highlights. It was difficult to discern the glass. A feeling, inexplicable but profound, of something about to happen, some impending terror, made her heart beat faster. The portal, the countless portals, opened farther and pivoted shut in a cascading torrent of sliding mirrors. The portal, the countless portals closed.

A thin, cadaverous man, Barburg, slumped against a mirror somewhere. He was dead; a dagger protruded from his heart, and scarlet stained his shirt. His dead eyes stared at her, and panic descended, for the corpse in hosts and hordes was everywhere, reflecting in all the mirrors and halls even as her own image. She was surrounded by an army of dead men, their eyes glaring at her even in death. There were thousands of Jeans, and every Jean accompanied by a corpse.

She ran into glass and bruised herself. She felt along the smooth surface, and the thousands of other Jeans felt along the walls of their separate, unending prisons, a panorama as terrifying as it was strange. Then she stumbled against the corpse, and it slumped lower, sprawling on the floor. The contact made her whole being shudder. She felt curiously anaesthetized, as though each nerve had been tied in a separate knot, so tightly that she could not scream. She watched, in a sort of conscious nightmare, while all the duplicating and receding images of the dead man slumped lower in all the other halls and upon countless floors.

Pushing with all her strength against the mirror in front of which the corpse lay, she forced it to pivot far enough for her to slip through. The murderer might be waiting outside, but a live man was preferable to a dead one.

She paused with quick apprehension in the dark passageway, but heard nothing to indicate the presence of any one else. She drew a small fountain-pen flash and a flat automatic from the pockets of her slacks. The thin beam poked around and picked out a door. She opened it carefully and let out a little yip when she saw the altogether too life-like gorilla. People passing looked at her idly. She heard a barker at one end of the inclosure. To her right, the curtain was partly pulled back from a booth labeled MADAME SERPA, and among other things she saw a fine collection of daggers like the one that had killed Barburg.

What would Frost do under the circumstances? She thought of several moves—to enter Madame Serpa's stall, to ask passers-by if they had seen any one come out of the door, to look around for clues. After a few seconds of indecision, she pocketed her automatic and went back to the corridor. There were two more doors, she found, an eastern entrance to a crowded dance floor, and a western exit to the open parts of Platinum Park, where other visitors went their way.

While Jean was walking along the corridor, her light crossed the point of a brad protruding from the wooden side. Billions of brads were never so royally decorated as this one, for it wore a crown of crimson, and a couple of drooping stands. One of the threads was dark-gray, and the other so blue as to look black. Jean detached them from the drop of blood. She looked at them, and slowly a half-satisfied expression came over her face. She snapped the threads and tucked one set away. The other she carried in her left hand and trotted around to the front of the Magic Hall.

"Don't let any one else in," she told the ticket collector. "There's a dead man inside—Barburg, one of the owners."

"Go climb a tree," he scoffed.

Jean flared up. "Go look for yourself. Then go climb a couple of trees!"

She hurried toward the Whirlwind. It surprised her that the roller coaster was not running, but crowds were running toward a single objective. Excited tumult filled the air. None of the group she expected remained on the loading platform of the Whirlwind. Its second ascent showed a jagged rip high above the ground.

VIII.

Inspector Frick bucked the rush with a skill born of war and riot experience. He heard piercing whistles cut through the uproar. Alert policemen were already summoning assistance and sending in for the riot squads. But Frick remembered his duties only with an automatic instinct. All his anxiety went for the welfare of Ivy Frost. He caught sight of the splintered coaster car, and near it the still, crushed form of Moss.

Swept on in the tide, he got a fleeting glimpse of the mechanical and human débris.

Toward him worked a dynamic figure that towered above the throng and elbowed it aside.

"Ivy! How——"

Frost stopped him. "I had a hand parachute. I expected this. The parachute was strong enough for two, but Moss lost his head and committed incidental suicide."

They made headway against the surge. Frick asked: "What happened? How did the accident come about?"

"It didn't happen. It was deliberately planned. A wedge-shaped obstruction had been planted between the tracks. Operating from a distance, the murderer sprang it above the level of the tracks as the car approached, and the car simply catapulted off. The murderer was in that group on the loading platform. The wiring from the wedge ran along the framework of the roller coaster to one edge of the platform."

"But why didn't it work the first time you went around?"

"Obviously, because some one in the party happened to be looking at the murderer. He could not act without being noticed until general attention was focused upon me in the coaster car. But as soon as he acted, the stage was set for him to trap himself. He is in that group, and cannot get away without immediately drawing suspicion. In addition, I placed my assistant where she could clearly watch the actions of all concerned. And, finally, I concealed a miniature motion-picture camera to photograph the scene and show the murderer at work."

They broke free of the main jam and headed for the platform. Frost glanced at it, asked with a harsh challenge in his tone: "Where is the group? I gave specific instructions for it to be kept there intact until I had finished my operations."

The inspector squirmed uncomfortably. "Well, Ivy, you didn't tell us what you were up to. You didn't say that this was the trap."

The professor drawled with biting sarcasm: "And if I had made such an announcement, do you seriously delude yourself into believing that the murderer would have made any move? The whole success of the trap depended upon its being known to none but myself."

"But nobody knew what you were up to. There didn't seem to be much point to it. I suppose the others got tired watching, or swept aside when the crowd went wild."

Jean Moray, flushed from running and excitement, scampered toward them.

"And what did you see?" Frost inquired.

"Barburg—murdered—in the Magic Hall!" she gasped.

Frick, with a startled expression, sprinted away. Frost said: "What did you see on the platform of the Whirlwind?"

Her eyes opened wide in guileless innocence. "Why, how could I see anything on the platform when I was finding a corpse inside?"

Frost carefully drew out a very long cigarette which he lighted and inhaled. Rian came out from among the roller-coaster supports, carrying an object that he was examining with open curiosity. He didn't see Frost and Jean until he was within a few paces. Then he looked up from the object.

"Uh—hello! Look what I found hidden down there. Some bird must have been taking pictures and went off and forgot his camera. Ain't that the nuts?"

Frost mused softly, meditatively: "I arranged a perfect trap, but the suspicion is dawning upon me that I observe a perfect mess."

If he had gone into a rage, or unloosed a blistering barrage from his extensive vocabulary, he could not have achieved a more excoriating effect. Frost surveyed the collapse of his plans with an Olympian serenity. The human causations may have interested him briefly, but he showed no inclination to waste time on unprofitable regrets or to linger among the ruins.

Rian muttered, "Uh, is something wrong?"

"I'll take my camera, if you don't mind. Did you happen to notice the actions of any of the suspects before you began your tour of exploration and discovery?"

Rian reddened, thought hard for a few moments. "Well, Barburg was standing near me, and I heard him say something about going to see about a cracked mirror. That was while you were riding the roller coaster. I didn't pay much attention because I saw something flash in the sunlight under the scaffolding or whatever you call it, so I went down there to have a look and found the camera."

"And while you were gone, Barburg walked to his death in a passageway behind the Magic Hall. Who told Barburg that a mirror was cracked?"

"Search me, I don't know." Rian raced after Frick.

Jean handed Frost one set of the threads. "This is the only clue I found. They were caught on a nail in the wall."

The professor studied the strands with analytic eyes, absorbed as though reading the pages of an informative text. "It is impossible to predict the value of these," he judged. "I will have Frick round up all the suspects again. That may take hours, and meanwhile they have ample opportunity to change socks and clothes.

"Even if the murderer was brought here immediately and confronted with the evidence while still wearing the fabrics from which these came, the circumstance would be cause for suspicion rather than conviction. He could claim that he had walked through the passage before the murder. Unless several reliable witnesses can be found to testify that they saw him go into the passage shortly before the murder or come out immediately after, the threads will not be of major help.

"It would be difficult to locate such witnesses even by public appeal, if they exist; and if found, their testimony as to time and identification could be invalidated by any competent criminal lawyer during cross-examination."

Jean said contritely: "I'm sorry about the roller coaster fizzle. But the way it turned out, it was a good thing I went inside the Magic Hall."

Frost uttered truths without reproaching her. "I assigned you to the Magic Hall primarily to watch the Whirlwind and to obtain direct testimony against the murderer. From the spectacular nature of Reisenham's death and with the assistance of several other deductions, I knew that he would utilize equally prominent media for further operations.

"The roller coaster and the Magic Hall were the most suitable for his plans. If what I anticipated took place at the Whirlwind, you were in a position to support my deductions. If the other alternative occurred in the Magic Hall, the identity of the murderer would be solved by elimination of all the suspects at the Whirlwind.

"Unfortunately, since human beings do not possess an extra eye in the back of the head, it was impossible to watch simultaneously the roller-coaster tracks and the group on the platform, aside from attempting to save Moss' life. The discovery of murder is but a starting point. The major importance lies in prevention and solution of crime."

The professor hiked off toward the Magic Hall, a veil of abstraction in his eyes.

Jean, watching him leave, tried to guess what new processes of thought occupied his attention. It was curious how readily Frost managed to penetrate into the minds of other people, and how difficult it was to estimate what went on in his head.

Jean had very positive ideas in view, but it was a testament to the force of Frost's character that she wasted many seconds staring after him and attempting to figure him out before she started putting her own theories into action.

Then she hastened out of Platinum Park and got into her roadster. Traffic was heavy pouring away from the city, but the incoming stream a mere trickle. She drove mainly with the intention of going places and doing things in a hurry. A lovely smile and an enchanting face work wonders. She got by with some petty violations of traffic laws, at practically no delay. She felt quite pleased after each demonstration of her devastating influence upon the male of the species. These demonstrations almost recompensed her for her failure to make a dent upon the unyielding armor of Frost.

She wove in and out through traffic, found the accelerator an interesting toy to play with, got a kick out of some fancy driving. She did not take chances and was by no means a reckless driver, but her assurance and nimble dodging left many a frazzled nerve in her wake.

Jean reached Manhattan and headed for a specialty shop on Fifty-seventh Street. She stopped there for several minutes, came out wearing over her halter a lustrous blouse decorated with an artful green figure which she had not intended to purchase, but which she couldn't resist the moment she saw it. She continued uptown to the West Seventies.

The address she halted in front of was a narrow brownstone house five stories high, of former dignity but now in its decline. She walked up the steps and looked at a row of corroded buzzer buttons and weathered cards. One of them bore the name: Ginger Lary.

Jean didn't press the buzzer because the door, though shut, was unlatched. She climbed two flights and went along the corridor to a rear room. She listened, dropped a hand in her pocket and felt the reassuring cool grip of the automatic. She rang the room bell.

Nothing happened. She waited an interval, rang again more insistently. She heard the muffled sound of running water which ceased, then a door closed. She repeated the ring after another brief pause. She didn't hear the footsteps she expected, but a key turned and the door opened a little. "Who is it?" a voice called in slightly annoyed tones.

Jean pulled out the automatic and shoved hard on the door. "Stick 'em up! Fast!"

The surprised occupant of the room reached for the ceiling, her warm, brown eyes big with respect for Jean's pistol. "Ginger" Lary was a couple of inches shorter than Jean. She was slim, had rich, wine-dark hair, thick and soft, with mahogany hues and highlights. All her coloring was vivid, from hair and eyes to skin as duskily golden as a ripening peach. Her features had a natural attractiveness with soft, rosy lips, a short and truculent nose.

"What do you want?" Ginger asked indignantly. "Who are you and what's the gag?"

"Get dressed! We're going places."

"Oh, we are, are we? Guess again."

Jean said: "You're wanted in connection with the murder of Leo F. Barburg at Coney Island this afternoon."

Slowly the color drained from Ginger Lary's cheeks; her eyes grew frightened, stricken. She was young but looked weary and older. Her arms dropped to her sides. A mask of defeat and despair altered her face. All at once she flung herself on a studio couch, sobbing into her arms, her shoulders quivering.

A lot of thoughts swirled through Jean's head at that moment. Ginger Lary was no hard-boiled gun moll or gangster type. She didn't resemble an adventuress wise in the ways of the world. She was just a good-looking kid who had got herself into a jam. In spite of her original intentions, Jean's sympathy went out to her.

Without further ado, Jean marched across the room, sat down beside the bowed figure, and put her arm around Ginger's shoulders. "Come on, Ginger," she urged gently, "spill it."

IX.

The sun was setting. It hung low in the west, a ball glowing red through the haze and murk of the atmosphere. Mugginess lingered on in Coney Island. Attendance had fallen off from its peak, but sweltering multitudes still thronged the beach and board walk.

They taxed the facilities of all the amusement centers, with the single exception of Platinum Park, which was closed to the public. The fickle crowds that had promptly flocked into it after discovery of the skeleton rider, had just as promptly flocked out of it after the Whirlwind disaster.

The wildest sort of rumors circulated—that the police were suppressing information about other deaths, that every device in the park had been tampered with and turned into a dangerous instrument of destruction, that corpses were buried all over the grounds, that even to enter the park meant a risk of life. The police finally cleared the park of visitors and closed it as a precautionary measure.

The group clustered in the manager's office at Platinum Park suffered from the heat like every one else, except for Frost who, as he towered above the others, appeared indifferent to such minor topics as weather and temperature. Frost was speaking to those assembled.

"At the heart of this mystery stands the new attraction called the Werner Turner. It has a direct connection with everything that has happened here, from the disappearance of Reisenham to the murder of Barburg. When I first arrived here this morning, I reached this conclusion by means of logic, analysis, observation, synthesis, and deduction. The facts had to be tested by theory, and the theory tested by facts.

"The Werner Turner bears the given name of Reisenham, but from all evidence, Reisenham was a business man purely and simply, without an inventive streak in him. His name might have been a front for the other partners; but by a single question I found out that they were likewise devoid of mechanical aptitude. They lacked knowledge of so elementary a principle as the universal joint. The making of money seems to have been their main interest.

"I wired to Washington and discovered that Reisenham had patented the Werner Turner early this year. That fact immediately raised a question: How did Reisenham who was not an inventor hit upon so profitable an invention? The answer is, he didn't. From this point on, all other answers clearly ensue and the problems explain themselves."

"I don't see that they do," Inspector Frick said, after waiting for Frost to proceed.

"Isn't it obvious? Some one else invented the Werner Turner. He either did not have the funds to patent it, and brought his idea to Reisenham, or Reisenham overheard him explain the principle and nature of his invention. In either case, Reisenham got there first and received the patent rights. The inventor, realizing what had happened, appealed to Reisenham; and we may be sure that Reisenham was deaf to such appeal.

"Judging by the success of the attraction here and at other amusement centers to which rights have been leased, a fortune is involved. The royalties this year alone should amount to more than half a million dollars. There was little hope for the inventor to prove his claims and obtain legal redress. If he lacked funds to patent his invention, he certainly had no money to hire high-priced counsel and fight his case through the courts.

"He decided to take his own revenge. He made an appointment with Reisenham in the basement of the repair shop. Here occurred an unforeseen twist that proved greatly to the inventor's advantage.

"The inventor probably made the appointment by telling Reisenham that he had another new idea in mind; but the inventor actually intended to threaten Reisenham or kill him if a share in the royalties was not forthcoming. Whether or not Reisenham believed the inventor is immaterial, for Reisenham himself had reached the conclusion that only death would put an end to the inventor's persistence.

"Thus, neither one cared to be seen going to that appointment. Reisenham must have used some simple disguise such as dark glasses and mustache when he entered Platinum Park through the adjoining side show; only thus can be explained Reisenham's reasons for and success in getting to the shed without being recognized the night he disappeared. Keeping the appointment resulted in his death. The inventor stuffed the body behind a pile of old doors and lumber slanted against a corner of the room.

"The body was not discovered the following day. For one thing, the shed is only in occasional use and at irregular intervals. Days and weeks sometimes lapse before any one has a reason for going to it. Any one who did enter it the day following the murder saw nothing unusual, partly for the excellent reason that the inventor had smeared tar over the bloodstain on the floor."

"You didn't tell me that before!" Frick exclaimed.

"You didn't ask me," Frost retorted. "The inventor may have secreted himself in the shed again the night after the murder, carried the body to the excavation while the workmen were elsewhere, and covered it loosely with sand; or he may have waited till a subsequent occasion, and reopened the spot. He needed very little time. The morning crowds would obliterate any traces of his work in short order; and no one who did notice the patch would attach the least significance to it. The precise hour and evening that he worked are immaterial. It should be remembered that Variss was off duty on both those nights; but when on duty thereafter, his schedule of hourly inspection was common knowledge to every one concerned.

"This procedure, however, would require that the body be interred, disinterred at a later date, and part of it reinterred at still another date—a highly improbable sequence with highly probable risks of discovery. The alternative is that the inventor simply left the corpse in the shed basement. He expected it to be found, but it was not. At this season, repair work is held to a minimum because the whole park will be overhauled when it closes for the winter. Consequently, no one used the shed.

"As the days passed, with Reisenham officially listed among the missing, the inventor must have thought often about the hidden body; and gradually his original plan assumed a new shape. His vengeance would go farther. The corpse had not come to light; he himself would make it emerge into the open, but in such a manner that it could never be identified, so he thought.

"Reconstruction of his actions would, I presume, present a terrifying picture to many minds. I can visualize him returning to that dark basement, aware of the corpse rotting in a corner, forcing himself to approach that gruesome form. The hatred that impelled him onward must have been so powerful that it brushed horror aside.

"I will not enlarge upon the details. The evidence tells the story. Modern scientific methods make it difficult to destroy identifying characteristics of a body. Even corpses immersed in water for months, or in the last stages of decomposition, have been identified through dental work, scars and marks, hairs, deformities, fingerprints, etc. But the very thoroughness with which Reisenham's body was reduced to a skeleton had the reverse effect. It simplified identification, as I have already shown."

Madame Serpa's face had a greenish tinge. Hermes, the magician, squirmed uncomfortably. Markey listened, soberly intent.

Frost continued: "Having the solution and knowing the identity of the murderer now, I would ordinarily have turned the information over to the police for whatever action they chose, since this was not one of my private cases. At the request of Inspector Frick, I went on, for there remained the problem of apprehending the inventor. He had done his task so thoroughly that there was no objective evidence to incriminate him, and the circumstantial evidence incriminated a great many other persons. I therefore led him into a trap of his own devising.

"While surveying the park, I noticed the wire on the Whirlwind framework. I deduced for various reasons that he never intended to operate the device he had installed. It would have been discovered during the next periodic inspection. The mere fact of its existence would have so alarmed the public as to cause a heavy loss in attendance not only at the Whirlwind but in all of Platinum Park.

"I made my plans and took a ride on the roller coaster. The murderer by then knew that I was closing in on him. It was I whom he feared. If he could do away with me, he probably would never be caught, for his was a mental determination that would never crack in a police grilling. And when Moss made the fatal blunder of jumping into the car, the murderer had what he thought was a golden opportunity to round out his vengeance at one blow."

Frost lighted a cigarette and inhaled deeply. "In order to make his own plans, the murderer had to know long in advance what I would be doing and when. What he did not know was that he alone among the suspects had the knowledge. The others first heard of it only when they were rounded up and brought to the platform of the Whirlwind," Frost said, with a sardonic glance at Sam Variss.

All heads turned. There was an instant's silence before Variss spoke, in a tired voice: "You win. You've told it all except for a couple of things.

"The night Reisenham came down to the basement in the shed, I didn't know he was armed. I intended to threaten him first, though he had stalled me along so many times I was mad enough to kill him. While we were arguing, he told me to get some papers he'd left on the ground floor, and like a dumb cluck, I started off. Then it struck me as being queer so I turned around and the skunk had a pistol with a silencer attachment.

"Naturally, I moved fast and my one shot finished him. Then I found out that his pistol had jammed as those with silencers are likely to do. That explained something that bothered me—why I'd been taken off the Werner Turner and put on night duty. Reisenham had gotten to hate and fear me almost as much as I did him. He made it easier for himself if it came to a show-down.

"I didn't drag the body to a corner. I stuffed it in the big boiler and put the cover on, where I wish it was, still.

"This afternoon, on the platform, I whispered to Barburg that a mirror was cracked behind the Magic Hall. Tell him anything that costs money and he jumps to see how much it'll cost. The second time you started around, Barburg was leaving. People were moving around and the group breaking up. It was easy to walk to the end of the platform and kick the button because a couple of others walked by there, too. Then I—"

There was a commotion at the door. In walked Jean with her prize. Ginger Lary ran across the room like a frightened faun, and Variss folded an arm around her protectively.

X.

For once, even Frost seemed surprised. Inspector Frick was a study in consternation. A hum of voices and questions arose. Jean stamped a foot imperiously. "Shut up! All of you! I'll do the talking now and you can do it later!"

The vehemence of her command silenced them. Jean rattled on: "I've a lot of things to say and I'm going to say them now. In the first place, I just hope you bring a murder charge against Ginger Lary, the girl over there, for Barburg's death. You can try from now till doomsday and I'll bet dollars to roses you never get to first base with any jury I ever heard of.

"She's the real reason Reisenham died before he expected to, and, personally, I think it was a grand idea. If you want some real crooks, you'd have to go a long way to beat Reisenham, Moss, and Barburg. They're cheap frauds.

"Ginger and Sam Variss were going to get married this spring. They had a lot of plans when Sam got royalties for his invention. He didn't get any royalties because Reisenham stole his idea and patented it. So Ginger and Sam didn't, because it's a hard grind when you get only fifteen or twenty dollars a week as a night watchman. I gather that Sam's a sort of quiet soul, hasn't many friends, and doesn't talk about himself, which is why nobody seems to have heard of Ginger.

"Anyway, Ginger was in the passageway back of the Magic Hall. She had a blackjack and a dagger that Variss stole from Madame Serpa. The dagger was for protection. She was to hit Barburg with the blackjack and knock him out. Variss said he would see to it that Barburg went into the passageway. Variss knew that Frost was closing in on him; but, obviously, Variss couldn't be at the Whirlwind platform and in the passageway at the same time. That would throw the whole case open again. And Ginger and Variss had an agreement not to see each other for a month after today.

"The idea went haywire because it worked too well. When the roller coaster went off, everybody started for the wreck. No one paid much attention to any one else; but if Variss hung around the platform of the Whirlwind, he'd be conspicuous because he'd be alone.

"Ginger figured Barburg would be blinded from sunlight when he stepped into the passage, but he wasn't. He must have had eyes like a cat. He dodged the blackjack, made a dive for her, and started choking her. She stopped fighting at that stage and let him have the dagger. She was scared and figured it was his life or hers. Barburg staggered against the mirror and it swung. She closed it and ran. That's all there is. This whole mess would never have happened except for Reisenham's meanness. He was the real criminal. He got exactly what he deserved and I'm glad!"

The inspector fidgeted. When she halted for lack of breath, he shifted her attention: "Do you mind telling how you plucked this woman out of thin air?"

"I didn't. In the scuffle with Barburg, Ginger kicked and a nail tore her skirt and hose. She didn't know it at the time, but I found the threads. The rest was easy. They were high-grade and handmade. I can't tell you how I knew. You get to know fabrics by feeling them. And a woman on Ginger's mission would dress to be inconspicuous in darkness. That's the only reason she'd wear a dark-blue skirt and gun-metal hose. About the only place I know of that has things that feel like those threads is an Irish store on Fifty-seventh Street, so I went there and asked, and I was right."

Frick looked openly bewildered by her line of thought. "What made you think that the threads came from a woman's apparel rather than a man's?"

It was Jean's turn at being stumped. She blinked her eyelids, taken aback. "It just didn't enter my head that there was any question about it," she confessed. "The moment I saw them, I wondered why any woman would wear such a color combination."

Frost strode toward the door. As if awaiting his signal, the others began a bustle of various activity. The inspector hurried after him, caught up with him outside.

"Wait a minute, Ivy," he implored. "Miss Moray is right. We have enough to indict the two, but getting a conviction is another matter. If this comes out in court the way it stands, there's a good chance they'll beat the chair or maybe win acquittal."

With a note of finality, Frost stated: "Ethics and punishments are not for me to decide. My interest lies in the solution of crime, the detection and apprehension of criminals. All aspects of the mystery have been clarified."

The professor was gone.

Jean climbed into her roadster with a feeling of utter content. She didn't know what his mood or attitude was. But she hoped she had got under his skin. Her face wore the contented smile of the cat that licked up all the cream.

FROST

First Edition

2000

Frost by Donald Wandrei was published by Fedogan & Bremer, 3721 Minnehaha Avenue South, Minneapolis, MN 55406. Thirteen hundred and fifty copies of the trade edition and one hundred copies of the limited edition have been printed from Century Old Style by the Maple Press Company.